Praise for the novels of

SHARON
SALA

"Sala's characters are vivid and engaging."
—*Publishers Weekly* on *Cut Throat*

"Sharon Sala is not only a top romance novelist,
she is an inspiration for people everywhere
who wish to live their dreams."
—John St. Augustine, host,
Power!Talk Radio WDBC-AM, Michigan

"Veteran romance writer Sala lives up to
her reputation with this well-crafted thriller."
—*Publishers Weekly* on *Remember Me*

"[A] well-written, fast-paced ride."
—*Publishers Weekly* on *Nine Lives*

"Perfect entertainment for those looking for
a suspense novel *with emotional intensity.*"
—*Publishers Weekly* on *Out of the Dark*

Also by Sharon Sala

Originally Published as Dinah McCall

Look for Sharon Sala's next novel
BLOOD TRAILS
available in October 2011

SHARON SALA

Blood Ties

MIRA®

MIRA®

ISBN-13: 978-0-7783-1264-2

BLOOD TIES

For questions and comments about the quality of this book please contact us at
Customer_eCare@Harlequin.ca.

www.MIRABooks.com

Printed in U.S.A.

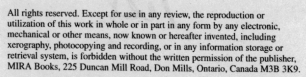

From the moment of inception,
we are forever marked by the DNA of our
parents' lineage. The physical characteristics of
their people become the faces of our own.
We walk through the world living our own
insular lives, sometimes forgetting that
we still bear their history, good or bad.

Time and circumstance can change our bodies
and faces, but nothing changes the ties
marked by blood. They can either be the
saving grace, the incontrovertible truth or the
final straw that seals a person's fate.

I see myself in the faces of my elders and in
the faces of my children. A part of me will live
forever through the blood ties of those to come.
It behooves me to be the best that I can be while
I am on this earth, so that the legacy
I leave behind me is one of honor, not of shame.

And so I dedicate this book to all my people—
to the ones who came before me
and made me proud to bear their name
and to the ones will who come after.
I hope and pray they do the same.

One

My life is a lie.

Savannah Slade stood before a mirror, staring at her own image as if she'd never seen it before. She knew the statistics: twenty-two years old, barely five feet four inches tall, shoulder-length white-blond hair and big blue eyes. She had a baby-doll look, but there was nothing babyish about her.

Her recently deceased father, Andrew Slade, had raised his daughters to be tough and self-sufficient, and she'd always considered herself that and more. But today she'd learned a devastating secret at the reading of his will. Andrew wasn't her father, and her sisters weren't really her sisters. The journal she was holding held even more secrets—secrets that, if revealed, were going to shatter more people's lives than just her own.

She opened the journal that Coleman Rice, the family lawyer, had given her. Her hands were still shaking. Even though she'd already read the entire book twice over, she returned to the first line. No matter how startling the information, there was no mistaking the truth.

You are not my child, and my darling Hannah was not your mother. Your real mother's name was Chloe Stewart, and when I first met her in Miami, Florida, she was dying of cancer.

She backed up to her bed, then sat down with a thump, swallowed past the lump in her throat and continued to read.

She said she was not married to your father but his name was Gerald Stoss, oldest of twin boys born to Rupert Stoss, and the heir to a massive fortune. She claimed Gerald did not know of your existence until she learned she had inoperable cancer. After that, she contacted him for help. He was devastated to learn your mother was dying, but he assured her he would take care of you. In fact, bring you both into his home and care for her during her last days, and claim you as his rightful heir.

Savannah shivered. So she was a bastard child. Not unusual. If that had been the only revelation, this would have been a bit easier to accept. But such was not the case.

She laid the journal aside and walked to the windows overlooking the south side of the ranch, then leaned her forehead against the panes. If only she could close her eyes and wish this horror story away.

A hard wind suddenly whipped around the corner of the ranch house, reminding her that spring had yet to make a full-fledged appearance in Montana. The weather had been chilly ever since the funeral, and now, three days later, was still the same. The house was warm, the two-story rock-and-cedar structure a strong bulwark against the unforgiving winds that continued to blow. But Savannah garnered no comfort from the familiarity. The family home no longer represented safety to her, and she wondered if she would never know peace again.

Everything she and her sisters had known from as far back as she could remember was a lie—a convoluted fabrication of bits of their pasts that Andrew had woven into their lives with him.

She felt sick. According to the lawyer, each of them, at different phases of their lives, had been taken in by Andrew, but only after their respective mothers claimed that the girls' lives were in danger. At this point, Savannah was so shocked and angry at the entire revelation that it was difficult to grieve for Andrew's passing. She looked back at the bed and the journal she'd just abandoned. The sight of it taunted her. Unable to leave it alone, she sat down on the mattress, searched for the phrase that had left her speechless and read it again.

They said they would kill you, just like they'd killed your father.

Savannah's gut knotted as she scanned through the next two pages of information. What kind of a family had she been born into? If this story was true, she'd just gone from being the baby of the Slade family to the heir to a massive fortune first amassed in the early 1900s by Austrian immigrant Anton Stoss.

It was a long, convoluted story, but the bottom line was that, although she was illegitimate, inheritance in this case was not based on legal marriage. Instead, the heir of each generation would always be the eldest and firstborn. And even though her father had been a twin, he was the oldest by two minutes, which made him the heir, and since she was *his* only heir, the vast inheritance was supposedly hers.

According to the journal, when the family learned that Gerald had fathered a child with a woman who was dying of cancer, and that he intended to bring the woman and toddler into the family and claim the child as his heir, his twin, Joseph, had been furious. According to what Gerald had told Chloe, Joseph resented not being named a dual heir—that he'd lost the right by virtue of being born a mere two minutes later.

Savannah turned the page. Andrew's familiar handwriting jumped out at her.

Your mother, Chloe, belonged to the church in Miami, Florida, where I'd been asked to hold a revival. She was in the front row every night, her bald head wrapped in a scarf, her skin pale and ashen. You were but a two-year-old toddler, oblivious to the fact that your mother was dying. Your sister, Maria, was already with me and sat nearby on the same pew, so that I might keep a close eye on her. Every night, when your mother would stand and ask for healing, Maria would scoot over and play with you while we prayed for her.

Then the last night came. She arrived carrying not only you but a stuffed rabbit and a satchel. After the service, she waited until everyone else was gone before telling her story between harsh, choking sobs. My heart ached for her as her story unfolded, and it was then I began to realize that, once again, God had more in mind for me than just preaching His word. According to her, your father, whom she appeared to love deeply, had been killed that very day in a car accident. But it was the phone call she got later that changed her grief to fear. A man told her bluntly that if she tried to make a claim on the Stoss fortune on your behalf, you would meet the same fate your father had met. They said they would kill you, just like they'd killed your father.

After a long, involved conversation, she convinced me that she had no other options. I looked at you, sleeping peacefully in Maria's lap, and gave in to the inevitable. She gave me a letter entrusting you to my care. A copy of it is in the back of this journal, along with a copy of your birth certificate listing Gerald Stoss as your father. The originals of both documents are with my lawyer, Coleman Rice. Suffice it to say, by the time I left Miami, I had acquired another daughter.

Savannah closed the journal and set it aside. Before Andrew's abrupt and unexpected death, she'd known her place in the world—right here on the Triple S, a huge, sprawling ranch a few miles from Missoula, Montana.

Although she had not been out of college long, her affinity with numbers had led her to take over the ranch bookkeeping, as well as the breeding registrations for the horse and cattle operations, leaving the role of "woman of the house" to her oldest sister, Holly. Maria, her middle sister, had opted for working with the livestock as well as training the horses.

Andrew's best friend, thirty-nine-year-old Robert Tate—Bud to the family—held the job of foreman. And now, after the reading of the will, Bud also held equal ownership in the Triple S.

This had been her world, but if she was to follow her

curiosity and instincts, it was the world she was about to abandon.

Savannah put on her coat and scarf, and began searching for her car keys. There was one person she had to face with this news before she left for Miami, and he wasn't going to like what she had to say. Telling her childhood sweetheart and almost-fiancé, Judd Holyfield, that she was leaving Montana wasn't going to be easy. When she left her room, her purse was on her shoulder and her car keys in her hand.

"Hey, honey, where are you going?"

Savannah paused in midstride. Ever since Andrew's death, Bud had taken his duty as foreman beyond the bunkhouse to the big house. She should have known she would never make it out of the house without Bud finding out.

"I'm going to Judd's."

Bud eyed the frown lines between Savannah's eyebrows and knew she was dealing with more than grief.

"Does he know what's happened?"

"Not yet."

"What are you going to tell him?"

Her chin jutted. "That the woman he thinks he loves is a fraud, then see how it goes."

Bud frowned. "You know him better than that, or at least you should. That's not going to make a damn bit of difference to him."

"I know, but it still has to be said, and he's not going to like the fact that I'm leaving Montana."

"So take him with you."

She shifted angrily. "I may be the smallest Slade on the place, but I don't need a babysitter. Size is a state of mind. I can be as tough and as tall as I need to be."

Bud loved these women more than he had a right to, hated that the family was coming apart and didn't know how to pull them back into the fold.

"I know, honey. I didn't mean to imply you were helpless. I worry, okay? But damn it, Savannah, Andrew took you in because you were in danger. Even though you've grown up, there's a strong possibility that the danger still exists—maybe more than ever."

"I know that, but right now, the only danger I'm about to be in is with Judd. Say a prayer for me. I'll see you later."

Bud flinched at the sound of the closing door, mumbled a quiet prayer for the family, then grabbed his jacket and Stetson and headed for the stables. At least the horses still needed him, which was more than he could say for Andrew's daughters.

"Hey, boss! Look out!"

Judd Holyfield reacted to the warning and yanked the reins of his cutting horse just in time to keep from being gored by the horns of an angry mama cow. The rangy brindle was pissed that they'd separated her from her baby and was pitching a royal fit. "Hurry up and get a band on that calf!" Judd yelled, keeping his rope taut and the cow at bay.

The little bull bawled as the cowboys upended it. While one cowboy held the calf down, another grabbed the bander and deftly slipped a short thick rubber band over the creature's small downy sac before letting him go free. The thick rubber band would slowly stop circulation, which would eventually cause the anatomy in question to shrivel up and drop off. It was bloodless and a far less painful method of castration than the old method of cutting had been, but it had to be done when the calf was small or it wouldn't work. As soon as the calf was set free, Judd loosened the tension on his rope and slipped it off the horns of the mama cow in question. She bellowed loudly, which brought her baby running, and off they trotted.

"That's the last one," Judd said as he reined in his horse.

"Hey, boss, looks like you've got company."

Judd turned in the saddle. When he recognized Savannah's car, he frowned. She was driving fast, which meant something was wrong.

"Three of you clean up here, then take a load of hay over to the back forty and feed the yearlings. Pete, take my horse to the barn. Brush her down good, and then make sure she has food and water. I'll be back later."

He dismounted, handed over the reins and started toward the house. He was there by the time she pulled up and parked, and he could tell by the look on her face that she wasn't happy. As she got out of the car, her body language worried him even more.

What the hell happened?

"Hi, sugar." He opened his arms. She walked into his embrace without a word, burying her face against his chest. "What's wrong?"

"We need to talk."

Everything had been turned upside down since Andrew's sudden death, and he assumed this was more of the same.

"Let's go inside. I have a fire going in the den and some chili I could heat up. Are you hungry?"

Savannah shrugged. It was after three, and she realized they'd all skipped lunch, which wasn't so surprising, considering what had been happening.

"I guess. Are you?"

He grinned as they walked up the steps and into the house. "Remember who you're talking to."

Savannah smiled, trying to keep up with his humor. "Right. Sure, I'll eat with you."

The busywork of heating chili, filling bowls and making coffee dispelled some of Savannah's nervousness. By the time they sat down, the butterflies in her stomach were barely fluttering. After all, this was Judd. She'd loved him forever. She knew her unexpected news wouldn't affect him nearly as much as the fact that she intended to leave Montana, and still without committing to an engagement.

By the time they sat down, Judd was the one who was anxious. He'd never seen Savannah like this. He waited until she'd taken a bite before he followed suit. They ate in silence. Finally she shoved her bowl aside and leaned her elbows on the table.

"We got a big shock during the reading of the will."

Judd frowned. He'd known that was happening this morning, but no one had been expecting any surprises. "What kind of shock?"

Savannah clutched her hands together to keep them from shaking.

"Andrew wasn't my real father."

It was the last thing he had expected her to say. "You're kidding!"

"I wish. But that's not all. None of the three of us are real sisters."

A tear rolled out of her eye and down her cheek. The sight of it cut Judd to the bone.

"Savannah…sweetheart, I'm so sorry." He got out of his chair and quickly circled the table, pulling her up and into his arms. "So you guys were adopted. That's not such a big deal, is it?"

"If only that were the case," Savannah said. "But… we were never adopted. Not legally. It's all a big complicated mess, but he left each of us a journal explaining how we came to live with him and what happened to our real parents. Remember he used to be an evangelical preacher? And that he traveled all over the States holding revivals?"

"Yes, I knew he'd done that when he was younger. Why?"

"The bottom line is that all three of our mothers were in some kind of danger when he met them, and as a result, all of us were in harm's way, too. Maria witnessed her mother's murder when she was four, although she has no memory of it. Holly's mother was convinced her husband was a serial killer. She was going to the police with the information, but she wanted Holly out of the way of the media spotlight. She planned to come get her after everything was over. Only she never came, and Dad guessed her husband killed her, because she never got the chance to go to the police, either."

"What about you?" Judd asked.

She shivered. "Dad…Andrew met my mother in Miami. I was two, and she was dying of cancer. She wasn't married to my father, but when he learned what was happening to her, he was going to bring her into the family and care for her, as well as claim me as his heir."

Judd frowned. "Heir? As in the family was well-to-do?"

Savannah sighed. "Heir as in the family had—has—a vast multi-billion-dollar empire."

Judd stared, unable to believe the words coming out

of her mouth. She was an heiress? How did that fit into a Montana cattle ranch? "So what happened?"

"According to the story in the journal, his family, in particular his twin brother, was unhappy with the news. It meant he would not be in line to inherit, as he'd supposed. My mother told my fa—Andrew that they killed him and made his death look like a car accident, then called my mother and told her that they'd kill me just like they'd killed him if she tried to make a claim on the fortune."

Judd's eyes widened. "Oh, my God! What's the family's name?"

"My father's name was Gerald Stoss."

"Stoss as in Stoss Industries?" Judd asked.

She nodded.

"Holy…that's… So are you going to make a claim? Wait! How can you prove you're Gerald Stoss's daughter if he's dead?"

"Coleman Rice said they can test my DNA against the living family members to prove I'm related. Gerald's twin brother is still living. Plus Gerald's listed on my birth certificate, and there's a letter from my mother that includes more details I suppose would enhance my claim in court."

"So Coleman is going to submit your petition for the DNA test?"

"Not exactly."

"What do you mean…not exactly?"

"I'm going to Miami to talk to the police. If my mother was right, someone murdered my father and got away with it."

Judd's heart sank.

"But what will talking to the police do when you have no way to prove anything?"

"I have my journal."

"Does it say who killed him?"

"It says who was behind his death, although it was ruled an accident."

"Then it proves nothing."

Savannah pushed out of his arms. This was exactly the reaction she'd expected.

"Look, Judd...this isn't something I can ignore. I'm still going."

His eyes narrowed. "I'm going with you."

Her chin jutted angrily. "No, you're not. This is about me. This is something I need to do on my own."

He reached for her in panic, desperate to make her understand.

"Honey, for God's sake, if someone really killed your father, how do you think they're going to react to your appearance?"

She shrugged. "I don't think they'll be all that happy about it, but I'm not going to confront them on my own. Of course I'll contact the police first, and then I'll contact a local lawyer and go from there."

Judd turned away. He needed to put some space between them before he said or did something that made things worse. He knew how hardheaded she could be, but he couldn't wrap his mind around the danger this could put her in.

Savannah could only imagine what he was thinking. He'd already asked her to marry him, and she'd hesitated. He'd withdrawn the request and told her that he would ask again when she was ready. This must seem like she was rejecting him all over again.

"I love you," she said.

He turned abruptly. "Really?" Sarcasm coated the word and his face.

She crossed the room and put her arms around him, but he didn't react. It felt like hugging a statue.

"I'm sorry you don't understand, but—"

"Oh, I understand perfectly. You just inherited a few billion dollars and don't want to tie yourself down to a cowboy."

Savannah slapped him before she thought, leaving the bright red imprint of her hand on his cheek.

"That's an insult! I may have some identity issues, but that part of me doesn't change! I don't ever want to hear anything like that come out of your mouth again. Do you hear me?"

Judd's face was stinging, but he knew he'd had that coming.

"Fine. Consider it an honest reaction to shock and fear that the woman I love is about to walk out on me again."

Savannah was so mad she was shaking as she clutched her hands against her stomach.

"I know. I get that. But this isn't some joyride. You have to try to see this from my point of view! Everything I thought I knew about myself was a lie. I can't start a new life with anyone when I have this past full of secrets and lies." Tears were rolling down her face as she finally let go. Her heart was pounding so hard it hurt to breathe. "I feel empty, Judd. Everything I thought I knew about myself was based on my family and the Triple S. Now I find out all this crap and that the first two years of my life are a big unknown. I need answers, and hopefully those will bring some long-overdue justice for the man who fathered me."

They stared at each other without moving—the shock and anger between them a living thing. Finally, Judd managed to ask, "When are you leaving?"

"In the morning."

"Damn," he muttered and swiped a shaky hand across his face.

Savannah took a quick, shallow breath. "I don't want to leave like this."

Judd's vision blurred as he swung her off her feet and into his arms, striding out of the kitchen and down the hall toward his bedroom without speaking.

No words were necessary.

A healing needed to take place between them, and making love was the ultimate cure.

Two

Clothes were shed faster than the tears in their eyes. Neither could get past the reality that this relationship was on the verge of coming apart. Fear lent urgency to the act as they fell into bed in a tangle of arms and legs. When the occasional sob escaped with a kiss, no one noticed. It was all about lust and passion.

Judd was a big man. He dwarfed Savannah physically, but she was a match for him in every other way. She met him kiss for kiss, stroke for stroke, until they were both verging on madness.

When Judd pinned her to the mattress, both with his weight and his grasp, his need to dominate her was apparent. Instead of pushing back, she welcomed it, wrapping her legs around his waist and her arms around his neck as he slid inside her. Then all of a sudden, he stopped.

"Don't hate me," she whispered.

"Don't leave me," he countered.

A sob rolled up her throat.

The sound tore at Judd's heart.

"Don't...don't...please, baby, don't cry."

"I'm not leaving you. I just need to do this before we begin a life together."

Judd shuddered. There was a knot in his gut, but the need to claim her was greater. He began to move, thrusting hard and steady. The gentleness usually present in their lovemaking was gone, replaced by passion born of desperation. He couldn't take his eyes from her face—memorizing every nuance, every curve, every aspect of her features. When her eyes closed and her body arched beneath him, he knew she was close to coming apart in his arms. He wanted that. He needed that confirmation that he was still the man who centered her world, and so he kept moving—harder, faster—pushing her to the ultimate submission.

Savannah wanted to feel it—that soul-shattering climax of heat and lust. It was what had always been perfect between them, and she needed it now.

"Love you," she gasped, then choked on a scream as she came in a freefall of pounding heat, shuddering from the power of his body and the ever-spreading ripple effect rolling through her own.

He followed her in a climax that hit him so hard he blanked out. There was no thought in his mind—no reality save the lust that left him momentarily deaf, dumb and blind. It wasn't until he heard her sobbing against his chest that sanity returned. He wrapped her in his arms and, with a groan, rolled them over until she was stretched full-length atop his body, unable to speak, unable to move.

He tangled his hands in the fall of her hair as his throat tightened around the words he wanted to say, but instead of speaking, he closed his eyes and held her.

That was when Savannah panicked. If she didn't leave

now, she would never leave—could never leave—and the decision would haunt her for the rest of her life.

She rose up on her elbows, staring down into his face.

Judd opened his eyes. She'd already withdrawn emotionally. He could see it. All he had to do was accept it.

"Is this it?"

She nodded.

His voice broke. "You're killing me."

Her vision blurred. "I have to do this."

He knew her well enough to know her mind was set. "Promise you'll call me every night."

"I promise."

"Promise you won't put yourself in danger."

"I promise."

His voice lowered to a whisper. "Promise you'll come back to me."

"I promise," she said, and then kissed him hard and swift before rolling off his body and reaching for her clothes.

Judd wouldn't watch. Instead, he rolled over to the other side of the bed, then got up and strode into the bathroom, shutting the door firmly behind him.

Savannah flinched at the sound, but when she'd finished dressing and he still hadn't come out, she realized he wasn't going to. She glanced back at the rumpled bed. Their goodbyes had already been said.

"Judd?"

He didn't answer.

"I love you."

His silence was frightening, but she'd made her proverbial bed. Now she had to lie in it. She walked out of the bedroom and then back down the long hall through which he'd carried her earlier. The closer she got to the front door, the faster her steps became, until by the time she got to the car she was running.

She left the same way she'd arrived—in a cloud of dust.

Miami International Airport, late the next day

A cabdriver loaded Savannah's suitcases into his trunk, then opened the door for her to get in.

"Where to, miss?"

"The InterContinental Hotel, just off Biscayne Boulevard."

The driver closed her door, circled the cab and jumped in behind the wheel before pulling away from the loading zone with a quick burst of speed.

Savannah leaned back and took a deep breath. So this was Miami. The sky was blue, the water bluer. There were palm trees all over the place, and it was hotter than hell.

Note to self: should have packed different clothes. No. Wrong note. Have never owned clothes that would work here. Which meant she would have to go shopping. Normally that would have been a thing to look forward to, but not this time around. She hadn't come here for fun in the sun.

Her first glimpse of the hotel was from a distance, but she recognized it from the website. She'd searched online for Miami hotels and chosen this one, not just because it overlooked the bay, but because it was also near Palm Island, which was the location of the Stoss estate. It wasn't so much a case of wanting to look at what supposedly belonged to her as not wanting to turn her back on the enemy.

By the time they reached the hotel, Savannah was hot and out of sorts. Part of her wished she hadn't rejected

Judd's offer to come with her. She didn't like confrontations, and she knew there was nothing but confrontation in her future. She paid off the taxi driver and followed the bellman who carried her bags and led the way to registration. Savannah strode across the open lobby with her chin up, and her stride swift and sure. Heads turned as she passed, admiring her curvy body and platinum-blond hair, but they would have been mistaken if they thought her just another pretty face. Savannah Slade was not only book smart, she was Montana tough and determined. By the time she got registered and in her room, it was close to sundown. Ignoring the suitcases she had yet to unpack, she walked out onto the balcony. As promised, the view from the thirtieth floor was spectacular. She gripped the handrails as she lifted her face to the breeze.

Gulls circled in the sun-bleached sky, and she took a deep breath and closed her eyes. Even the air smelled different here. It was hard to believe she'd been born here. It felt and looked like a foreign country.

The sound of a helicopter flying by drew her focus. She watched as it came over the top of the hotel and then swooped toward Dodge Island, which was directly across the water. Beyond that lay Palm Island and the Stoss estate. She knew Judd's concerns about her safety were not unfounded. Getting to the truth of her past was going to be difficult, if not dangerous, especially if what her mother had believed turned out to be true.

First things first, she thought, and went back into her room. She needed to unpack, shower and change, then go get some food. It was almost sundown, and she hadn't eaten since 5:00 a.m.

Judd was walking into the kitchen from the back porch when he heard the phone begin to ring. He dropped his gloves onto the sideboard and bolted, grabbing the receiver on the third ring.

"Hello? Savannah?"

The sound of his voice was what she'd been waiting to hear. All the tension slid out of her body as she rolled over onto her side, the phone still cupped to her ear.

"What if it hadn't been me?" she asked.

"Then I would have come across like the lonesome man I am."

"I just left this morning."

"I know. But knowing how far away you are makes it worse. Did you get there okay?"

"Yes. Long flight, but I'm here. I went downstairs and ate dinner. Just got back to the room. I'm on the thirtieth floor. The view is amazing."

"Can you see the water?"

"The hotel is *on* the water. It's hot here. I have to go shopping tomorrow. I don't even own clothes that would be comfortable here. It feels like another planet."

She was rambling. Judd heard the uncertainty in her voice but knew better than to ask about it. She'd made her need for independence painfully clear.

"I can only imagine. No palm trees in Montana."

She laughed softly. "No. No palm trees. I'm going to talk to the police either tomorrow or the next day for sure. It's hard to guess how it will go, but I'll let you know."

"Be careful."

"I will. Bye, Judd."

"Bye, sweetheart."

"I love you."

Judd shoved a hand through his hair, and then leaned against the wall and closed his eyes.

"I love you, too," he said softly, then hung up the phone.

He stared blindly at the dirty dishes still in the sink. That damn faucet in the utility room was still leaking. He could hear the drip from here. He could wash the dishes and fix the leak, but he couldn't fix the hole in his heart.

Even though Savannah heard him disconnect, she still held the phone against her ear, not ready to give up the connection.

"I'm sorry I keep hurting you," she whispered, then finally hung up the phone.

Savannah was trying to get free from the ropes that bound her hands behind her back and held her ankles together, but they had been tied too tight. She could feel the vibration of the airplane engine as the plane taxied down the runway. Faster and faster it went, until it lifted off. There were two loud thumps as the landing gear came up. When the plane began to climb, she began sliding toward the back of the plane. Desperation kicked her adrenaline into high gear as she rolled into the small galley, hitting a cabinet with a thud. Hope rose as she thought maybe now she could find something to cut herself free. Before she could act, hands were yanking her to her feet and she was being dragged toward the exit. Someone popped the door. A huge rush of wind whipped through the opening, making her stagger backward against her captor's chest. She heard a curse, then someone pushed her forward, closer and closer to the opening. She began to scream.

"Stop! Please! No! I'll go away. I won't tell. I won't tell! Just don't kill me!"

Then someone whispered harshly against the back of

*her ear, "You should never have been born," and gave
her one last shove.*

*Out of the plane she went, falling head over heels
with her hands still tied behind her back—falling, falling, falling, as the screams were torn from her lips,
falling ever closer toward the choppy blue surface of
the Atlantic Ocean.*

It was the phone that saved her. It began to ring just
before she hit the water, yanking her from the horror
of her nightmare. She sat up with a gasp, her heart
pounding and her hands shaking as she reached for the
receiver.

"Yes...hello?"

"Miss Slade, this is the front desk. We have a floral
delivery for you. May we bring it up?"

"What...? Oh, yes, all right," she muttered, and hung
up the phone.

She couldn't believe she'd slept the whole night
through without waking up. She glanced at the clock,
then did a double take. She never overslept, and it was
after 10:00 a.m. A quick calculation in her head explained the situation. It was only 8:00 a.m. back home.
Her body was still on Montana time.

Then she remembered that someone was coming with
a delivery, and flew out of bed and raced to the bathroom. When she came out, her hair had been combed
and she was wearing a robe. She was scrambling through
her purse for tip money when she heard a knock at the
door.

She rose up on her tiptoes to peer through the security
peephole, saw a man in a bellman's uniform holding a
vase of flowers and opened the door.

"Good morning, miss," the bellman said. "Where would you like me to put these?"

"The desk is fine," Savannah said, standing by the door as she waited for him to come back out. She handed him a couple of bills as he walked past, added a quick thanks as she shut the door, then went to check out the flowers.

They were pale pink carnations, with a cloud of baby's breath scattered throughout. A wave of homesickness washed over her when she read the card. "Remember, you're not alone. I'm only a phone call away. Bud."

She pressed the card to her heart. Pink was her favorite color, and Bud knew it. He was like a brother, and the closest thing she had left to a father figure. He and Judd were the only people from her past who weren't tied to the lies.

She laid the card down on the desk, brushed her fingertips lightly across the flowers, then headed for the shower. Even though her body thought it was still early, she was going to have to adjust to Miami time to get anything accomplished. After a quick shower, she chose the lightest weight clothing she'd brought and a comfortable pair of shoes, then left her room. She needed clothes, a rental car and a map of the City of Miami. Her belly growled, reminding her she also needed food. So breakfast first, then the world.

It was just after 3:30 p.m., and Savannah had been at the Mary Brickell Village since right after breakfast. She slipped her newly purchased sunglasses onto her nose as she exited Frida Kahlo and started across the parking lot toward her rental car—a gray Ford Focus. She'd accomplished a lot since waking up this morning. The hotel had helped her rent the car, furnished her with a map of Miami and then directed her to the trendy shopping area just south of the hotel. She'd hit every boutique and bought enough clothing to last at least a week, along with a couple of pairs of sandals. The quick breakfast she'd eaten hours earlier was long gone. She was hot, tired and too hungry to wait until dinner to eat her next meal.

She dumped her bags in the trunk of the car and decided to head back to the hotel. She could order room service, then study the city map to see how to get to police headquarters. She also needed to call Coleman Rice to see if he could recommend a lawyer here. She would rather not pick one cold from the phone book, but if it came down to it, she would.

She couldn't think about this mess without feeling overwhelmed by the enormity of what she was about to undertake. Except for the written words of a dead woman, she had no proof to back up the claim that Gerald Stoss had been murdered. But she could certainly find a lawyer and begin the process of trying to prove she was his heir.

After one last glance at the map to remind herself of where she was going, she pulled out into traffic and headed north, back to the hotel. The trip didn't take long. She pulled up to valet parking, got her shopping bags out of the trunk and her claim ticket from the attendant, then headed into the hotel.

"Do you need some help, miss?" a bellman asked, eyeing the armful of sacks she was carrying.

"No, but thank you," Savannah said.

A few minutes later she entered her room, kicked off her shoes, dumped the bags beside the bed and then grabbed the phone and ordered room service. It would take a while for the food to arrive, but she didn't like to eat alone in public, though she had already gone that route last night.

While she was waiting for lunch, she began removing tags from her clothes. The closet was too small for what she'd brought and what she'd just bought, so she packed her old clothes in her suitcases. She would have to ship stuff back when she finally went home, but that was something she would deal with later. Right now she just needed the space. Forty minutes later there was a knock on her door. Her food had arrived.

She opened the door, inhaling the delicious aroma as the bellman wheeled the room service cart in and began transferring her order to the table. As soon as he was finished, she signed the ticket, adding a tip, and then opened the door for him to exit.

"Enjoy your food, miss," he said as he pushed the cart past her.

"Yes, thank you, I'm sure I will," she said.

She was waiting for the cart to clear the doorway when a tall, curvy redhead came out of the room next to hers, slung her purse over her shoulder and strode toward the elevators without acknowledging Savannah's presence. Savannah watched her go, then pushed the door shut and locked it behind her.

Lunch beckoned. Savannah grabbed her plate of sliders and fries, crawled up on the bed and turned on the TV, upping the volume as she settled down to eat. Since she'd missed lunch, she'd already decided this was going to count as an early dinner and had added a big piece of pie to her order. The miniburgers were juicy and cooked to perfection. The fries were hot and salty, a perfect accompaniment, but she was making sure to save room for the key lime pie still on the tray.

As she was eating, a loud boom suddenly rattled the sliding doors leading out to her balcony. She looked out to see a growing spiral of dark smoke rising in the air. Curious, she set her food aside and ran to the balcony door, but she couldn't see beyond the buildings on Dodge Island to see what had happened.

She noticed a man standing on the balcony next to hers. He'd obviously heard the explosion, as well, and gone out to investigate. She watched him smile to himself as he slipped his phone into his pants pocket. Unwilling to be caught staring, she darted back to the bed, retrieved her food and kept on eating. A few minutes later, the television programming was interrupted by a news bulletin.

"We interrupt this program to bring you breaking news. A speedboat has just exploded in Biscayne Bay, between MacArthur Causeway and Palm Island. Authorities have shut down boat access to the area while the incident is being investigated. The explosion was less than five hundred yards from the secluded estate belonging to Joseph Stoss and his family. Stoss, the CEO of the corporation, who lives on the estate along with other members of the Stoss family, was not available for comment. Our own news helicopter was in the area when the explosion occurred, and was on the scene only seconds behind the arrival of the harbor police. This is live footage of the burning craft. As yet, the name of the boat and its owner is unknown. There have been no reports of survivors, or how many people might have been on board. We'll keep you apprised of updates as they occur."

At the mention of the Stoss name, Savannah's interest in the incident escalated. Once again she scooted her plate aside as she bounced off the bed, but this time she went out onto her balcony.

Two police helicopters were circling the area. In the bay below, boats that had been speeding up and down the shoreline were temporarily docked, and in the distance, she could hear police sirens. She quickly realized she wasn't the only curious onlooker. Dozens of hotel guests had come out onto their balconies, too. The same man she'd seen earlier was still there. She purposefully ignored him until he spoke.

"Quite a spectacle, isn't it?"

The man was an early-thirties Latino wearing a tailored white Cuban shirt and pale gray slacks. His smile invited her to respond.

"I was thinking more toward tragedy," she said. "The report they gave on the television said no survivors had been found."

"Ah…a soft heart to go with the pretty face," he said. "And what is your name, *señorita?*"

When she hesitated, he kept pitching. "My name is Alejandro Montoya."

Savannah couldn't help but wonder how many women he'd picked up with that soft-heart line and thought of the pretty redhead who'd come out of the same room a few minutes earlier.

"Savannah Slade."

"So, Savannah Slade, will you allow me to buy you a drink?"

"I don't think so."

"Maybe later, then?"

Sometimes persistence was a good thing, she thought, and sometimes it was a nuisance.

"Let's just say I'm not available and leave it at that, okay?" Then she smiled to soften the rejection and

slipped back into her room, taking care to lock the sliding door and pull the curtains behind her.

A news anchor was still talking about the explosion
over a repeat of the earlier footage. She switched the
plate with her half-eaten food for the one with her key
lime pie.

The pie was sweet and cold, with a refreshing tang—
definitely not a regular on Montana menus.

"Mmm, I could get addicted to this," she said aloud,
and dug into the pie for a second bite.

Suddenly she glanced up at the television, then fumbled for the remote and upped the volume further, catching the explanation of the clip they were showing in
midsentence.

"—taken in December of last year during a fundraiser for the state Arts and Humanities Council. The
woman on Joseph Stoss's arm is his widowed cousin,
Elaine Stoss Hamilton. The man beside them is another
cousin, Michael Stoss. Still no word on whether any of
the three were at home when the explosion occurred,
and a statement has yet to be released by the family."

Savannah's heart began to pound. So that was Joseph
Stoss. Had her father looked like him? Had this man
really been responsible for Gerald's death?

She leaned forward, the pie forgotten as she stared
at the faces, imprinting the images on her memory. In
pursuing her claim to the Stoss fortune, she would be
seeing them soon enough. Andrew had taught all the
girls to face their fears head-on, but now that she had
faces to go with the names, it made them a shade too
real for comfort. Even if they had nothing to do with
Gerald's accident, they were still going to view her as
an interloper and act accordingly. It wasn't going to be
pretty.

Three

After a very restless night, Savannah gave up trying
to sleep and was up and dressed before 7:00 a.m. She
kept staring at the phone and thinking of Judd. It was
not quite 5:00 a.m. in Montana. She'd talked to him last
night but wanted to hear his voice again. If she called
and woke him up, he would think something was wrong,
and that was the last thing she wanted.

Confidence had to be the word for the day.

She reached for the journal, flipping through the
pages until she found where she'd left off last night and
began to read, even though she'd read it so many times
before that she could almost recite it by heart.

You came to me with a worn-out blanket and a
stuffed rabbit you called Baby. For months, the
only thing you would allow to cover you at night
was that blanket. I knew you were suffering from
the absence of your mother, but you had no words
to voice it. It broke my heart to know that, as you
began to learn more and more words, you'd quit
saying Mama. Even in your little baby mind, you
somehow knew she was gone from your life. I

tried so hard to make you feel loved. Maria turned herself into a little mother and never relinquished the job until I married Hannah two years later.

Your first Christmas with Maria and me, I bought you a baby doll. You thought it was pretty and played with the clothes, taking them off and putting them back on a dozen times. But when it came time for sleep, it was always Baby, the pink rabbit, that you tucked beneath your chin.

Savannah's hands were trembling as she finally laid the journal down in her lap. All she could think was "poor little baby." How confused she must have been.

Too disturbed by the story to read any more, she fussed with her hair and clothing until it was finally past 7:00 a.m., grabbed her bag, stuffed in the copies of the journal she'd made for the police, then headed out the door for breakfast.

A waffle and coffee later, she was on her way to get her car out of valet parking. Thanks to a very helpful concierge, she had directions to the main office of the City of Miami P.D., and as luck would have it, it wasn't that far from her hotel.

With the city map on the seat beside her, she checked the area he'd circled, then drove out of the hotel parking lot toward the street that would take her to Second Avenue. Suddenly she could hear the sounds of screaming sirens and, like the rest of the traffic, braked to a stop on the right. Moments later, two blue-and-white police cruisers, followed by a fire-and-rescue truck, went speeding through an intersection just ahead.

The sirens reminded her of the ambulance that had come speeding onto the Triple S after her father's collapse. They hadn't been able to save him. She hoped the people waiting for that ambulance were more fortunate. Once the traffic was clear, she proceeded through. Minutes later, she pulled into the visitors' lot at the police department and parked.

Now that she was here, her nerves kicked in. She checked for the third time to make sure she had copies of the journal, as well as copies of her mother's letter and her birth certificate, and then headed into the building. After a request to speak to a detective in Homicide, she was given a visitor's pass and escorted to the desk of Detective Frank Barber.

The detective was on the phone when she entered the room but quickly hung up as she was introduced and seated at his desk.

"Miss Slade, I'm Detective Barber. How can I help you?"

Savannah eyed him closely, trying to judge his demeanor. His salt-and-pepper hair was military short, his brown slacks and camel-colored sports coat both lightweight, as was the light blue polo shirt he was wearing beneath his jacket. His deadpan expression reminded her a little of the actor Tommy Lee Jones, and she guessed him to be in his mid-fifties. She pulled out the journal and papers that she'd brought, and then laid them in her lap.

"I've recently come into some information that I believe will change a twenty-year-old death from being ruled an accident to a homicide."

Barber's interest shifted as he picked up his pen. "You're claiming someone was murdered?"

"Yes."

Barber frowned. "And how do you know this? What is this person's name?"

Savannah knew how crazy this was all going to

sound, but the only way to get it told was to start at the beginning.

"It's complicated, okay? Let me go back to the beginning. I'm from Missoula, Montana, and last week my father, Andrew Slade, suddenly passed away. During the reading of his will, I learned some extraordinary facts regarding my past."

Barber shifted wearily in his chair. Yesterday's boat explosion had just turned into a murder investigation after remnants of a bomb were found attached to a piece of floating wood. He had no idea how many victims there were, or their identities, but they were still pulling body parts out of the bay. An eyewitness had come forward early this morning and identified the boat as *Her Alimony,* belonging to a CPA named Paul Wilson, who worked for a large shipping company. Finally he had a starting point to his investigation, and now he'd been sidetracked by this woman and her meandering story. He combed his fingers wearily through his hair, massaging the back of his neck, then leaned forward, resting his elbows on the desk.

"Miss Slade, I don't mean to interrupt you, but let's cut to the chase. I had a long night, and today's not going to be any better."

Savannah frowned. "And I didn't come to Florida for fun in the sun. I just came into possession of these facts, and I feel they should not be ignored. You want a shorthand version? Fine. During the reading of my father's will, I learned that he was not my real father, that my sisters were not my real sisters, that I was born here in Miami to a young, unmarried woman named Chloe Stewart, who when Andrew Slade, the man I knew as my father, met her was dying of cancer. According to the story Chloe told Andrew, when my birth father learned of my mother's illness and my existence, he readily agreed to acknowledge me as his child and bring us both into his family. He intended to care for my mother until her death, and to claim me as his only living heir. Also according to my mother, his twin brother disagreed with his decision. There was a family fight, and supposedly his brother had my father killed, making his death seem like an accident. Then the family called my mother and told her that if she tried to make a claim to the family money on my behalf, they would kill me just like they had killed him."

Barber's interest shifted again. "That's quite a story. What do you have to back up this claim?"

Savannah fidgeted slightly. This was where it was going to get sticky. "I have a journal written by Andrew Slade, telling me everything he knew, and a letter my birth mother wrote on my behalf, stating this as the reason she wanted Andrew Slade to take me and raise me as his own."

Barber frowned. He felt like he was being played. "Why would she give her child to a man she didn't know...or did she? It's more likely he's your real father and—"

"No. When he first met Chloe Stewart, I was a toddler and she was already dying. Once my birth father was killed, she panicked. She had no way to protect me, so she gave me up to save me."

Barber leaned back in his chair, making no attempt to hide the sarcastic tone in his voice.

"To a total stranger. She just gave away her baby to a total stranger. Really?"

Savannah panicked. He was slipping away, and she didn't know how to stop it.

"But it happens every day when children are orphaned

and there's no family to take them. They're given to total strangers under the guise of an organized child-protection system, and we all know what a mess that's become. Twenty years hasn't made any difference in the level of care orphans receive. Chloe would have had no idea what kind of people would raise me. At least she'd seen and talked to Andrew Slade—an evangelical preacher who already had one child very near my age."

Barber glared. That made sense he couldn't argue with, but he still didn't believe the story. "Are you sure you weren't kidnapped? Maybe this was a story he cooked up to cover his butt after—"

Savannah slapped the flat of her hand on the desktop. "I didn't come in here to debate the wisdom of a dying woman's decision on who ended up raising me. I came to tell you that someone committed murder twenty years ago in this city and got away with it. Here's a copy of everything I was given at the reading of the will. It's a copy of the journal Andrew kept of everything he knew about my past, along with a copy of Chloe's letter to him and a copy of my birth certificate." She slid everything across the table toward him. "I didn't come to you to try to claim my inheritance. I'll do that through a lawyer. I'm here because I believe someone got away with murder."

Barber stifled a curse as he scanned a couple of pages in the journal, then sorted through them until he found Chloe Stewart's letter and Savannah's birth certificate.

"It says here that the child's name is Sarah Stewart. I thought you said your name was Savannah Slade."

"I know. That's the name Andrew Slade gave me. But I was born Sarah Stewart."

He frowned, scanning down the page. "So your parents weren't married. Does she name your father on your birth certificate?"

"Yes…there," she said, pointing to the line.

Barber read it, then did a double take and read it again.

"What the hell?" He looked up. "It says here that Gerald Lee Stoss was your father."

Savannah nodded. "Yes, I know."

"*The* Gerald Stoss of the Stoss family on Palm Island?"

Savannah braced herself for the reaction. "Yes."

Barber's jaw dropped. "Let me get this straight. You came in here to accuse the existing Stoss heirs of murder, and you intend to make a claim on the estate for yourself?"

She didn't comment on his question. "I would also like a copy of the report taken at the scene of his accident."

All of a sudden Barber thought of the explosion near the Stoss property.

"Where were you yesterday afternoon?"

Savannah frowned. She couldn't imagine where he was going with this. "Shopping for clothes at Mary Brickell Village. What I brought with me was too heavy for this weather. Then I went back to the hotel. Why? What does that have to do with anything?"

"There was an explosion in the bay near the Stoss compound yesterday afternoon."

"Yes, I know. I heard it from my room and saw smoke from my balcony."

Barber scooted to the edge of his seat. "What hotel are you staying in?"

"The InterContinental Hotel, just off Biscayne Boulevard."

Barber's eyes narrowed. "You come to Miami to claim a fortune and just happen to be staying at a hotel that close to the estate?"

Savannah was losing control of this conversation and didn't know how to pull it back. "No. I chose that hotel on purpose. I admit I was curious, but look at this from my point of view. I'd just learned my whole life is a lie. I came here to find the truth, so it made sense to find a location nearby. My balcony overlooks the bay and the island where the estate is located. I'd rather be facing them than worrying about what might happen to me when my back was turned."

"Are you saying you're *afraid* of them? Have you met them? Have you already confronted them about your claim?"

"Of course I'm afraid of them. According to my journal, my life was already threatened once by the family, remember? I have no reason to assume that twenty years has softened their hearts or their consciences. No, I have not met them nor confronted them. I'm not a fool. As I said, I'll deal with them through a lawyer."

"Is there anyone who can corroborate your whereabouts during the time of that explosion?"

His question was like a slap in the face. She didn't bother to hide her shock.

"You aren't even listening to what I'm saying, are you? Why would I need an alibi for that boat explosion? What does it have to do with what I just told you? I just got to Miami late yesterday evening. I don't know anyone here, and I damn sure didn't know the owners of that boat."

"But the explosion happened just offshore from the

Stoss estate, and here *you* are, claiming to be an heir to the family fortune."

Shock was turning to anger. It was all she could do to control the tone of her voice. "If you're saying the explosion was aimed at the Stoss family, then you need to be looking into who owned the boat that exploded, or the people who were on it. They're the ones who were near the estate, not me. I was in my hotel room, eating food I'd ordered from room service. And if you think I'm some down-on-her-luck gold digger, you couldn't be more wrong. I did not grow up poor. My sisters and I, along with a family friend, just inherited our father's ranch. One hundred square miles of prime ranch land. That's 64,000 acres, with over 4,000 head of cattle, 112 horses, six employees and I don't know how many pieces of farm equipment. We're not in hock to any bank. We're solvent and more than comfortable. I have a master's degree in accounting *and* my CPA credentials. I am the accountant for the ranch and all the family holdings, and I'm damn good at what I do." She stood abruptly. "It's blatantly obvious that you have no interest in the fact that Gerald Stoss might have been murdered twenty years ago, so I suppose our business here is done."

She reached across his desk for her papers, then stopped herself.

"Are you going to give me a copy of that accident report?"

Barber frowned. "I'd have to do some digging to find it. Twenty years is a long time."

Savannah pointed to the papers she'd given him. "You keep those, and you dig out that accident report and look at it, too. Check my story. Check the facts. Our lawyer's name is on the paperwork. Coleman Rice. Call him.

Look up the name Andrew Slade and the Triple S Ranch in Missoula, Montana. You'll see I'm not lying."

She started to walk away, then stopped and turned, quietly staring at the detective's face as if memorizing his appearance.

"What?" Barber asked.

She shrugged. "Just wondering. Your reaction to my accusation that someone in the Stoss family was responsible for murder was not only vehement but completely dismissive. I didn't think people in law enforcement were supposed to blatantly ignore an accusation of murder. At the least, it should have sparked a little curiosity and a desire on your part to revisit the report of Gerald Stoss's death. So either you're not a very good cop, or you're in their pocket. I was trying to decide which category you fall into."

Barber's face turned red with anger, but before he could answer, she walked away. He had to admit, she'd taken him by surprise, but he wasn't a rookie. He'd been in the business too long to fall for a con like that. She'd come to establish herself as an heir to a fortune, and an accusation of murder would be one hell of a way to get the rest of the family out of the picture. She'd woven quite a story, which he would check out, but her accusations still rankled. He couldn't arrest Savannah Slade outright for suspicion of being a con woman, and he wasn't convinced she had nothing to do with that explosion, but he had to give it to her. He'd never met a con artist who'd decided to use law enforcement to help her run her scam. And what he *could* do was alert the Stoss family to her presence and intent.

Joseph Stoss glanced at his reflection as he walked into the Stoss Building. He knew he looked good for his age. At fifty-two, he wasn't more than five pounds heavier than he'd been at twenty-one, and he had a full head of thick blond hair that was set off by a smooth Miami tan, compliments of his love of sailing. He nodded at the doorman as he strode through the lobby, eyed the fresh flower arrangements and the enormous free-form stone sculpture sitting right beneath the atrium dome. It was supposed to represent achievement and integrity, which were the traits upon which the Stoss fortune had been founded. It wasn't his taste in art, but it didn't matter. The artist was famous, and the piece had cost a fortune. It was all about the power that money could buy. That was what the Stoss name meant to him.

When he got to the elevator, he swiped his ID card and then stepped inside. The doors were closing when his cell phone began to ring. He glanced at the caller ID, recognizing the name of the detective who'd left a message earlier about the boat explosion in the bay. He hadn't returned the call, but now was as good a time as any to see what the man had to say.

"Joseph Stoss."

"Mr. Stoss, this is Detective Barber, Miami P.D."

"Yes. I'm sorry I didn't return your call last night. I was out of Miami on business and didn't get back home until very late."

"No problem," Barber said.

"I was told the P.D. is investigating the possibility that the explosion was an attack aimed at the Stoss family. Do you have information for me regarding the explosion? Have you identified the owner of the boat? Do you know who was on it when it blew up?"

"That avenue is just a theory we are investigating. We're getting in some new info this morning. When I know more, I'll let you know. However, that's not why I'm calling."

The elevator doors opened. Joseph strode out, nodded a hello to his secretary, indicating he was going to finish his call in private before he gave her any instructions, and headed into his office.

"Then what can I do for you?" he asked as he closed the office door behind him.

"Have you or any member of your family recently been contacted by anyone claiming to be a child of your deceased twin, Gerald Stoss?"

Joseph's heart skipped a beat. He reached for the desk to steady himself, then dropped into the seat.

"No. Why?"

"A woman just came by the department with some wild story about being his daughter. I thought I should give you a heads-up in case she starts running some scam, or trying to charge stuff all over Miami and have it billed to you. Stranger things have happened, you know."

Sweat beaded on Joseph's upper lip. His thoughts were in turmoil. *What the hell? After all these years...* Then he took a deep, calming breath. He couldn't let on that he was rattled.

"What was her name?" Joseph asked.

"She said her name was Savannah Slade."

Joseph scribbled the name on a notepad while trying to maintain calm.

"Hmm, doesn't sound familiar, but thank you for the warning, although I can assure you this isn't the first time someone has tried to scam the family."

"I guessed as much," Barber said. "As for the explosion, if I find out that your family was in any way a target, I'll be in touch."

"Thank you, Detective."

"No problem," Barber said and hung up, then glanced down at the papers the Slade woman had left with him, eyeing the damning name on her birth certificate.

Almost immediately, he began having second thoughts about making that call to Joseph Stoss, but the family had more money and power than God here in Miami, and he didn't want to suffer the flack that would come later if this all went to court and it got out that he'd known of her claims and not warned them.

At this point, he might not be able to stop the woman from running a scam, but at least he'd given her intended victims a warning. For now, he had an unknown number of murders to solve. He dropped her papers into a desk drawer and reached for the new info he'd received about the boat.

Joseph pocketed his cell phone, then leaned back in his chair, took a deep breath and closed his eyes. His gut knotted. He'd known at the time that leaving her alive was a loose end, but the woman had been dying. At the time, his own son, Tony, had just turned one. He'd been so wrapped up in fatherhood that he'd gotten soft, thinking of a baby only a year older than his. He figured the kid would wind up lost in the welfare system, and that would be that.

Fuck.

The intercom buzzed. He sat up with a jerk and grabbed the phone.

"Mr. Amini is here, sir."

"Thank you, Darla. Send him in."

Joseph stood. He would deal with loose ends later. Right now there were contracts to sign and money to be made, and the more of that, the merrier.

* * *

Savannah was angry at the detective's reaction, even though she'd known going in that it would be a hard sell convincing anyone to look into Gerald Stoss's death. Money always bought power, and there was enough of both behind the Stoss name to discredit anything she might have to say. But she hadn't been prepared to become a suspect in some random boat explosion. Andrew had raised his girls to be honest and true to themselves. And now she had to find out her own truth—no matter how ugly it might turn out to be.

She got to her car, dug her cell phone out of her purse and called the family lawyer, Coleman Rice. The secretary answered and promptly put Savannah on hold. A few moments later, Rice was on the line.

"Savannah! Good to hear from you. How can I help you?"

"I'm in Miami."

"My goodness, you didn't waste any time."

"Well, sir, in a way…twenty years have already been wasted."

"Yes, yes…of course," Coleman said. "What do you need?"

"The name of a good lawyer here in Miami. One who's tough and mean and not afraid to buck power. I don't suppose you'd happen to know someone like that?"

"Hmm, not right off the top of my head. Let me think a bit, and I'll call you back within the hour. Will that do?"

"Yes, sir, that'll do just fine. Call my cell."

"I will," Coleman said. "You take care."

"Don't worry, I intend to do just that."

* * *

It was twelve-thirty before Joseph had a break. He reached for the phone and buzzed his secretary.

"Darla, call my driver to pick me up ASAP. Also, cancel my two o'clock appointment and reschedule for later in the week. Something has come up. I'll be home for the rest of the afternoon if you need me."

"Yes, sir," she said, and calmly flipped through her Rolodex for the needed number as Joseph hung up in her ear.

He frowned. There was no sense him being the only one whose day had been ruined. He hit number two on his speed dial and waited for the call to be answered.

It was picked up on the second ring.

"Michael Stoss."

"It's me, Michael. What are you doing?"

"I'm about to tee off," Michael said as his caddy handed him his driver.

"Cancel your tee time. I need you to come home," Joseph said.

Michael Stoss wasn't like his cousin Joseph. He didn't have the ambition or, he admitted, the intelligence to run Stoss Industries. But he was still man enough to stand his ground when it mattered, and playing golf was Michael's passion.

"I'm not canceling anything," Michael said. "Whatever's going on, you deal with it. You're the one who's getting paid the big bucks."

"Shut up and do as I say, Michael. I need you and Elaine at the house. Now. We have a problem."

Michael frowned. "What kind of problem?"

"It relates to Gerald."

"Gerald is dead and buried."

"Not all of him," Joseph muttered.

Michael's gut knotted. He dropped his cell into his pants pocket, then handed the driver back to his caddy, along with a hundred dollar bill.

"Sorry, Billy. I'm going to have to cancel. Family business."

"Sure. No problem, Mr. Stoss. Want me to put your clubs back in your locker?"

"Yes, thanks," Michael said, and made himself smile, but his heart was hammering as he fished out his car keys and headed for the parking lot.

Joseph sighed. One down. One to go. He hit three on his speed dial. When it went to voice mail, he cursed, then left a message in a tone of voice she wouldn't misunderstand.

"Elaine, whatever the fuck you're doing, stop it and get your ass home now. We have a problem."

He disconnected angrily, then strode out of his office and back to the elevator. A thousand scenarios were swirling through his head as he walked out of the building toward the waiting limo.

Goddamn you, Gerald. This is all your fault.

Savannah was sitting at a red light when her cell phone rang again. She started to let it go to voice mail and then saw it was Coleman Rice.

"Hello, Mr. Rice. Do you have a name for me?"

"Thomas Jefferson."

She grinned. "You're kidding, right?"

"Nope. He's in the phone book. Give him my name and remind him he owes me."

"What does that mean?" she asked.

"Nothing that concerns your needs," Coleman said. "You can trust him."

"I don't want *Sesame Street* nice," she warned him.

Coleman laughed in her ear. "Trust me. *Nice* is not an adjective I would ever use in reference to the man. It'll be okay. Just call him."

The light turned green. "Okay. Thank you," she said, then dropped the cell phone back onto the seat and accelerated through the intersection.

Four

Savannah strolled out of the hotel with a to-go drink and a sandwich, heading toward the sunny walkways of Bayfront Park just north of her. She needed some fresh air and time to herself—time to think. After a short walk she came to an open-air amphitheater and found a seat in the shade to eat her food.

The turkey wrap she'd chosen from the restaurant lunch menu looked appetizing, but she was so distracted by what had happened at the police department that she barely tasted it as she ate. She kept replaying her conversation with the detective, wondering what she might have said that would have made him react differently, but came up blank. The irony of a random act of violence happening so close to the Stoss estate and coinciding with her arrival was bizarre. All she could do now was hope he got curious and looked into the report on Gerald Stoss's death, then hope there was something suspicious about it that would give him the impetus to investigate further.

All in all, a lot had happened this morning, but none of it in the way she'd hoped. She needed advice. She'd tried calling Maria, but the call had gone directly to voice mail. Holly had already planned to travel to Missouri today, so there was no need trying to play phone tag with her between flights. The urge to call Judd was so strong she actually put down her sandwich and picked up her phone, then stopped. She'd talked to him last night. If she called again today he would think she couldn't handle what was happening. Frustrated, she put her phone back in her purse and picked up her food.

A pair of gulls swooped down in front of her, obviously begging. She picked some bits of the tortilla wrap off the sandwich and tossed them in the grass, smiling at the fuss and squawking that ensued.

The anger she'd felt at being questioned about that boat explosion was like a knot in her gut, and she had a bad feeling this wasn't the last she would hear about it. But she wouldn't be caught unaware again. It was time to contact the lawyer Coleman Rice had recommended. She tossed the last bits of her sandwich into the midst of the gulls, then reached for her phone. She'd already entered Thomas Jefferson's office number in the address book, so she pulled it up and made the call, hoping Coleman Rice hadn't steered her wrong.

The phone rang and rang, and rang again, and just when Savannah thought her call was going to go to voice mail, a man answered gruffly.

"Jefferson Law Office. Hang on a minute, will you?"

Savannah didn't even get the chance to respond before she was put on hold. She grinned. Whoever was answering the phone seemed to be having a bad day, as well. When the Beatles' "A Hard Day's Night" began to play in her ear, she laughed out loud, which sent the gulls skyward.

She brushed the crumbs off her lap, then gathered up

her garbage and carried it to a nearby trash can as she waited for her call to be answered. All of a sudden the gruff voice was in her ear again.

"Jefferson Law Office. You still there?"

Savannah smiled. "Yes, I'm still here."

"What can I do for you?"

"I want to make an appointment with Mr. Jefferson."

"Why?"

She arched an eyebrow. This wasn't the most professional secretary she'd ever encountered, but to each his own.

"I have a complicated situation that's going to take a lawyer to work out."

"I don't do divorces."

"I'm not married."

"Good for you," he drawled.

Savannah was starting to get the drift of this conversation and realized she wasn't talking to a secretary, after all.

"I'm sorry, but are you Mr. Jefferson?"

She heard a sigh.

"Yes. My secretary just quit."

"Oh. Well, my condolences."

"I don't suppose you type?"

"No, and I'm not looking for a job. I need a lawyer, and you were recommended."

"Out of curiosity, who recommended me?"

"My family lawyer, Coleman Rice, gave me your name."

"Holy shit! Are you kidding me? Is he still living up in the northern wilds somewhere?"

She frowned. "Missoula, Montana. Look, maybe this wasn't—"

"Be here by nine o'clock tomorrow morning. What's your name?"

"Savannah Slade."

"Do you have my address?"

She read off the address she'd gotten out of the phone book.

"Yes, that's it. Ah, damn…phone's ringing again. See you in the morning."

The line went dead in her ear. She had asked for someone rough and tough but was beginning to wonder if she was going to get more than she'd bargained for.

The roar of a racing engine caught her attention, and she turned toward the water just as a speeding boat breezed past, leaving a rooster tail of water in its passing. The man behind the wheel was tanned and laughing, seemingly happy with the bikini-clad woman at his side. Savannah's shoulders slumped as she started walking back toward the hotel. If only her life could be that simple. Watching that couple's happiness only made her miss Judd even more. She pulled her cell phone back out of her purse as she moved into some shade and, before she could talk herself out of it, called his number.

Judd had taken a truck into Missoula just after sunup to pick up a load of cattle cubes and block salt. He'd had to wait longer than usual to get it loaded, which had defeated his purpose of getting an early start on the day's work. By the time he was on his way back to the ranch, it was midmorning and he was frustrated. He was driving with one eye on the clock and the other on the gathering storm clouds when his cell phone began to ring. When he saw Savannah's number pop up, his heart skipped a beat. He answered quickly, elated that she was calling.

"Hi, baby. You have no idea how glad I am to hear your voice."

Savannah exhaled slowly. His whiskey-soft voice was just what she needed to hear.

"Hi, Judd."

"I'm missing you," he said softly.

"I'm missing you, too. What are you doing?"

"I'm on my way home with a load of cattle cubes and salt. What are you doing? Are you okay?"

She sighed. Now that she could hear him, she began to relax. "I'm fine. I'm in a park just north of the hotel. I needed to get out and find some fresh air and sunshine."

"You sound frustrated."

He could read her too well. "I'm okay. But my trip to the police department didn't go the way I'd hoped."

"They didn't believe you?" Judd asked.

She laughed, unaware of how bitter it sounded. "Not only did I get read the riot act for being some upstart coming in to con the famous Stoss family out of a fortune, I wound up being questioned about an incident that happened near their house the day after my arrival."

"What the hell? Are you in trouble?"

"No, no, nothing like that, but I guess you could say that, for the cops, it was beyond the laws of coincidence that a boat should happen to explode just offshore from the Stoss estate right after I hit town. Then I showed up to talk about Gerald Stoss's death twenty years ago, they put two and two together and got twenty-two, and the rest is history."

"You *are* in trouble, aren't you? Damn it, I knew I should have gone with you."

Savannah's head was beginning to hurt, which unintentionally sharpened her words.

"No, Judd! I'm not in trouble. I'm just griping. I don't need a keeper, and I have an appointment tomorrow morning with a lawyer recommended by our very own Coleman Rice, okay? Don't start putting words in my mouth or you're going to make me sorry I called."

Judd took a deep breath, resisting the urge to argue back. Their personalities were so alike—both of them take-charge people—that it often caused friction between them. The last thing he wanted to do was tick her off. He needed to keep the line of communication open between them so he would know she was all right. So instead of firing back, he took a deep breath and made himself calm down.

"Sorry. Didn't mean to push the detonate button, okay?"

Savannah closed her eyes against the burn of quick tears.

"I'm the one who should apologize. I'm just frustrated, and I shouldn't be taking it out on you. I'm sorry, Judd…really sorry."

"Forget it," he said softly. "I already have. So what are your plans for the rest of the day?"

She swiped angrily at the tears on her cheeks.

"I'm going back to my hotel room to make some calls. I'd like to see if I can find the location of my birth parents' graves. What about you?"

Judd eyed the clouds gathering on the horizon. "I'm going to do my best to get home and get this stuff unloaded before it starts to rain. Take care of yourself, sweetheart."

"I will. I love you," she said.

"I love you more," he said softly.

The line went dead in her ear.

She dropped her phone into her purse, gave her face

a quick swipe, making sure all the tears were gone, and began walking back to the hotel. This was one of those "just got thrown off the horse" days, but she was ready to climb back on.

Joseph Stoss had never lost a night of sleep over killing his brother. For him, it had amounted to nothing more than a phone call, then waiting for Gerald to leave the house in his BMW. Everyone knew Gerald drove too fast. So when he rammed into the back end of a semi on the way to Coral Gables, no one was surprised. It was a logical assumption that he'd been speeding. The car had exploded on impact. Bystanders had pulled Gerald's body from the burning wreck, but he was already dead, and before the fire department could arrive, the car was fully engulfed.

The Stoss family appeared properly shocked and saddened, then sent Gerald's body to Montreal to be buried in the family mausoleum with all the pomp and circumstance befitting their social status, after which Joseph quietly stepped into the role of CEO. Life moved on, leaving him as the sole beneficiary of the massive fortune, which meant he was now furnishing a roof over his cousins' heads as well as his. That they chose to live with him didn't bother him, as long as they didn't give him grief.

As he drove back to the estate, Joseph's stomach was in knots. Who could have known that the loose end he'd left dangling would return all grown up, dragging enough rope with her to hang all of them? He had to do something fast.

He pulled up in front of the mansion and strode between the three-story pillars and inside without pausing to admire that which was his, as was his habit. The housekeeper met him in the hall.

"Estella, are Michael and Elaine here yet?"

"They're in the library, Señor Joseph. Do you want me to bring you anything?"

"No. And make sure we're not disturbed."

"Sí, señor," she said quickly, and walked away.

Joseph walked purposefully through the foyer and down the hall to the library. As he entered, his cousins, who were sitting on a sofa, turned to face him. When he closed the doors behind him, they both stood.

"What in hell is going on?" Michael snapped.

"I was in the middle of a meeting," Elaine added.

Joseph wasted no time giving them the news. "It seems that Gerald's bastard child is all grown up and has returned to Miami to lay claim to her inheritance."

Michael paled, staggered backward and dropped into a chair. Elaine slapped a hand over her mouth, as if to stifle a scream, and then moved to the wet bar and poured herself a drink.

Joseph cursed beneath his breath. Typical. He wondered why he'd even bothered to let them know.

"What are you going to do?" Michael asked.

Joseph glared. "Me? Shouldn't that be 'we'? You two are just as affected by this as I am."

He glanced at Elaine, who was tempering her panic with whiskey. It figured. Elaine's tendency toward liquor as a mood regulator was less than attractive.

"Is it really Gerald's child? How can you be sure? What was it? After all these years I've forgotten," Elaine asked.

"'It,' as you so succinctly put it, is a girl. According to the police detective who called me, her name is—"

"Police? Shit! Why are they calling? Does she have something that would implicate—?"

Joseph glared. "Shut up, Michael, and let me finish, will you? According to the detective who called, she indicated her intent to make a claim on the family money, and he called to give me a heads-up. That's all."

Elaine began pacing. "Did she leave a name, or say where she's staying? Have you seen her? Does she look like a Stoss?"

"The detective said she was calling herself Savannah Slade. I haven't seen her and don't know where she's staying, but I'm assuming in a hotel. It can easily be checked out."

"Why was she at the police department to begin with?" Michael asked.

Joseph frowned. "I don't know. The detective who called just asked me if anyone had contacted the family recently to make a claim on the estate."

Michael stood. "There had to be more than that. You don't go to the police to claim an inheritance. You go through the courts, a lawyer, ask for DNA, the works. The police department doesn't figure into that scenario."

The knot in Joseph's gut got tighter. Shit. He hadn't thought of that. Michael was right. She shouldn't have been at the police department at all, unless... Double shit. That phone call he'd made all those years ago to Chloe Stewart might be coming back to haunt him. *I'll kill the child just like I killed Gerald.* At the time, he'd been desperate to scare her away from going to court on her daughter's behalf. But the woman was dead. He knew that for a fact, because he'd watched the obituary notices faithfully until he'd seen hers published. It wasn't like she could show up and testify against him in court. She wouldn't have had any kind of a recording of his threat, because she hadn't been expecting his call. Even if she'd told someone, or written it down, it was still a dead woman's word against the word of a Stoss.

He glared at Michael, then strode to the wet bar where Elaine was pouring her second drink and took the decanter out of her hands.

"For God's sake, that's enough!"

Elaine glared at him as she carried her glass back to the sofa. She looked at Michael, as if waiting for him to do something, then took a sip. But Michael was through talking. He'd already done his part. He'd thrown out a few questions to prove he was concerned, but the way he saw things, it was up to Joseph to fix the problem he had created.

Joseph strode back to where they were sitting. He wanted to shout at them, but this was a conversation for hushed tones.

"Like it or not, this is what's happening. If you're approached by this Slade woman at any time, don't say anything. Don't do anything. Just tell her to call me. I'll take care of the rest."

"Are you going to get rid of her like you did Gerald?" Michael asked.

Joseph's gasp of disapproval sounded more like a hiss.

"You stupid bastard! Do not *ever* say those words aloud again."

Michael shifted nervously in his seat. "I just meant—"

Joseph grabbed him by the shirt and yanked him out of the chair. "Everything I did, I did for all of us. Don't ever forget that. You and Elaine knew what was happening, and neither of you spoke against the idea. You're both as liable as I am. The next time you start to open your mouth, ask yourself if the question you're about to voice could put you behind bars." He turned loose Michael's shirt as if it was suddenly foul and pointed a finger at Elaine. "That goes for you, too." Then he stomped out of the library.

Elaine's voice trembled. "What are we going to do, Michael?"

Michael was pissed that he'd let himself be manhandled, but he was no match for Joseph, either physically or mentally.

"We're going to let Joseph fix it, just like we did before, because that's what Joseph does." He smoothed his hands down the front of his shirt and lifted his chin. "I'm going back to the golf course. I won't be home for dinner."

Elaine sniffled, downed the last of her second drink and pushed herself up from the chair.

"He made me miss my meeting and my lunch. I'm going to find Cook and have him make me some food."

"Whatever," Michael said. "Just keep quiet about all this, understand?"

She nodded.

Michael strode out of the library, leaving Elaine alone in the room. For a few moments she stood without moving, eyeing the rich color of the beautifully paneled walls and the floor-to-ceiling shelves. When she turned, she caught a glimpse of herself reflected in one of the windows.

She was still slim and fit for forty-six, her hair still the same shade of blond that marked all true Stosses, even if it now came out of a bottle. Her breeding and education were impeccable, but that had not been enough to keep a man. Twice married and twice divorced, had it not been for her social standing and the family money, she would have been the odd woman out within her social group. She didn't exactly love her life, but she certainly didn't want to go to jail.

Her stomach growled, a reminder of the lunch she'd missed, but instead of going in search of Cook to make her some food, she went back to the wet bar and poured that third drink.

Armed with the name of the boat that had exploded, as well as the name of the owner—Paul Wilson, who was an accountant for a shipping company—Detective Frank Barber had located Mrs. Wilson and now he and his partner, Al Soldana, were on their way to the couple's home. Barber had already checked to see if a missing person's report had been turned in on the man, but it hadn't. So either Paul Wilson and his wife had died aboard the boat, or there was a whole other reason why a wife wouldn't be concerned that her husband hadn't bothered to come home last night.

The Wilson home turned out to be located in an upscale neighborhood, which figured, considering *Her Alimony* had cost a pretty penny on its own.

"Nice digs," Al remarked.

"Yeah," Frank said as he pulled into the driveway and parked beneath a pair of matching palms.

He pocketed his keys as they headed for the front door. Al made a face as he pointed to the ornate doorbell in the shape of a lion's head.

"How the hell do you ring that?" he muttered.

Barber reached in front of Al and stuck his finger in the lion's open mouth, sending a cascade of chimes echoing inside the house.

Moments later Frank glanced through one of the frosted-glass door panels. "Someone's coming."

The door swung inward, silhouetting a slender redhead with shoulder-length hair. She was wearing rhinestone-encrusted gold sandals, red minishorts and a tight white T-shirt.

Barber's first impression was "boob job," and then his thoughts shifted as he pulled out his badge. Al followed suit.

"Ma'am, I'm Detective Barber and this is Detective Soldana, from the Miami Police Department. We'd like to speak to Paul Wilson. Is he here?"

The lady's smile shifted to a slight puzzled frown. "I'm his wife, Rachel. Is something wrong?"

"Ma'am, is he here?" Frank repeated.

"I'm sure he's at the office. I've been out of town the past week and just got back today."

"We've already contacted his office. They said they hadn't heard from him since yesterday."

Her eyes widened, then her chin began to tremble.

"I had no idea. Why didn't they call me? I just got home around noon and assumed he was at the office. Has something happened? What aren't you telling me?"

"May we come inside?"

"Oh. Yes, I'm sorry. Follow me," she said, and led the way through the marble-floored foyer into a vast living room with floor-to-ceiling windows. "Please, have a seat." She gestured toward a solid black sofa while she chose one of a pair of chairs upholstered in bloodred leather.

Al eyed the black-and-white cowhide rug splayed on the floor between them, then glanced up at the art hanging on the wall. Two black streaks running diagonally across the canvas, with a wide slash of red in between. His son could have painted something better. The couple definitely had a thing for red, white and black, though. Even the lady of the house was dressed to match.

Frank took out his notebook.

"Mrs. Wilson, can you tell me the last time you talked to your husband?"

Her hands were clasped together in her lap, but it didn't hide the fact that her whole body was beginning to shake.

"Uh, yesterday, I think… Yes. It was yesterday. I called to tell him what time my flight would come in. He said he'd see me at dinner. It's the housekeeper's day off. I was making beef Wellington. It's Paul's favorite. Please, detectives. You're frightening me."

"Is your husband the owner of a boat called *Her Alimony?*"

Rachel put a hand to her stomach, as if stilling an internal panic.

"Yes, he bought it after his ex-wife remarried. We both thought it was funny."

Frank sighed. He hated family notifications, and it was time to tell her what they knew.

"Mrs. Wilson, we're here because *Her Alimony* exploded in the bay off Palm Island yesterday. We don't know for sure how many were on board, but there were no survivors."

Rachel Wilson screamed as she jumped up from the chair. "No! No! Please God, no! Are you telling me my husband is dead?"

"At this point, we can't positively confirm it, although we do feel it's likely."

"God! Oh, my God! This can't be happening!" Rachel moaned, then began to sob.

Frank grimaced. He still wasn't through breaking her heart.

"Mrs. Wilson, I'm sorry to be asking you this at such a stressful time, but we need a DNA sample from your husband. Like his toothbrush or hairbrush."

She shuddered as she looked up. "I'm sorry…what did you say?"

"We need your husband's hairbrush or toothbrush, something that would have his DNA on it, so we can identify the remains."

She kept staring, as if she couldn't wrap her head around what he was saying. Then she got up, walked across the room and took a picture from off the top of a black baby grand.

"Here's a picture of us taken last year in Avila, Spain."

Frank frowned. "Ma'am, a picture isn't going to do the medical examiner any good."

"Why not?"

"Because the bodies were recovered in pieces."

The shock on her face was profound. The tone of her voice rose as she spoke. By the time she asked the last question, she was screaming.

"Pieces? Pieces? My husband's body is in *pieces?*"

"Shit," Al muttered.

Frank continued to explain. "We can't be sure whose bodies we've recovered until we can match DNA to body parts, which will help us identify who and how many were on board. Would he go out of town without telling you? Did he ever loan out his boat?"

Rachel kept shaking her head. "No, no, no, this isn't happening."

"Ma'am, if you'll just show me the bedroom and

bathroom where your husband's clothes and toiletries are, I'll get the samples myself," Al said.

"Up the stairs, first door on your right," Rachel mumbled, then staggered.

Frank grabbed her arm before she fainted on him. He had some more questions to ask, and they weren't going to make the situation any better. What the M.E. did know from the body parts that had been recovered was that at least one of the people on board had been a young white woman.

"Just a couple more questions and then we'll be through," Frank said. "How about we sit back down?"

"Yes, yes…we'll sit," Rachel mumbled. She eased herself down into the chair as if every joint in her body had begun to ache.

"Were there any problems in your marriage?" Frank asked.

For a few moments she didn't speak, and Frank was beginning to think she hadn't even heard him.

Then she suddenly jerked and met his gaze straight on.

"Why would you be asking me something like that? What would the condition of our marriage have to do with identifying a body?"

"Just trying to cover all the bases," Frank said. "We know there were at least two people on board, a male and a female. We can't notify next of kin until we identify who they are. And I was wondering if—"

Rachel's fingers suddenly curled into the arms of the chair.

"Oh, my God. You're asking me if Paul was cheating on me, aren't you? Paul is dead, and you think he was having an affair?"

"We can't verify his death as yet, and we're trying to—"

"No. If there was a man on that boat, it was Paul.

And if there was a woman on board, I have no idea who it might be, because if he was cheating on me, I didn't know it. Okay? Is that clear enough for you?"

At that point she broke into sobs, and she was still crying when Al came back with the items they needed all bagged and tagged, and ready for the crime lab.

"Is there anyone we can call for you, ma'am? A neighbor? A relative…maybe your pastor?" Frank asked.

"I can't think. Maybe Julie. She lives in the white brick house next door. I'll call—"

Frank turned to Al. "Why don't you go next door and see if the lady is home? If she is, bring her back with you, okay?"

Al was out the door within seconds.

Frank walked over to a wet bar, dug through the minifridge and pulled out a bottle of water, then poured some in a glass and carried it back to her.

"Drink this, Mrs. Wilson."

Rachel took it blindly and sipped it because he said so. Frank felt bad for her, but he'd had to ask.

A couple of minutes later the front door flew open, slamming against the wall with a solid thud, followed by the sounds of running feet. He turned just as a forty-something brunette came hurrying into the room.

"Rachel! Rachel! Oh, my God, Rachel. I'm so sorry, darling. What can I do?"

The newcomer threw herself down onto the floor beside Rachel's chair and pulled her into her arms. The sympathy was obviously more than Rachel could bear, and her sobs became louder.

Frank sighed. "Ma'am, this is my card. If Mrs. Wilson should happen to hear from her husband, or from anyone

else who might know more details, call that number.
We'll let ourselves out."

Julie took the card, then turned her attention back to
her friend. The sounds of Rachel Wilson's thick, choking
sobs were behind them all the way through the house
and then out the door.

"Damn, that was rough," Al said as they headed for
the car.

Frank nodded. "Yeah. Nothing like finding out your
husband is probably dead and the woman with him
might be a lover. So let's get this stuff to the crime lab
and hope we get at least one positive ID."

Savannah was back in her hotel room, bored and
antsy. If she'd been home, she would have been in the
office at the ranch, or helping Holly cook, or riding with
Maria. Since her appointment with the lawyer wasn't
happening until tomorrow, she decided to see if she
could find out where her parents had been buried.

She logged onto Google, then typed in *Gerald Lee
Stoss Obituary*. A long list of links popped up, but she
quickly found what she wanted in the obit files of the
Miami Herald. It didn't take long to see that she wouldn't
be visiting his grave anytime soon. He'd been buried in
the family mausoleum in Montreal.

She moved on to her mother. She knew nothing
about Chloe Stewart except that she must not have had
any other family, or she wouldn't even have considered
giving her toddler to a stranger. An overwhelming sad-
ness for the mother she'd never known swept through
her. How frightening it must have been, with no one to
help, knowing she was dying and that her baby girl was
in danger.

Savannah's vision blurred as she crawled up onto

her bed with her laptop. She had no real idea of how to begin the search, so she simply searched online for death records for Miami, Florida, and waited to see what happened.

Again, multiple links popped up. She chose one, and as she typed in the name *Chloe Stewart,* for whatever reason, it slowly became real to her. Chloe was the woman who'd given her life.

She'd named her Sarah and tucked her in bed at night, and cared for her when she was sick. But there'd been no one left to take care of Chloe when *she* got sick. As far as Savannah knew, Chloe Stewart had died alone.

It broke her heart.

She swiped at an errant tear as she began to focus on the info coming up. All she had was a name and a probable year of death. Andrew hadn't known Chloe's address or where Sarah had been raised. He'd only seen Chloe at the services where he was preaching. He didn't know what kind of a job she'd had. Nothing but that she was dying and scared to death her daughter would meet the same fate as her father.

Savannah had no date of birth to go on, no date of death, which left her with more questions than answers, so she wasn't surprised when her search came up empty. So she logged out of that website and decided to try newspaper morgues. Obituaries were part of every newspaper. If she narrowed her search to a couple of specific years and then down to the name Chloe Stewart, it should work. She couldn't imagine there being any great number of young women with the same name dying within such a short span of time.

A short while later, she hit the jackpot.

Five

Savannah clicked on the obit, unconsciously leaning toward the computer screen as she read.

> Stewart, Chloe Ann, 24. Born August 30, 1966. Died December 12, 1990 after a brief illness. She was an employee of Conroy Pools and Spas for more than five years and is survived by her daughter, Sarah, age 2. Graveside services will be held December 22, 1990, at Graceland Memorial Park North at 10:00 a.m.

There were only a few other Stewarts who'd passed away in Miami during that time period, but none with the first name Chloe.

Savannah stared at the screen for the longest time, wondering what on earth her mother must have said to the people who knew her to explain why her daughter was no longer around. But her mother had known she was dying. She'd probably told them that, because she was so sick and unable to care for her child anymore, she was with relatives. It would have made sense and satisfied the Stoss family, should they have chosen to make their threat real.

She grabbed the phone book and flipped to the yellow pages, looking to see if Conroy Pools and Spas was still in business, but it was not. Too many years had passed to go looking for past employees. She wouldn't know where to start. This was harder than she had imagined. What surprised her was the emotional connection she was beginning to feel toward a woman she couldn't remember. Still, after the roadblocks she'd been encountering, she did have a location for her mother's grave site. That was something.

She glanced at the clock. It was almost 4:00 p.m. There was plenty of time before sunset. Quickly jotting down the name and address of the cemetery, she checked MapQuest for directions.

One last task was to get the location of her mother's grave on the cemetery grounds, but she wasn't sure how to go about that. She made a call to city hall and, after being transferred three times, found a person who could answer her questions. Two more phone calls later she learned that the cemetery office was located on the premises, and that when she arrived, she could go to them for assistance. It was all she needed. Within minutes she was gone.

The sun was hot, the sky a clear and cloudless blue that reminded Savannah of the color of robins' eggs. For the first time since her arrival, she was driving away from the ocean toward Coral Gables. Even though she'd been here a few days now, the sight of palm trees was still a bit surprising. She was stopped at a red light and humming absently to herself, waiting for the light to change, when she became aware of being watched.

She glanced over to the lane beside her and saw a white BMW. Her gaze went from the car to the driver. The fact that she recognized him was a shock, as it apparently was to him, as well, when he realized he'd been caught staring. He frowned briefly, then seemed to reconsider his attitude, flashed a white smile and blew her a kiss before turning right at the intersection.

Savannah grimaced as she drove straight through. That was the man who'd been in the room next to hers and had tried to pick her up. Only she knew he wasn't there anymore, because she'd heard a family with children in there last night. What was his name? Alexander? No…Alejandro. Alejandro Montoya. Odd coincidence, seeing him again, she thought, and then promptly forgot about him as she neared her turn.

A short time later she saw the large rock gates of Graceland Memorial Park North a few blocks ahead and quickly changed lanes just in time to take the turn onto the cemetery grounds. Once inside, she slowed her speed and followed the signs to the office, marveling at the beauty of the place and how well the grounds were kept. She parked at the office, then got out, adjusting her sunglasses as she walked. The sun was warm on her bare shoulders, the breeze lifting the thick fall of white-blond hair from her neck as she reached for the doorknob. Oddly enough, all the nervousness she'd felt earlier was gone. The peace and tranquility of the place was a balm. A blast of cool air hit her as she walked inside. The man sitting behind a desk looked up, then smiled as he stood and came to meet her.

"Welcome to Graceland. I'm Carl Morrow. How can I help you, Miss…?"

"Savannah Slade."

"So, Miss Slade, are you interested in purchasing a family plot?"

"No. I'm trying to locate the grave of my birth mother. She was buried here on December 22 of 1990."

"You're certain she was buried in this cemetery?"

Savannah hesitated, then nodded. "As certain as I can be. Her name was Chloe Ann Stewart. She was twenty-four years old when she died."

The man's expression shifted to one of instant sympathy.

"Oh, dear, so young when you lost her." He eyed Savannah closer. "You must have been a mere baby when she passed."

"I was two," Savannah said. "Needless to say, I have no memory of her, which I regret. Uh, about that location?"

"Certainly, certainly," Morrow said, and gestured toward the chair on the other side of his desk. "Please have a seat while I check our records."

As he turned to his computer, Savannah felt as if she was standing on the precipice of unraveling a twenty-year-old secret. Finding her mother's grave would be the first piece of actual evidence toward realizing her purpose for coming here.

She eyed Morrow curiously as she waited, wondering what kind of a personality it took to work among the dead. The sunlight coming through the stained-glass window behind him bathed his snow-white hair and light-colored sports coat in a rainbow hue of colors, making him appear almost angelic. Maybe that was the answer.

"Ah, yes, here it is," Morrow said as he made note of the location, then exited that site and clicked on another.

"I'm printing you a map of the cemetery. I'll mark your mother's final resting place, as well."

Savannah heard the sound of a printer kick on as Morrow got up and walked into the room behind him. A few moments later he came out, carrying a layout of the cemetery with a specific area circled.

"You'll find her grave where I marked an *X*. As you can see on the map, I've circled the section where it is. From here, you'll need to drive north a short distance, turn at the Beth Israel Garden, then park and walk a short distance to this area. You'll see another of our mausoleums close by. It's the Mausoleo Cubano. We like to think of it as a tribute to the souls who died attempting to reach freedom in our great country."

"Thank you very much," Savannah said.

She drove away, counting down turns and landmarks until she came to the area he'd circled. Once parked, she took the map and started walking. The place was so beautiful, but she couldn't appreciate the beauty for reading names on the tombstones. Somewhere behind her the sound of a lawn mower broke the fragile tranquility, reminding her that life still existed in this place. She kept glancing at the map and then back up at the cemetery, fixing her present location in relation to the *X* he'd marked on the map.

On foot, the place was larger than it looked, and the humidity was getting to her. She stopped to dig a tissue out of her purse, then dabbed at the sweat on her upper lip, wishing she had a bottle of water. A small white egret flew past her line of vision. She turned to watch its graceful flight, thinking Miami was definitely a one-eighty from Missoula.

Sighing, she turned back to the task at hand, centered herself once again from the map and kept walking toward a mausoleum she'd been using as a landmark. According to the map, the grave she was seeking should be just a few yards south of…

She stopped as her eye caught a name.

Stewart.

Her heart started pounding. She read the name twice to make sure she was right, then dropped to her knees.

Nothing was different than it had been seconds ago. The sun was still hot. The lawn mower was still running somewhere nearby. But she was shivering, and she felt like crying. She reached toward the name, tracing the letters with the tip of her finger.

"There you are," she said softly. "It's me, Mother. It's Sarah."

The words on the stone began to blur as she rocked back on her heels, staggered by the unexpected emotion.

"I'm sorry, so sorry, that your last days on earth were lived alone and in fear. I want you to know that your decision to give me to Andrew Slade was a blessing. I was raised with so much love and comfort. I came back to find you, and to make things right."

Afterward, she sat without moving, absorbing the quiet and the peace that came from knowing a piece of the puzzle had fallen into place. It took a few minutes longer for it to soak in that there were wilting flowers at the base of the tombstone. That meant someone was still around who'd cared about Chloe Stewart!

She stood abruptly. What if she could find out who it was? She remembered the lawn mower she'd heard earlier and did a three-sixty, looking to see if any grounds crew were in the area. A man with a Weed Eater was trimming around tombstones about fifty yards ahead.

Grabbing her purse, she started toward him. When she was a few yards away, he saw her and stopped. She waved, indicating she wanted to talk. He killed the engine and started toward her.

"Yes, miss, is there something you need?"

She smiled. "The answer to a question…if I'm lucky. I need to show you something."

He took a handkerchief from his back pocket and wiped sweat from his brow as he fell into step beside her.

"How can I help you?"

"I just found my mother's grave, and there are flowers on it. I was wondering if you'd know who's leaving them, or if you've seen anyone there before."

"Show me where she's at," he said, and followed her back across the expanse.

"Here. Chloe Ann Stewart was my mother. She died when I was two, so I have no memory of her. But someone is leaving flowers on her grave, and I thought you might have seen who it was. I would love to talk to them."

"I've never seen who's putting the flowers here, but I know fresh ones are always replaced the day after we remove the dead ones."

"How often do you do that? Remove flowers, I mean."

"We'll pick them up tomorrow, which is Thursday."

"And there are always fresh ones the next day?"

"Pretty much."

"Any certain time of day? Morning? Afternoon?"

"I don't come on duty until after noon, and they're always here when I clock in and begin trimming."

"Thank you. Thank you so much," Savannah said.

"My pleasure, miss," he said, and nodded before heading back to work.

Savannah looked down at the tombstone one last time, put on her sunglasses and returned to the office. The manager, Carl Morrow, was still behind his desk. When he saw her come in, once again he stood.

"Did you find what you were looking for?" he asked.

"Yes, and thank you very much. I have one more quick question. There were flowers on the grave—fairly fresh ones. I know you would have no way of knowing who comes and goes with them, but is there anything in your records that tells who paid for her burial plot?"

He hesitated briefly, then put his hands together as if he was about to pray. Savannah thought he was going to refuse her request.

"I'm not sure," he said. "Twenty years was a long time ago. Records weren't on computer at that time, and by the time names were entered, details weren't always included, but I'll see what I can find."

"Thank you. I really appreciate this," Savannah said.

He smiled absently, his mind already on the task ahead as he disappeared into the back room.

Thankful for the cool air circulating in the room, Savannah sat down to wait. A few minutes later he returned carrying a very large book.

"This is an old register. The kind we used to use before everything was put on computer. It's for the year 1990, so whatever information we have on that particular plot would be in it."

Savannah leaned forward to watch as Morrow sat back down at his desk and began his search.

"Do you know the exact date of her death?" Morrow asked.

"December 12, 1990."

"Ah, yes, yes," he muttered, and flipped toward the back of the book.

His plodding manner was making Savannah nuts. She wanted to yank that book out of his hands and look for herself.

Finally he paused, his forefinger on a notation half-way down the middle of a page.

"Here we are. A plot was purchased for Chloe Ann Stewart on…" He frowned. "That's odd. The plot was purchased on December 22."

"What does that mean?" Savannah asked.

"Ten days is a long time between death and burial. I suppose there are all kinds of reasons. However, it is a bit out of the ordinary."

Savannah sighed. One mystery solved. One more mystery added to the mess that was her life.

"Does it say who bought the plot?"

"Phyllis Palmer. She actually bought two plots. The one your mother is buried in, and the one next to it."

"Seriously?"

"Yes. It says so right here."

"What does that mean?" Savannah said.

"It doesn't have to mean anything," Morrow said. "But usually when that happens, it's for a family member."

Savannah gasped. She'd never thought of the possibility of finding any members of her mother's family. She'd just assumed that because Chloe had given her baby away to a total stranger, there hadn't been anyone else.

"Do you have any contact info? Anything that would help me locate this Phyllis Palmer?"

"First let me check to make sure she's not already buried there," Morrow said. "Did you happen to notice who was on either side of your mother's grave?"

"No, I didn't pay any attention."

He swiveled his chair around to his computer and quickly typed in the name Phyllis Palmer. Then he frowned.

"There are a couple here already. Let me check something."

Savannah's hopes fell as Morrow continued to talk.

"The first one on the list died in 1937, so that's not your Phyllis Palmer. Let me check the date on the other one…1980. Hmm, maybe…no, this one was only four years old. As far as I can tell, the lady who purchased this plot is not buried here. However, I cannot deny the possibility that she might have passed and been buried elsewhere. Sometimes that happens when different family members take control of an estate and 'do their own thing,' so to speak, rather than follow a loved one's wishes. Let me look at the plat map of the cemetery used for selling plots. It won't tell me the names of the deceased, but I can tell if anyone is buried on either side of her."

"That would be great," Savannah said, and then added, "I suppose that page is too big to copy, but could you write down whatever info you have for me?"

Morrow nodded as he continued to scan the plat. Then he looked up. "There's no one buried on either side of her, and…here's the info you needed," he said, and handed her the paper.

Savannah dropped it into her purse as she stood. "Thank you so much for taking the extra time to help me."

"It's been my pleasure," Morrow said.

Savannah quickly left the office. Within minutes she was on her way to the hotel. She glanced at her watch. Almost 7:00 p.m. She was tired and hungry, but elated. She'd found her mother's grave. She had a possible lead on a relative, and an appointment with a lawyer tomorrow to help her begin her claim on the Stoss estate. The one thing that kept niggling at her conscience was the fact that the police had shown no interest in pursuing her story about her birth father's death. Maybe after she met with Thomas Jefferson she would go back to the precinct and talk to that detective again. Maybe he'd looked at her papers and decided there really was some basis for what she believed. She certainly wanted a copy of Gerald Stoss's accident report. She was pretty sure that would be considered a matter of public record, so she could get a copy without a problem. But if she was wrong, she would ask her lawyer to get involved.

Satisfied with her day, her thoughts immediately went back to Judd. She couldn't help but wonder what he was doing. She'd never been this far away from him—ever. Not even when she was in college. He could get hurt or sick, and she wouldn't know it. Suddenly she wanted to hear his voice—just to know that all was right with his world. He would be the first person she called when she got back to the hotel.

Judd was fixing a stretch of fence bordering the highway in front of his house instead of moving part of his herd to the upper pastures as he'd planned. He was doing it because an hour earlier his neighbor, Dan Sugarman, who had spent the day drinking at Avery's Bar, had tried to drive home drunk as a skunk. It was obvious from the tracks left behind in the pasture that he'd driven straight through the fence without braking.

One of Judd's hands heard the commotion, yelled at Judd and the other men who were inside the barn unloading hay and they all ran to help. Their immediate presence had kept the cows from getting out, which was the only saving grace of the entire debacle. Dan was taken away in a highway patrol car for driving while intoxicated, and Judd was left with a fence to patch. He was just stretching the last wire on a four-strand barbed-wire fence when his cell phone rang. He started to let it go to voice mail, and then thought it might be Savannah. The least he could do was check.

"Hey, Randy, finish this up for me, will you?" he asked, and stepped back as his hired hand grabbed the stretchers and finished up the last of the repair.

When Judd saw the caller ID, he started to grin. "Hey, sweet thing, how's it going?"

"Judd, you won't believe what I found today."

He smiled. The excitement in her voice had to mean it was a good thing.

"What?"

"My mother's grave. And guess what else I found out? There's a possibility that I might have a living relative from her side of the family."

"No way! I guess I thought that she was alone in the world, considering she gave you to a stranger."

"I know. I thought the same thing. I don't know the facts yet, but I have a lead."

"Tell me more," Judd said as he got into the truck and started driving back toward the house.

"When I found her grave, I saw flowers had been placed there. They were wilted, but fairly fresh...you know, several days old. I asked around, and found out that someone comes and puts fresh flowers on the grave once a week. The day they come is the day after tomorrow, so I'm going to stake out the cemetery and hopefully see them."

"That's great, sugar. Wouldn't it be something if you find out you actually have other family besides the Stosses?"

Judd pulled up in front of the house, then killed the engine. He sat, listening to the animation in her voice and wishing she was sitting beside him and not on the other side of the country.

"Yes. So here's what I know so far. A woman named Phyllis Palmer paid for my mother's burial plot, and get this—she also bought the plot next to her. The manager at the cemetery office said that's usually what people do when they're related. So…"

"So if she's still living, she might be the person putting flowers on the grave, right?"

"Who knows?" Savannah said. "I'm just happy. Finding the grave is the first piece of my puzzle to be solved, and look where it might lead."

"Did you find the location of your father's grave?"

"Yes. Unfortunately, he's buried in a family mausoleum in Montreal. Evidently that's where the family originated."

"What about that detective? Are they still on your case about that boat explosion? Shoot me for caring, but I'm still worried about that hanging over your head."

"No, they aren't, thank goodness. But I'm going to try and get a copy of the accident report on my birth father's death, and I thought I'd stop by the detective's desk again and see if he's had a chance to read any of the journal pages I copied for him."

Judd closed his eyes. The sound of her voice amped the perpetual ache in his gut that had begun the last day they'd made love and wouldn't be going away until he had her in his arms again.

"So I guess you have no idea when you'll be coming back?"

Savannah heard the longing in his voice. She couldn't let herself go there or she would be crying.

"No. At least, not yet. I'll meet the lawyer tomorrow and find out where I stand, and what it will entail to file suit."

Then she hesitated and Judd heard the brief intake of her breath. "What's wrong, honey?"

"Do you think I'm being mean and greedy with what I'm going to do?"

He frowned. "You mean making a claim on the family money? Hell, no. If you're the legal heir, you're the legal heir. That won't change despite what others have done to change it. I'm just worried sick that once you begin the process, whoever took out your father will take aim at you."

Savannah shuddered suddenly, as if a ghost had just passed by. She'd thought the same thing herself, but she didn't know any way around it. Her only other option was to go home and forget this part of her life had ever existed. And that wasn't going to happen.

"I'm being careful. I'm not going to confront anyone face-to-face or anything like that."

"If you piss off powerful people, they can find you anywhere. Remember that."

"I will."

"Think of me tonight when you go to bed," Judd said. "I won't be there in body, but I will in spirit."

She did start to cry then. If she didn't hang up now, Judd would be on the first plane out tomorrow.

"I will. Dream of me, too, and hopefully I'll see you soon. Love you."

"Love you more," Judd said, and then the connection ended.

He flipped the phone shut and got out of his truck, his feet dragging as he walked into the house, wishing he could be on the first plane out the next morning.

Six

Joseph Stoss was on a mission to control the unexpected arrival of his brother's bastard. He knew what had to be done but needed information about the woman to make it work. He had to come up with a plan that would make her demise seem like an accident, or his family would immediately be under suspicion, given her visit to that cop. He needed an idea of her daily routine before he could make a plan, so he began by having her tailed. He needed pictures, as well as a detailed report on her activities, and had sent a man whose specialty was, for lack of a better word, cleanup work for Stoss Industries.

It would be the repetition in her routine where she would be most vulnerable, the places or people she visited regularly, giving them a place they could predict she would go, where they could set their trap. It would be her downfall. He had no qualms about getting rid of her. She was a throwaway, a blip on his very busy radar, but he wasn't sharing details with his cousins. He didn't need or want their opinions. As long as he continued to foot the bills for the lifestyles to which they'd become accustomed, they were more than happy to look the other way.

Then Michael showed up for breakfast and ruined what had started out as a good day.

Michael Stoss knew he was physically attractive. All Stosses were. His stylishly long hair was as white-blond as the rest of the family, and his classic features were enhanced by a golfer's tan and good clothes. His father had always claimed clothes made the man, so he'd adhered to that theory religiously. Between his good looks and deep pockets, he had his pick of pretty young men. Today he had a lunch date with his latest, along with an afternoon rendezvous, which was why he came into breakfast with a bounce in his step. When he saw Joseph, he frowned. Joseph had a tendency to take the wind out of his sails.

"Morning," he said as he moved to the sideboard and served himself some eggs and toast. "I thought you'd be long gone."

"And I thought you'd still be in bed," Joseph countered as he gave Michael's appearance the once-over. "You're all decked out. What's up? Meeting with your latest boy toy?"

Michael glared. He knew Joseph looked down on the fact that he was gay. It was one more black mark in the long list of things in which Joseph found him lacking. But he didn't care. He just had no desire to join the business. All he wanted was to reap the benefits of having been born a Stoss.

"At least I have a partner," Michael said as he carried his plate to the table and sat down. "Neither you nor Elaine seem to be able to keep one."

Joseph sneered. "I have my son. I have Tony, who at this point in my life matters more than any woman, although I could have anyone I want. I just happen to get more joy out of making money than spending it on some bitch. When I decide I want someone, I do all right, and you know it. You're just jealous because I have the life you want."

Michael jammed a bite of eggs into his mouth. Joseph was wrong. He didn't want any part of Joseph's life, but he did want to make sure he wasn't in any danger of losing his own lifestyle because of the upstart claiming to be Gerald's heir.

Michael peppered his eggs and smeared some jelly on his toast before taking a bite. Between chewing and a quick sip of coffee, he casually dumped a loaded question into Joseph's lap.

"So what have you decided to do about that woman?" he asked.

Joseph glared. "I'm dealing with it. That's all you need to know."

"Dealing with what?" Elaine said as she entered the breakfast room still wearing her nightgown and a robe.

"The upstart who's claiming to be Gerald's heir," Michael said.

Joseph's eyes narrowed as he watched Elaine skip over most of the food and head for the coffee.

"You look like hell, Elaine. What's wrong? Another hangover?"

"Shut up, Joseph," Elaine drawled, and carried her coffee and plate to the table.

Joseph eyed the single piece of dry toast in the middle of the plate. Her food choice had answered his question. Damn. How had he managed to get stuck with a drunk and a queer for family? Thank God for Tony. He was the future of the Stosses, and Joseph would be happy when he was no longer at school in Geneva, when he would be home with them all the time.

Elaine picked at her toast as she eyed the men. As always, the antagonism between them was so thick she could feel it. If she didn't hate living alone so much, she would leave. The family had a villa in Italy and another in France. She loved France, and it had been almost a year since she'd been there.

"I've been thinking about taking a trip to the family place in France. What do you think? Anyone up for a little trip? Maybe Tony could join us there on break."

Joseph glared. "Perfect. Just perfect. Do you do anything with your brain but pickle it? Does it make no difference to you that some illegitimate bitch has come to Miami to lay claim to what's ours? I don't think leaving the country is the best way to deal with her, do you?"

Elaine flinched as if she'd been slapped. She hated conflict, and being the butt of constant derision from both Michael and Joseph. But they'd grown up this way, and age had only deepened the habits they'd long ago set in place. She tore another piece off the toast, dunked it in her coffee and then nibbled at the corner, testing to see if her stomach was ready for food.

"I'm leaving," Joseph said as he pushed back his chair and stood. "Remember what I said yesterday. If that woman contacts either of you, or comes to this house making demands, don't deal with her on your own. Call me."

"Whatever," Michael said.

Elaine shrugged.

"Perfect," Joseph muttered, and then left the room. By the time he got out to the waiting limo, he'd already put them out of his mind.

* * *

Mateo Bonaventure was a short, wiry Latino who had been working for Stoss Industries for twenty years. He wore his hair long and in a slicked-back ponytail, and had a tattoo of a scorpion on his neck and a gold tooth that was occasionally visible when he smiled.

His first job had been "smoothing the way" for Joseph Stoss to take control of the family business, and he'd done a lot more smoothing since. When he'd found out yesterday that Mr. Stoss wanted him to tail a woman named Savannah Slade, who was in truth probably Gerald Stoss's illegitimate daughter, he thought it ironic. His first job for the company had been getting rid of Gerald Stoss, and now here he was, getting set to dispose of the very female who'd been the reason Gerald died. It was a true full-circle moment.

It hadn't taken Mateo long to call around and find the hotel where Savannah Slade was staying, and he'd been waiting in the lobby of the InterContinental for over an hour. His contact here had already informed him that she was still in her room. And there was another contact at the concierge desk who was going to give him a nod when she exited the elevators.

He sipped a cinnamon cappuccino as he waited, hoping she wasn't one of those women who slept until noon. Another half hour passed before he saw the concierge trying to get his attention. He stood abruptly, watching the stream of people just coming from the elevators, wondering if he could pick her out. Then he saw a small slender blonde with a confident stride and a jut to her chin that said she meant business, and smiled. She even looked like a Stoss with that odd white-blond hair like Joseph and Michael, short and slender like Elaine. No wonder Joseph wanted her gone before she got a chance to take her claim to court. She would probably win the case on looks alone.

He glanced at the concierge, who confirmed she was the one. Pleased that he'd been right, he followed her outside, taking care to stay a few yards back. As she waited for a valet to retrieve her car, he made a run for his own, then drove to an exit where he could see her. He couldn't help but notice what a beauty she was. It was a pity she was going to die.

When Savannah finally found Thomas Jefferson's office, she was verging on a headache and wished she'd stopped long enough to get a coffee before she'd left the hotel. But she'd overslept, and her choices had been to be late for her appointment or skip breakfast. The meal had been the one to take the hit. After finally finding a parking garage a couple of blocks away, she got out and started backtracking.

Mateo watched her pull into the garage, waiting to see where she went from there. His eyes widened perceptibly when he saw her go into the Towers. It was a fortress of a building, housing all kinds of firms, from brokerages to diamond buyers.

By the time Savannah entered the building, she was hot and sweaty and verging on being in a mood. This lawyer had sounded a bit off on the phone. If this turned out to be a wasted trip, she was going to be mad at Coleman Rice. She paused just inside the doorway to assess her options. There was a central desk in a large open space, and a uniformed man sitting behind it. Obviously one had to sign in here to get farther. No problem.

"Hello," she said as she reached the desk. "My name is Savannah Slade, and I have a 9:00 a.m. appointment with Mr. Thomas Jefferson."

The guard eyed his clipboard, then looked up at her. "May I see some identification, please?"

Seriously? Savannah thought as she dug out her driver's license and handed it over, wondering what kind of people would need such stringent protection. Then she shrugged it off and waited.

Moments later, the guard handed back her license and pointed toward a bank of elevators to the right.

"Mr. Jefferson's office is on the ninth floor. Room 900. First door to your left off the elevators."

"Thank you," Savannah said, and headed toward the elevators.

The doors opened silently within seconds of her punching the button to go up. She glanced back at the guard as she started to get in and realized he was still watching her. On an impulse, she waved.

He quickly looked away, startled that he'd been caught staring.

She was still grinning when the doors closed behind her, then up she went all the way to the ninth floor, and into the offices of Mr. Thomas Jefferson, Esquire.

The woman sitting behind the desk looked up and smiled politely.

Ah...a new secretary, Savannah thought as she stopped in front of the desk.

"Savannah Slade. I have a 9:00 a.m. appointment with Mr. Jefferson."

The secretary scanned a list near her Rolodex. "One moment please." She hit a button on the switchboard and spoke into her headpiece. "Savannah Slade is here. Yes, sir. Right away, sir."

"This way, Miss Slade."

Savannah followed the secretary across the room to a large black door adorned with an enormous relief carving of a dragon spanning the length and breadth of its surface. The door was completely black except for the dragon's eyes and tongue, which were a bright Chinese red. Savannah was still gawking as the secretary ushered her in, then gestured toward a coffee bar near the wall.

"Can I get you anything, Miss Slade?"

"A coffee, black, would be wonderful."

"Please, have a seat," the secretary said as she turned to pour the coffee.

Savannah eyed the office, noting that the Chinese decor had been continued throughout. From the stylized furnishings to a massive desk reminiscent of the door itself to a few tasteful pieces of hanging art, it fostered a feeling of culture and of peace. The office was amazing, but the lawyer was nowhere in sight.

"Where's Mr. Jefferson?" Savannah asked as the secretary handed her the coffee.

"He should be—"

The wall behind the desk suddenly parted, silently sliding into pockets in the wall.

Savannah gasped.

The black man silhouetted in the doorway was, without doubt, the biggest human being she had ever seen. His bald head gleamed beneath the overhead lighting; his shoulders seemed too wide for the doorway. His dark eyes swept up, then down, her person so fast she felt as if she'd just been electronically scanned. When he stepped through the doorway, the room seemed to shrink. He was an imposing man in every way.

And then he smiled, and charm oozed. "Savannah Slade?"

She nodded.

"Thomas Jefferson," he said as he extended his hand.

Savannah felt like he could swallow her whole. Instead, it was her hand that disappeared, but only for a moment.

He pointed to her cup. "Try the coffee and tell me if you like it. I'm experimenting with a mocha hazelnut roast. It's sweet, but that's not a deal breaker for me."

Savannah took a sip. First, because she badly needed the caffeine, and second, because she was afraid to tell him no.

"It's actually very good," she said.

He sat, leaning back in his chair and beaming like a proud papa.

"So, to save us some time this morning, you should know that I called Coleman last night. I'd completely lost touch with him. Your call was a delight. After trading a few old stories, I asked him about your situation. He told me what's going on with you, and also faxed me a copy of your birth certificate. Gerald Lee Stoss is named as your birth father. I know about the journal. I will need to put the original in the safe with your other records, but Laura can make you a copy."

"I have it with me," Savannah said, and pulled it out of her bag.

Thomas buzzed his intercom. "Laura, I need you, please."

The secretary appeared almost instantly.

"Make a copy of that journal for me, will you?"

Savannah handed her the journal, and the woman disappeared.

Thomas eyed her curiously. "May I say, you certainly have a mess on your hands. I want to make sure I understand why you're here. You do intend to make a claim on the Stoss estate?"

Savannah nodded. In a way, the fact that he already knew her story made all of this easier.

"Yes, but not because I'm mercenary or all that desperate for money."

"Then why?" he asked.

"Because according to the journal my father... Andrew Slade...left me, I'm the reason my birth father was murdered. The police don't seem interested in my claim that his family was responsible for his death. It doesn't seem fair that he died trying to do what was right by me. The best way I can see to get justice for him is to take away what the family was willing to kill for, which is the money."

Thomas's eyes narrowed thoughtfully. "You know what?"

She shook her head, suddenly nervous that he was about to tell her that he wouldn't help her.

"There's actually a really big person inside that tiny body of yours," Thomas said. "As for taking on the Stosses, it would be my pleasure."

Savannah sighed with relief. "Oh, thank you. For a moment I thought you were going to turn me down."

He grinned. "Not a chance. I don't like Joseph Stoss, and he doesn't like me. I wouldn't miss this for the world."

Thank you, Coleman Rice, Savannah thought, and took another sip of her coffee.

"The first thing we're going to do is get a DNA sample from you. Joseph was Gerald's twin. There will be enough markers in his DNA to prove you're related. That plus your birth certificate and the contents of the journal should do the job."

"You think it will be that easy?" Savannah asked.

"Oh, no. They'll fight this. Never doubt it. But we'll persevere, and we will win."

"Good."

"Now. Tell me what the police said to you and who you talked to."

Savannah began to relate the story, including Detective Barber's attitude and subsequent dismissal.

"Did you get a copy of the accident report on your father's wreck?"

"They wouldn't give me one."

"I'll take care of that," he said, and made himself a note. "Anything else you want to tell me?"

"Detective Barber questioned me about the boat that exploded near the Stoss estate. Despite me telling him I had just gotten into town, he kept pushing, saying that my staying at the InterContinental Hotel, which has a view of the island where the Stosses live, and the explosion happening the day after my arrival, was too coincidental for his liking."

Jefferson's smile shifted. His eyes narrowed. "Anything else? If you've done anything that might come back on us, you should know that what you tell me is confidential, that it falls under attorney/client privilege."

Savannah stood abruptly, put both hands on the desk and leaned forward until she could see her own reflection in his eyes.

"No, and if you ever ask me that question again, consider your ass fired."

The smile reappeared. "Coleman said you would surprise me. Sorry, but I had to know. If I'm going to represent you to the best of *my* ability, I have to know everything about *you*."

She was still pissed. She backed off, but she wouldn't sit down.

"Then know this, sir. My whole world has just been ripped apart. First by my father's death, then learning he wasn't really my father, learning my sisters aren't really my sisters, that my birth father was murdered and that I'm supposedly the heir to a massive fortune I need to take away from the people who murdered him. I have an almost-fiancé back in Missoula who's not happy I'm here. *I'm* not happy I had to come here. But I don't back down from a fight, and this is going to be a big one. I told Coleman Rice I didn't want a lawyer who was *Sesame Street* nice. I wanted someone tough, who wasn't afraid of a fight. But I *don't* want someone who doesn't believe me one hundred percent. So. Are we on the same page or what?"

Thomas stood. Now he was towering over her, but his demeanor was anything but threatening.

"Yes, ma'am, I believe we are."

Savannah sighed, then dropped back into the chair and dug out her checkbook.

"How much of a retainer do you want?"

"We'll begin with a thousand dollars."

She wrote the check in dark, angry strokes, then tore it off and laid it on the desk between them.

"So what do we do first?"

"I need your DNA sample. Do you have time now?"

She nodded.

"Good. I'm taking you to a lab I use when I want fast results. I'll have the papers drawn up notifying the Stoss family of your intent and demanding DNA samples from them, as well, when we file suit. They'll have to comply as part of the court process."

Savannah's heart thumped nervously. "Do you think

I should make living arrangements somewhere other than a hotel?"

He frowned. "Why?"

"Twenty years ago they threatened to kill me, just like they killed Gerald Stoss. Once they get those papers, I'm thinking I could be a sitting duck."

"Hmm, you may be right. Let me think about what might be a safe place for you. In the meantime, you should be all right. It's going to take a couple of days to get all the paperwork together, and I want to take a look at that accident report, as well."

"I was going to stop by the police department later today and see if Detective Barber has made me a copy. I asked for it once already."

"If he balks, give him my name."

Savannah nodded. "Uh, I have a question."

"Of course."

"That guard down in the lobby…?"

"What about him?"

"Are armed guards the norm here in Miami? I couldn't help but wonder who else has offices in this building?"

He frowned. "Coleman didn't tell you?"

"Tell me what?"

"Part of it has to do with the diamond merchants. But the reason I'm here is a little less obvious. I beat Joseph Stoss in court, and he doesn't like being beaten. I've made other enemies over the years. I like feeling safe."

Savannah nodded.

Thomas pointed to her coffee. "Drink up. It'll take about fifteen minutes for my limo to get here. We'll go to the lab, get the DNA sample and then I'll drop you off at your hotel."

"I drove here."

He frowned. "Where did you park?"

"A parking garage a couple of blocks up."

"Then I'll drive you to your car, but next time, take a cab. I can always have my driver bring you back to the hotel."

"Do you do that for all your clients?" Savannah asked.

He smiled. "Only for the ones who threaten to fire my ass."

She blinked.

He laughed out loud, and the sound echoed within the walls.

"There are some sweet rolls beside the coffee urn. Help yourself. I'm going to see about the limo."

He left the office through the outer doors as Savannah began to relax. This was going to be okay, after all. Her stomach growled as she eyed the glass-covered platter with the assortment of sweet rolls, and she didn't hesitate. She chose a bear claw sprinkled with almonds, carrying it back to her chair and eating as she went. The food was just what she needed to settle her nerves, and by the time they left for the laboratory, Savannah and Thomas Jefferson, Esquire, were on a first-name basis.

Mateo was still in his car a block away from the building, watching the entrance for sight of the blonde. She'd been inside almost thirty minutes when a long white limousine pulled up in front of the entrance.

He sat up straight, wondering who would be getting out. Instead, it was who was about to get in. Two people emerged from the building. He recognized the Slade woman immediately. Then he saw the huge black man towering over her, and his heart skipped a beat.

Jefferson! The boss wasn't going to like this.

He grabbed the phone and hit speed dial as the limo pulled away from the curb. He let a couple of cars get between them, then followed, curious as to where they were going. Just when he thought his call was going to go to voice mail, Joseph answered.

"What?"

"She just got into a limo with Thomas Jefferson."

"Son of a bitch! How did she hook up with him? Where are they going?"

"I'm behind them as we speak."

"Stay with them," Joseph snapped. "I want to know everything they're doing."

"Yes, sir. Actually they're turning into a parking lot."

"Where is it?"

"It's the parking for Deloyd Laboratories."

Joseph frowned. He couldn't figure out why they'd be going to—

And then it hit him. DNA testing. They weren't wasting any time setting the wheels in motion.

"We've got to amp this up before it hits the courts," Joseph said. "Keep following them, and call me tonight. This is getting serious."

"Yes, sir," Mateo said, and disconnected quickly so he could find a place to park.

Frank Barber had just been given a whole new handful of reports on the Wilson case. Thanks to the DNA samples they'd turned in and the urgency of making sure the Stoss family was not a target, the medical examiner had rushed the tests and confirmed Paul Wilson as the deceased male. This left Barber about eighty percent sure the explosion had nothing to do with the Stosses, and that it had been a coincidence that the boat was in such close proximity to the Stoss property. Now all he needed was an ID on the female and maybe they would have something to go on.

His partner, Soldana, was at the company where Paul Wilson had been employed, interviewing the people he'd worked with. If Wilson was having an affair, someone there would likely know about it. He thought about how devastated Rachel Wilson had been and felt bad that he'd had to break the news to her like that. Finding out your husband was not only dead but had most likely died with a lover would be a whole hell of a lot to cope with.

No sooner had he thought of Rachel Wilson than he looked up to see her being escorted toward his desk.

He stood abruptly. "Mrs. Wilson?"

Rachel nodded. "Detective. I called Paul's best friend last night. After a short screaming fest, he confessed to me that he'd known about the affair, and that he also knew the woman."

Barber took her elbow. "Please, have a seat."

"No, but thank you. I only came to give you a name."

He grabbed his notepad. "I'm sorry you're having to go through this, but this is very helpful."

"Her name was Deborah Wilson. Paul's ex."

"I thought you said she'd remarried."

"She had."

"I don't suppose you would happen to know where she lived? I'd be curious to know why her husband hasn't reported her missing."

Her glare deepened. "She got the house when she and

Paul divorced. It's in Coral Gables." She handed him the address. "Her husband's name is Carter Finch."

"Thank you, Mrs. Wilson. I know this was difficult for you."

Her chin was trembling, her eyes welling with tears that she dabbed with a tissue.

"Yes. Well. I'll be leaving now," she said.

"Let me walk you to the elevator," Barber said.

She nodded. "Thank you."

He slipped a hand beneath her elbow and escorted her out of the room and down the hall to the elevator. He punched the button, then glanced up. "The car's coming up now. It won't be long. Thank you again for coming in."

"You're welcome," she said, and dabbed at her eyes again as the doors opened.

To Barber's surprise, Savannah Slade stepped out as Wilson's widow walked in. But instead of claiming his attention, Savannah stopped and stared back into the car as the doors went shut. When she turned around, she was frowning.

"Who was that woman?"

He sighed. "Miss Slade…what do you want?"

"I came to see if you had that copy of the accident report on Gerald Stoss."

"No, I don't. I haven't had time to—"

"Fine. I'm not going to argue with you. My lawyer said if you gave me a hard time, to mention his name."

Barber glared. "I don't like threats."

She shrugged. "It wasn't a threat, and I don't like being ignored."

"So who's this big-shot lawyer you've hired?"

"He's actually a personal friend of the family lawyer from back home. His name is Thomas Jefferson."

Barber's eyes widened. "Seriously?"

"Seriously."

"Shit."

"I had a feeling you might say that," Savannah stated. "About that woman who was getting on the elevator. Who was she?"

"Why?" he asked.

"I've seen her before. At my hotel."

"Not that it's any of your business, but her name is Rachel Wilson. She's the widow of the man who died in the boat explosion."

"Oh. I'm very sorry for her loss." Then something clicked in her memory. "That's actually the day I saw her. She was coming out of the room next to mine. I'm on the thirtieth floor."

Barber frowned, remembering Rachel Wilson had told him that she'd been out of town and had just returned to Miami around noon the day after the explosion.

"You must be mistaken."

"No, I'm not. She came out of the room just as I opened the door for room service. I saw her clearly. Why? What does it matter?"

Barber's heart skipped a beat. When people lied, there was always a reason behind it.

"You're sure?"

"I saw her as clearly as I'm seeing you. She's not a woman you would easily forget. She came out of the room directly next to mine. A few minutes later, as I was sitting on my bed eating, I heard the explosion. I got up and walked to the patio door, but I didn't go out onto the balcony because of the man next door."

Barber was starting to get a sick feeling in the pit of his stomach. One of these two women was lying to him, and the way he looked at it, the woman with the most reason to lie was the dead man's widow, not a stranger to Miami.

"Shit," he muttered. "Come with me."

Savannah followed him to his desk.

"Please, have a seat," he said.

She sat.

"Why did you say you didn't go out onto the balcony?" Barber asked.

"Because, like I said, there was a man out there and I didn't feel like talking to anyone. He must have been making a phone call, then been interrupted by the explosion, because I saw him drop the phone into his pocket."

Barber felt the blood draining from his face as he reached for the stack of new reports, and began shuffling through them, looking for one from the bomb squad. He found it, scanned the info and then looked up at Savannah as if he'd never seen her before.

"This man. Would you know him if you saw him again?"

She nodded. "Actually, I know his name, because a few minutes later, when the news began covering the event and I learned it was close to the Stoss estate, I let my curiosity get the better of me, and I did go out onto the balcony. He was still there."

"So how do you know his name?" Barber asked.

She nodded. "He introduced himself and tried to pick me up, but why does this matter?"

Barber grabbed a pad and pen. "What name did he give you?"

"Alejandro Montoya, and oddly enough, I saw him again yesterday when I was on my way to the cemetery where my mother is buried. He was driving a very new, very sporty white BMW. He acted kind of weird for a person who'd tried to pick me up the day before."

"Like how?" Barber asked.

"He frowned and looked away, and then did a quick about-face and looked at me and waved before driving away."

"Sit tight," Barber said, and turned to his computer and started to type. Within seconds, a picture popped up.

After quickly scanning the man's arrest and conviction record, he turned the screen toward Savannah. "Is this him?"

She leaned forward. "Yes! That's him. Why? Is he bad?"

"According to his rap sheet, he's very, very bad. You don't want to run into him again, okay?"

Savannah's heart skipped a beat. "I don't understand. I swear, I had nothing to do with that poor man's boat exploding. I am not threatening the Stoss family. I haven't even contacted them yet."

Barber felt sick to his stomach. He had a horrible feeling he'd done this woman a disservice, but it was too late to take back what he'd done. The report he'd just looked at had confirmed that the detonating device on the bomb had probably been a cell phone. It was too damn big a coincidence that Rachel Wilson had been seen coming out of the hotel room of a man who was suspected of making a living by blowing up things— and people—for money, and that Savannah Slade had seen him standing on the balcony with a phone in his hand only seconds after the explosion. Forgetting for a moment that Savannah was still sitting there, he reached for his notepad and began making notes to himself.

Check Rachel Wilson's bank account.

Check her phone records to see who she'd been calling recently.

Then he frowned. Why hadn't Carter Finch contacted the police about his missing wife? How did he play into this?

Barber reached for his cell and hit one on the speed dial. Within moments Al Soldana answered.

"What's up, Frank? I'm already in the car on my way back to headquarters."

"I've got an address in Coral Gables." He read it aloud.

"Okay, got it," Al said. "Who lives there?"

"Rachel Wilson was just here, said she called her husband's best friend last night and pushed until he admitted Paul was having an affair, but get this…it was with his ex-wife, Deborah. Deborah is now married to a man named Carter Finch. If she's the dead woman in the water, I'm curious as to why he didn't report her missing. And there's more." He suddenly remembered Savannah and glanced her way. She was clearly confused as to what was happening. "I'll explain when I get there. Wait for me before you go in."

"No problem," Al said.

When Barber disconnected, Savannah shifted nervously.

"Am I in trouble? Are you accusing me of something?"

"I'm not accusing you of anything, ma'am. But I think you might have just blown my case wide open."

"Am I free to leave?"

"Yes, ma'am. And I promise, as soon as I get this case wrapped up, I'll pull the accident report on Gerald Stoss and read what you gave me. Deal?"

She nodded, then handed him her card. "My cell

phone number is on there. I'm not sure what's going on, but I'm thankful you finally believe I had nothing to do with the boat exploding."

"Yes, ma'am. And stay safe," Barber added as she got up to leave.

"Why wouldn't I?" she asked. "What do you know that I don't?"

He thought of the phone call he'd made to Joseph Stoss, then reminded himself that, so far, this woman's story was just that: a story. There was no reason to believe her life was in danger.

"Nothing. It's just what homicide cops say."

"Oh. Well, thanks."

"And thank you," he echoed.

It wasn't until she began to walk away that he focused on the unusual color of her hair—almost a white-blond—and that was when it hit him. She had the same color hair as Michael and Joseph Stoss. Admittedly, she could have colored it thinking it would make her case that much stronger. But if she hadn't, it was a great big coincidence that it was such a noticeable match—unless she really was related. He shrugged off the thought. Right now he had a murderer to arrest.

Seven

Savannah left the police station more confused than she'd been before she went in. The only thing she knew for sure was that Barber wasn't looking at her for the bombing, and that she might have just become a witness in a murder. How had all this gotten so mixed up? She just wanted to solve her own father's murder, not get involved in someone else's problems.

The good news was that having a lawyer meant she was no longer in this alone. She started the car and jacked up the air-conditioning, then decided to call him before she got back into traffic. He would want to know the latest.

As the phone rang, the new secretary answered.

"Jefferson Law Office."

"Laura, this is Savannah Slade. I was just there this morning, remember?"

"Yes, Miss Slade. How can I help you?"

"Is Mr. Jefferson in? There's something I need to tell him."

"Yes, he is. One moment please."

Again, "A Hard Day's Night" began playing in her

ear. Knowing the man behind the choice of music, now it made sense.

All of a sudden Thomas's voice was booming in her ear.

"Hello, Savannah. What's up?"

"I just left the police station. I didn't get the accident report yet, but something happened that has certainly changed Detective Barber's attitude toward me."

"How so?"

"On the day after I checked into the hotel, I happened to see a woman coming out of the room next to mine. She turned out to be the widow of the man who died in that boat explosion. I saw her at the police station, and out of curiosity I asked Detective Barber who she was. When he asked why I wanted to know, I said because I'd seen her once before and was curious as to who she was. He asked where I'd seen her, but when I told him, he said I was mistaken. After assuring him I wasn't, and telling him what else I'd seen right after that, it appears I've become an unwitting witness in a homicide investigation."

"Are you serious?"

"I wish I wasn't, but yes. Supposedly she'd told the police that she wasn't even in the city at the time of the explosion, but I blew that alibi. Later I saw a man from the same room out on the balcony with a cell phone only seconds after the explosion, and it seems the bomb was detonated with a cell phone, so—"

"Shit, woman. Are you telling me you also saw the bomber?"

"I think so. Maybe."

"Have they asked you to try to identify him?"

"Actually, he tried to pick me up a short while later. I refused his invitation, and then I saw him again

yesterday in his car. He'd told me his name and everything, so now the police know who she'd been to see."

"Did they say why she would have had her husband
killed?"

"I think he was having an affair with his ex-wife."

"Ouch. You do have a way of stepping into it, don't
you?"

Savannah leaned back against the seat and closed her
eyes.

"All I want to do is find the truth about my father's
death, not get mixed up in all of this."

"I know, but you're already there. Mixed up in it, I
mean. This is one of those times when life reminds us
we're not in control. I suggest you keep a low profile
until everyone has been arrested. The last thing you
want is for this bomber to realize you're the one who
fingered him."

Savannah's voice began to shake. "Am I in danger?"

"You could be."

"What do I do?"

"Go back to the hotel and stay there until you hear
from me."

Her voice broke. "I'm scared, Thomas. I don't
know who I'm more afraid of—the Stosses, or these
people."

"It's going to be okay. Just know that I promised
Coleman I'd take good care of you, and I always keep
my word."

"Okay. I'm leaving now, and thank you."

"Don't thank me yet. We're barely getting started.
Now get yourself back to the hotel and hunker down.
Looks like we've got a fight on our hands."

Savannah's hands were shaking as she laid the cell

phone back in her purse and put the car in gear. It never even occurred to her to check the mirror to see if she was being followed.

Barber met Soldana outside the residence of Deborah and Carter Finch.

Al got out of his own car as his partner pulled up.

"Hey, Frank. I turned up some interesting information when I went out to Wilson's work."

"Like what?" Frank asked.

"His current wife was once his mistress. She's the reason his first marriage broke up."

Frank frowned. "It happens. But it doesn't tie in with why Deborah Finch's husband didn't report her missing."

"Yeah, you're right, but you said you have more. What's up?"

"You remember that woman I told you about who said she was Gerald Stoss's daughter?"

"Yes, what about her?"

"So, she came by to ask for a copy of the accident report in his death and saw Rachel Wilson as she was leaving the office. She asked who she was, then mentioned she'd seen her before. And get this—she said she'd seen her at the hotel coming out of the room next to hers only minutes before the explosion. And *then* she said when she heard the explosion, she ran to her balcony window and saw a man standing on the adjoining balcony drop a cell phone into his pocket."

"I don't get it," Al said. "What's that—"

"Remember, Rachel told us she'd just gotten back into town shortly before we came to notify her, not the day before. And that's not all. I got a report back from the bomb squad after you left. They say the bomb was probably detonated by something like a cell phone."

Al nodded. Things were beginning to fall into place. "We need to check hotel security. See if they caught Rachel Wilson's visit on tape. And maybe check to see who the man was in the room next door."

"The Slade woman already gave me a name. She said later she went out onto her balcony and he was still standing on his. She said he tried to pick her up, even told her his name. Good thing she passed on his invitation. He might have been wanting to get rid of any witnesses."

Al pointed toward the house. "So what's up with this place, then?"

"This is where Paul Wilson's ex lived with her husband. It's time to get his take on this story."

The detectives headed up the sidewalk to the front door and rang the bell, then rang it again...and again.

"I guess no one's home," Al said.

Frank frowned. This didn't feel right. On impulse, he grabbed the doorknob and turned it. The door swung open.

They looked at each other, then into the foyer.

Frank stepped across the threshold. "Man...they sure like it cold in here. The temperature has got to be down in the sixties." Then he called out, "Mr. Finch? Carter Finch? Miami P.D."

Something squawked. Al looked at Frank. "That sounded like a parrot."

Frank nodded, then stepped farther into the foyer and called out again.

"Hello! Miami P.D."

Another squawk ensued, followed by a "Hey, good lookin'."

Al grinned. "Make that a talking parrot."

Suddenly Frank frowned. "I think I know why it's so damned cold in here," he said, and took a handkerchief out of his pocket at the faint scent of decomposing flesh.

Al caught the same scent and reached for his own pocket.

Frank kept on walking, moving into the living room toward the sofa. Within seconds, he stopped. A dead man lay sprawled on his back on the floor—a gun near his right hand, a hole in his right temple and an even bigger hole on the left, where the bullet had exited.

Al circled the sofa and moved toward a massive glass coffee table. "Is that a suicide note?"

Frank stepped closer, reading the note the man had left in plain sight. "'God forgive me, but Paul and Deborah got what they deserved.' Looks like we found Carter Finch. Now we know why he didn't report his wife missing."

All of a sudden they heard cautious footsteps in the entryway, and then someone running, followed by a woman calling Finch's name.

"Carter? Carter!"

Frank turned and headed toward the foyer, meeting a woman just at the entrance to the living room.

Startled by the sight of a stranger running toward her, she turned and ran screaming for help.

Frank ran after her. "Miami P.D., ma'am. We're from Miami P.D."

She staggered, then stopped just inside the doorway, her hand over her breast as if to steady the frantic beating of her heart. She was forty-something and a well-dressed woman, and by the size of the diamonds on her fingers, well-heeled, too.

"What are you doing here? Where's Carter?"

"Call it in," Frank said to Al, and then produced his shield as he led her just outside. "What is your relationship to Mr. Finch?"

She started crying. "I'm his sister, Sheila Chin. Please. What's happening?"

"When was the last time you talked to your brother?"

"Two days ago."

"Are you sure?" Frank asked.

"Positive. I was watching TV when they interrupted about that boat explosion in the harbor, and I called him up to ask if he'd seen it. Then that night my daughter went into labor. Her second child. I called to tell him he was an uncle again, but he didn't answer, so I left a message. I spent most of the day at the hospital yesterday, and it was only last night, as I was getting ready for bed, that I realized he'd never called me back. But it was late and I didn't want to wake him up, so I called again this morning. This time when he didn't answer, I got worried and…well…here I am." She grabbed his arm. "Please, what's wrong?"

"Ma'am, we found a body in the living room and—"

She screamed and pushed past him.

"Al! Stop her!" Frank yelled, but it was already too late. Although she'd stopped on the back side of the sofa, she could see the body on the floor on the other side.

"No, no, no," she moaned, and then covered her face and began to sob.

"I'm sorry," Frank said. "Is that your brother?"

"Yes. Oh, God, what happened? Was it a break-in?"

"Do you know if your brother and his wife had been having problems?" Frank asked.

She staggered, then turned her back on the body and leaned against the sofa.

"Not that I know of. Where's Deborah? Oh, my God! Did they kill her, too?"

"Ma'am, we don't think this was a robbery. It appears Mr. Finch might have taken his life. There's a note and—"

Shock, followed by anger, swept over her face. "No way! Carter would never kill himself!" she shouted, and spun, staring down at the body in disbelief. All of a sudden she gasped and pointed. "The gun! Look at the gun!"

"What about it? Do you recognize it?" Frank asked.

"That's not right. Carter was left-handed."

Frank looked down at the body. "Al. What did the note say again?"

"That Paul and Deborah got what they deserved."

Frank sighed. This kept getting better. What had first seemed like an explanation of suicide now appeared to be a cover-up, setting this man to take the fall for the murder of Paul Wilson and Deborah Finch. Only whoever had done the job hadn't done his homework. If Carter Finch was a lefty, he would never have picked up or fired a gun with his right hand.

Frank could hear the sound of approaching sirens. Within minutes the place would be crawling with crime scene investigators and police, and he needed to get Sheila Chin's statement. He walked her out to his cruiser, handed her a large pad of paper and a pen and asked her to write down exactly what she'd just told him.

She did as he asked, then handed him the pad with shaking hands.

"Can I call my husband?"

"Yes, ma'am, and I'm sorry for your loss."

He walked a short distance away, giving her some privacy, but it turned out to be an unnecessary action. The moment her call was answered, she tried to speak, then began to sob. He winced. This was the part of his job that totally sucked.

By the time Savannah had returned to the hotel, she was paranoid, imagining she saw Montoya's white BMW at every turn, imagining she would never see Judd or her sisters again. Today had proven one thing to her. This had gotten too complicated. She couldn't do this by herself anymore. She handed her car keys to the parking valet, pocketed her receipt and stopped in one of the hotel shops long enough to buy a cold drink and a couple of snacks. She had to force herself not to run for the elevators, and when she finally got in, she moved to the side with her back against the wall and stared down at the floor, ignoring the couple who were already there and the man who hurried in after her. When the car stopped at the thirtieth floor, she darted off and hurried toward her room. By the time she reached it, she was running. The card key was in her hand. She swiped it quickly, then pushed inside. Only after she'd turned the dead bolt and put the chain on the door did she begin to relax.

Her legs were shaking. She couldn't quit thinking about what had just transpired. Her own reason for coming to Miami had gotten lost in what she'd inadvertently seen.

Judd. She needed to talk to Judd. She glanced at the clock. It was just after five in the afternoon. That would be just past three o'clock back home. She didn't know what he might be doing, but he was about to get interrupted.

She opened her Dr Pepper and took a quick sip, then set it aside, kicked off her shoes and crawled up on the bed with her cell. Just the thought of hearing his voice was enough to settle her nerves. She punched in the number, then reached for the bag of potato chips, tore it open and stuffed one in her mouth as she waited for the call to go through. Three chips and five rings later, the phone went to voice mail. Disappointed, she left a quick message for him to call her and disconnected.

She would call Bud. He would be the voice of calm and tell her what to do. But before she could dial the number, her phone rang. Thinking it was Judd, she answered with a smile.

"Hi, you," she said.

"Honey, it's me, Bud."

"I was just about to call you."

"Are you sitting down?"

Her smile shifted, then disappeared. "What's wrong?"

"Holly's on conference call. I wanted to tell you both at the same time."

"Tell us what, Bud? Talk!" Holly yelled, obviously upset at having been put on hold.

Savannah held her breath.

"Maria is hurt. Someone put a bomb in her car. She wasn't in it when it went off, but was very close by. She's in the hospital under police protection. The hospital called me. I immediately got put through to the detective who was in her room at the time."

Savannah gasped, then closed her eyes, imagining her vivacious sister injured badly enough to end up in the hospital. "Oh, my God. How bad is she hurt?"

Holly started to sob. "Is she going to be all right? Please, Bud, tell us she's going to be all right."

"I don't know anything more than what the cop told me. What you do need to know is it looks like Maria has made a conquest. Whoever this cop is, he's taken this attack on her very personally. I was getting ready to fly out there when he told me I could come if I wanted, but that I needed to know he wasn't leaving her side and wouldn't let anyone hurt her again."

"What should we do, Bud?" Holly asked. "Do you think we should all fly to Tulsa?"

"I don't know. I think I'm going to wait to make a decision until I hear from him again. I've got a mess on my hands here at the ranch, and I hate to leave right now."

"What's wrong?" Savannah asked.

"We had a freak snowstorm last night. It'll melt soon, but right now we're a little short on hay and trying to feed cattle in two feet of snow."

"Oh, my," Holly said. "I've been so focused on what's happening here that I haven't even watched the weather once since I left."

Savannah realized now was not the time to let them know what was happening to her. Compared to Maria, she was fine.

"Me, either," she said. "So you think we should wait until you call us again to make a decision?"

"Yes."

"Okay," Holly said, and then added, "Are you okay, Savannah?"

"I'm fine. How about you?"

"I'm good. Take care," Holly warned.

"Both of you take care," Bud said. "I don't want to make another phone call like this. As soon as I hear an update, I'll call the both of you. And just so you don't forget, I miss you—both of you."

"We miss you, too," they said in unison. "Bye."

The connection ended; Savannah dropped her cell phone onto the bed, and then curled into a fetal position and cried herself to sleep.

Mateo had followed Savannah up to the thirtieth floor, waited a few seconds after she got off, then glanced up at the floor number as if he'd just realized this was his stop.

"Oops. Hey. This is my floor, too," he said, and grabbed the door to keep it from closing on him and slipped out.

He stepped around the corner. But when he saw she was running, he frowned. Either she knew she was being followed or something had spooked her big-time.

When she suddenly stopped, he ducked into an open doorway leading to the ice machine, hoping she hadn't spotted him. He waited a couple of seconds, then looked out. She was already inside.

He checked out her room number, then hurried back to the elevator. Stoss wanted an accounting of her activities, and he himself wanted some food and a cold beer. Hopefully he could produce a satisfactory report on the first, then dig into the second without further delay.

Joseph was just leaving his office for the day when his cell rang. He recognized Mateo's number, and made a U-turn and stepped back into his office for privacy's sake.

"Yes?"

"She's had a busy day. After going to Jefferson's office and then with him to the lab, he brought her back to a parking garage. She got her car and drove directly to the police station. She was in there less than an hour, came back out to her car and made a phone call. Then she drove back to the hotel. I got in the elevator with her and followed her off on the thirtieth floor, where she ran all the way to her door."

"She made you! That's why she was running," Joseph snapped. "Damn it, you're better than this."

Mateo's eyes narrowed angrily. "She did *not* make me. This I know for sure. She didn't look around when she got back to the hotel as if searching for someone. She never looked over her shoulder when she got to the elevators, and she never looked at anyone else who was in the car with her. When she got off, she was already running. She didn't see me, but something has her spooked."

Joseph cursed beneath his breath. "It's got to be that damned lawyer. Of all the lawyers in Miami, why did she have to pick him?" Then he frowned. "Unless she knew about my history with Jefferson and did it thinking it would throw me off. If that's true, then I've been underestimating her, which isn't good."

"So what would you have me do?" Mateo asked. "I can get to her now, take her out in her room, and no one would be the wiser."

"No. Too much hotel security. Just make sure you keep tabs on her tomorrow and keep me informed."

"So you don't want me to stake out the hotel tonight?"

"No. Just start tailing her in the morning. I need to think about this some more."

"Yes, sir," Mateo said, and disconnected, smiling. He could almost taste that cold beer already.

* * *

Rachel Wilson was in the den pouring her second martini of the evening. She'd been getting flower deliveries and sympathy calls all day, ever since the news had gotten out among their friends that Paul was dead. She was confident she had a handle on just how much devastation to let show. After all, she had two roles to play: the grieving widow, and the woman who'd been betrayed. Between the sympathy of her social circle and being the recipient of Paul's two-million-dollar life insurance policy, she was feeling smug, and she'd only had to invest fifty thousand to make it happen. That was a nice return, if she said so herself. The doorbell began to ring—again. She took a quick sip of the martini, then set it aside as she went to answer.

Pausing a moment to catch her breath, she shifted her expression to the one she called "troubled sorrow" and opened the door. To her surprise, it was the detectives who'd talked to her earlier about Paul's accident.

"Detective Barber. Detective Soldana. To what do I owe such a late visit?"

Frank glanced at his watch. "It's not quite eight o'clock, and you know detectives work all kinds of hours."

"I suppose. At any rate, do come in."

"We won't be long," Frank said as they followed her into the living room and took a seat. "We just need to clear up a few things and then we'll be going."

"Of course. Anything I can do to help," Rachel said, and sat down in one of the single red chairs opposite the sofa.

"It's good you feel that way," Frank said, taking the lead as they'd planned.

"What do you mean?" she asked.

"We thought you'd like to know that we located Carter Finch."

She nodded thoughtfully, waiting. When neither of them spoke, she shifted in her seat and smoothed at a loose curl on the side of her forehead. The silence continued so long that she got nervous and spoke.

"So what did Carter have to say about Deborah?"

"Not much. He'd been dead a couple of days when we found him."

She gasped, her eyes widening in what she hoped was disbelief.

"Oh, no! How terrible! What happened?"

"He was murdered," Al said.

A momentary frown creased her forehead. "Murdered? But I thought—"

Frank leaned forward. "You thought what, Mrs. Wilson?"

She flushed, then licked her lips before speaking, as if gauging her words to make sure she gave nothing away.

"Why, I mean…how odd. What happened?"

"Someone tried to make it look like a suicide," Al said.

"Tried to… I don't understand?"

"I'll bet you don't," Frank said. "Here's the deal. Whoever you hired to do the job didn't do his research. Carter Finch was left-handed, only your guy left the gun he'd supposedly used to kill himself near his right hand, instead."

She jumped to her feet, her hands curled into fists.

"I don't know—"

"Sit down, Mrs. Wilson. We're not through with you," Frank said.

Rachel sat as panic enveloped her. This wasn't supposed to be happening.

"I assure you, I had nothing to do with this," she said, then started to cry. "I wasn't even in Miami when it happened."

"That's a lie," Frank said. "We have surveillance footage from the hotel showing you coming out of a room on the thirtieth floor only minutes before the explosion. We also have bank records showing you withdrew fifty thousand dollars three days ago."

"I can explain that. I took that money with me. I was out of town...shopping and spending time with my friends. I told you."

"We know what you said, but that's not what the facts prove."

"Facts? What facts?" she shouted. "I did nothing, I tell you. Nothing."

"Nothing except pay Alejandro Montoya to kill your husband and his mistress while they were out on that boat together. It must have stuck in your craw to know what was happening. During a visit that Detective Soldana made to your husband's workplace, he learned that while he was still married to Deborah Finch, you were the 'other woman.' You had an affair with him while he was married, and he dumped Deborah for you. Life goes on. You two marry. She remarries. Everyone is living happily ever after—until you find out that he's gone back to her."

Her heart was pounding so loudly she couldn't hear—she couldn't think. She had to regain control of the situation.

"I don't know anyone named Montoya. I didn't pay anyone to commit a murder. You're wrong, I tell you.

You're wrong. I want my lawyer. I have nothing else to say to you."

Both detectives stood. "Then there's nothing else we have to say, except please stand up. Rachel Wilson, you're under arrest for the murders of Paul Wilson and Deborah Finch. You have the right to—"

Rachel started weeping, drowning out most of the Miranda warning as if her tears could negate the words' meaning. But it didn't matter. Frank Barber finished his due diligence in informing her of her rights as Al handcuffed her. When they started toward the door, she began to plead.

"Please. You can't do this. I'm innocent. I don't know anyone named Montoya. I have nothing to do with this."

"By the way," Frank said. "I don't suppose you'd know where Mr. Montoya is at this moment, because if he's making plans to leave the country, you're going to take the heat for this all on your own."

She yanked on the handcuffs, forcing them to stop.

"What if I do?"

"What if you do what?" Al asked.

"What if I know where he is? If I give him up, can we make a deal?"

Frank had heard it all before, but it never failed to amaze him how perps were so willing to turn on each other to save their own hide.

"We don't have any authority to make deals," he said, and pulled, forcing her to continue walking, but she was talking fast.

"You have to stop him! He's going to get away, and I'm not taking the blame for this all by myself. You have to understand. He played on my weaknesses, empathizing with me when I learned Paul was cheating, making promises to me."

"You've already asked for an attorney, Mrs. Wilson. We're taking you to headquarters, where you'll be fingerprinted and booked into jail. You'll have your phone call then, and I suggest you don't speak until your lawyer arrives."

"I take it back! I take it back! I don't want a lawyer. You have to listen. Montoya's leaving the country tonight. If you don't stop him, he'll be in Brazil by morning."

"Which airline?"

"I don't know. I swear."

"I'll call it in," Al said as Frank opened the back door to their cruiser and put her inside.

Rachel's tears were drying. She was moving from shock to anger. How had this gone so wrong so fast? This wasn't supposed to happen. Damn Paul for being a cheat. Damn Carter for being left-handed. Damn Montoya for screwing it up. Damn all men in general. And that was when it hit her. There wouldn't be many men where she was going, except maybe the guards.

Al finished his call, and then got into the car. "They're already notifying airport security. They'll stop him."

Frank put the car in gear and drove away. This had been one seriously unexpected day. But the biggest twist of all was that their break had come from a woman he'd suspected of running a con.

At the least, he would definitely look into her claims. At the most, he might wind up owing her one big-ass apology.

Eight

The half-eaten food from the room service tray was on the floor outside Savannah's door. She'd awakened around nine o'clock and ordered dinner, then hadn't been able to eat for thinking about her sister Maria in ICU in some strange hospital, in danger for her life and without any friends or family there. Bud had said a policeman had taken a personal interest in her, but that was no substitute for a loved one when something this awful happened.

She still wanted to pitch everything and get on the first plane to Tulsa. She'd called Holly earlier, but it hadn't made her feel any better. Holly was just as upset as she was, and of the same mind. But Bud had asked them to wait until he heard from the policeman again, so now they were waiting. Bud had been a guiding force for them almost as much as Andrew had, and it was instinct to obey.

It was after eleven. She kept thinking about Maria, praying over and over that she would live. The television was on, but the volume was turned down to little more than a murmur. She was propped up in her bed with her legs under the covers and the air conditioner blowing full blast, reading yet another passage from her photocopy of the journal her father had left her. She missed holding the real thing. It had been a tiny link to Andrew. But even in the copy, the strokes and curls of her father's handwriting were so familiar, though the words he'd written were still a shock. She turned to yet another chapter of how her past had unfolded.

When you first came to live with Maria and me, you called me Mama. It was Maria who first taught you to say Daddy. You took to it like the proverbial fish to water. Suddenly every male was Daddy. The man at the feed store. The teller where we went to deposit checks from the cattle sales. The postman where we went to buy stamps. It took you a while longer to understand that Daddy didn't represent all men. That it was a word meant just for me.

When you'd been with us for about eight months and were nearing your third birthday, you woke up with fever and vomiting, sick from some passing childhood illness. It was around midnight. A couple of hours passed as you continued to battle bouts of nausea, with me holding you and trying to figure out what to do to keep you from getting dehydrated to the point of danger. As time moved toward morning, we were both exhausted. You were worn out and clung tightly to me each time I tried to clean you up. Your behavior was almost frantic—as if you feared each time I put you down that the familiar might be taken away from you again.

I could only imagine previous times like this, when your mother, Chloe, would have been the midnight angel who gave you comfort, and how confused you must be, wondering where she was and who I was, and how this transfer had come to pass.

Finally the fever broke and the nausea was over. I had you bathed and in a clean nightgown. When I picked you back up, you had your blankie and Baby, your stuffed rabbit, under your chin. I sat down in the rocker by your bed to rock you back to sleep. Your eyes were growing heavy—your breathing easier since the fever had broken. You had a bunny ear in one hand and my finger in the other. We rocked and rocked, and I thought you'd finally gone to sleep. But when I started to get up and put you in your bed, you opened your eyes and looked straight into mine, and said, "Daddy." Needless to say, I sat back down with you and held you until morning.

After that, you never said it to anyone other than me. I don't know what happened in your little head, but somehow you figured out that Daddy wasn't just a name for men, but the word for someone who loved you and took care of you. I think I cried a little that night, knowing that I was reaping the joy of raising you only because a good woman had died.

Savannah closed the journal and then leaned her head against the headboard as tears rolled down her face. The poignancy of that passage was almost too painful to bear. She'd loved her father dearly but had no idea what a truly special man he'd been. The fact that he'd had to die for her to find this out was even more devastating. She would never have the chance to thank him. All she could do was her best to right the wrong that had put her in his keep.

She glanced at the television as she reached for a tissue, then began scrambling for the remote and upping the volume just in time to hear the on-site journalist covering a piece of breaking news: Detectives Barber and Soldana ushering a woman into the station in handcuffs.

"...break in the boat bombing that killed local residents Paul Wilson and his ex-wife, Deborah Wilson Finch. It's reported that Wilson's current wife, Rachel Wilson, learned her husband was having an affair with his ex-wife and hired a hit man to blow up the boat. She has admitted to her part in the bombing. We received word only seconds before this broadcast that the accused hit man was arrested at the gate to his departing flight to Brazil only minutes before takeoff."

"Hallelujah."

It felt as if the weight of the world had just been lifted. Yes, she still had to deal with the mess that had brought her to Miami, but becoming involved, however innocently, in this murder investigation had been horrifying.

Within minutes of the broadcast, her cell phone began to ring. When Savannah saw who was calling, it felt like the icing on the cake.

"Judd! Thank God."

Judd frowned. That almost sounded desperate.

"Hey, sweet thing, what's going on?"

She shivered with sudden longing. Just the sound of his voice was enough to tie a knot in the pit of her stomach.

"I have things I need to tell you."

Unconsciously, Judd's fingers tightened around the receiver.

"Talk to me, honey."

"Oh, Judd, it's all such a mess. The day of my arrival, I was in my hotel and saw something happen that broke a murder case wide open. I didn't even know that it mattered until today, when it accidentally came out when I was talking to the homicide detective handling my case. He's also the lead detective in that boat bombing I told you about. The one they thought I might be involved in. It wasn't an accident, and the explosion killed two people. What I saw broke the murderer's alibi."

"Sweet heaven, Savannah."

"I know, but until today, I didn't know that what I'd seen even mattered."

"Okay, I get that, but damn it, Savannah, I'm thinking you need a keeper."

"I was beginning to think that, too. I was scared I was going to wind up being the only witness, and what if they came after me, too? My lawyer was already on top of it, looking for a safer place for me to stay, when I saw the broadcast showing the wife being arrested. Even better, she admitted it, and the hired killer has been arrested, too, which I hope lets me off the hook of having to testify."

"I'm so sorry," Judd said. "Sorry you were scared. Sorry you went through all that by yourself."

She thought of Maria and pinched the bridge of her nose to keep from crying. But even that didn't stop her voice from beginning to shake.

"That's not the worst. Bud called late this afternoon. Maria is in a Tulsa hospital."

"No? What the hell happened?"

"Someone put a bomb in her car. She wasn't in it

when it went off, but she was close enough to get injured. We don't have a prognosis yet, but Bud said he'll call Holly and me as soon as he hears."

The silence was telling. Savannah could almost hear the thoughts spiraling through Judd's head.

"I know," she said softly. "I know it could happen to me, too."

"I can't take this anymore," he muttered. "You're the most important person in my life, and you're going through this hell on your own. What are you still trying to prove, Savannah?"

"I'm not trying to prove anything, Judd. This is something that landed in my lap, and I'm doing my best to get through it."

"Alone."

Tears suddenly blurred her vision. The urge to give in was so strong. She was scared. She did feel like too many things were out of her control. She sighed.

"I know you guys got a freak snowstorm the other day. I know you have your hands full on the ranch right now, but I'll make a deal with you, okay?"

"I'm listening."

"My lawyer is in the process of getting the paperwork together to file against the Stoss family. I'll admit, after learning about what happened to Maria, I'm really scared about what will happen. They wanted me dead when I was two. That's not going to change. Grown, I'm an even bigger threat. So how about I give you a call when I find out when the papers are going to be filed? You can fly out and stay with me until I can go home. I'm expecting that once I've made whatever court appearances I have to when the process starts, it will probably be weeks, even months, before things go to trial, so I'll be able to come home."

"What about the time between now and the filing?"

"I should be fine. The Stoss family still doesn't know I'm here...or even that I still exist. At this point, there's absolutely no reason to assume I'm in danger."

"Yeah, okay. So you promise you'll call me before this happens, right?"

"Yes, yes, I promise."

"Okay. Just so you know, I miss you like crazy."

"Oh, Judd, I miss you and love you, too."

"Love you more," Judd said. "Bye, honey."

"Bye."

She heard a click, and then he was gone. Still restless, she tossed her cell phone on the bed and walked out onto her balcony.

Outside, the Miami heat was tempered by a cool ocean breeze that lifted the hair from her neck. If only her troubles could blow away as easily. She leaned against the railing, looking out across the harbor to the little islands connected by man-made causeways. It felt surreal, knowing she had family somewhere out there who'd been willing to kill a member of their own for money. One of her father's favorite quotes had been the verse from the bible about the "love of money being the root of all evil." In this case, it certainly held true.

For now she felt safe, but only because the Stosses were unaware of her presence. At least, after talking to Judd, she had something to look forward to. Knowing he was only days away from being in her arms sent a shiver of longing through her body. He was the Alpha and Omega to her world, and losing him wasn't an option. She knew she'd pushed him way past the point of reason. He was a man with a bone-deep need to protect those he loved, and after the past three days, she was ready to admit she was in over her head.

But with the arrest of Rachel Wilson and her hired killer, at least she was now free to move about on her own again, which was a huge relief. Tomorrow she was going back to Graceland Memorial cemetery in the hopes of catching the person who regularly left fresh flowers on her mother's grave. The gates opened at daybreak. She would be there, waiting to get to her mother's grave. If she was lucky, she might actually find someone who'd known her—who could answer some of the many questions Savannah had about her.

With a last look across the water, she turned her back on the moonlight and went inside, taking extra care to lock the sliding doors behind her. Setting her alarm for an early rising, she crawled into bed and quickly fell asleep.

Savannah had just gotten up to go to the bathroom, and was debating with herself about getting another couple of hours' sleep or just waiting for the sun to come up so she could go stake out the cemetery, when her phone suddenly rang.

She grabbed it on the second ring, recognizing Bud's number on the caller ID.

"Hello?"

Bud heard the fear in her voice and wanted to allay it as soon as possible.

"Maria woke up. The detective just called me. His name is Bodie Scott, and I'm telling you that so you'll remember it, because it appears he's fallen hard for our girl."

The release of panic was so strong that Savannah started to cry. "Thank God. Thank God. Is she going to be all right?"

"Bodie said she has a concussion, fractured rib,

stitches to close the cuts from flying debris and a lot of contusions, but nothing life-threatening. She definitely had angels watching out for her. I've already called Holly. I was going to do another conference call, but she wouldn't hear about it. Said she wasn't going to be put on hold again to learn if her sister was alive. Pretty much read me the riot act, and you know me, when it comes to Holly, I always fold."

Savannah laughed through tears. "When it comes to Holly, we all fold. For someone so sweet and soft-spoken, she can be daunting."

"That I know," Bud said. "So is everything really all right with you?"

Savannah sighed. One day she would tell him—she would tell all of them—what she'd unwittingly stepped into, but not until they were all back home together.

"It is now," she said. "I talked to Judd late last night."

"Dang, I never thought to call him about Maria," Bud muttered.

"I told him. Needless to say, the news only made him worry about me more."

"And don't you think with good reason, honey?"

"Yes. We made a deal. As soon as the lawyer gets the papers ready to file on my behalf, I'll let Judd know. He will be here with me before it happens, so I'm not alone when the proverbial shit hits the fan."

"Thank God. Look, I know it's early there. Go back to bed. After this news, we can all rest easier."

"Can Maria take phone calls?"

"I don't think so. At least, not yet," Bud said. "She's in ICU."

"Be sure and keep me updated on her progress or I'm going to worry."

"Absolutely," he said. "Love you, sugar."

"You, too," Savannah said.

She hung up the phone, checked the alarm to make sure it was still set for six-thirty and crawled back into bed. Tears were drying on her face as she fell asleep.

Even though he'd missed a whole lot of sleep last night, Frank Barber walked into headquarters with a bounce in his step.

A cop exiting the door as he came in saw him and gave him a quick slap on the back.

"Nice catch you and Al made last night."

Frank grinned. "Yeah, thanks," he said, and headed for the elevator.

A lawyer and a couple of clerks he knew joined him as he got in.

"Good job, Frank. Didn't see that one coming," the lawyer said.

Frank nodded. "Got a lucky break."

The car stopped. He got off. "Have a good one," he said as the doors closed behind him.

He walked into the office and went straight to his desk. Savannah Slade and her story had been the last thing on his mind before he went to sleep and the first thing he thought of when he woke up. He grabbed his coffee cup and headed for the break room, filled it quickly, then headed back to his desk.

His chair squeaked as he eased down into the seat, reminding him that he'd been going to call maintenance for a week and get someone up here with some WD-40. He hated hearing things squeak. After a quick sip of coffee, he picked up the phone, punched in a number and requested a copy of the twenty-year-old report on Gerald Lee Stoss's accident. Then he reached into his desk drawer and took out the file with all the papers Savannah Slade had given him, settled back in his chair and began to read.

Between taking phone calls and some follow-up paperwork to turn in regarding last night's arrest, it took him most of the morning to read through all the stuff she had left with him. Just before noon, the accident report he'd requested showed up. He gave it a quick read-through, didn't find anything obvious that would lead him to believe someone hadn't done their job, and then looked for the autopsy report. Only there wasn't one. Frowning, he looked again, made another call, waited four minutes on hold, only to find out that, at the request of the family, an autopsy had never been done. Stoss had been boxed up and shipped off to Canada to some family mausoleum before his body barely had time to get cold.

Odd, he thought as he hung up the phone. Not unusual, but definitely odd, like they just wanted him out of sight.

It was already past noon. He vaguely remembered Al mentioning that he was taking the afternoon off for personal business, and thankfully Homicide was having itself a slow day. He decided to go get something to eat before some new shit hit the fan, which it was bound to do. Everything he'd read about Savannah Slade's story was rolling through his head. And like the detective he was, he kept looking for discrepancies, expecting to find something that would unravel all her claims. He couldn't stop thinking how far-fetched all this was—like something out of a Hollywood movie. People didn't just wake up one day and find themselves the heir to a billion-dollar-plus fortune. Stuff like that didn't happen in real life. Not unless you got lucky enough to win the lottery. But she'd helped them out in a real big way, and then there was that birth certificate. The least he owed her was a thorough look-see.

The next time Savannah woke up, it was because her alarm was going off. Remembering what lay ahead, she jumped out of bed. By the time the sun was fully up, she had showered and dressed and was on her way to claim her car. The new sun was still in its gentle mode, bathing the water and the city in a fading array of soft pinks and yellows. But within minutes of her hitting a freeway, it was a viable force, well on the way to a promised eighty-five degrees by late afternoon.

She had a to-go coffee in the cup holder, a paper bag with an apple and a croissant and a handful of napkins in her lap. She ate the apple as she drove, then reached for the coffee as she braked for a red light.

From the corner of her eye, she saw a white car pull up beside her. Her heart skipped a beat as she gave the driver a quick look, then breathed a sigh of relief when she realized it was just a woman in a white Mazda, not Alejandro Montoya in his white BMW. She was just being silly. Montoya and the redhead were behind bars.

When the light turned green, she sped on through the intersection, secure in the assumption that she had several days before she had to start worrying again.

Savannah wasn't the only one getting an early start on the day. It had been pure luck that Mateo had shown up in the hotel parking lot just as she was walking out the front door. He pulled into a side parking lot and watched them bring up her car. Stunned that she was on the move so early in the morning, he whipped his car around and quickly followed her as she drove away from the hotel.

However, she wasn't through with surprises for him. When he saw her drive through the gates of Graceland Memorial cemetery, he frowned. If he followed her in, theirs would be the only two vehicles in the entire place. There was no way he could follow her in there without being seen. Frustrated by the unexpected twist, he scrambled to find a place where he would be able to see her the moment she came out and settled down to wait.

This time, there was no need for Savannah to stop at the office for directions. She still had her map from the day before yesterday. She drove as far as she could go, then took her coffee and croissant, and got out of the car, locking it behind her before heading for her mother's grave and a bench beneath a shade tree about twenty yards away from it.

She hurried toward the site, praying it was still devoid of fresh flowers. To her relief, the ground was bare of anything but the grass, which meant whoever was putting out the flowers had yet to arrive. She took a quick look around, saw nothing but gulls and a seemingly endless array of grave markers, then moved toward the bench and settled down to finish her on-the-go meal.

It didn't take long for a small bird to drop down from the upper branches of the tree under which she was sitting and start pecking the ground for crumbs from her croissant. Just like the day she'd walked to the park adjoining her hotel and fed the gulls part of her sandwich, she was sacrificing part of her breakfast to even more birds. What was it about birds in a city? Like ants, they must have learned long ago that wherever people were, crumbs were bound to follow.

She polished off the croissant and the last of her coffee, then tossed the empty cup into the sack and looked around for a garbage bin, only to realize how dumb that was. The only people inhabiting this place no longer had a need for food, and she doubted the people who came to visit were in the mood to eat.

She tucked her trash into a corner of her bag and then reached for her cell phone. She could give Holly a call to help pass the time. But her call to Holly went straight to voice mail, which meant her sister was probably on a mission of her own.

Resigning herself to a solitary wait, she pulled her journal out of the bag and began flipping through the pages again, even though she was coming to know some of the stories by heart. When she got to the place marked Your First Day at School, she stopped and began to read.

Your mother, Hannah, had brushed your hair until it looked like silk. We still hadn't cut it beyond an occasional trim, and it was hanging below your shoulders. When you dressed up to go to church, you honestly looked like a little angel, with your porcelain-doll face and big blue eyes, wearing pretty little dresses and all that white-blond hair. But on this morning you came striding into the kitchen, wearing jeans and a T-shirt instead of the pretty outfit your mother had picked out for you, and asked for her to help you fix your hair.

I could tell she was a bit dismayed that you'd chosen not to wear the new dress, but she didn't mention it. She did, however, point out that she'd already brushed your hair, and reminded you of the blue barrettes she'd put in it to keep it out of your face.

But you stood firm, handing her the hairbrush and one of those twisty things you girls used to put up your hair, and asked her to please put it in a ponytail. When she asked why, you said, "Because I know I'm gonna have so much fun at recess, I don't want my hair getting in the way." We had to laugh. It was typical of your positive attitude. Then Holly and Maria came into the kitchen, both wearing jeans and T-shirts, and both of them with their hair up in ponytails that they'd done for themselves, and it quickly became clear. You might have been the baby of the family, but there wasn't a thing that Holly or Maria did that you didn't try to do, as well.

So Hannah took that hairbrush, put your hair up in a ponytail and then grabbed the camera. You know the picture. It's the one hanging in the hall of you, Holly and Maria, all dressed alike, hair alike, holding hands.

And that's how you three have gone through life. So whatever doubts you're going through while you're reading these words, remember your sisters. They'll always have your back.

The sound of a small engine suddenly starting caught Savannah's attention. She looked up and saw a grounds worker starting up a Weed Eater. As long as the grass kept growing, the work here was never really done. She closed the journal and dropped it back in her bag. It was odd how much comfort she got from the stories.

She glanced at her watch, surprised by how much

time had passed. It was almost ten o'clock. The beige cargo pants and pink cotton pullover she'd chosen this morning were comfortable, but she was tired of sitting. Deciding to walk around the area a little, she got up and stretched, slightly stiff from having sat so long.

Just as she started to walk away, she noticed a blue Chevrolet coming up the road. She paused, watching... hoping. When the driver parked a few feet from where Savannah had left her own car, her heart skipped a quick beat. An older woman emerged, carrying something wrapped in green paper. Savannah could see it from where she was standing. Still, it didn't mean this was "her" person. She didn't even know whether the person leaving the flowers on Chloe Stewart's grave was male or female.

She continued to watch, taking note of everything about the woman—from her slightly stooped shoulders to the neat pale green pantsuit she was wearing. She was taller than Savannah, which meant nothing. She had no idea which side of her family had been responsible for the gene that had influenced her height or lack thereof.

As the woman came closer, Savannah could finally see her face clearly and the somber expression she was wearing. If she'd seen Savannah, she gave no hint of the fact. Her gaze was focused on the rows of graves, and she was going to pass within twenty yards of where Savannah was standing.

Savannah wanted to call out. Ask her who she was and where she was going, but she made herself wait. Those answers would come soon enough if the woman went to her mother's grave.

Even though Savannah had been waiting for over two hours for this moment, when the woman finally stopped and knelt down beside Chloe Stewart's grave, she was stunned.

This *was* the person she'd been waiting for, and all of a sudden she was scared. Who was she, and what would happen if Savannah introduced herself?

She made herself move. The first step was the hardest, but once she began, it was all she could do not to run, until finally she was there.

"Hello," she said.

The older woman jumped, obviously startled, then quickly rose, facing Savannah with a slight frown.

"Yes?"

Savannah pointed to the flowers lying against the tombstone.

"Those are very pretty."

The woman sighed and looked back at the bouquet. "Yes, they are." She brushed at the knees of her pants and began to walk away.

"Wait!" Savannah said, hurrying to catch up. "I need to ask you something…something about the woman buried here."

The woman's frown deepened. "Who are you? Why are you asking this? What do you want?"

Savannah clutched her purse to keep her hands from shaking.

"My name is Savannah Slade. A few days ago I learned that I was actually born Sarah Stewart. Chloe Stewart was my mother, and since I have no memory of her, I was hoping, since you obviously knew her, that maybe you would be willing to tell me a little about her."

The woman jerked as if she'd been slapped, then clutched Savannah's shoulders, her fingers curling so tightly into her flesh it was almost painful.

"Are you serious? Are you truly Chloe's child?"

"Yes, ma'am. I'm sure of it. I have the birth certificate and everything to prove it."

"Sweet Lord," the older woman said, and then staggered.

Savannah caught her arm, steadying her before she fell. "Are you all right? There's a bench just over there. Would you like to sit down?"

The woman nodded blindly, letting Savannah lead her back to the bench where she'd been sitting.

"Here you go. It's a bit cooler here, with the shade," Savannah said, and then sat down beside her.

The moment she sat, the woman began to stare at her intently, as if searching for confirmation.

"You're truly Chloe's daughter?"

"Yes, ma'am, I am. Did you know her well?"

The woman swayed where she sat, then reached for Savannah's hand. "Not as well as I should have, or I would have known about you."

"I'm sorry. What do you mean?"

"My name is Phyllis Palmer. Chloe was my daughter from my first marriage, which makes me—"

Savannah gasped. "My grandmother! It makes you my grandmother! I never thought… I wouldn't let myself hope…" She wanted to hug her, but didn't know what the woman was feeling.

Phyllis turned loose of Savannah's hand and cupped the side of her face instead. "You don't look a lot like her, but you have her eyes. Chloe's eyes were so big and blue…." She began to weep. "I should have known. I should have known. What happened to you? Did she give you up for adoption after she became ill? I don't understand."

Savannah hesitated, but there was no easy way to say this.

"It's actually kind of a great big mess. Chloe had an affair with a very rich man. He didn't know about me until she found out she was sick and dying. To his credit, when he learned of my existence, he quickly came to her rescue. I was two. He was going to take her into his family, care for her until the end and claim me as his heir. When his family found out about her and about me, they were not happy. It had something to do with the way their money was dispersed throughout the family. It's always to the oldest child of each generation, and my sudden arrival on the scene meant that I was about to become the next heir."

"I don't understand," Phyllis said. "Chloe left a letter with a lawyer. Upon her death, the letter was to be mailed to me. When the authorities finally located me, she'd been dead for over a week, but she said nothing about what happened to you."

"Ah," Savannah said. "That explains the gap between her death and when she was buried, which was something I learned as I tried to find her grave."

"Yes, yes, I was horrified," Phyllis said. "No, devastated. We'd been at odds ever since my marriage to my second husband. She hated him. Swore he tried to…tried to molest her, and I didn't believe her. To my everlasting dismay, I chose him over her, and she never forgave me. She left the day after we fought, and I never heard from her again."

Phyllis took Savannah's hand again, needing the physical contact to believe what was happening was true.

"So many years lost with her, and now so many years lost with you. What have I done? *What have I done?* Obviously she didn't want me to have anything to do with you or she would have called when she knew she was dying."

"There's more," Savannah said. "My birth father died in a car accident soon after she'd told him about me. The day she found out my birth father was dead, she got a phone call from his family, warning her not to try and make a claim on the family fortune on my behalf. They told her if she did, they would kill me, just like they'd killed him."

Phyllis gasped. "What are you saying?"

"That my mother gave me away to keep me alive, and then died alone to make sure no one would ever know where I'd gone."

Nine

Phyllis Palmer was stunned. She couldn't wrap her head around the implications.

"You're serious."

"Yes, ma'am, very serious."

Now Chloe's refusal to tell her about the baby made sense, Phyllis thought.

"Do you know the name of your father? Is it on your birth certificate?"

"Yes, ma'am, it is."

Phyllis gave Savannah's hand a quick squeeze. "Please, I would love it if you would call me Grandma. Chloe was my only child. After she died, I lost all hope of ever being a grandmother."

Savannah threw her arms around the woman's neck and hugged her.

"I never had a grandma before, so this is a first for both of us."

Phyllis held Savannah close. "Dear girl, my dear little girl. You have made me very happy."

Savannah couldn't stop smiling. "There are so many things I want to ask you. I don't know what your schedule is like, but if you could spare some time for me to—"

"Now. Tomorrow. Anytime. For the rest of my life."

Savannah's smile widened. "I choose now."

Phyllis dug a tissue out of her purse and began wiping at her tears. "But not here," she said. "This place always makes me sad, and today I am filled with gladness. Will you come to my home?" Then she stopped, struck by an old memory. "Oh, my goodness! I just remembered something."

"What?" Savannah asked.

"When I went through Chloe's apartment to pack up her clothes for the Salvation Army, I found some things…mementos I suppose, that I guessed were special to her. Even though I didn't know the significance of them, I still couldn't bear to throw them away. I kept them in a box in my attic. There are a lot of pictures of her with a very handsome young man." She ran her fingers through the tips of Savannah's hair. "A man with hair the same color as yours."

Savannah started to shake. "My father?"

"Possibly…probably. Anyway, I think you should have them."

Savannah jumped up. "Yes! Now is perfect! That's my car parked next to yours. Are you okay to drive? I mean, you're not too upset or anything?"

Phyllis stood, straightened her jacket and then dug her keys out of her bag.

"Thanks to you, I'm better than I've been in years, and yes, I'm fine to drive, although you're a dear for asking. You can follow me to my house. I don't live far."

They held hands all the way to their cars, talking as they went.

Phyllis was already buckled up and starting her car before she remembered Savannah hadn't told her the name of her father, then shrugged it off. She would find out when they got to the house.

Savannah put her car in gear and began to follow her grandmother out of the cemetery. As happy as she was, she knew that once she told her grandmother the name of her birth father, Phyllis was bound to realize that the danger to her newfound granddaughter still existed, and in a very big way.

When Mateo saw cars coming out the cemetery gates and realized one of them was his mark, he slapped the steering wheel with relief. This sitting around was driving him crazy.

"Finally!" he said, and started his engine. But instead of turning back toward the hotel, she turned in the opposite direction and quickly slipped into the flow of traffic. "Now where are you going, *mija?*"

He had to hurry before he lost her, then made sure to keep at least one car between them at all times. It wasn't until she turned off the main thoroughfare and into a residential neighborhood that he realized she was actually following the blue Chevrolet in front of her. Once again, she'd surprised him. He'd thought that the visit to the cemetery was going to be the weak spot—the place where routine began. But she hadn't gone back to the hotel like she had before. All he could do now was continue to follow and hope he wasn't spotted.

He was about a block behind when he saw the blue Chevrolet make a right turn into a driveway. Savannah took the same turn and pulled up behind the other driver. He tapped on the brakes, slowing down his approach to make sure they went into the house together. He was about a half block away when they got out. But when he saw them embrace, he began to smile. Maybe *this* could turn out to be a possible chink in the Slade woman's armor.

In Mateo's line of business, it was always good to find more than one means of persuasion. Collateral damage was often useful in getting someone to see things his way. He drove slowly past the house as the women went inside, made a quick mental note of the address, then had to find a place to park that would not draw attention to his car. He needed to call Stoss. It might interest his employer to know of this new twist. Stoss would know people who could give him quick access to information on who this older woman was and if she mattered in the scheme of things.

He drove a couple of blocks up, then turned around so he could watch the front of the house and parked in front of an empty house with a for-sale sign in the front yard. He didn't know how long this was going to take, and a strange car parking for an extended period of time in a family neighborhood often raised an alarm. If there was some kind of neighborhood watch, or someone questioned him as to his presence, he could always claim he was waiting for a Realtor to show him the house. Satisfied with his plan, he reached for his phone.

Joseph eyed the gaggle of paparazzi gathered around the restaurant as his driver pulled the limo up to the front walk. He was meeting the mayor for lunch and wondered what rumor they were chasing now. It was always something. Still, he had a public image to maintain, so he smiled and waved briefly as he got out of his limo and walked toward the entrance.

"Mr. Stoss. Mr. Stoss. Is there any truth to the rumor that you're going to buy Condor Airlines?"

Joseph was past ever being surprised by the media these days. Someone somewhere along the chain of command, either on his payroll or that of the bankrupt airline, had obviously spilled the beans for a nice chunk of change.

He didn't bother to answer. It never mattered what he said, anyway, because the press always put their own spin on the story they wanted to tell. It was his opinion that true journalism was all but dead. These days, it was all about the scandal. At the thought, the hair rose on the back of his neck, knowing what a field day they would have with the knowledge that Gerald had a living heir. But Joseph wasn't a man who dealt in possibilities. His money was always on the sure thing. He walked into the restaurant with his head high and a swagger in his stride.

The hostess saw him coming and stepped up to meet him.

"Welcome, Mr. Stoss. We have your table ready."

"Has my guest arrived?" he asked.

"No, sir. When he does, we'll make sure to escort him to your table."

"Thank you," he said, and then followed her through the restaurant, nodding now and then when he saw a familiar face among the diners.

A waiter appeared within seconds of his having been seated and took his order for a cocktail. Another brought a basket of his favorite artisan bread and a small bowl of hummus, then left him to enjoy. He was smearing hummus on his first slice when his cell began to vibrate.

He glanced down at the ID, then quickly took the call.

"Yes?"

"She went to Graceland Memorial again this morning, but when she came out, she followed a car driven by an older woman to her home. When they got there, they embraced and then went inside. I have the place staked out right now."

Joseph frowned. Who could she possibly know here? He needed all the info he could get on her before he began cleaning house, just in case there was more than one place in need of cleaning.

"Give me the address," he said, and took down the info. "Just keep tabs on Savannah for now. I'll let you know about the other one later."

"Yes, sir," Mateo said, and hung up.

Joseph glanced around to make sure he was still alone, and then quickly dialed another number.

"Stoss legal department, Penny speaking."

"Penny, this is Joseph Stoss. I need you to run down an address for me ASAP. Find out who lives there, who owns it, in case it's a rental, and call me right back."

"Yes, sir. Right away, sir," she said.

He gave her the information, then hung up without so much as a goodbye.

It was just the way Joseph conducted all his business—quietly but definitively.

"Come in, dear," Phyllis said as she led the way into the house. "I'm partial to air-conditioning, so it's nice and cool in here."

"It feels wonderful," Savannah said.

"I don't know how long you were waiting out at the cemetery, but if you would like to freshen up, the guest bathroom is just down that hall."

"I was there a couple of hours or so, and I *would* appreciate that. I'll be right back," Savannah said.

"I'll get us something cold to drink. I have iced tea, or if you prefer, I have soda."

"Iced tea, please," Savannah said, and then hurried down the hall as Phyllis went into the kitchen.

A few minutes later Savannah came out, then followed the sounds into the kitchen where Phyllis was making their drinks.

"Your house is so homey," Savannah said. "Isn't this what they call a Craftsman-style house?"

Phyllis smiled. "Why, yes, it is. The wood floors are original to the property, as are the kitchen cabinets and crown molding throughout the house. It's not luxurious, but I'm comfortable here."

She handed Savannah her iced tea, then led the way back into the living room. The moment they sat down on the sofa together, they both took a quick sip of their tea, then set the glasses down on the coffee table in unison. When they realized what they'd done, they laughed.

"This is a bit awkward," Phyllis said. "I know nothing about you. Do you have other family? Where did you grow up? Tell me. I want to know everything."

"I've lived all my life—at least, the life I remember—in Missoula, Montana. My...father's name was Andrew Slade. My mother's name was Hannah. I have two older sisters, Holly and Maria."

She didn't bother going into details now. What she wanted most was to hear about Chloe and see those pictures Phyllis said she had, but Phyllis was the one wanting to learn more.

"How on earth did that come to pass? Did he adopt you?"

"No, not legally. As for us sisters, none of us are biologically related, although we didn't know that until Daddy's death."

"Then how?" Phyllis asked.

"Long story short… Dad used to be an evangelical preacher, and he traveled all over the country holding revivals. During his travels he met three different women, our birth mothers, who believed that their daughters' lives were in danger. It's complicated, but as best we can tell, he decided it was something God had sent him to do, and he wound up taking each of us to keep us safe."

"Dear Lord," Phyllis said. "Oh, wait. You said your birth father's family was well-to-do and had threatened your life, but you didn't tell me who they were. Do you know if they're still in the area?"

"They're here, all right. Confronting them is part of why I came to Miami. I've already hired a lawyer to present my case."

Phyllis frowned. "But that could be dangerous."

"I'm prepared to deal with it."

"What's their surname?" Phyllis asked.

"Stoss. My birth father's name was Gerald Lee Stoss. He was the child of Rupert Stoss."

Phyllis gasped. "Not *the* Stosses who live on Palm Island?"

Savannah nodded.

"But they're billionaires. They have more money and power than pretty much anyone in the country."

"It doesn't change the truth," Savannah said. "They killed my father because he wanted to claim me as his heir. I have a birth certificate and DNA on my side. And hopefully those photos you mentioned will be added evidence."

Phyllis jumped to her feet. "Oh, yes, yes, the photos. The box is in a closet in the attic. It won't take a minute. I'll be right back."

Savannah took another drink of her tea, and then leaned back and glanced around the room. The furniture was a mixture of contemporary and traditional, but all in very feminine tones. The bouquet of flowers on the dining room table in the adjoining room was all white, as were the sheers at the windows. It was apparent that Phyllis Palmer liked neat clean decor. Then she saw some pictures hanging on the opposite wall and got up for a closer look.

There was one of an elderly couple cutting a cake together. She saw a big *50* on the cake and realized it must have been an anniversary. Maybe her great-grandparents!

"Wow, fifty years," she muttered, and moved to the next one.

It was a photo of Phyllis, but at a much younger age, with a young man in uniform and a toddler clinging to her knee.

"That's a picture of your grandfather and me. His name was Corey Stewart. He was in the service when he died. The baby is Chloe. She was six months old when he left. He died within six months of being deployed."

Phyllis set the pictures she was carrying down on the coffee table, then walked over to where Savannah was standing.

"Oh, my gosh," Savannah said. "That's around the age I was when my mother died."

Phyllis's eyes welled. "We were so happy then." Suddenly she looked very old. "If only I could take back the damage that was done after I remarried. I would do it in a heartbeat."

This was a touchy subject, but Savannah had to ask.

"You said my mother didn't like her stepfather, and that she said he tried to molest her?"

Phyllis nodded, unable to speak for the tears still in her eyes.

Savannah couldn't imagine anything more devastating to a child, no matter the age.

"How old was she when you remarried?"

"Seventeen. She'd just graduated high school when Buck Palmer and I got married."

"How could you *not* believe her?"

"Looking back, I don't know, but at the time her dislike for him was so strong, I thought it was just her trying to get him out of the house. She told me what he'd done. I didn't believe her, and it crushed her. I could see it in her eyes. But before I had time to mend any kind of fences between us, she was gone. I looked for her for years, but to no avail, and never heard from her again until I got that letter from her lawyer."

"You're not still married to the man, are you?" Savannah asked.

"No, and the irony of that is that we separated within a month of her leaving because of what she'd told me."

Savannah took Phyllis by the hand. "Show me the pictures. I want to see what my mother looked like all grown up."

"Of course," Phyllis said, and led the way back to the sofa.

Savannah scooted close to her, then leaned forward as Phyllis took the first photo off the pile.

"This is Chloe. I don't know where it was taken or

how old she is here, maybe twenty or so. But she looks happy."

Savannah took the picture, staring intently at the face of the woman in the shot.

"She was taller than I am, and her hair was dark. You were right. I don't look anything like her, do I?"

"Not much," Phyllis said. "But if I close my eyes when I hear you talk, I would swear it's Chloe speaking."

That was exactly what Savannah had been needing to hear. "Really?" she said.

Phyllis smiled and nodded, then dug through the pile of pictures and pulled out several in which Chloe was standing in the arms of a tall and handsome young man. They were smiling widely for the camera in a couple of them, and there were a few more of the couple on what looked like a yacht out in a harbor. Almost instantly, Savannah saw her own features reflected in the young man's face, including his white-blond hair.

A huge lump formed at the back of her throat as an ache for what might have been swept through her.

"How sad. So much joy on their faces, and then I think about how both of them wound up. If only I'd been old enough to remember them."

When she started to hand the pictures back, Phyllis stopped her.

"They're your parents. You keep them," she said. "They may help you fight your case, and no matter what, you're the one who should have them."

"Thank you! Thank you so much," Savannah said. "I'm going to take these to my lawyer when I leave here."

At the thought of Savannah leaving so soon, Phyllis glanced at the clock.

"It's nearly lunchtime. Please say you'll eat with me before you go?"

"I would love to, if you'll let me help."

Phyllis beamed. "Yes! And while we're working, I want you to tell me about yourself. What do you do for fun? Do you have a job? There are a thousand things that I need to know about my brand-new granddaughter."

Savannah laughed. "Only a thousand?"

"At least a thousand," Phyllis corrected. "So let's get started."

Savannah slipped the pictures into her purse, then left it on the sofa as she followed Phyllis into her kitchen.

Mayor Harwood had already left and Joseph was signing the tab for their lunch when he felt his cell vibrating in his pocket. It was his legal department. Just what he'd been waiting for.

"This is Stoss. What do you have for me, Penny?"

"The property you asked about belongs to a seventy-two-year-old woman named Phyllis Palmer. She bought it twenty years ago."

"Hmm, okay. Now I have another task for you. I want you to put together a complete dossier on Ms. Palmer. Where she was born? Where she's from? Maiden name…the whole nine yards. Oh. And run her name in conjunction with Graceland Memorial Park North and see what comes up, will you?"

"Yes, sir. Do you have a time frame on this, sir?"

"Still ASAP."

"Yes, sir," Penny said, and disconnected.

Joseph frowned. The name "Palmer" didn't ring a bell, but back in the day, he hadn't done any kind of background check on Chloe Stewart. He'd never seen the need, since she was dying. Another loose end that should have been dealt with at the time, like leaving that brat alive.

He called Mateo back.

"Yes, sir?" Mateo said.

"You still outside the house?"

"Yes, sir," Mateo repeated.

"Good. The plan stays the same. Follow the girl when she leaves and give me a report at the end of the day. We're running out of time, though, so we're going to have to make a move soon. If I need you to address the old woman, I'll let you know later."

"Yes, sir," Mateo said.

The line went dead. He made another call, this time to his driver, and told him he was ready to be picked up. By the time he made his way out of the restaurant, the limo was waiting for him at the curb.

"Back to the office," Joseph said as he got into the car.

His day wasn't close to being over.

Phyllis put the last dirty glass in the dishwasher, then shut the door.

"That's it," she said.

Savannah was wiping off the kitchen table. "I'm finished, too," she said, and left the dishcloth on the counter. "Lunch was wonderful, but I really need to get those pictures to my lawyer."

"Will you come back…at least before you return to Montana?" Phyllis asked.

"Of course. I don't have all that much to do while my lawyer's getting the papers ready to file."

"I'm still amazed that you managed to get Thomas Jefferson to represent you. He's a really big deal here in Miami."

"I didn't know any of his background until you mentioned it during lunch. He was just a friend of our family lawyer back home. At least now I know why he said he and Joseph Stoss didn't like each other. I can't believe that he actually sued Stoss Industries on behalf of his client and won."

"Forty million dollars," Phyllis said, then grinned. "However, you might not think it's so great if you wind up inheriting the Stoss fortune. That's forty million you'll never see again."

Savannah shook her head. "Like I said before. It's about justice, not money. Back in Montana, we're what I would call very well off ourselves. I never wanted for anything I needed and was raised with a whole lot of love. That's pretty much all that anyone could ask for."

"You're a good girl," Phyllis said as she hugged her. "I'm so glad we've found each other."

"Me, too," Savannah said. "I'll see how tomorrow starts off, and maybe give you a call later and drop by. If you're not busy, I'd love to take you to dinner."

"I'm never busy," Phyllis said. "I'll wait to hear from you, to make sure, but tomorrow night is good for me."

"Great." Savannah gave her a quick kiss and retrieved her purse. "I'm off, and thanks for the directions on how to get to my lawyer's office from here. If this keeps up, I'll be a pro at learning how to get around this city."

Phyllis stood in the doorway, waving at Savannah as she drove away.

Savannah called Jefferson's office on the way over. She didn't have to talk to him so much as she wanted him to have the pictures to add to their case. But she lucked out. According to his receptionist, he was on his way back from the courthouse and would have a few minutes in which he could see her before his next appointment.

Savannah was grateful, and took care to make the proper turns that would get her where she needed to go without delay. She was surprised when she realized she was coming up on his office from the opposite direction this time, and quickly pulled into the parking garage she'd used before, then made a dash for his office.

Ten

This time when Savannah walked into the building, the guard in the lobby recognized her and didn't bother asking for her ID as she signed in.

"You're free to go up, Miss Slade."

"Thank you so much," she said, and flashed a smile that made the older man blush.

She rode the elevator up to the ninth floor, smiling at the secretary as she walked into the office.

Laura smiled. "Good afternoon, Miss Slade. Have a seat. You actually beat Mr. Jefferson back to the office, but he should be here anytime."

"Good. I was afraid I'd be too late."

A couple of minutes later Jefferson entered, his briefcase in one hand and a can of Pepsi in the other. When he saw who was waiting in the outer office, he smiled.

"Savannah! I didn't expect to see you today. What's up?"

"I have some more info for you," she said.

"Great. Laura, when's my next appointment?"

"In about fifteen minutes, sir."

"Perfect." He motioned to Savannah. "Come with me."

She followed him into the office and took the chair

on the other side of his desk. He set his briefcase on the floor, the can of soda on the coffee bar and dropped wearily into his chair.

"Long day in court. What do you have?"

Savannah took the photos out of her purse.

"Pictures of my mother with Gerald Stoss."

All of a sudden, his weariness disappeared. "You're kidding!" He reached out as she dropped them into his hands. "How did you come by these?"

"I found my grandmother, Chloe's mother, when she came to visit my mother's grave. We introduced ourselves, and I wound up following her to her house, even had lunch with her. She had a small box of my mother's things that she'd kept when she had to clean out her apartment. The photos were in it, although she didn't know who the man was."

He flipped through the pictures one by one, pausing to tap his forefinger on Gerald Stoss's face.

"There's no mistaking who this is…or you, for that matter," Thomas said, then looked up and grinned.

Jefferson's comment eased her last concern that the man might not actually be Gerald Stoss.

"Did you know him?" Savannah asked.

"No, but I remember when he had that wreck. His picture was all over the papers. It was the talk of Miami for weeks."

"What did they say about it? Did anyone think it was suspicious?" Savannah asked.

"No. Quite the contrary. Most people thought it was a shame, but not a surprise."

"Really! Why?"

"Because he always drove too fast. At least, that was the rumor. Like I said, I didn't know him."

"I can have the pictures back when this is over, right?"

"Absolutely. In fact, I'll have Laura make copies for both of us, and we'll put the originals in my safe. No need taking a chance on having something happen to them until this is all over."

"Do you have any idea when the papers will be ready to file?"

Jefferson flipped through his calendar. "I'm guessing a couple more days. Why?"

"I promised my boyfriend, Judd, that I'd call him before that. He doesn't want me here by myself when it goes public."

"Not a bad idea," Jefferson said. "I've got a handle on a safe place for you to stay, too. I just need another day or so to confirm."

"Do I need to give you any money ahead of time for that?"

"No, no, it's not a hotel. I have a friend who owes me a favor."

She frowned. "I don't think it's a good idea to take my problems to someone's family."

"My friend is ex-CIA. He lives alone and in a place with some damn good security."

"Still, it seems a—"

Suddenly the big man with the easy smile was gone, startling Savannah.

"Don't argue. You're going to need all the backup you can get when this hits the news. Between the Stosses and the media, your life is going to turn upside down. Besides, I owe Coleman Rice a big favor and you're my payoff. Don't deny me the chance to wipe the slate clean between us."

"I never thought about the media," she said.

"So start thinking, because they're a huge fact of Stoss family life."

"Duly noted," she said as she stood. "I won't take any more of your time. I just wanted to make sure you had these right away."

"That was a piece of luck, running into your grandmother like that," Thomas said.

"It wasn't an accident. I knew from talking to a groundskeeper at the cemetery that someone put down fresh flowers once a week, and always before noon. So I staked out the cemetery and waited."

Thomas made no attempt to hide his surprise. "You never cease to amaze me, girl."

"Thank you. I think."

He eyed her thoughtfully. "It was a compliment. Stay safe and I'll be in touch."

"Thank you so much—for everything."

"Nothing to thank me for yet. Are you going back to the hotel from here?"

"Yes. Oh. I almost forgot. There's one other thing. It has nothing to do with *my* case, but everything to do with my family."

He frowned. "What's that?"

"You know how I told you each of my sisters is on a similar quest? So I got a phone call from Bud, our foreman, last night. My sister Maria is in Tulsa to do what I'm doing here in Miami. It seems she rattled some pretty big skeletons, because someone put a bomb in her car. It went off before she got in, but she was seriously injured. She's in the ICU, expected to recover fully, but she's still not out of the woods."

Thomas's frown deepened.

"My God. I'm sorry to hear this, but glad she's going to be okay."

Savannah nodded. "We are, too, but it's made my other sister, Holly, and me even jumpier than we were."

"Like I said, you'll be safe staying with my friend, and in the meantime, pay attention to your surroundings and the people in them."

"I will," Savannah said. "And thank you for seeing me on such short notice."

Thomas walked her to the door with a hand on her shoulder, then gave it a quick squeeze.

"Be careful."

Savannah nodded, then waved goodbye to Laura as she left the office. Her mind was a jumble of emotions as she rode the elevator down. It was almost four. She wanted to return to the hotel before the five o'clock rush hour traffic hit. As she was walking back to the parking garage, her phone rang. When she saw it was Holly, her heart skipped a beat.

"Holly? Is everything all right?"

"Yes, honey. I'm sorry I scared you. I just talked to Bud, and told him I would give you an update on Maria and save him a call."

"Great! Her recovery is still progressing, right?"

"Yes, and better than they expected. I wanted to talk to her, but Bud said when he spoke to her cop again, he said she wasn't up to talking, that she keeps going in and out of consciousness because of the drugs they're giving her."

"Shoot. I was hoping to call tonight."

"It's okay. Here's the *big* reason I'm calling. Bud says his intuition was right. The cop *has* fallen for Maria big-time."

"Oh, my God! I can't believe it!" Savannah said. "They just met."

"Sometimes that's how it happens," Holly said. "Anyway, it made me feel better knowing someone's really invested in her safety."

"I see what you mean. So how are things going with you?"

She heard her sister sigh. "I won't go into details, but it isn't looking good. No one knows what happened to my mother, and according to my research, the serial killer was never arrested."

"Oh, Holly. Be careful. I couldn't bear it if something happened to you, too."

"Same to you, baby sister," Holly said. "Have you made any progress?"

"I no longer need to testify in a murder case that happened the day I got here."

She winced as she heard Holly scream, and prepared herself for the grilling to follow.

"What the hell do you mean, 'testify'? What did you see?"

"Oh, it's a long complicated story."

"Does Bud know?" Holly asked.

"No, and don't tell him. Judd does, and he's coming out to stay with me before we file the papers on the Stoss family and the whole mess goes public."

"Are you scared?"

"Yes," Savannah said as she reached the parking garage and headed toward her car. "Are you?"

"Yes."

"Hell of a mess we're in, isn't it?" Savannah muttered, digging into her purse for the car keys.

"Yes, it is," Holly said. "Just remember, if you need a long-distance hug, call me."

"You, too," Savannah said. "And thanks for letting me know about Maria. She's been on my mind all day."

The call ended just as she spied her car. Now that she was no longer talking, she tuned in on the sound of her own footsteps and how they echoed as she walked, heightening the fact that she was alone in a very large, empty place. Anxious to get out, she lengthened her stride and hit the remote so that the car door would be unlocked by the time she got there. It wasn't until she drove out of the garage and back into the sunlight that she felt as if she'd left danger behind.

Joseph Stoss would have been horrified if he'd known that his cousin Elaine's curiosity was about to override her better judgment. She hadn't been able to quit thinking about Savannah Slade. What did she look like? What did she know? She bugged Michael about it constantly, until he caved and got the information she wanted. Once Elaine found out where the Slade woman was staying, she spent the entire morning thinking about it. She knew the hotel. She'd actually been a speaker there once, during some women's conference. She knew the layout—at least where the bar and a bathroom were. For Elaine, that was usually enough. The more time that passed, the more compelling the urge to see the woman for herself. Once she got to that point, she began thinking of reasons why it was a good idea. Joseph always said you should know your enemies. So she needed to know what Savannah Slade looked like. If she was ignorant of her enemy, she might become an easier target.

By midafternoon she'd convinced herself that she was just going to go to the bar and have a couple of drinks, and wait for fate to drop Savannah Slade in her lap. It was something to do until her dinner engagement tonight. It occurred to her that she might not recognize her target, but it was her style to play things by ear, secure in the knowledge that whatever happened, she wouldn't be the one to pay the price.

She started to get her car keys, then realized she'd already had a bit too much to drink today to get behind the wheel. Joseph had the family chauffeur, so she called a cab and got herself to the hotel without any trouble.

The day was clear, the sky virtually cloudless. Just the way she liked it. As she got out of the cab, the warm air on her bare legs reminded her of her childhood and a time when anything seemed possible.

She caught the eye of a woman passing by, who smiled and nodded, then did a double take, as if recognizing who she was. That was when Elaine realized she'd missed a step in her plan. In Miami, there were few places she could go without being recognized. Usually, when things like that happened, at least a mention of it would make the evening news. If it happened here and someone mentioned it on air, Joseph would kill her.

Suddenly paranoid, she turned and headed to the valet stand. They would hail her another cab, and she could get out and go home before something went wrong.

Her heart was hammering, her steps a bit unsteady from the amount of liquor she'd already drunk, and her equilibrium hadn't caught up with her resolve to escape. Before she'd gone five steps, she began to stumble. Then she caught her toe, and before she knew it she was falling. The impact was painful and jarring as she landed on her hands and knees.

Panic hit as she keyed in on the sounds of running feet. Shit. She'd only made things worse.

Savannah had just dropped her car off at valet parking and was about to go inside the hotel when she saw a lady stumble, then fall.

"Oh, my gosh," she said, and dashed forward to

help the woman up. "Bless your heart," she said as she reached for the woman's shoulder. "Are you all right? Do you think you can stand?"

Elaine was in shock. This couldn't be happening. And the misguided efforts of her Good Samaritan were only calling more attention to the incident.

"I'm fine, I'm fine," Elaine muttered as she struggled to her feet, wishing to hell the woman would stop talking. It wasn't until she tried to stand and staggered again that she realized she'd broken the heel of one of her peep-toe pumps.

Savannah caught the woman by the elbow as she swayed on her feet. "Here, let me help you," she said. "I think you've broken your heel. Do you want to go inside? I'm sure there's someone on staff who can help you."

Elaine wouldn't even look at her, and when she saw two bellmen coming toward her, she knew she had to get away fast before this became a full-blown incident.

"No, no," she said. "I'm fine. I just want a cab. Someone hail me a cab."

The palms of her hands were stinging horribly, as were her knees. That was when she looked down and saw that they were bleeding.

The first bellman arrived just then and said, "Ma'am, you're bleeding. Let me help you inside."

"No. I don't want to go inside. I want a cab. I want to go home."

Elaine turned to walk away and found herself face-to-face with the woman who'd been helping her. Her heart stopped. She knew that face—the white-blond hair, the ice-blue eyes. It was like looking at a female version of Gerald. She couldn't believe the perversity of fate. She'd come to spy on Savannah Slade, only to find herself at the woman's mercy. She didn't know whether to laugh or run.

Now that they were face-to-face, Savannah could smell the liquor on the woman's breath, which explained the stumbling and then the fall. But it didn't change the fact that the woman's injuries must be painful. She dug a handful of clean tissues from her bag.

"At least take these," she said.

Elaine blinked, then looked down. "Thank you," she mumbled, and began dabbing at her bloody knees as a cab pulled up beside her. Grateful for a timely exit, she got in as quickly as she could manage and never looked back.

"Where to, ma'am?" the cabbie asked.

"Just drive," Elaine said.

As Savannah watched the cab drive away, she couldn't help thinking the woman had looked familiar, which made no sense. She didn't know any women here but her grandmother, Phyllis. What bugged her was the weird way in which the woman had looked at her when she'd turned around—as if she'd seen a ghost, which again made no sense. Savannah chalked it up to the woman's embarrassment at being caught drunk and let it go as she entered the hotel.

As she was walking through the lobby toward the elevator, the notion returned that she'd seen that woman somewhere before. Then she shook it off. The last time that had happened, she'd gotten herself mixed up with a murder.

"I'm not going there again," she said, then got into the elevator.

By the time Elaine got back to the mansion, she was bordering on hysteria. She staggered up the stairs and then down the hall to her room, ripped off her clothes and then got into the shower. The warm water stung her chafed knees and palms, but it didn't matter. She considered the pain her penance for the mistake she'd just made, and by the time she got out of the shower, she had a story in place. She wasn't going to lie about falling, just the place in which it happened. And if she was lucky, tomorrow this would be nothing but a bad memory.

Mateo had been a short distance behind Savannah's car and had pulled into the hotel parking lot to make sure she was going inside, hopefully for the evening.

He saw her hand off her keys to the attendant, pocket the stub and then pause. It took him a few moments to realize something had happened. When he saw her bolt forward, his gaze immediately shifted. And then he saw her down on her knees, helping a woman who'd apparently just fallen. It wasn't until the woman stood and turned around that his heart skipped a beat.

It was Elaine Hamilton, and he was pretty sure the boss would not be happy about the incident. The way he'd understood it, they didn't want the Slade woman alerted in any way. He had no way of knowing if Savannah Slade knew her enemies, but if she did, they'd just been made. He called Joseph.

"Sign here, here and here, Mr. Stoss," his secretary said, then waited for Joseph to finish.

"FedEx these. Overnight priority," Joseph said as he handed back the contracts.

"Yes, sir. Right away, sir."

The door closed with a distinct click, and the quiet that ensued was welcome. Joseph leaned back in his chair and allowed himself a brief moment of respite. As he closed his eyes, he wondered if he had enough time to work in a massage before he went home today. He felt the beginnings of a headache and knew it was from stress. But who could blame him? As if the pressure of the business itself wasn't enough, he had this pending lawsuit hanging over his head. It occurred to him to wonder why he hadn't heard from her yet and guessed that damned lawyer, Jefferson, was planning on one big move. He had half a mind to call Mateo right now and tell him to get it over with, but he had to be cautious. There could be no hint of suspicion as to how she died. Especially since the police already knew of her presence and what she planned to do. The Stoss family would be the first ones on the top of the list if she died under suspicious circumstances.

While he was still thinking about the massage, his cell phone rang. Back to business, and it was Mateo.

"Hello."

"Boss. I think we've got trouble."

Joseph sat up, instantly alert. "What happened?"

"I was following the Slade woman as you instructed. She went back to the hotel and I was watching to make sure she went inside when she suddenly stopped out in front of the entrance. Some woman had fallen, and she was helping her up and—"

"Damn it, Mateo, get to the point," Joseph muttered.

"The woman who fell was your cousin, Mrs. Hamilton. And Savannah Slade was the one who helped her up. They looked each other straight in the face before your cousin jumped in a cab and the Slade woman went into the hotel."

At first Joseph was so shocked he couldn't talk.

Then, when he could, the first words that came out were curses.

"Son of a bitch! Elaine was at the InterContinental Hotel?"

"Yes, sir."

"You're sure?"

Mateo frowned. "Yes, sir."

"Did they speak?"

"Yes, but I couldn't hear what was being said. I could only see their lips moving."

Joseph was livid. "Damn it to hell, why must my life be plagued with imbeciles?"

"I think the Slade woman is in for now. Do you want me to take her out tonight?"

"No. I need to talk to Elaine to find out what went on before I make a decision. Go home. I'll call you if I need you."

"Yes, sir," Mateo said, and hung up. He was glad to be rid of the Stosses for the day and headed home, thankful he would be in his condo before rush hour.

Joseph glanced at the clock. Four-thirty. He flipped through his calendar. No more appointments today. There were papers he could review, but after this revelation, he knew he would never be able to concentrate. Pissed beyond words, he called his driver.

"Taylor, I'm ready to go home. Is that Kentucky whiskey still in the minibar?"

"Yes, sir," Taylor said.

"See you in five."

He dropped the phone into his pocket, tossed a couple of files into his briefcase and headed out the door. Elaine had better be home when he got there or he was going to put a hit out on the bitch, so help him God.

He paused at his secretary's desk. "Darla, call my cell if you need me. I'm going home for the day."

"Yes, Mr. Stoss. Have a good evening."

"Right," he muttered. "You, too."

The limo was waiting for him when he exited the building. He slid into the backseat, reached for the whiskey bottle sitting in the rack by the minibar and poured himself a shot, neat. He had it down before Taylor got behind the wheel, then nursed his second drink all the way home.

The front door swung open. Joseph strode angrily into the house, slamming the door shut behind him. Seconds later, the housekeeper came flying down the hall.

"Estella, is Elaine here?" Joseph roared.

"*Sí*, Señor Joseph. She is upstairs in her room."

Joseph handed her his briefcase, then strode through the foyer and up the front staircase without another word.

Thankful he was mad at someone besides her, Estella took his briefcase to his office, then made herself scarce.

Michael heard the commotion as he carried his cocktail out of the library. He saw the look on Joseph's face, heard Elaine's name and knew something was up. Part of him wanted to stay out of it, but his alliance with Elaine was what kept them from sinking under Joseph's overbearing manner.

He downed the cocktail, set the glass on a table in the hall and ran up the stairs just in time to see Joseph storm into Elaine's room without knocking. That was when he knew it had to be bad. He ran inside just as

Joseph pushed Elaine against a wall. She was sobbing as she struggled helplessly to get free.

"Joseph, don't! Let me go. Let me go!"

Michael leaped forward. "Stop! Stop! What the hell's wrong with you?" He pushed between them just as Joseph took a swing at her, blocking the blow.

He couldn't believe this was happening. He caught sight of a visibly throbbing blue vein along Joseph's temple, and when he looked into his cousin's eyes, Joseph's pupils were blown. *What the hell? Is he high?*

Then Joseph took a swing at Michael. He blocked that one, as well, then shoved Joseph hard against the wall.

"I said stop, damn it!"

Michael glanced at Elaine. She was cowering in the corner and blubbering, which meant she was probably drunk.

Joseph was so angry, he was shaking. He glared at Elaine as if she were little more than a piece of filth.

"You've got about five seconds to explain what the fuck you were doing at the InterContinental Hotel this afternoon and make me believe it, before I choke the everlasting life out of your worthless hide."

Elaine was too drunk to pull it together and resigned herself to die.

Michael wasn't as amenable. Still pissed, he stepped into Joseph's line of vision, forcing Joseph to talk to him instead.

"Joseph! She's too drunk to talk, and you know it. And while we're at it, if you ever threaten her life or mine again, you need to remember that you're not the only one with connections to the bad boys. You're just as big a pain in my ass as I am in yours. The only difference is, I usually ignore you. But I *can* be pushed too far. You can be mad as hell at either of us, but you do not fucking get to threaten our lives. You are no bigger a deal in the eyes of the law than we are, and if you're gone, I inherit. Do we understand each other?"

Joseph shuddered, trying to pull himself down from the edge of the insanity and rage.

"You don't know what she did," he muttered.

"No, but I'll bet if we all calm down, you'll be happy to tell me."

Joseph shoved a hand through his hair in an angry gesture, then turned around and slapped the wall before moving to the opposite side of the room. He had to. If he didn't put some distance between himself and Elaine, he *would* kill her.

Michael hid a slight shudder and calmly sat on the side of the bed, making sure to stay between the other two.

"Now. What's all the ruckus?" he asked.

Joseph glared at Michael. "I'm the one asking questions."

Michael shrugged.

Joseph pointed at Elaine. "What did you and Savannah Slade have to say to each other this afternoon? Were you giving her a warm welcome into the family? Or was it just a case of morbid stupidity that you chose to draw her attention to yourself?"

Michael lurched from the bed and turned to stare at his cousin in disbelief.

"Tell me you did not do that!"

Elaine covered her face and slid to the floor, sobbing uncontrollably.

"I didn't mean… I only thought… Joseph always said…"

Joseph was screaming. "Shut up! I don't want to hear

excuses. I just want to know what you two said to each other."

Michael was still in shock. "Shit, Elaine. What were you thinking?"

"I didn't say anything to her. I fell down. All right? Look at my hands! Look at my knees!"

Both men saw the raw, bloody abrasions.

Michael winced.

Joseph glared.

"What the fuck were you doing there to begin with?" he asked.

Elaine was still bawling. Tears were mingling with snot to the point that Michael nearly gagged. He grabbed a handful of tissues and threw them in her lap.

She wiped her face, then her nose, before she managed to answer. "I wanted to see what she looked like. You always say we should know the enemy. How could I protect myself from her if I didn't know what she looked like? Tell me! How was I supposed to stay safe?"

Joseph slapped the wall to keep from slapping her. The sound echoed with a flat thud.

"I don't know. For starters, maybe stay the hell away from the hotel where she's registered?"

Elaine started sobbing all over again, but Joseph wasn't finished.

"She talked to you, and I know it. Tell me what she said."

"She didn't know who I was, and I didn't know she was anywhere around. I didn't even know what she looked like, remember? She just happened to see me fall and came to help me up. She asked me if I was all right. I told her I just wanted someone to call me a cab. She tried to get me to go inside, but I said I wanted to go home. She handed me some tissues because my knees were bleeding. I got in a cab and drove away. That's all. I swear!"

Michael frowned. "I don't get it. If you didn't know what she looked like, then how did you know it was her?"

Elaine shoved the hair away from her face and then started to laugh. It was a deep, ugly sound that bore no traces of mirth.

"How did I know who she was? Have you seen her? Has either of you seen her?"

"No, but I have a man tailing her," Joseph snapped.

"Damn it, Elaine. Spill it. Who did you talk to? Who at the hotel knew you were looking for her? That could point an even stronger finger of suspicion at us when she's dead. Who pointed her out to you?"

"No one," Elaine snapped. "No one *had* to, because she looks so damned much like Gerald it scared the shit out of me, that's how I knew!"

The silence in the room was as shocking as the fight had been. This wasn't something Joseph had expected to hear. Even Michael got the message. In this day and age of DNA testing, if hers even came close to matching theirs, they were toast.

Eleven

Joseph stared at the pair of them for almost a minute without speaking. As much as he regretted what Elaine had done, what she'd just told him was valuable information, enforcing his need to act swiftly.

"You do know that you've put the whole family in jeopardy here."

Elaine staggered to her feet. She wouldn't turn her back on Joseph, but she wasn't through talking.

"No, I haven't. I wasn't the one who killed Gerald, then left his brat alive. I'm not the one who's put us all in jeopardy. That was you."

Joseph wasn't going to accept that responsibility.

"Technically, that's not correct. I didn't touch him, but just like you two, I knew it was going to happen, so in the eyes of the law, that makes us all equally guilty."

Michael's stomach knotted.

Elaine's revolted. She dashed into the bathroom just in time to throw up in the sink.

"I am surrounded by idiots," Joseph muttered, then pointed at Michael. "You think she's worth saving, fine! Now she's your responsibility. If she fucks up again, we're all going down, and you'll have only yourself to blame."

He left angrily, stomping down the hall to his own room, then promptly locking himself inside. All he needed was a few minutes of quiet. But it wasn't happening. No sooner had he settled into his easy chair than his cell phone rang.

He was about to blow a second fuse when he saw who was calling. Taking a deep breath, then exhaling slowly, he answered.

"Hello, Penny. What did you find out about Phyllis Palmer?"

"Quite a number of things, Mr. Stoss. I've attached the info in an email. Just wanted you to know the report was finished and on the way in case you needed the info tonight."

"Thank you, Penny. Have a good evening."

"You, too, Mr. Stoss."

The dial tone was all the impetus he needed. Information was always power, and right now he needed to swing the balance of power in his favor. He hurried to his office, anxious to see what she'd discovered. It took only moments to pull up the email and open the attachment. As soon as he printed it out, he sent an email back to Penny instructing her to delete everything regarding this subject and scrub it from her hard drive.

It wasn't anything she hadn't done before, and he knew she would think nothing of it as she promptly followed his orders.

He took the papers from the printer, then kicked back in his chair and began to read, scanning past the minutiae to the main points.

Phyllis Palmer: born Phyllis June Wyman in
Detroit, Michigan
Married Corey Stewart—1964
One child: Chloe Stewart—born August 30, 1966/
deceased December 12, 1990
Corey Stewart—deceased September 1967
Married Charles "Buck" Palmer—April 14, 1983
Divorced Charles Palmer—December 1, 1983
Moved to Miami, Florida—December 24, 1990

Joseph paused. Good God. The old woman was Chloe
Stewart's mother. Savannah Slade's grandmother. He
didn't know how they'd found each other, and it didn't
matter. Now there were two people who threatened his
welfare. He scanned through the rest of the report, then
got up and fed each page through the shredder.

Without knowing what Thomas Jefferson was planning, he knew there was no more time to waste. Once
again, he reached for his cell phone and called Mateo.

Mateo had just been seated at his favorite restaurant
when his cell vibrated. He waved the waiter away before
answering.

"Yes?" he said softly.

"The old woman is her grandmother. It goes down
tomorrow. I want you to take the Slade woman out first.
Make it look like an accident. Then get rid of the old
woman, too. Go through the house. Remove anything
that connects them to us, then toss the house and make
it look like a robbery."

"Yes, sir," Mateo said.

"Call me when it's done."

"Of course."

"Have a good evening," Joseph said.

"Thank you, sir," Mateo said, and disconnected.

Then he waved at his waiter, who quickly reappeared
with a basket of chips and a small bowl of Killer Hot
Salsa, which was Mateo's favorite.

"Cerveza, por favor."

"Sí, señor," the waiter said, and scurried away.

The boss had told him to enjoy the evening, and
Mateo intended to do just that. He scooped a chip into
the thick red sauce and popped it in his mouth, enjoy-
ing the quick bite of heat that hit his tongue while he
waited for his beer. This particular job had turned out
to be boring. At least tomorrow would bring it to a suc-
cessful end.

Savannah felt good about the events of the day. Maria
was healing. She'd found a grandmother and more info
to strengthen her case, and the papers regarding her
lawsuit would soon be ready to file, which meant Judd
would be here soon.

It was a little before 5:00 p.m. by the time she got to
her room. She kicked off her shoes and then crawled up
on the bed to call Judd. If she was lucky, he might be
able to get a flight out tomorrow. She knew it was short
notice, but nothing they hadn't expected. And since it
was only 3:00 p.m. there, it should give him time to call
a travel agent before they closed for the day.

She made the call, counting the rings until she heard
that deep, husky voice.

"Hey, darlin'," Judd said.

A low ache curled in the pit of her stomach. "Hey,
yourself."

"How's Maria?"

"Better. Still in and out of it, Holly said, but part of
that's due to meds."

"Thank God. So, do you have news for me?"

"It's why I'm calling. My lawyer says he'll probably file the papers within a couple of days, so…"

Relief washed through Judd so fast it made him light-headed. It was what he'd been waiting for. "I'm calling a travel agent right now. I'll call you back with times as soon as I get a flight, okay?"

"Absolutely," Savannah said. "And, Judd…"

"What, honey?"

"I can't wait."

She heard a low groan and then a chuckle, which made her smile. "You are one evil woman, Savannah Slade. You know what I'm thinking."

"I'm feeling the vibe already."

He laughed. "I'll call you back in a few."

"I'll be waiting."

Savannah hung up, then threw herself backward onto the mattress, her arms out-flung as her longing for Judd spiraled into a full-blown ache. It suddenly occurred to her as she was waiting for him to call back that she'd told Phyllis she wanted to take her out to dinner tomorrow night. But that wasn't going to happen if Judd was coming. She wanted them to meet, but she intended her first night with Judd to be for them alone. As soon as she got a definite time on his arrival, she would call Phyllis and ask her to lunch instead.

About ten minutes later, her cell phone rang. She answered quickly.

"Hello?"

"Miami International Airport. Flight 2126. Continental Airlines. Seven-thirty tomorrow night."

"Yay!" Savannah said as she wrote down the info.

Judd chuckled. "That reaction is the understatement of the week. I've never missed anyone as much as I've been missing you."

"Same here," Savannah said. "I'll meet you at luggage claim, okay?"

"Absolutely. Take care of yourself until I get there, okay?"

"Don't worry about me. It's all under control."

"Okay, honey. I've got a lot of arranging to do before I leave. Gotta call Pop, and get him to come out and ride herd on the ranch and the hands until I can get back."

Savannah grinned. Judd's father had retired from ranching less than three years earlier and moved into Missoula proper. He hadn't stopped complaining since.

"That should make him happy," she said.

Judd chuckled. "You know it. See you tomorrow night."

"I love you, Judd."

"Love you more."

The connection ended, but the emotional tie was as strong as if he were standing in the room. Now all she had to do was change meal times with her grandmother and she would be good to go.

As she made the call, she couldn't quit thinking about how amazing it was that she actually had a grandparent. The phone rang a couple of times before her grandmother answered.

"Hello?"

"Hi, Grandma, it's me, Savannah."

"Hello, darling. How sweet of you to call."

"I have a favor to ask," Savannah said. "I know I said I wanted to take you out to dinner tomorrow, but my boyfriend, Judd, is flying in tomorrow night and I have to pick him up at the airport, so I was wondering if we could do lunch instead?"

"Of course," Phyllis said, then laughed. "It's not like

I have any kind of a social calendar. I'm pretty much available at all times."

"Perfect!" Savannah said. "So how about I pick you up around eleven o'clock? That will give us time to get to a restaurant before the noon rush."

"Works for me," Phyllis said. "Where are we going? I ask so I'll know what to wear."

"I was going to ask you to suggest a place," Savannah said.

"Do you like Indian?" Phyllis asked.

"Yes, I do."

"Great. There's a good place not far from here. You get to my house, and I'll navigate from there."

"Perfect, and thanks for understanding, " Savannah said. "See you tomorrow."

"Yes, see you tomorrow," Phyllis said.

Elated that the change of plans had not been an issue, Savannah found herself suddenly starving, so she bounced off the bed and went to change clothes. Even if she didn't know a single soul in the place, she was going to go down to a proper restaurant and eat food from a table instead of her mattress.

Dinner in the hotel had come and gone, and Savannah was still too antsy to go to bed. Instead of going back to her room, she was browsing through the gift shop. She'd already found a cookbook of Cuban recipes she was going to take home to Holly, and a snow globe with a palm tree and a beach for Maria's snow globe collection. But no matter how long she looked, she couldn't find anything appropriate for Bud. She still felt guilty that she'd gone off and left him with the burden of book-keeping as well as everything else he was doing, but she didn't think a miniature palm tree dangling from a key chain was going to do it for him.

After a fruitless search, she decided to wait until Judd got there and get a guy's point of view as to what Bud might like. She paid for her other purchases and went back to her room.

Today had been exhausting, and she was so focused on tomorrow, she couldn't wait for this day to be over. She couldn't remember the last time she'd gone to sleep before 10:00 p.m., but this just might be the night.

She got into her pajamas and crawled into bed, planning to watch a little TV. Propping some pillows up behind her, she pulled up the covers to her waist and turned it on. After flipping through a few channels, she found a show she liked and settled down to catch up with the story line. Somewhere between a gunfight and a commercial, she fell asleep, and then she dreamed.

She was standing in a cemetery, searching for something, but she could not remember what. Tombstones were everywhere, like trees in a forest, and all of them so tall she couldn't see over them. Every time she tried to walk out, another tombstone would pop up, blocking her exit. At first it had been nothing but an aggravation, but the more times it happened, the more panicked she became. Then she began to hear voices—first her father, then Maria, then Judd—but their voices kept echoing, and she couldn't pinpoint a direction. Sometimes they called her Sarah, and sometimes Savannah.

When she screamed for help, the voices disappeared. She began to run, dodging in and out among the tombstones, calling over and over for someone to help.

Suddenly she tripped and fell. Pain shot through her hands and up her arms, and the skin was ripped from her knees. When she tried to get up, she kept slipping in blood. Then there was a soft voice behind her.

"I'll help you," a woman said.

"Thank you, oh, thank you," Savannah sobbed. "I can't find my way out."

The woman's voice turned into what sounded like a sneer. "You aren't supposed to. This is where you belong."

Savannah rolled over onto her back and looked up, thinking she'd seen the woman somewhere before.

"What do you mean?"

The woman pointed. "See, I was right."

Savannah's gaze shifted to where the woman was pointing, and then she saw the name on the tombstone— her name, Savannah Slade—and started to scream.

Savannah sat up with a jerk, her heart pounding, her face bathed in sweat. She threw back the covers and rolled out of bed. The dream had been so real that, for a moment, the covers had felt like dirt covering her body. She stared at the television in confusion, wondering why it was on, and remembered she'd been watching it when she fell asleep. She dug through the covers, looking for the remote to turn it off.

The sudden silence was startling. A slight thump sounded in the hall outside her room. She flinched as she looked over her shoulder, half expecting that woman from the dream to be standing in the room behind her, but there was no one there. She glanced at the clock. It was twenty minutes after three. Too early to get up.

"No big deal. I'm just losing my mind."

She glanced toward the balcony, visible through the sheers, and realized she'd fallen asleep without even pulling the drapes. The lights on the water pulled at her senses. Fresh air. That was what she needed. Something to wipe away the horror of that dream.

She unlocked the sliding door and inhaled deeply as she walked out onto the balcony. The sharp tang of sea air centered her focus like a shot of smelling salts. She told herself to think of something positive, but nothing came forth but the dream, which seemed to be stuck in rewind. It was that tombstone bearing her name that had freaked her out. Was that a portent of things to come?

The night sky was clear and beautiful beyond the shore—a vivid interpretation of the infinity of the universe—but the stars in Montana seemed closer and brighter. It made her homesick, wishing she was back on the ranch, listening to Andrew snore down the hall from her room, hearing the lowing of an occasional mama cow out in the pasture searching for her baby.

But the only thing left of Andrew was his spirit. She didn't know how that transition from death to life beyond actually worked, but she wished to God there was a way to "dial in" for emergencies.

God help me.

She felt lost. Her hands were shaking as she pushed the hair back from her face.

"Daddy…I don't know what to do. Did I make a mistake by coming here? If I challenge the Stoss family, is it going to get me killed?"

She waited for what seemed like forever, listening for an answer that never came. Finally the chill of the Atlantic breeze got to her and she went back inside, locking the door, then pulling the drapes. She had to get some more sleep or she would never get through tomorrow.

Judd's face slid through her mind, bringing the comforting knowledge that this time tomorrow she would be lying in his arms.

It was enough to get her back in the bed. She kicked at the covers, then pulled until they were straight. After removing the extra pillows, she finally lay down and closed her eyes.

A minute passed, and then another, until her breathing slowed and she was asleep. The fear that the horror would come back became a reality as the dream resurrected itself. All of a sudden she was back at the cemetery, but this time standing at the entrance beneath the great stone arch.

Within seconds of her arrival, the woman was back, standing amid the headstones and beckoning for her to come in. In that moment, reality tore through the dream-sleep, rudely yanking Savannah awake.

"Oh, my God, oh, my God."

She reached for a light.

The woman in her dream was the woman who'd fallen in front of the hotel, and she *had* seen her before. And now she remembered where.

This time when she got out of bed she grabbed her laptop and went straight to Google, then did a search on "Stoss family."

Dozens of links popped up. She scanned down the list, looking for one that referred to the only female of the three, and then clicked. The story that popped up was a piece written on a charity fundraiser, accompanied by a photo of the four organizers, one of whom was listed as Elaine Stoss Hamilton.

Savannah's gaze went straight to the woman on the end. Well-dressed. Well-groomed. Perfectly elegant in every way.

And it was the woman in her dream—the woman who'd been outside the hotel, the drunk who'd looked at Savannah as if she were seeing a ghost.

"Sweet heaven," Savannah muttered. "What does this mean?"

Elaine had behaved almost as if she'd recognized Savannah, but that made no sense. They'd never seen each other before. The Stoss family would have had no way of knowing who she was, and the papers had yet to be filed, so it made no sense that the look had been one of recognition. But it had happened.

Savannah kept staring at the photo, as if waiting for the woman to explain herself. The odds of the two of them meeting accidentally in a city the size of Miami had to be astronomical.

So how—why—did Elaine know her? Seeing Savannah, regardless of why Elaine had been at the hotel, should not have elicited such shock.

Savannah didn't know what all this meant, but she had a feeling it wasn't good. She needed to let someone know. But not the detective. He had yet to acknowledge she even had a reason for concern. Her lawyer, he was the one who needed to know. At the least, it might make a difference in his timing for filing the papers.

She got her cell phone, scrolled through the address book, then dialed Thomas Jefferson's office. Of course he wouldn't be there, but he would get the message first thing this morning. Then, if he thought it mattered, he would call and tell her what to do.

Convinced that she'd made the right decision, she waited for the machine to pick up. There was no time to leave details. When it beeped, she kept her news brief.

"Mr. Jefferson, it's Savannah Slade. A weird thing happened yesterday evening. Elaine Stoss Hamilton was at my hotel. To make a long story short, when she saw me, the shock on her face was evident. I don't know how it happened, but I believe they knew I was here and what I'm planning to do. At the very least, they know I'm here now. Let me know what you think. You can reach me on my cell anytime."

Satisfied that she'd done all she could for now, she laid the phone by her bed, then crawled back under the covers and turned out the lights. This time, when she fell asleep, it was peaceful, and when she woke, it was morning.

Savannah was in the shower when she heard her cell phone begin to ring. She grabbed a towel and then made a dash into the bedroom, answering before the call had time to go to voice mail.

"Hello," she said, breathlessly.

"Get packed."

Her stomach knotted. It was Jefferson, and the tone of his voice was not encouraging.

"Is this about the message I left you last night?"

"Yes, but you were vague. Tell me details. How did this meeting go down?"

Savannah began to explain, ending again with Elaine Hamilton's odd reaction to seeing her. "She looked like she'd just seen a ghost. She stared and stared at me, and then jumped into a cab and took off. But how could they know I'm here?"

"Who else in Miami besides me and my secretary knows why you're here and— Oh, shit. You told that detective, didn't you?"

"Yes, but you don't think—"

"Yes, that's exactly what I *do* think. I told you the arm of the Stoss family is long and strong. There's no telling who the detective told. It's not as if your request was confidential. There is no police/client confidentiality agreement like there is between a lawyer and client.

Almost anyone could have called the Stosses hoping to make a little money on the side. Hell, it might not even have been about the money so much as the perception of what the Stosses should be protected from. If your request was in any way viewed as a scam you were going to run on them, I can see a cop giving them a call and letting them know. Damn it. I let this get by me, and I shouldn't have. I should have known it would happen."

Savannah's heart was pounding. "You're scaring me."

"You have every right to be scared. If Elaine was scoping out the enemy, you've been made. So get packed and come to my office. I'll have my friend here waiting. You'll leave with him from my office."

"What about my car?"

"Just leave it in the parking garage. I'll call the rental agency tomorrow and have it picked up from there."

"Oh, wait! I need to call Judd." Then she glanced at the time. "Oh, no. I can't. He's already in the air. I was supposed to pick him up at the airport at seven-thirty this evening."

"One thing at a time, Savannah. You can leave him a voice mail. I'll pick him up myself. We'll make it work."

"There's more. I was supposed to have lunch with my grandmother. I need to call her and tell her there's been a change of plans."

"Do what you have to do, but get over here fast."

"All right," Savannah said. "I'll be there as soon as I can get packed and checked out."

"Drive carefully."

"I always do, and, Thomas…"

"Yes?"

"Thanks."

"I already told you, don't thank me yet. Thank me when it's over."

The line went dead.

Savannah's heart was hammering as she hung up the phone. Her hands were sweaty, and she wished she'd never argued with Judd and had let him come with her to begin with. She needed him here.

One more call that had to be made, and she dreaded the explanation. She punched in the numbers, waiting anxiously for Phyllis to pick up. Just when she thought it was going to go to voice mail, her grandmother answered.

"Hello?"

"Grandma, it's me, Savannah."

Savannah could hear the smile in Phyllis's voice as she answered.

"Hi, sweetheart, I hope you're calling to tell me you're coming early."

"No, sorry, Grandma. I'm calling to tell you that I can't come at all."

"Oh, dear, I'm sorry to hear that. Are you okay?"

"Not really," she said. "Despite our best efforts, we think the Stoss family already knows I'm here and why I came. Basically, my lawyer is about to put me in what amounts to protective custody."

"Oh, no. I was afraid something like this might happen. Have you been harassed? What's happening?"

"It's kind of a long story. As soon as I get settled, I'll call you, okay?"

"Yes, of course. The most important thing is your safety. Take care of yourself."

"Yes, I will, Grandma," Savannah said.

"I know we haven't had time to get to know each

other yet, but I wanted you to know how much I'm looking forward to the future."

"Me, too," Savannah said.

"I love you, dear."

Savannah smiled. "Love you, too, Grandma. I'll call
as soon as I can."

Savannah hung up the phone, then began to pack.

Mateo had been planning for days how he was going
to make this go down. Stoss wanted an accident. But
guaranteeing she would not survive it was tricky. The
only times he had free access to her was when she was in
her car or at her grandmother's house. Ideally, it would
have been easy to take them both out at once inside
the old lady's house. Make it look like she'd been there
when the robbery had gone down. But Stoss obviously
didn't want the cops making the connection between
the two women. The fact that the Slade woman had already involved a lawyer only added to the problem. The
more people who knew her story, the harder it would
be to make the cops believe her death had not been
planned.

So once he'd gotten the go-ahead, he'd spent the night
in preparation. Getting into the parking garage at the
InterContinental where the cars were valet parked and
staying undetected had not been easy. He'd spray painted
the lenses of the security cameras, then set about rigging
Savannah Slade's car. Afterward he'd spent an extra five
minutes leaving graffiti tags all over the walls and posts
on that floor, so that when security went to check out
the cameras, they would assume they'd been put out of
commission because of the taggers.

Once he'd finished, he'd slipped out of the garage and
run through three blocks of alleys to where he'd parked,

then driven to an all-night diner to eat breakfast. It was just past 5:00 a.m. when he drove back to the parking lot across from the hotel entrance, taking care to find a spot where he could watch who came and went, and settled down to wait for the Slade woman to leave the hotel.

The sun came up. Traffic began to increase. Shuttle buses began their daily runs between the hotel and the airport, and still Mateo waited, confident that he could not be seen through the darkened windows. When the air grew too hot for comfort, he started the engine and turned on the air conditioner, and then took a drink from the bottle of water in his console. Mateo Bonaventure was a man who came prepared.

At ten minutes after ten, Savannah Slade came out of the hotel and went straight to valet parking, which he had expected. What he hadn't expected was the suitcase she was pulling. As she waited, it became apparent that she was overly anxious about something. She kept scanning the area and looking over her shoulder, gauging everyone who came close to where she was standing.

Mateo gritted his teeth, a habit he had when he was disconcerted. She was running. He would bet his life on it, and he would also bet that the stunt Elaine Hamilton had pulled was what had precipitated this unexpected exit. So be it. She wouldn't run far. Not after what he'd done to her car.

The boss always got what he wanted.

Twelve

Savannah didn't feel easy until she was driving away from the hotel. The attendant had already turned on the air conditioner, and the interior of the car was cooling rapidly as she pulled out into the main flow of traffic.

She was still in shock and wishing she'd thought to call Bud just to let him know what was happening. She wanted to hear Holly's voice, too—to know someone she loved was aware of the shift in her plans. Her life was out of her control, and it didn't feel right. How had everything gone so wrong when she'd been so careful to do things right?

The light was turning red as she neared the first main intersection. As soon as it changed back to green, she accelerated through, heading due north, then began signaling to change lanes. But there was a dark SUV driving in the lane beside her that wouldn't yield. The windows were so heavily tinted that she couldn't see into the car, but she hoped the driver could see her glare of disapproval.

She sped up so that he could see her turn signal and assumed he would slow down to let her in. To her surprise, he sped up just enough to close the gap, completely blocking her. Her frustration turned to concern. There were cars in front of her, cars behind her, and this car beside her had her pinned in.

"Fine. You won't let me ahead of you. I'll just slow down and get in behind you."

But when she tapped her brakes, the dark car braked, too.

Suddenly the car in front of her turned right, leaving her enough space to accelerate and get in front of the SUV. But this time when she hit the accelerator, the car shot forward far faster than she'd expected. Startled, she stomped on the brakes, but they wouldn't respond. In a panic, she was forced to swerve onto the shoulder of the road to keep from rear-ending the car in front of her. She kept stomping the brakes, but the car wasn't responding. In fact, it kept going faster and faster, until the car was out of control. She began honking the horn, desperate to alert the other drivers as she swerved in and out between them.

All of a sudden she saw the MacArthur Causeway looming. She didn't want to get on that highway. It was bordered on both sides by nothing but water. There was a side street coming up. She was going to take it and, if she had to, smash her car into the palm trees along the highway rather than hit another car.

Suddenly the dark SUV was back, and to her horror, it swerved right at her. To keep from crashing into the church van in front of her, she swerved, missed her side street and wound up exactly where she hadn't wanted to be—hurtling down the causeway at breakneck speed, dodging traffic and honking her horn, while praying she wouldn't end up like her father, dead in an accident that was not of his making.

The dark SUV was gone.

She started to cry. She didn't want to die, but it looked like it could easily happen. Her cell phone was on the seat beside her. She had to let someone know what was happening. Taking a chance, she steered with one hand long enough to feel around and find the phone.

If she could just dial without taking her eyes from the road, at least she could alert Thomas Jefferson as to what was happening. She dialed by feel alone, praying it was the right number, then was forced to grab the wheel with both hands, which sent the phone onto the floor.

She screamed. Her tires squealed as she narrowly missed a car full of teenagers. Then she saw traffic slowing down and realized there was construction on the bridge and lanes were narrowing. To her horror, she'd just run out of room to drive without crashing into another vehicle. The only place left to drive unimpeded was the narrow space between the right lane and the bridge railing. The tires were humming as she shot into the space at full speed. Then sparks began to fly and the car began to vibrate. It took her a moment to realize it was because the car was literally scraping against the railing—metal on metal.

She didn't know if the call had gone through, or if anyone was on the other end of the line, but she started shouting, saying what she needed to say, and praying someone had picked up and was hearing her.

Laura loved her new job at Jefferson's law office. She didn't know why the previous secretary had quit so abruptly. The man was easy to work for. She was in a good mood, thinking about the new apartment she'd just leased, when the phone began to ring. Still smiling, she picked up the receiver.

"Jefferson Law Office, how may I—"

She stopped. Someone was screaming and talking, but the sound was too garbled to understand.

She saw the caller ID and screamed herself. "Mr. Jefferson!" She screamed again as she put the phone on speaker. "Mr. Jefferson!"

Then she ran into his office.

Thomas was working on a summation when his door flew open, hitting the wall. He jumped, frowning in disapproval as Laura came running into the room, her face devoid of color.

"What on earth is the matter with—"

"Mr. Jefferson! Mr Jefferson! You've got to hear this! It's Miss Slade."

She put his phone on speaker just in time for him to hear the panic in Savannah Slade's voice.

"I need help! I'm on the MacArthur Causeway. Accelerator is stuck…going ninety miles an hour! Dark SUV with black windows forced me onto the bridge. Help me! I'm on the MacArthur Causeway and my car is out of control. The accelerator is stuck at ninety miles an hour. Dark SUV with black windows. Find the driver. He's the one who killed me!"

Thomas jumped to his feet. "Laura, tell her we heard her! Say it over and over. Maybe she'll hear," he said, pulling out his cell. "I'm going to call the police."

He was already dialing 9-1-1 as Laura began to shout. He moved into the outer office, only to realize he could still hear Savannah's panicked message there, too. The moment he heard the dispatcher, he began relaying the info in short choppy sentences to make sure the woman understood who and what was involved, then quickly added, "Her name is Savannah Slade, and someone is trying to kill her. She's going to go off the causeway into the water. Tell Harbor Patrol before it's too late."

When he realized Savannah had quit talking, his heart dropped. He spun toward the phone just as a high-pitched scream cut through the silence, immediately followed by the sound of an impact, then the grinding sound of crushing metal, followed by a long moment of silence, and finally a gut-wrenching splash.

She was in the water.

Savannah knew she was going over the railing, and at that moment panic ended. Although everything began to happen in slow motion, her mind was still spinning. If she had a chance of surviving, she was going to have to get out of the car before it sank. She hit the button that rolled down her window, knowing the door wouldn't open against the pressure of the water. She would have only a few brief moments to climb out after she went in the water.

She braced herself, her hands on the steering wheel as the car finally ran out of room and slammed full-on into the railing. Despite her seat belt, the force was so strong that her head popped forward, slamming her chest against the steering wheel, before her head jerked backward against the headrest. The air bag had deployed. The taste of blood was in her mouth. She could feel it running down the side of her face as the car went airborne.

The sudden silence was surreal. The rush of air flowing through the open window brought her thoughts into bittersweet focus. Sunlight glittered on the water below like a million tiny diamonds scattered across the surface. Judd's face flashed before her eyes.

She didn't want to die.

Then…impact!

Water began pouring into the vehicle like a flood over a dam as she struggled to unlock her seat belt. Her heart was hammering, her hands shaking so hard she couldn't find the latch. Water was up to her shoulders, and then her chin.

God help me.

Suddenly she was free, but when she tried to climb out, the pressure of the water kept pushing, pushing, pushing against her, and the air bag was in the way.

And then the car went under.

Harbor Patrol was already en route when they saw the car go airborne. For a few seconds it seemed suspended in midair, and then it was going down, hitting nose first before it began to sink. Crew members were already in place, ready to go into the water when the car suddenly disappeared. Seconds later the boat reached the area and swerved as the pilot killed the engine. Moments after that, two men were in the water.

"There's a body!" someone shouted.

The men came up, then began swimming toward her. The first swimmer reached her and immediately flipped her onto her back.

"She's not breathing!" he yelled.

The second swimmer arrived. Together, they began towing her toward the patrol boat.

Once there, other crew members hauled her out of the water and began performing CPR as the swimmers climbed back on board. The engine roared to life. The patrol boat began speeding toward shore and the waiting ambulance.

A chopper from a local television station was already on the scene, circling overhead like a vulture that had spotted a kill. It had been filming her wild race on the streets nearly from the start. They'd seen her swerve onto the causeway, seen her trying to dodge traffic before she'd been forced onto the shoulder of the highway. They'd seen the impact, and then the car sailing over the railing and into the water. The live feed continued to broadcast as Harbor Patrol pulled her body out of the bay, and it was still broadcasting the attempt to resuscitate her as the City of Miami watched.

Jefferson's police scanner was squawking as he sped through the city in his big Hummer. He'd been listening to the police band and knew when they pulled her out of the water and then when she was being transported to Mount Sinai Medical Center. He wouldn't let himself think that she might already be dead. If she was, it would be his fault. He'd been too damned complacent, thinking about the coup he was going to pull on Joseph Stoss and not enough about the ramifications. He'd known she'd been to the police before she'd come to him, but he'd never factored it in. Stoss was too big a deal not to have people on the inside of every branch of city government, and he should have known it. He didn't want her death on his conscience.

When he pulled into the E.R. parking lot, he saw patrol cars and several unmarked cop cars already there. Detectives. He wondered if the son of a bitch who'd blown her off at the station had gotten the news that someone had tried to kill her. If he had, Jefferson couldn't help but wonder what the man's reaction was going to be now.

Jefferson wheeled into the first empty spot he came to. When he got out of his car, he was running.

* * *

Frank Barber was at his desk, doing follow-up on a dead gangbanger whose body had turned up in the bay last night, when his partner came flying into the room and headed for the television.

Al yelled as he grabbed the remote, "You gotta see this!"

Frank reached the television and saw a car weaving in and out of traffic on the causeway. "The Channel 6 News chopper is filming a speeding car on the causeway? What's the deal?"

"All I know is they said the car was out of control and that the accelerator was stuck. But get this. Dispatch said the name of the driver was Savannah Slade. Isn't that the name of the woman who helped us break the Wilson case?"

Frank's gut suddenly knotted as he pictured the pretty blonde behind the wheel.

"Oh, shit."

"Oh, man, she's going over!" Al yelled. By now everyone in the office was watching, and when the car took out part of the railing as it went over, there was a collective gasp, followed, when it hit the water, by a collective groan.

Frank wouldn't let himself think that she was already dead.

"Where's Harbor Patrol? Did someone call Harbor Patrol?"

As if on cue, the camera in the chopper shifted just enough to catch sight of a patrol boat speeding toward the point of impact.

"They're gonna be too late," Al said as the car went under.

The chopper was circling now, filming the arrival of the boat and the two men who went in the water.

Suddenly someone pointed to the top of the screen.

"Look! Look! Isn't that a body? It is! It just came to the surface."

Frank began to yell, as if they could hear him.

"She's facedown. She's facedown, damn it! Somebody pull her out!"

The camera suddenly zoomed in on the two swimmers, and then the rescue itself. But Frank couldn't watch anymore. He grabbed his gun out of his desk and headed for the door.

"Where are you going?" Al said.

"To the hospital."

"Wait for me," Al said, and hurried after him.

Phyllis was carrying a bag of groceries from the car to the house when a dark SUV pulled into her driveway. She paused on the porch, watching as a middle-aged Latino man with a long black ponytail got out and came up her walk.

She was taken off guard by his ease and his smile.

"Good morning, *señora*," the man said. "My name is Mateo. I am a friend of your granddaughter, Savannah."

Phyllis frowned. Savannah hadn't mentioned anything about making friends here in town, and she was already supposed to be in protective custody. Even stranger, he had both hands in his pockets and had yet to take them out.

"How can I help you?" she asked.

Aha, Mateo thought when she didn't deny knowing Savannah Slade. Instant confirmation that he had the right woman.

"May we go inside? I just need a few moments of your time."

"I don't think so," Phyllis said, and began backing toward the door.

Mateo blinked as the smile slid off his face. "Your way or mine, but either way, we're going inside," he said.

It was when his hands came out of his pockets and Phyllis saw that he was wearing surgical gloves that she understood she was going to die.

Her scream was cut short as he pushed her inside the house, shoving her so hard against the wall that she lost her breath. The sack of groceries slid to the floor between them. Suddenly his hands were around her neck, and she began kicking and scratching at his face, anything to try to get free.

But Mateo didn't move or even shy away. Even as her fingers were digging into the skin of his cheek, he remained steadfast, squeezing, squeezing, until the light went out in her eyes. Her arms went limp; her body began to slide down the wall as her eyes rolled back in her head. Mateo followed her down then, just to make sure it was over, gave her head a quick twist. The snap of bones in her neck was the last sound she made.

He stood and stepped back, frowning at the sting of the scratches on his face, then took out a handkerchief and pressed it to his cheek as he went about tossing the house to make it appear as if she'd walked in on a robbery in progress.

Once he was finished, he closed the door behind him and got into his car and drove away. All in all, the day had not gone as smoothly as he'd planned. He needed to check in with the boss, ditch the car and lay low until all this blew over.

* * *

Joseph had already heard about the crazy incident on the MacArthur Causeway from an employee. He'd watched Savannah Slade's car speeding out of control, seen her hit the bridge, then go into the water. It wasn't until the car went under that he realized he'd been holding his breath. The commentary the network was running over the live feed was vague. What he didn't like was the fact that they knew the woman's name and that her car was out of control. That wasn't what he'd ordered. It was supposed to be a sudden and devastating crash. He didn't want the public invested in her drama, or to know that whatever was happening was out of her control, which might lead to suspicions of foul play. How the hell had Mateo fucked this up?

He tried to reach the man, but the call went straight to voice mail. A few minutes later, Mateo called him back.

"It is done," Mateo said.

Joseph was furious. "It's all over the fucking TV is what it is. That's not what I ordered, and you know it."

Mateo was ready for the accusation. He knew just where to shift the blame.

"When she came out of the hotel this morning, she was running."

Joseph frowned. "What do you mean?"

"She had her bag packed and kept looking over her shoulder as she waited for her car to come from valet parking. Whatever Elaine said to her yesterday set her off. I had no idea where she was going and had to make the best of a bad situation."

Joseph cursed. "Perfect. Just fucking perfect," he muttered. "What about the old woman?"

"As you asked."

"At least you got that much right," Joseph snapped. "Get rid of your car and get out to my hangar at the airport. You're going to visit your mother in Panama. Officially, you do not work for me, so there's no paper trail from me to you. Let's keep it that way, shall we?"

Mateo was already packed.

"Yes, sir. If you need me, you know how to reach me."

Joseph hung up in his ear. He needed to notify the pilot. Once he had that set in motion, he decided to make one more call. It was time for Bonaventure to retire.

The ambulance was two minutes out from Mount Sinai when the EMT working on Savannah Slade suddenly yelled, "I've got a pulse!"

She went from being a body to a tangible rescue as she gasped, choked, then vomited up water.

They ceased CPR as she began breathing on her own, while the EMT slipped an oxygen mask onto her nose and started assessing vitals. She was beginning to exhibit signs of consciousness. When she tried to pull the mask off her nose, he knew he had her back.

Moments later the ambulance reached the E.R. entrance. Within seconds they were wheeling her inside, moving her from the gurney to a hospital bed as the EMT related her vitals to the attending doctor.

Knowing that she'd been the victim of an accident before the vehicle had gone into the water, the E.R. team began working on her again, cutting the clothing from her body to check for injuries. The E.R. doctor was a man named Adam Miesner, who immediately began assessing her brain function, trying to get her to respond.

"Savannah...I'm Dr. Miesner. You had an accident. Do you remember? You're in the emergency room." He took her hand. "Savannah. Savannah? Can you hear me? If you can hear me, squeeze my hand."

There was a slight pressure on his fingers, enough to convince him that she could hear what he was saying.

"Okay. Great, you can hear me. You were in a wreck. Can you tell me where it hurts?"

She began to moan. He couldn't tell if she was trying to talk, or if her pain was increasing with returning consciousness. The nurses had removed the last of her clothing. Now he could see the bruises forming beneath her skin and was most concerned about the obvious—a large one on her chest.

"Get X-ray in here. It appears she hit the steering wheel. I want film on her from the waist up."

He checked her pupils. They were dilated. Concussion. There was a gash at her hairline that would have to be closed.

The moment the nurses removed the last of her clothing, she began to thrash, as if she knew she was naked and in some sort of peril. She began shaking her head from side to side, fighting against the oxygen mask and pushing at the hands on her bare skin.

Miesner grabbed her wrist. "Miss Slade...you're safe. You're in the E.R. You're safe."

The words seemed to register. She quit rolling and kicking, but she still fumbled at the mask.

Miesner spoke again as he pulled her hand away from her face. "Miss Slade, it's okay. That's an oxygen mask. You need to leave it alone. Do you hear me? You need to leave it alone."

Her body stilled, but then tears began welling from beneath her eyelids.

"Savannah, do you hurt? Can you show me where you hurt?"

Her eyelids were fluttering as she reached toward her chest.

"Your chest hurts? Okay. We're going to take care of you."

All the while he was talking, he was checking her from head to toe, his practiced eye noting swelling and bruising. When he palpated her stomach to check for internal bleeding and found it still soft and pliable, he counted it one less problem with which to deal.

A nurse was swabbing the cut along her hairline, readying it to be stitched, when Savannah suddenly opened her eyes. Her confusion was evident, but her eyes were focusing, another good sign.

"Savannah, I'm Dr. Miesner. You had an accident. You're in the emergency room, and we're taking good care of you. Do you understand?"

She blinked, and then her eyes closed.

The mobile X-ray arrived in Savannah's room, while out at the reception area, a very large black man and a cop brandishing a badge reached the admitting desk at the same time.

"Savannah Slade," they said in unison, then stopped and stared at each other.

Thomas pushed ahead. He was too frantic to be concerned with manners. "Ma'am, an ambulance just brought in a woman named Savannah Slade. I'm not asking you to divulge anything improper, but the police band said she wasn't breathing when they pulled her out of the water. So please, could you just check and see if she's alive?"

It was the tears in his eyes that tipped the scales. The

receptionist hesitated briefly, then picked up the phone and dialed.

Barber shifted nervously from foot to foot, waiting to hear the answer as the receptionist made the call. A few moments later she hung up.

"They revived her. She's breathing on her own. Beyond that, you'll have to wait to talk to her doctor. I told them she had people in the E.R. lobby waiting for word."

She pointed to the chairs.

"Praise God," Thomas said softly, then added, "Thank you, ma'am. Thank you for that," and headed for the seating area.

Barber followed and sat down in the chair beside him. Al got a call and had to leave.

"I'm her lawyer," Thomas said shortly. "Who are you?"

"Detective Barber, Homicide."

Jefferson's expression shifted. "Oh. Yeah. The cop who blew off the information that the Stoss family had killed one of their own and threatened her life. How do you feel about that now?"

An angry flush crept up Frank's neck, but he held his tongue. "They're pulling her car out of the water. I'm going to reserve comment until I get the report from CSI."

Thomas knew his size was an intimidation factor all on its own and was just pissed enough right now to use it. He leaned forward.

"Just in case you're interested, she was on the phone with me all the way across the causeway. She said a dark SUV with tinted windows forced her onto the bridge. Like the driver knew she wouldn't be able to control the car and had nowhere to go but into the bay."

Barber's eyes widened. This was news he hadn't heard. "I don't suppose she got a tag number?"

Thomas didn't bother to hide his sarcasm. "At ninety-plus miles an hour, with nowhere to drive except against the bridge railing, I'm pretty sure she wasn't taking names or numbers."

"Look," Barber snapped. "I get what you're feeling. But you know the law. You can't just accuse someone of a crime without a single shred of evidence. Especially when billions of dollars are at stake."

"When billions of dollars are at stake, this kind of shit is what happens," Thomas countered. "We haven't filed a single paper with the court. There is no way on God's earth that a member of the Stoss family should know she's even in Miami to claim her inheritance, let alone that she also came to seek justice for her birth father's death. The only people who knew what she was planning to do beside me were the people she went to first—the cops. No one knew, and yet Elaine Hamilton confronted her at her hotel late yesterday evening, stared her down as if she'd seen a ghost, then got into a cab and bolted like a skunked dog. Less than twenty-four hours later, this happens. Sounds pretty damned fishy to me."

Before Barber could answer, Thomas went at him again.

"As for the way things went down today, I consider it quite a coincidence that Gerald Stoss died in exactly the same way twenty years ago—in a speeding car. Twenty years ago they said he was driving too fast. Twenty years later, we have cell phones, and Savannah Slade was savvy enough to make an SOS call and tell us exactly what was wrong and why it was happening before she hit the bridge and went into the water."

Barber wasn't about to agree, but he was listening.

Thomas glared, then got up and put a three-chair space between them before he sat back down. He leaned back and folded his arms across his chest. He'd said his piece. The only person he wanted to talk to now was the doctor.

An entire hour passed and was well on its way to a second, and still they waited.

Thomas had checked in with Laura twice. He'd had her cancel his appointments for the rest of the day, then notify the man who was to have provided her protection. After that he spent the rest of the time trying not to think that Savannah Slade's survival might have come at the cost of her future. He couldn't imagine anything worse than someone as vital as she had been spending the rest of her life in a vegetative state. Just the thought of it made him madder and more determined to advocate on her behalf.

All of a sudden he remembered he was supposed to pick up her almost-fiancé, Judd Holyfield, from the airport this evening, and he added that to his calendar, making sure to set the alarm on his BlackBerry as a reminder.

Meanwhile, Barber had been up and down, on his cell phone a half dozen times to Al, and then to his lieutenant, keeping up with the investigation from their end while still waiting for permission to question Savannah Slade. A large part of his concern was based on guilt. He kept reliving the moment when he'd made that call to Joseph Stoss and wondering how it might have changed the outcome of this tragedy.

Every time the door leading back to the E.R. opened, both men turned to look. Finally a doctor emerged and headed for the waiting area.

"Any family for Savannah Slade?"

Both men stood.

The doctor approached. "I'm Dr. Miesner. Are you family?"

"I'm her lawyer," Thomas said.

Barber flashed his badge. "I'm investigating her accident. When can I talk to her?"

The doctor frowned. "No family?"

Thomas spoke up. "Yes, in Montana. She has a grandmother here. Her name is Phyllis Palmer. She lives in Coral Gables, but as far as I'm aware, she doesn't know about the accident."

Barber frowned. "I didn't know she had any family here."

"You didn't ask," Thomas snapped. "Please, Doctor. Right now I'm all she has."

The doctor began to explain. "She was successfully resuscitated. I don't detect any cognitive damage as of yet, but there are substantial contusions to her chest area. She said the air bag deployed, but not until after she'd hit the steering wheel. Whether it was faulty or she's not remembering correctly, I can't say. I put four stitches in a cut in her hairline, but there don't seem to be any broken bones."

"Thank the Lord," Thomas said. "Can I talk to her?"

"We're moving her to a room. Check with the nurses' station on the fourth floor. They'll tell you where she is."

"Make sure it's a private room, because she's going to have a guard on her door," Thomas said.

Miesner frowned. "I'm sorry?"

"Her accident wasn't an accident," Thomas said. "Someone tried to kill her."

Miesner's eyes widened as he glanced at the cop for confirmation.

Barber pushed forward. "That has yet to be determined. I need to talk to her."

"Then follow me," Thomas snapped. "You can talk to her with her lawyer present."

He walked away, giving Barber no option but to follow.

Thirteen

Thomas and Barber got onto the elevator together. The car started up as Barber took out a notepad.

"Give me her grandmother's name and address. I'll send a car to notify her."

Thomas called his office. "Laura, it's me. I need you to look up the info on Savannah Slade's grandmother, Phyllis Palmer. Phone number, address, whatever we have."

"Yes, sir, just a moment and I'll pull it up. Okay, um, here we go. Are you ready?"

"Hang on. I'm going to give the phone to a detective. Tell him the particulars, then you can hang up."

He thrust the phone at Barber. "Here."

Barber tucked the phone between his ear and shoulder, and quickly took down the info.

"Thank you, ma'am," he said, and gave the phone back to Thomas.

The doors opened. They walked out together and headed for the nurses' station.

"I'll be right there," Barber said as he paused by a waiting room. "I'm going to dispatch the car. You find out what room she's in."

Thomas kept on walking. He didn't like the cop's attitude, but there was little he could do about it. He asked for the floor supervisor, then explained who he was and the situation they were in, and told her that a guard was going to be put on Savannah's room.

That changed the attitude at the desk considerably, as did the cop who appeared flashing his badge. A few moments later they were walking into Room 440, and the sight stopped Thomas in his tracks.

Savannah looked like a child lying in the middle of that bed. Her blue hospital gown nearly swallowed her, and her hair was still damp and in obvious tangles. The bruising on her face was startling, already turning varying shades of bloody purple, as was the seeping bandage at the top of her head. Her lip was swollen, and one of her eyes was already turning black. There was an IV in her arm, and a couple of machines were hooked up to her body—registering her vitals, he supposed. Whatever they were, they only made her look smaller than ever.

"Son of a bitch," Thomas whispered.

Barber moved past him, heading for the bed. Thomas frowned, then followed, stationing himself on the opposite side.

Barber paused, eyeing the machines. A nurse came into the room, gave them a sharp look and then moved Barber aside to check Savannah's readings.

"Visiting hours aren't until 2:00 p.m.," she said.

Barber flashed his badge again. "I have Dr. Miesner's permission to question her about the accident."

"I'm her lawyer," Thomas said. "He's not talking to her without me."

"Keep it short," the nurse said, then left the room.

Barber stepped up beside the bed, then touched Savannah's arm.

"She feels cold."

Thomas pulled up a blanket from the foot of the bed.

Barber laid a hand on her arm. "Miss Slade. It's Detective Barber, Miami Homicide. I need to ask you a couple of questions. Can you hear me?"

Savannah stirred, slowly opening her eyes.

Barber could see she wasn't focused and wasn't sure how much good this was going to do.

"You had an accident. Do you remember?"

She was so long in answering he didn't think she was really conscious. When she finally spoke, her voice was so soft he had to lean down to hear her.

"He tried to kill me."

Barber felt sick. She might look like hell, but it seemed she hadn't forgotten a thing.

"Who tried to kill you, Savannah?"

"…no face…dark windows…dark SUV."

"Son of a bitch," Thomas muttered.

Savannah stirred at the sound of his voice.

"I'm here, honey," he said, and laid his hand on top of hers. Her fingers curled, instinctively clinging to his strength.

"What happened to your car? Why couldn't you stop?" Barber asked.

"Wouldn't stop. Going fast…so fast…"

"Were your brakes out, as well?"

She frowned, struggling to open her eyes. "Don't know…just kept going faster and faster."

Barber made a few notes, then came at her from another angle.

"Miss Slade, your lawyer said Elaine Hamilton was at your hotel yesterday evening. Did you speak to her?"

Savannah nodded weakly. "She fell… Drunk, I think. Helped her up."

Barber sighed. That made sense. Everyone knew the woman was a lush. What he couldn't figure out was why, if the Stosses were truly behind this, the woman would have shown herself that way.

"Did she say anything to you?" Barber asked.

"Call a cab. Wanted to go home."

"Did you know who she was?"

Savannah shook her head. "Not then. Later. Remembered seeing a picture."

"Have you had any contact with the Stoss family since your arrival?"

"No. Just that." Then she tugged on Thomas's hand. "Call my grandma.…"

"I've already sent some people to notify her," Barber said.

Savannah looked up into Thomas's face. Her chin began to quiver, and her eyes filled with tears.

"The water. I couldn't get out. Thought I was going to die."

"I know, honey," Thomas said. "I'm so sorry."

"Judd. I want Judd."

"He'll be here tonight. I'll bring him straight here," Thomas said. "I promise."

Savannah closed her eyes.

Barber frowned. "Who's Judd?"

"Judd Holyfield, her boyfriend back in Missoula. I'm picking him up at the airport this evening."

Barber made a note of the name, then dropped the notepad and pen in his pocket and laid a hand on her arm again.

She looked up.

"Miss Slade. I'm leaving now. I'll be in touch."

"They killed my father. Don't let them kill me, too."

A fresh wave of guilt made Barber's stomach knot. "I'll have a guard on your room. You just focus on getting well."

Savannah's grip tightened on Thomas's hand.

"I'm still here, girl. I'll be here, at least until the guard shows up. And maybe by the time he comes your grandmother will be here, too. You just rest."

"Judd," she said.

"I won't forget him," Thomas said.

Savannah closed her eyes.

It was after 4:00 p.m. when a police cruiser pulled into the driveway of Phyllis Palmer's house. Officers Rex and Hale walked up the sidewalk to the front porch and rang the bell.

When no one answered, they glanced back at her car in the drive, and then rang the bell again, followed by a loud knock.

"Miami P.D.!" Rex called out, but there was still no answer.

The curtains were pulled back from the windows on either side of the door. Hale walked over to one window and leaned forward, shading his eyes as he looked inside. All of a sudden he jerked back.

"We've got a body," he said tersely. "Try the door."

The doorknob turned freely, and the door swung inward. Both officers entered with their guns drawn and did a quick sweep of the house before coming back into the living room.

"Call it in," Rex said as he looked down at the crumpled body of the elderly woman lying against the wall.

Hale reached for his radio.

Phyllis Palmer had just become a statistic.

Savannah was still in shock. She kept waking up in the hospital bed, gasping for air as she relieved her near-drowning again and again. The nurses who came and went were both kind and capable, but the police guard outside her door was enough to start the spread of gossip. No one knew for sure why someone wanted her dead, but they were well aware that someone important considered her in danger.

Twice she'd asked if there had been a call from her grandmother, and each time they told her no, her concern grew. She didn't know Phyllis Palmer well, but all she could think was that she'd either read Phyllis wrong or something was happening that no one wanted to tell her about. Thomas would tell her the truth, but he'd left to pick up Judd at the airport. She would have called Detective Barber, but she didn't have his number.

At that point there was a knock on her door, then a doctor entered, followed by a nurse she hadn't seen before.

"Good evening, Miss Slade. I'm Dr. Polo. I'll be in charge of your case while you're here. I hear you got yourself on TV when you went for a swim this morning. Thought I'd come by and get myself an autograph."

His lighthearted attitude and friendly smile were just what she needed. By the time he pulled his stethoscope out of his pocket, she was already at ease.

"Let's see how your lungs are faring," he said, and did a quick check of her breathing. "Shirley, may I see her chart?"

The nurse handed it over.

Savannah tried to judge what he was thinking by the

expressions on his face but couldn't get a reading. Finally she just came out and asked, "When can I leave?"

He smiled as he handed her chart back to the nurse. "Let's table that decision until tomorrow morning. You swallowed a goodly portion of the Atlantic this morning before they fished you out of the bay. I'd like you to stay at least until I'm certain you're not going to develop any problems with your lungs, okay?"

Put like that, she had no room to argue. "Okay."

He patted the covers on top of her foot. "You get a good night's rest, and we'll talk tomorrow."

Jefferson had been on the phone nonstop ever since he'd left the hospital, trying to juggle his court appearances tomorrow with today's appointments that he'd had rescheduled. Laura had turned out to be a lifesaver, staying until well after 7:00 p.m to make sure all the calls had been returned and the times confirmed while he left for the airport.

Parking was always a hassle, and he didn't want to be late picking Holyfield up. He knew that Savannah had sent the man a text about the change of plans, but he wouldn't know until he got there if Holyfield had checked his messages. He didn't know how the man was going to react to the news of what had happened, but he knew that if he himself received that kind of news about someone he loved, he would probably go ballistic. With that depressing thought in mind, he finally found a parking spot and headed inside the terminal.

The moment the wheels touched down, Judd breathed a huge sigh of relief. His seatmate, an older woman who'd been quiet all the way from Denver, reached over and patted his hand.

"I had no idea you were an anxious traveler. You did great."

Judd smiled. "No, ma'am. That sigh of relief wasn't because I was afraid of flying. It's because I'm about to see my sweetheart again."

Her eyes lit up as her smile widened. "Oh, how romantic," she said. "Miami is a beautiful place for lovers. Have a wonderful time."

"Thank you, ma'am. You, too."

The plane began to taxi toward the terminal, and the business of gathering up belongings took over everyone's focus. When the flight attendant gave the okay for phones to go on, the first thing Judd did was check his messages. When he saw the one from Savannah, he grinned, expecting some kind of a "Hurry up, I can't wait for you." What he got wiped the smile off his face. "Have a problem. Thomas Jefferson will pick you up. Look for giant black man in fancy suit. Will explain all later. Love you."

"Damn it," he muttered, then grabbed his carry-on from the storage bin and strode out of the plane, trying to figure out why Savannah's lawyer would be picking him up instead of her.

He got to baggage claim and was waiting for the bags to unload when someone tapped him on the shoulder. He turned around to find himself face-to-face with the biggest man he'd ever seen. That he was black was almost inconsequential.

"Judd Holyfield?"

Judd nodded. "Thomas Jefferson?"

Thomas nodded.

Judd shook his hand. "Out of curiosity, how did you recognize me?"

Thomas grinned. "She said to look for the tallest man

in baggage claim wearing cowboy boots and a Stetson. How did she describe me to you?"

Judd smiled. "A giant black man in a fancy suit." He eyed Thomas's clothes. "Nice suit, but what's the deal? Why couldn't she pick me up herself?"

Thomas frowned. "Let's get your luggage first. We'll talk in the car."

Judd didn't like it, but he didn't argue. Whatever was going on with Savannah didn't need to be aired where anyone could overhear them.

A short while later they were in the parking garage. Thomas tossed Judd's bags into the back of his big white Hummer.

"Nice ride," Judd said as he slid into the front seat.

Thomas grinned. "It's pretentious, I know. But in my line of work, first impressions are everything."

Judd buckled up as Thomas started the engine.

"Okay, we're in the car," he said. "Start talking."

Thomas frowned. "You're not going to like it."

Judd's gut knotted. "Just tell me she's okay."

"Yes, she's okay. Now."

Judd's calm demeanor was suddenly gone. "Don't fuck with me, Jefferson. This is my woman we're talking about. Spit it out."

Exactly how I would have reacted, Thomas thought as he drove out of the terminal and then through the tollgate.

"Someone tried to kill her. Her car went off the causeway and into the bay this morning. Harbor Patrol pulled her out. She wasn't breathing. They resuscitated her on the way to the hospital. She looks like hell, but she's going to be okay. The hell of it is, she was on her way to my office. We realized someone must have leaked her presence to the Stosses, and I had a man all ready to protect her until the story broke. His name is White-side. He's ex-CIA and a friend of mine. The way we figured it, once the news got out that she was claiming to be the rightful heir, she would be safe. No way would the Stoss family dare to touch her after that."

Judd felt like he was going to pass out. He heard the man talking, but the words had all run together after "she wasn't breathing." The only thing keeping him from losing it was the fact that Jefferson had begun with the end of the story, rather than the beginning.

Thomas kept waiting for an explosion, but it didn't come. Then he saw Holyfield's hands. They were white-knuckled fists. Shit. One of the quiet ones. Those were the ones you couldn't read.

"Is anyone under arrest?" Judd asked.

"Not yet, but the Miami P.D. is on it."

"They know it's the Stoss family, don't they?"

"I think they suspect them, but there's no proof yet," Thomas said as he braked for a light.

"Take me to their house. I'll get all the proof they need."

Thomas's opinion of the man shifted again. Quiet *and* dangerous.

"Don't think I haven't considered that myself. How-ever, I promised Savannah I would bring you to the hospital this evening, and that's exactly what I intend to do."

Judd shuddered, then swiped his hands across his face. He felt like throwing up. When the car began to move again, he flinched, momentarily startled by the motion.

"How far to the hospital?"

"About fifteen more minutes," Thomas said.

"Can you do it in ten?"

Thomas sighed. "I can try."

He stomped the accelerator, and the Hummer shot forward. Hopefully none of Miami's finest would be on patrol between here and the Mount Sinai hospital.

Frank Barber had been a cop for twenty-four years, eighteen of them in Homicide. It took a lot to rattle him, but finding out that Phyllis Palmer had been murdered had shaken him to the core. He felt the noose of guilt tightening around his soul and wondered how he was going to live with all this after it was over.

According to the M.E, the old lady had probably died within an hour of her granddaughter's wreck. The fact that it appeared to be a robbery gone bad was, in his opinion, a load of bullshit. This was a simple case of tying up loose ends, but why? Was the Slade woman right? Did the family have Gerald Stoss killed twenty years ago? If so, how in the hell was he going to prove it?

Then it hit him. He didn't have to prove anything about that death. He just had to find the link between them and what had happened to Savannah Slade. And from what he knew, Elaine Hamilton was definitely the Stosses' weakest link.

However, the worst part of his day wasn't over. Now he had to tell Savannah Slade what had happened to her grandmother. By the time he reached the hospital and found a place to park, his gut was burning. He popped a handful of antacids as he headed inside.

Savannah had been up and walking around her room to keep from having a meltdown, dragging her IV on a stand as she went. No one would tell her a thing about why her grandmother hadn't shown up or called, and

Judd still wasn't here. She didn't know whether his flight had simply been delayed, or if something awful had happened.

She'd finally climbed back into bed and was propped up with the television on. Still, she couldn't concentrate on the shows and kept flipping from one channel to the next. When the door suddenly opened, her heart leaped. It had to be Judd. Then Detective Barber walked in, and she didn't bother to hide her disappointment.

Barber saw her disappointment and knew that whatever else was going on in her world, he was about to make it worse.

"Good evening, Miss Slade."

"What are you doing here?" she asked. "Where's my grandmother? Did anyone ever give her the news about what happened to me?"

"I sent a car over to her house myself," Barber said, and then moved to the side of the bed. "But I have some bad news. I'm so sorry to have to tell you this, but the officers found Mrs. Palmer dead."

Savannah felt the blood physically draining from her face. The room began to spin. The detective's words were all running together in one giant roar. She kept seeing the expression on Phyllis Palmer's face when she'd told her she was Chloe's daughter. The laughter that they'd shared. The stories Phyllis had told her about her birth mother. The scent of freesia, which Phyllis had said was her favorite perfume, as she'd kissed Savannah goodbye. This couldn't be happening. This couldn't be over before it had even begun.

In a panic, she grabbed Barber's arm. "What? What did you say?"

Barber felt sick. The shock on Savannah Slade's face was apparent.

"I said your grandmother was dead when the officers arrived. It appeared as if she'd been to the store, then come home and walked in on a robbery in progress."

It was too much to process. Savannah couldn't take any more. She screamed then, and put her hands over her ears, unwilling to hear any more.

"No! No! Stop talking! Stop talking!" she sobbed.

"I'll get your nurse," Barber said, and reached for her call button, but she slapped his hand away.

"You're lying! Get away from me *now!*"

Then she threw back her head, and the sound that came up her throat—the sound that had begun as another scream—emerged as a wail of such despair that Barber wanted to cry.

Thomas and Judd were just getting off the elevator when they heard a scream. Before Thomas could comment, Judd grabbed him.

"That's Savannah! What's her room number?"

"Four-forty, but how do you know that's—"

Judd was already running.

Thomas had no choice but to follow.

Judd flew past the nurses' desk so fast that they never even saw his face, only the back of his head as he raced past. A nurse was about to call for security when Thomas caught up.

"It's all right," he said quickly. "He's with me." Then he bolted down the hall, trying to catch up.

The guard on the door stood as Judd rounded the corner on the run and was reaching for his gun when Thomas saw him.

"Don't shoot! Don't shoot! He's part of her family!"

The guard hesitated, and at that moment they all heard the second scream.

The guard jumped, then turned toward the door as Judd flew past him.

Judd's heart was pounding, his mind focused on nothing but Savannah. He hit the door with the flat of his hand, sending it slamming against the wall.

Barber jumped, then spun.

Savannah saw Judd's face, then crawled out from under the covers onto her knees and, despite her IV, leaped into his arms.

He caught her in midair, his heart pounding so rapidly he could barely breathe. Her body had been ravaged beyond all he could have imagined, but she was alive. She was naked beneath the gown, but it was so oversized, it only emphasized how small she really was. He was afraid to hold her for fear of causing her more pain, but so grateful she was alive that he couldn't bring himself to let her go.

"I'm here, baby, I'm here."

Savannah was shaking so hard she could barely speak. "Oh, Judd, oh, Judd, my grandmother is dead. They killed her. They killed her. I didn't even get a chance to know her, and now she's gone, too."

Barber frowned. "Mister, you need to—"

Judd looked over his shoulder and spoke, his voice devoid of emotion. "Butt out. Savannah Slade is mine."

Jefferson sailed into the room before Barber could answer, sized up the situation in one glance, then stepped between the two men before Holyfield got himself arrested.

"Ease up, Barber. He's her boyfriend. His name is Judd Holyfield, and you can understand if he's less than thrilled about how we've been taking care of the woman he loves."

Savannah was sobbing so hard it was making Judd sick. "Get out," he said softly. "All of you."

Barber shrugged. He wasn't used to being on the receiving end of orders from civilians, but had nothing to say in his own defense.

Jefferson took him by the arm. "I would appreciate it if you would fill me in on what's happened. Outside this room, of course." Then he led the detective out into the hall, quietly closing the door behind them.

Worried that she was going to pull out her IV, Judd carefully carried Savannah back to the bed, kissing her face, her neck, the side of her cheek—everywhere he could find that hadn't been hurt—while the tears ran down his face.

"Baby, baby," Judd whispered as he sat down on the side of the bed, still holding her in his arms. "What did they do to you?"

He saw the bloody bandage at her hairline, and the bruises on her legs and arms. But when the gown slipped off her shoulder and he saw the bruises on her chest, he felt like he'd been gutted.

"What caused that?"

"The steering wheel, I think. It was when I hit the railing, just before I went off the bridge. Something was wrong with the air bag. It didn't deploy on time, and then it nearly got me drowned because I couldn't get out." She started to rock back and forth in a slow, jerky motion, her voice growing softer, her face suddenly devoid of emotion. "I thought I would drown. I wouldn't see you again. I couldn't get out. I couldn't get *out*."

Quietly, Judd untied the back of her gown and let it slide all the way down to her waist. The shock of what he saw was more than he could take. His hands were shaking as he pulled the gown back up, but when he tried to retie it, he couldn't see for the tears.

Savannah cupped his face with her hands, and then kissed him so fast and hard it took his breath away.

"I didn't think I would ever see you again."

"I'm here, baby, I'm here."

Her face crumpled. "Detective Barber just told me they found my grandmother dead. He said she had surprised some robbers in her house, but that isn't true. They killed her because of me—because they're afraid of what I might have told her."

"Can the cops prove it?" he asked.

"Not yet, but they will. I'll make sure of that."

Fourteen

Mateo filed the VIN off his SUV, stripped it clean and waited for sundown. Once it got dark, he drove out to the Everglades, took a small motorbike out of the back, then drove the car off into the water. To his surprise, it didn't sink all the way, but there was nothing he could do about it now. He got on the bike, started it up and headed back into the city, then went back to his condo and called a cab. After a ten-minute wait, the cab arrived.

It wasn't until the cab sped away that he began to breathe easy. He was on his way to the hangar where the company jet was housed. He knew the pilot would be waiting. The boss was hell on details. He didn't like loose ends. He got out at the gate and paid the driver. Floodlights lit up the area around the hangar as the cab sped off. Mateo hefted his suitcase one more time, and started walking across the tarmac toward the plane. The door was open. The steps were down, just waiting for him to climb up. It felt good to know he was going home for a while. Even though Miami had similar weather, he missed the lifestyle of his native Panama.

As he neared the plane, the pilot appeared at the top

of the steps. Mateo waved. It wasn't the first time these two employees of Stoss Industries had flown together.

"Nice night for a trip," the pilot said as Mateo climbed up into the plane.

He handed his suitcase to the pilot to stow in the closet beside the galley and headed toward the elegantly appointed seating area.

As usual, there was a bottle of his favorite champagne on ice, with a silver platter with fruit and sandwiches beside it.

Breathing a weary sigh of relief, he shed his jacket and tossed it aside as the door slammed shut. That meant they would be taking off. He sat down and buckled up, absently rubbing the deep gouges in his cheek where the old woman had dug her nails before pouring himself a glass of champagne, and reaching for a sandwich.

The plane was cleared for takeoff and taxiing down the runway when a second man slipped from the cabin toward where Mateo was sitting, his back to the door.

The garrote was around Mateo's neck before the champagne had cleared his throat. It bubbled back up his nose and out of his mouth as the assassin gave the wire a sharp yank.

The champagne glass fell onto the carpet. The sandwich Mateo had been holding dropped into his lap as his eyes rolled back in his head.

Satisfied that his part in this trip had just been finalized, the assassin, a man named Carl Tyson, moved quickly, taking care to strap himself in just as the plane lifted off. It was the first time he'd flown beside a dead man, but the dead man was far from his first kill.

Like an outdated computer, Mateo Bonaventure had just been phased out for an updated model.

* * *

Joseph was having a rare evening at home, and was about to sit down to dinner with Michael and Elaine when his cell vibrated. He pulled it out of his pocket long enough to look at the text.

It is done.

Smiling to himself, he dropped the phone back in his pocket, then calmly shook out his napkin and laid it in his lap.

Michael noted Joseph's pleased expression. "Anything we should know about?"

Joseph arched an eyebrow. "No. Pass the bread, Elaine."

Still struggling to make peace with him after her faux pas at the InterContinental, she picked up the bread basket and politely passed it down.

"Thank you," Joseph said.

He took a warm brioche and bit into it with perfect white teeth, tearing off a piece with relish. Then he reached for his wineglass and casually toasted the table before washing the brioche down with his favorite red.

Michael recognized the gleam in his cousin's eyes. There was some kind of secret celebration in progress, but he knew enough not to push.

Elaine lifted her glass in response, emptying it in one gulp without bothering with the bread. No need diluting the beginnings of a good high.

The only snag in Joseph's plan had been Mateo's failure to deliver on Savannah Slade, which meant another avenue had become necessary. Even as their meal was being served, one more strike against Savannah's life was about to take place.

* * *

Between the meds and Judd's presence, Savannah had finally fallen asleep. He stood beside her bed, judging the even rise and fall of her chest. She was finally out. He could barely stand to look at the end results of what she'd suffered. The bruises on her face continued to darken. Both her top and bottom lips looked sore and puffy. The stitches at her hairline, the bruises on her chest, the cuts on her hands and legs, were all evidence of how hard she'd struggled to climb out of that sinking car.

The rage he felt for the people who'd done this to her was almost overwhelming. He knew that, given the chance, he could easily wipe them from the face of the earth and never lose a moment's sleep over how he'd done it.

He glanced at his watch. It was almost midnight, but back home it was not quite ten. Bud would most likely be settling in to watch the late-night news and catch up on the events of the day. He knew no one from the hospital could have called the foreman, because all Savannah's contacts were in her phone, which had been in the car that sunk into the harbor. He'd been told the Miami P.D. had already retrieved the car and taken it to headquarters for the CSI crew to handle.

Judd brushed his finger along the curve of her cheek, then walked out into the hall. He stopped to talk to Pete Marsh, the officer on guard at her door.

"I'm going to make a call. I won't be long."

Marsh nodded.

Judd walked a short distance away to a windowed alcove to call the Slade ranch. The phone only rang a couple of times before Bud picked up.

"Hello."

"Hey, Bud, it's me."

"Judd! You're there, I take it. So did your plane get in on time? I'll bet Savannah was glad to see you. How's she doing?"

Judd exhaled softly. There was no easy way to say this.

"We've got problems."

Bud's elation faded. "What happened?"

"I'll preface this by saying she's okay now, but to make a long ugly story short, there was an attempt on Savannah's life today. It looks like someone rigged the accelerator in her car, and then, while it was out of control, forced her onto the MacArthur Causeway, which is basically a long-ass bridge over a whole lot of water. She hit the bridge, then went over the railing into the bay."

He heard Bud groan, then the sound of footsteps, which told him Bud was on his feet and pacing, which was what he always did in a moment of crisis.

"Shit!" Bud said angrily. "How bad was she hurt?"

Judd could tell from the tone of Bud's voice that he was at the end of his rope with worry.

"She hit the steering wheel with her chest. She has a concussion, some cuts and some of the worst bruises I've ever seen in my life. But the miracle is that she managed to get herself out of the car after it sank. She wasn't breathing when she was rescued by Harbor Patrol, but she seems to be okay now. They're keeping her in the hospital a couple of days to make sure she doesn't suffer any aftereffects to her lungs."

Bud felt sick. "I shouldn't have let them go. I thought it was a bad idea from the start. I don't know what the hell Andrew was thinking when he told them all this."

"Yeah, I'm beginning to agree. Anyway, I'll keep you

updated on her progress and where we go once she's released. However, I have one piece of advice for you. If you're as much in love with Holly as I think you are, pack your damn bags and go get her while she's still in one piece."

There was a long moment of silence before Bud finally spoke.

"How did you…? I didn't think anyone… Damn it! Does everyone know?"

"No. At least, I don't think so. I just recognized the signs. I've felt the same way about Savannah for as long as I can remember. And as soon as those damn papers she's been talking about are filed, I'm bringing her home."

"Yeah, okay…thanks for calling. Have you talked to Holly or Maria?"

"No. I'm leaving that up to you. Listen, I've got to go. I don't want to leave Savannah alone for too long."

Judd disconnected and stepped out of the alcove. When he looked up the hall, his heart sank.

The guard was no longer at the door.

"What the hell?"

He began to run.

Joseph Stoss made it his business to know who in places of authority had chinks in their armor. The ones he didn't know personally, he still knew about.

Allan Daly was one of those people. He had been a member of the Miami police force for almost ten years. Daly was smart, but he had problems, the worst of which involved his cocaine habit. He'd spent his family savings, borrowed money from every relative he had; his house was in foreclosure, his wife and kids had left him and for the past two years he had been stealing drug money from crime scenes before it could be logged into evidence. It wasn't something he was proud of, but he was hooked, and going to rehab would mean his problem would go public, which couldn't happen. He was on the take, and every bad man in the city knew it, which made Daly the kind of man Joseph needed.

Joseph knew that Savannah Slade was in the hospital and under armed guard. He needed someone who could get close enough to her to finish her off and make it look like the aftereffects of her wreck. All it would take was one syringe full of air injected into her IV and she would be gone. The death would be attributed to her injuries, the problem would be over and Tony's inheritance would no longer be in jeopardy.

Foolproof.

To make that work, he was going to ensure that Daly became one of the guards assigned to her door. The trick was to entice Daly with a prize big enough to make him willing to kill. In his case, a very large amount of money: enough to cover his losses, remove the lien on his house and keep him in cocaine for the next five years, or until he overdosed and died—whichever came first.

As for Daly, he had been in serious need of a fix when he was approached with the offer. He didn't know the man who asked or care why he wanted what he was asking for. Just the thought of getting out from under the burden of debt and having a nest egg for his old age was all it took for him to cave. And he knew exactly how to make things happen the way his mysterious benefactor wanted them to.

Everyone at the precinct knew he was short on money, so when he volunteered for guard duty, which would come in as overtime, no one thought a thing about it.

He walked into the hospital, armed and in uniform, with full approval from his lieutenant and hospital security, then casually made his way up to the fourth floor. His orders were to relieve Marsh at midnight, and he was right on time.

"Hey, Marsh. How's it going?"

Marsh stood, relieved that his shift was finally over. "Good. No problems. There's a man named Judd Holyfield who's the victim's fiancé or something. He's allowed to come and go as he pleases. Also her lawyer, Thomas Jefferson. Beyond that, it's just hospital staff—doctors, nurses…you know. If anything seems wonky, it's your job to challenge it."

"Got it," Daly said, and peeked inside the room. To his surprise, the woman was alone. "Where's the fiancé?" he asked as Marsh started to walk off.

"Down the hall making a phone call," Marsh said. "He won't be long. See you later."

"Yeah, later," Daly said.

His eyes narrowed thoughtfully as he looked up and down the hall. It was relatively quiet. Other than the murmur of voices at the nurses' station, there was no one in sight. He considered it an omen and slipped into the room where the Slade woman was sleeping. He quickly moved to her bedside and took the syringe out of his pocket. He popped the lid and was reaching for her IV when she suddenly moved and cried out.

At the sound, his heart nearly stopped. It took him a second to realize she was having some kind of nightmare.

He grabbed the shunt in the IV and jabbed in the needle just as the door flew open.

He gasped and stepped away from the bed, but not soon enough. And he'd forgotten the syringe. It was still dangling. He had a brief glimpse of someone really big and really fast, and then they both went down in a tangle of arms and legs.

Savannah woke up, saw people struggling on the floor and started screaming for help as she rang for the nurse. Within moments her room was full of staff, but all she could see—all that mattered to her—was Judd fighting with a cop. And then Judd swung a blow so hard that the cop's head flew back against the wall and he was unconscious.

Judd got up, dragging the uniformed officer with him, then slammed his body into the chair against the wall.

The charge nurse was in a panic.

"What do you think you're doing?" she cried. "Call security! I want this man out of here."

Judd glared. "And while you're at it, call the cops."

"You're out of your mind," the nurse said. "He *is* the cops. They just changed guards at midnight. He's supposed to be here."

Judd pointed to Savannah's IV. "Since when do cops administer meds?"

Savannah saw the syringe dangling from the IV and panicked. "Oh, my God, oh, my God!" She began tearing at her IV, ripping it out of her hand and flinging it onto the floor.

The shock on the nurse's face was evident as she quickly moved to the IV stand for a closer look.

"The syringe is empty. There's nothing in it."

Savannah's heart started to hammer against her chest as a new wave of fear swept through her. "What was in it? Was it poison? Am I going to die?"

The nurse started to remove the syringe, when Judd yelled, "Don't touch it! I want the cops to see this for themselves."

"Oh, sorry," the nurse said, and quickly turned to Savannah, trying to calm her. "Look, honey. Look. You're okay. The plunger hasn't been depressed. Nothing got into your IV."

Savannah was shaking. "I don't understand. If nothing is in it, then why—"

"Air," Judd muttered. "It would mimic an embolism, right?"

The nurse's eyes widened in disbelief. "If it had gotten into her vein, there wouldn't be anything we could do."

Judd looked at Savannah, then reached for his phone.

Barber was in shock all the way to the hospital. They now had confirmation that the brakes on the car Savannah had driven off the MacArthur Causeway had been tampered with, then this! The phone call he'd gotten from the lieutenant had been short and sweet. Get to Mount Sinai. One of their own had just tried to kill Savannah Slade. By the time Barber got there, black-and-whites were everywhere, along with at least two local news crews.

"How do they find out about this shit so fast?" he muttered as he entered the hospital and headed toward the elevators.

Before he got there, the doors opened and a half-dozen officers emerged. It took him a few moments to realize one of those officers was being taken out in handcuffs.

"What the hell?" He turned to watch their exit.

Al appeared at his elbow. "You won't believe this fuckup," he muttered.

"What's happening?" Frank asked.

"The cop's name is Allan Daly. He just tried to shoot a syringe full of air into Savannah Slade's IV."

Frank's eyes widened in disbelief. "You're shitting me."

"If only," Al said.

"I need to talk to her," Frank said.

Al shrugged. "Well, that's not going to happen."

Frank frowned. "Why not?"

"Because she's gone. Her boyfriend made a phone call. Fifteen minutes later some guy shows up at the door and escorts them out. I don't know where they went, and they weren't offering a change of address."

"What kind of guy?"

"Looked like a damn spook to me."

"Spook?"

"Yeah, spook. As in CIA. Had an uncle in the agency. They've all got this look, you know? Just a guess, but I'm just sayin'."

Frank shoved a hand through his hair in frustration. "I'd bet a month's salary that Jefferson is behind that."

"Just between you and me, it's a good thing someone's taking care of her, because she's got a target on her back bigger than Dallas."

"Damn it," Frank muttered. "God. Fucking. Damn it. This shit is going to stop."

Al frowned. "How do you propose to make that happen?"

Frank didn't answer. He wasn't about to admit that this whole mess had started because he'd made a phone call. And now he was about to make another phone call, and he was pretty damn sure Joseph Stoss wasn't going to like it.

Even though Savannah was wrapped up in a blanket and the temperature was in the seventies, she was shaking. The shock of all she'd gone through had exhausted her both mentally and physically. The fact that she was now in Judd's arms and going up to the roof of the Mount Sinai hospital was surreal. She could almost let herself believe it had all been a nightmare, except for the fact that Judd was so angry.

She could feel his heartbeat against the side of her arm. The scent of him was as familiar to her as her name. She didn't dare take her eyes from his face for fear if she looked away, he would disappear.

She wasn't exactly sure how they'd come to this moment.

When the man accompanying them had first appeared as yet another stranger, her first instinct had been to panic. But then he and Judd had shaken hands, and her fear had dissipated. She'd watched as they shared a brief moment of conversation, and then Judd had come over to the bed for her.

She hadn't asked for an explanation, and he hadn't offered one. All she knew was that his touch was gentle as he pulled the blanket over her, then scooped her up off the mattress. He told her he loved her, that she was no longer alone and that no one was ever going to hurt her again, and it was all she'd needed to know.

And now, watching the intensity on his face as the elevator continued to go up, she couldn't remember one good reason why she'd ever told this man no when he'd asked her to marry him. If she lived through this nightmare and he ever asked her again, there would be no more hesitation or denial.

"You two doing okay?" the stranger asked.

Savannah flinched. Judd had called the man Whiteside, but this was the first time she'd heard him speak.

"We're good," Judd answered, then winked at Savannah when he caught the panic in her expression.

When she relaxed against him and closed her eyes, he, too, relaxed, at least outwardly. But there was a rage within him that continued to grow. Someone was going to pay for what they'd done to Savannah and to her grandmother. He would make sure of it.

As for Whiteside, Judd had trusted him on sight. The man was a little less than six feet tall, maybe late fifties, early sixties. There was a scar across the bridge of his nose and another one down the back of his head. He looked a little like a professional wrestler, minus the crazy hair and earrings. He had one small tattoo on his forearm, and his hair, which was gunmetal gray, was buzzed off nearly down to the scalp, accentuating the presence of the scar. But for Judd, it was the gun in his waistband that was most reassuring.

Judd would have described the man as a minimalist.

Whiteside wouldn't have disagreed. He was a man who wasted no time or words in accomplishing what he needed to do.

Judd hadn't known at the time that the ride Whiteside had promised as soon as he arrived was a chopper, or that it was waiting for them on the roof of the hospital, until they'd gotten into the elevator and gone up instead of down.

When the elevator doors opened directly onto the roof, Whiteside glanced back at the big cowboy and the woman he was holding. The rush of wind was only slightly less wild than the sound of the spinning rotors.

Whiteside lifted the Stetson off Judd's head.

"If you don't mind, I'll carry it for you until we get in the chopper or it will wind up in the Atlantic."

"Thanks," Judd said.

Whiteside nodded, then pulled his gun and stepped outside. He swept the rooftop with a practiced gaze, then motioned for them to come out.

"Head for the chopper," he said, and then fell in behind them, his gun at the ready.

Savannah's eyes were open again, wide with renewed anxiety. Judd could only pray that was all that was wrong with her. There was a part of him that was afraid to take her out of the hospital, yet he didn't dare leave her there. He didn't know which was worse, playing roulette with her life and hoping she didn't develop pneumonia or throw a clot from her injuries, or staying and hoping to God someone else didn't try killing her.

Then they reached the chopper and the decision was taken from him as Whiteside got in, took Savannah out of his arms and strapped her into a makeshift bed behind the seats. Judd climbed in and buckled himself into a seat, then took his hat from Whiteside.

Seconds later, they were airborne.

Below, the lights of Miami were like a crazy quilt of colors. It would have been pretty if Judd hadn't known the evil that dwelled there.

Whiteside glanced over his shoulder once, eyeing Savannah, and then met Judd's gaze. The look that passed between them was silent but reassuring, as if they'd taken each other's measure and come away satisfied with what they'd seen.

Savannah hadn't spoken or moved since they'd strapped her into the chopper. Her gaze was wide and fixed on Judd. He was her touchstone to sanity. She didn't know where they were going, and right now she didn't care. It was enough that they had removed her from imminent danger.

Judd felt her staring, and he reached down and took her hand. She clung to him until the chopper started to descend, then grabbed onto her cot in sudden fear, wondering where fate had taken her now, and praying to God that it was somewhere the Stosses couldn't find her.

It wasn't until morning that Joseph found out his plans to get rid of Savannah Slade had failed again, and that the cop he'd been counting on to finish her off was in custody.

He didn't know how it had happened, or if the man was talking, but he wasn't as concerned with what Daly might say as the fact that Savannah Slade was still alive. Joseph never left paper trails between himself and the people who provided services outside the law. He was most concerned with getting rid of her before the media found out who she was and why she'd come. He was living on borrowed time. He had to come up with something brilliant, and he had to come up with it fast.

Fifteen

Savannah woke up. For a few moments, she couldn't remember where she was or how she'd gotten there, then remembered her grandmother was dead and that someone tried to kill her again. Judd's face flashed in her head. Judd! Her Judd. She exhaled softly as she realized she was lying in his arms. His chin was against the crown of her head, and his arms were wrapped around her, his hands locked beneath her breasts. She shifted slightly within his embrace and then sighed. Her life was in chaos, except for Judd—her one constant.

Judd was awake and had been for hours, but he wasn't about to move and disturb her. It wasn't until he felt the change in her breathing and the shift of her muscles that he slid an arm out from beneath her body and rose up on one elbow. "Hey, sweet thing, how are you feeling?"

"You're naked," she said.

He laughed softly. "You're feeling better than I'd hoped if that was the first thing on your mind."

"Where are we?"

"In Whiteside's home, only I'd call it more of a compound."

"No. I remember that much. I meant…*where* are we, as…are we in another city or what?"

"Oh. No. We're on his land outside the city in the Everglades. There's an eight-foot-high rock wall around the house and immediate grounds, with razor wire on top of that. He has the most intricate security setup I've ever seen wired into the house itself, and a fair-size radar dish on the roof."

"Why?" Savannah asked. "Who's he scared of?"

Judd shook his head. "Actually, you're looking at this backward. It's more of a case of uninvited guests who should be scared of him."

"Who does he work for?" she asked.

"He said he's retired. All I know is that he saved our butts last night, and for that I'll be forever grateful. Now back to you. Seriously, how do you feel? Does it hurt to breathe? Do your lungs feel heavy?"

"Yes, it hurts to breathe," Savannah said. "It has ever since I hit the steering wheel, but nothing worse than that. My lungs don't feel heavy, but I need to go pee. Help me up."

Judd threw back the covers.

She swung her legs off the side of the bed and then moaned. "Oh, my God. I am sore in every bone and muscle of my body."

"I've got you," he said, and scooped her up into his arms.

Savannah winced. "Wait. I think I can walk if I go slow."

"Maybe I just like doing this," Judd said as he carried her into the adjoining bath and set her down on her feet by the commode.

"You don't have any clothes. I'm sorry. But Thomas

is bringing some out this morning. Until then, you're
stuck with the hospital gown."

"I don't mind," Savannah said.

"Me, either," Judd teased as he flipped at the open
back. "I like the view."

She grinned, then winced as the motion stung her
still-swollen lips.

"You can go away now," she said, and shooed him
out the door.

Judd shut the door behind him, then went to get
dressed. After he'd put Savannah to bed last night,
he'd stayed up for another hour, talking to Whiteside
and Thomas. He knew the papers were being filed this
morning on Savannah's behalf, and that Thomas had
already fed the info to the media, along with photos
and enough information to knock the ground out from
beneath Joseph Stoss's feet.

Barber had called Jefferson right after Savannah
Slade's disappearance from the hospital and had to leave
a message. Jefferson never called him back.

When he woke up this morning to find it raining and
his newspaper ruined, it was just another flea of disappointment causing his life to itch. He tossed the paper
in the trash without giving it a glance, knowing he could
either buy another or read one at work.

Then he realized the hot water heater had gone out
in the night and he had to take a cold shower. After
that, he burned the toast he was making from the last
two slices of bread and called it quits. He was in a piss-
poor mood and about to leave for work when Jefferson
finally returned his call. He looked out at the downpour,
knew he would be soaked before he ever got into the

car, turned around at the doorway and went back inside to answer.

"Barber."

"Detective, I'm returning your call. How can I help you?"

"I need to talk to Miss Slade. Where is she?"

"Her whereabouts are no longer public knowledge," Jefferson said.

Barber frowned. "Look, I need her and Holyfield's statements as to what happened in her room last night. Except for a nurse who appeared after the fact, the only two people who witnessed Officer Daly's attack are both suddenly unavailable."

"I'll get them to you," Jefferson said.

"But I need—"

"It doesn't matter what you need," Jefferson interrupted. "However, I have something to tell you. It's actually more of a courtesy, just to let you know what is happening, rather than a request for your permission to do it."

"If you're about to do something illegal, you know I can't let—"

"As I said before, I'm not asking permission, and it's not illegal, so hear me out."

"I'm listening."

"This morning I filed Savannah Slade's petition to be recognized as Gerald Stoss's legal heir. We have her birth certificate listing him as the father, the journal given to her stating her birth mother's reasons for giving her baby to Andrew Slade to raise. I have her DNA test from a reputable local lab, which is going to force the Stosses to submit their DNA just to refute her claim, which is going to backfire in their faces. I have photos, taken before her birth, of her mother and Gerald

Stoss as an obvious couple. And just before deadline last night, I called a friend at the *Miami Herald* and gave him the entire story, along with the photos of Gerald and Chloe. And then we discussed the fact that Joseph Stoss's son is the heir apparent. However, if Savannah Slade's case is made, he stands to lose everything. Apparently you haven't seen the paper yet, or you would know that the story is the morning headline. As for the pictures, they're quite remarkable. When you see them, you'll know what I mean."

Barber was stunned. "Why taunt the family that way when I assume you're taking them to court in hopes of an amicable settlement?"

The tone of Jefferson's voice shifted to instant anger. "Oh, hell, no! This isn't a taunt. It's a warning. Savannah *will* be named the rightful heir. There's no question about it. And there's not going to be anything amicable about it once Joseph and his siblings are arrested for murder."

Barber frowned. "Then you know something I don't know, because last I heard, there wasn't a shred of evidence linking them to Gerald's death, or even linking them to the attack on Savannah Slade and the murder of her grandmother. For all intents and purposes, they appear to be three separate incidents."

"And that's where you and I differ on getting results," Thomas snapped. "I'm laying out the facts we do know to the general public via the media. Gerald Stoss died in a car wreck, supposedly driving too fast. His biological daughter returns to claim her inheritance and nearly dies in a car wreck, because the accelerator malfunctioned and she was going too fast. She survives the accident only to have a Miami police officer walk into her hospital room and make a second attempt on her life within the same twenty-four-hour period. Her grandmother is murdered on the same day of her wreck. Do I need to go on? Because I can. I heard about Daly's confession this morning. He was offered a million dollars to make her go away. That's a lot of money. So who do we know who has a lot of money and even more to lose if she wins her case? Many have died for far less than a multi-billion-dollar empire. You might not be able to arrest them, but so far, I have not stated one fact that is libelous. What I'm going to do is change the tone of public opinion, which will shift in our favor. And if you're as smart as I think you are, and if you want to solve this case half as much as I do, you'll go after the weakest link in that family."

"The weakest link?"

"Elaine Stoss Hamilton. She's a drunk, and I'd lay odds she's scared or she wouldn't have shown up like she did at the InterContinental to confront Savannah."

Barber's gut knotted. Yet another aspect of what had happened after that call he'd made. "I didn't know about that."

"You do now," Thomas said. "So I suggest you take yourself and your badge out to Palm Island and see how fast she crumbles."

"What are you going to do?" Barber said.

Thomas laughed. "Why? Don't you think I've done enough for one morning?"

Estella was afraid to go into the breakfast room with fresh coffee. She didn't know who had come down for breakfast yet and had no desire to look, having seen the headlines in the morning paper before she'd laid it on the table. So far she hadn't heard any loud voices or anything breaking, but it was early. She decided to make herself scarce, just in case.

Michael was the first to come down, but he never touched the paper until Joseph had gone through it. Joseph didn't like anyone reading it before him, and it wasn't that big a deal to Michael.

He was at the sideboard serving himself some waffles and fruit when he heard Joseph's footsteps in the hall. Like most of Miami, he'd watched the live coverage and seen the runaway car go over the railing on the causeway and into the water, seen Harbor Patrol arrive only moments before the body popped up in the water. He'd witnessed the rescue and heard all about the miracle of her surviving such a terrible incident. He knew in his heart that not a damn bit of it was an accident but was in no mood to discuss it, or be on the receiving end of Joseph's misplaced anger that his plans had gone awry.

He thought about abandoning breakfast and leaving for the golf course now, but then it was too late. Joseph was already in the breakfast room and pouring himself a cup of coffee, then loading his breakfast plate with bacon and eggs.

"Morning," Joseph said.

"Good morning," Michael responded, and took his food and sat down.

Joseph followed. He noticed Michael was wearing his lucky golf shirt. At least he knew where his cousin would be today. And since Elaine had yet to come down for breakfast, he could only assume she was sleeping off last night's drunk.

A typical morning on an atypical day. He had a lot of things on his mind, not the least of which was the fact that Savannah Slade still drew breath.

He reached for the paper without thought and popped

a piece of bacon in his mouth as he unfolded it. As he scanned the headline, he gasped, then choked. Bacon spewed across the table as he bolted up from his chair.

"Son of a holy bitch!"

"What the hell is wrong with you?" Michael muttered as he swiped at a piece of bacon that had landed on his shirt. Now he was going to have to go change.

Joseph flung the paper down in Michael's lap.

"That's what's wrong. If you weren't concerned before, now's the time to panic. Don't go anywhere. Don't answer the phone. Don't talk to the media. And for God's sake, make yourself useful today and keep Elaine under wraps. The last thing we need is for the media to get hold of her when she's drunk off her ass. No telling what she might say."

Then he called for his car, made a second call to the family lawyer and stormed out of the room.

Michael unfolded the paper, saw the headline and then the pictures in the story below and felt as if he was going to faint. He hadn't looked at a picture of Gerald in years. They'd all been put away after his death, but looking at it now and seeing the shot of the young woman right beside it, was a shock. Except for the subtle differences between male and female, the resemblance was startling. It was painfully obvious that twenty years ago, Gerald's claim that she was truly his daughter had been right. Now the world would know it, too.

Dear God.

They had underestimated Savannah Slade.

Whiteside was at the breakfast table when Judd came in. He looked up and smiled slightly, then looked past Judd to the doorway.

"Breakfast is on the stove. You might have to heat part of it in the microwave. Is Miss Slade awake?"

"Yeah, but she's minus clothing. I told her I'd bring her some food."

Whiteside frowned. "My bad. I should have thought of that sooner. Is she up to coming to the table, or would she rather eat in bed?"

"She's pretty sore, but I think she's okay to move around. It's more of a reluctance to flash us."

"Right," Whiteside said as he jumped up and left the room. He came back shortly carrying a neatly folded pair of gray sweatpants and a matching T-shirt.

"She's very small, but I think with the drawstring she'll be able to keep them up. They'll suffice until Thomas arrives with something better. Tell her I'd be happy if she'd like to come in for breakfast."

Judd smiled. "Will do, and thanks."

He hurried back through the house, missed the first hallway and had to backtrack to get to their room. The single-story house was laid out like a maze, and Judd couldn't help but wonder if that was yet another line of defense Whiteside had incorporated into the nearly five thousand square feet of house under one rambling roof.

Savannah was sitting up in bed with the television on when Judd walked in. She looked up and smiled when Judd laid a stack of clothes on the bed.

"For you," he said. "Whiteside apologizes for not thinking of sending some clothes sooner and hopes you'll join us for breakfast."

"Wonderful," Savannah said, and raised her arms to untie her gown, then winced.

"Let me, baby."

Grateful for the help, she turned her back to him. The

ties came undone, and the gown fell to the floor. Still a little wobbly, she leaned against the bed as she turned around to pick up the sweatpants, and as she did, she heard Judd grunt as if he'd been punched.

She looked up. He wasn't watching the television. He was looking at her. Then she looked down at her own body. The bruises were appalling, even to her.

"God, I hope these eventually fade or I'm going to look pretty weird in a bikini."

The skin on his face was as taut as a drum. "Don't make a damned joke about this."

He pulled the T-shirt on over her head, then helped ease her arms into the sleeves.

"Sit," he said.

She did, letting him maneuver her feet into the legs of the sweatpants.

He pulled them up as far as they would go, then leaned forward and brushed a kiss against the side of her face. "Okay, now stand up," he said softly, and when she did, he eased the sweats up over her hips and tied them off. "No shoes," he said, and scooped her into his arms.

"I can walk."

"You have no idea how far we are from the kitchen."

Savannah wrapped her arms around his neck and then kissed him.

Judd eyed her still-puffy lower lip and sighed. "I would kiss you back, but I'm too damned afraid to touch your mouth. Does your head still hurt?"

"Yes, but I think it's from the cut."

"If it gets worse, will you promise to tell me? I'm still uneasy that we took you out of the hospital before you were officially released. I had nightmares last night that you were getting worse. I was afraid you were having some kind of delayed reaction to your injuries and it was my fault for taking you away."

"I didn't die, and I'm actually hungry. Think we can talk about my welfare on the way to that kitchen you mentioned?"

"I'm taking you to the food now," Judd promised as he carried her out of the room.

Whiteside had two plates of food already reheated and was carrying them to the table when Judd walked in with her in his arms.

"Good morning, ma'am," Whiteside said as he pulled out a chair. "I'm glad you're feeling well enough to join us."

"I could have walked," she said as Judd eased her into a seat.

"It's quite a distance from your room to here. Probably just as well you didn't try. Do you drink coffee?"

"Yes, please. Black."

"Me, too," Judd said as he sat down beside her.

Whiteside brought the cups and set them down at their plates, and then refilled his own before joining them.

"Eat," he said shortly. "We'll talk once you're done."

They didn't have to be told twice. The food tasted good to Savannah, but even better was the feeling of relief she was experiencing, knowing that she was no longer alone in this battle and, at least for the time being, was actually safe.

As they were finishing breakfast, they began to hear an approaching helicopter. A few minutes later the doorbell rang.

"I'll get that," Whiteside said, and slipped out of the room. He returned shortly with Thomas beside him.

"Miss Slade, it appears you have a guest."

Savannah couldn't help but smile. Her lawyer was dressed to the nines in an oatmeal-colored suit, a pale yellow shirt and an off-white tie made of raw silk. The only things missing were a Panama hat and a big cigar.

Thomas was smiling, but there was a glitter in his eyes she hadn't seen before.

"I come bearing gifts." He dropped the bags he was carrying. "Laura did the shopping, so I'm assuming she thought of everything. I did tell her to make sure it was all soft, so you wouldn't be any more uncomfortable than you already are."

"Thank you so much," Savannah said. "Did you leave the sales receipt in the bag so I can pay you back?"

Thomas raised a hand in denial. "We'll worry about all that at a later date. We still don't know if your purse came up with the car, remember? I'll check on that today. If it's not in the car, it's at the bottom of the bay, in which case you'll need to request replacements for all your plastic."

"Oh, no! I didn't even think about that."

"No frowns," Thomas said as he unfurled the newspaper he'd been carrying under his arm and laid it on the table with a flourish. "Cast your eyes on that."

Whiteside had already seen it and was curious as to what Savannah's reaction would be. It didn't take long. The shock on her face was evident as she snatched the paper off the table.

"Oh, my God! What happened? How did they find out?"

Thomas grinned. "I told them."

That was not what she'd expected to hear. "You *told*

them? I thought we needed to keep this secret? What am I missing?"

"I filed the papers for your lawsuit against the Stosses this morning, and releasing all this information took the venom out of the scorpion sting, so to speak. If a hair on your head gets mussed now, they'll be the first people to be blamed. Should have done it sooner, but who knew your presence would be leaked so quickly?"

Judd was reading over Savannah's shoulder, and the more he read, the more shocked he became.

"Is all this true? About the heir?" he asked.

Thomas nodded.

"What heir?" Savannah asked.

"Joseph Stoss has a son who was the heir apparent until you showed up."

Savannah shuddered. "I didn't know about him."

"He's in school in Switzerland."

"I wonder what he's going to think about all this?" Judd said.

"Indeed," Thomas said. "I wonder."

Then his phone began to ring. He rolled his eyes and put it on vibrate. "Sorry. It's been ringing like crazy all morning."

"Why?" Savannah asked.

"Because I'm the lawyer on record, so everyone wants an interview, especially since you've suddenly gone missing."

Whiteside frowned. "I assume you took the precautions I mentioned to get here."

Thomas nodded. "Yes. Drove my car to airport parking. Went through the terminal, then out to where the chopper was waiting, but I need to get back. I have a dozen things to be done before the day is out."

"What should I do?" Savannah asked.

"For now, you rest and heal. Barber and I are working on a plan. When the time is right, we'll bring you in." He glanced at Judd. "Is there anything else either of you needs?"

"No. Thanks to your foresight in sending my suitcase along with Whiteside last night, and the stuff you brought Savannah this morning, we're set."

"I'll be in touch," Thomas said.

"I'll see you out," Whiteside offered.

Judd turned to Savannah as the two men left the room.

"How do you feel about all this?"

Her eyes narrowed. "I feel good. After what they did to me and my grandmother, I hope they're in one hell of a panic."

The news vans were outside the gates of the Stoss mansion when Joseph's limo drove through. Unused to being on the receiving end of scandal, he was furious.

"Fucking vultures," he muttered as he grabbed his phone and made a call to the police commissioner.

It wasn't until he was told that the commissioner was in a meeting and couldn't take his call that he realized it had already begun. Public opinion was already taking shape, and it was against him, and the commissioner could not attach himself in any way to someone who was not above suspicion. This wasn't good. As soon as he got to his lawyer's office, he would make them all sorry.

Still angry with the situation, he checked his messages. There were three from Tony, which was strange. Hopefully he wasn't ill. Before he could return the call, his phone began to ring. Tony again.

"Hello, son, great to hear from you," Joseph said, making sure to keep his tone light.

"Dad! I've been calling and calling. Why didn't you get back to me?"

"I'm sorry. Busy day. What's up?"

"Oh, hell, no. That's my question to you."

Joseph frowned. The tone of voice and the attitude weren't like his son. "What do you mean?"

"The *Miami Herald*. It might interest you to know that I read it online every day."

Joseph's gut knotted. "Oh. That."

"Yeah, *that!* So what the hell is going on? Who is this woman? Why didn't I know about her? Is she for real?"

"It's complicated," Joseph said.

It wasn't what Tony had expected to hear. "What are you saying, Dad? Is her claim valid? Is she telling the truth? Does this mean I'm not the rightful heir?"

"Don't worry," Joseph said. "I'm going to take care of it."

There was brief moment of silence before Tony spoke. "What did you just say?"

"I said I'll take care of it. You don't need to worry."

Silence.

Joseph frowned. Had they lost their connection? "Tony, are you still there?"

"I'm here. But I have a question. How are you going to make this go away? By making a third attempt on her life?"

"Anthony! You don't know what you're saying!"

Another long moment of silence, and then Tony spoke, but in a shocked and shaky voice. "Oh, my God, Dad. Did you just hear yourself?"

Joseph frowned. "I don't know what you mean."

"You didn't deny it. You bastard. *You didn't deny it.*
She looks just like Uncle Gerald, and she's a year older
than me. What's the matter with you?"

The line went dead in Joseph's ear.

Panic set in. He tried calling his son back, but there
was no answer.

"Perfect."

He looked out the window. They were at the lawyer's
office. He had no more time to worry about damage
control in another country, even when his own son was
involved.

He got out of the limo and walked into the building
with his usual amount of confidence, rode the elevator
up to the law offices of Stern and Stern, and strode into
the outer office.

The receptionist, who was normally chatty, stared a
moment and then quickly looked away.

Joseph frowned. "Paul's expecting me," he said, and
headed for the inner office to let himself in, as he'd
always done.

"I'm sorry, sir. If you would please wait a moment.
Mr. Stern is with a client. I'm sure it won't be long."

Joseph almost stumbled. "What do you mean, he's
with a client? I *am* his client! His only client."

She looked as if she was going to cry and breathed a
quick sigh of relief when her boss suddenly opened his
own door.

"Joseph, I thought I heard you. Come in, come in!"

Joseph stomped past him, ready to denounce Stern
and his client, when he realized the office was empty.

"What's going on? Your receptionist said you were
with a client. Don't I pay you enough of a retainer to
suffice?"

Stern frowned. "There's no need to raise your voice

with me," he said shortly. "I was on the phone with your son. I assume he falls under the auspices of a client, or was I mistaken?"

Joseph sighed. "Sorry. I misunderstood. I'm sure you can understand."

Stern just managed not to glare. "Not really," he said. "Sit down. We need to talk."

Disconcerted by his lawyer's attitude, Joseph chose a seat. As soon as Paul Stern sat down, Joseph leaned forward.

"That story in the paper… I want them to print a retraction. I want this spill of misinformation stopped. Draw up the papers. I am filing a libel suit against Savannah Slade and the *Miami Herald* for printing such trash."

Paul bit his lip to keep from saying what he wanted to say. He'd been through a lot of crises with Joseph before, but never anything this volatile or shocking. As for Joseph's immediate demands, they weren't going to be met.

"Actually, that can't happen."

"What do you mean, it can't happen? They alluded to the possibility that we had something to do with Gerald's death, with the Slade woman's accident, and with the murder of her grandmother. There is absolutely no reason why we would be upset by anything as ludicrous as this woman's claims. It's absurd. All of it."

"Seriously, Joseph? Did you just hear what you said? You're the one being absurd."

Joseph was in shock. "What the hell do you mean? You can't talk to me like that!"

"Actually, as your legal adviser, I can. It is my job to keep you from creating legal problems for—and, in this case, not making a laughingstock of—yourselves."

"I don't understand."

Stern's voice sharpened as he leaned across the table. "Don't mess with me, Joseph. You claim it's absurd to think you would have no reason to be upset by the idea of being usurped. I beg to differ. Right off the bat, there are several billion reasons for you to want to put a stop to someone claiming your place in the company."

Joseph glared. "You're telling me she can lie and get away with it?"

"No. I'm telling you that there's not one actual lie in the entire piece. Not one. And that's entirely due to the brilliance of her lawyer, Thomas Jefferson. Need I remind you that he's already beaten us in court once before? The piece does *not* say the Stoss family was responsible for Gerald's death. It does *not* say the family caused Savannah Slade's car to go off the causeway, and it also does not say you had her grandmother murdered. It merely stated a series of facts in a very clever order, leaving the readers to draw their own conclusions. Which brings me to the question I *have* to ask you. Joseph, are you or any member of your family responsible for what's been happening to her and her family?"

Joseph stood abruptly, his face pale from shock. "I can't believe you even asked me that!"

Stern frowned. "You did not answer my question."

"Oh, for God's sake, Paul. You should know me better than that."

Stern's frown deepened. "Damn it, Joseph. If you're not straight with me, there's no way I can protect you from surprises in court."

Joseph dropped back into his seat. It was beginning to sink in that Stern was serious.

"You believe that this…this…bitch actually has a case?"

"She's provided DNA. To refute it, we'll need a sample from you."

"Me? Why me? I'm not her father."

"No, but you were his twin, which means your DNA will be close to identical."

Joseph snapped. "Son of a bitch! He's dead, and he's still messing with my life."

Stern stared. "I assume you know enough not to say something that damaging in public. It not only makes it sound as if you're not sorry your own twin is dead, but that he was a thorn in your side during his lifetime."

Joseph shifted nervously, then looked away.

Stern continued. "That's not all she's got behind her. She has photos of her birth mother and your brother together in a very loving embrace. Add to that a birth certificate naming Gerald as her father, along with a letter from a dying mother claiming someone called her the day of Gerald's wreck, telling her that Gerald's death was not an accident, and that if she tried to make a claim to the Stoss money on her daughter's behalf, the child would meet the same end as her father. Then that child shows up twenty years later and what happens? Someone tries to kill her. What the fuck were you thinking?"

"I didn't know about any letter or birth certificate."

Stern shook his head. "Joseph, Joseph…the proper response would have been, 'I had nothing to do with it,' not a denial of knowing all the facts."

Joseph blanched. He'd as good as admitted to his lawyer that he was guilty. Still, the man couldn't testify against him, so what the hell?

"So you're telling me we're helpless to rebut the innuendos?"

"Pretty much."

"This is an outrage," Joseph said.

Stern shrugged. "Thomas Jefferson is a wily opponent."

"This is not a fucking tennis match. He is not my *opponent*. He is my *enemy*." Joseph stood. "I think we're done here. And just for the record, I don't like your attitude. You can be replaced, you know."

Stern stood, as well, staring straight into Joseph Stoss's eyes. "Replacement is much neater than disposal. It's a damn shame you didn't remember that sooner."

Joseph was so furious he walked out without another word. He was in the limo and on the way back to the mansion when it dawned on him that he'd never asked why his son had called their lawyer. Before he had a chance to call back and find out, his cell phone rang.

It was Michael. Now what?

Sixteen

"I don't get it," Al said as he glanced at his partner. "We have no evidence linking anyone in the Stoss family to what happened to Savannah Slade, so how is this supposed to work? We just knock on the door, throw out a bunch of accusations and see what happens?"

Frank signaled and shifted lanes as the car sped across the causeway on the way to Palm Island.

"Look, there's where she went over the railing," he said as they sped past the impact point of Savannah's wreck.

"I see it," Al muttered. "Damn it, Frank, were you even listening?"

Frank glanced briefly at his partner, then back at the road. "I hear you. And no, we're not throwing out blanket accusations. For starters, I want to hear how Elaine Hamilton explains away her visit to the InterContinental, and how she 'just happened' to bump into Savannah Slade."

Al frowned. "That's pretty flimsy."

"I've questioned people with less reason," Frank said. "Just because their last name is Stoss, that doesn't mean they're allowed to get away with murder."

"Shit, you aren't going to go out there and accuse them of *that,* are you?"

"I'm not going to say it," Frank said. "But before I leave, they're going to know it's what I think."

Al cursed beneath his breath. "I retire in five years."

"I retire in two," Frank countered.

"So let's not do anything rash that sets the police commissioner on our asses, okay?"

"We have a murder to investigate, an attempted murder under investigation, and we're the men with the badges."

Al knew when to stop arguing. He didn't understand why Frank had locked on to this with such passion, but he understood the need to clear the books, and if they could find out who'd killed Phyllis Palmer, then so much the better.

Finally they reached Palm Island, and then turned down the street leading to the Stoss estate. A pair of large iron gates barred entrance to the grounds. Frank pulled up to the intercom and buzzed.

A man's voice came over the intercom.

"State your business."

"Detectives Barber and Soldana, Miami P.D."

"Do you have an appointment?" the man asked.

Frank leaned out the window and stuck his badge up toward the camera.

"This is my appointment," he said sharply. "Open the damned gates."

The gates swung inward.

"Rich bastards," Frank muttered as he drove onto the grounds and proceeded toward the mansion.

Michael was a nervous wreck. The house phone had been ringing off the wall all morning, but he'd instructed

Estella to let everything go to voice mail. After Joseph left, he'd taken the paper and gone straight up to Elaine's room. Her reaction to the headlines had been horror, then panic.

"We're going to get arrested!" she wailed, and then burst into tears.

It had taken all his negotiation skills to calm her down without letting her resort to liquor.

He'd waited until she got dressed, and then they'd gone downstairs together. He sat with her while she ate breakfast and talked her into spending the morning in the library, playing cards. As the morning wore on, everything began to become surreal to him. Even the smallest details took on meaning. The smell of shrimp grilling as the cook made their lunch. The whisper-soft sounds of Estella's feather duster as she swept it along the bookshelves behind them. The clink of ice against their water glasses as they lifted them to drink. Even the constant ringing of the phone took on new meaning. When he was an old man, would he look back on this as the day that signaled the beginning of the end?

Elaine kept bursting into tears, but he kept letting her win, which kept her focused. Finally it was lunchtime and Michael was grateful for the diversion.

As they were putting up the cards, he thought he heard the doorbell, then decided it was just his imagination. A few moments later he heard the sharp click of Estella's heels as she came down the hall to call them for lunch. He was smiling as he turned toward the doorway.

"Mr. Michael. The police are here. They want to talk to Mrs. Hamilton."

It was the last thing Michael had expected to hear

her say, but before he could comment, Elaine screamed aloud and bolted up from her chair.

Michael spun. "For God's sake, shut up!" His mind was racing. "Put them in the living room. We'll be right there."

"Yes, sir," Estella said, and hurried away.

He turned back to see that Elaine was already at the wet bar, pouring herself a drink. She tossed it back like a sailor before Michael could stop her, and he decided not to make an issue of it. It might be what it took to calm her down.

"No more," he said. "Pull yourself together and act like an adult."

"Joseph said for us not to talk to anybody."

"Yes, well, even he doesn't get to tell the cops what to do," he muttered, but just to be on the safe side, he called Joseph. When he answered, Michael could tell he was in a bad mood. Great. He was about to make it worse.

"Joseph, it's me."

"I'm on my way home. Can't this wait?"

"Just once, would you shut up and listen?" Michael snapped. "The police are here. They want to question Elaine. I'll be with her, but I cannot guarantee what comes out of her mouth. Just so you know, I blame this entire fuckup on you."

He ended the call without waiting for Joseph to respond, then put his hand under Elaine's elbow and gave it a sharp tug.

"If you want to stay out of prison, get your damned act together. You don't know anything. You don't know what they're talking about. And if it gets dicey, you don't want to talk to them without your lawyer present. Understood?"

She nodded.

Michael rolled his eyes. There was no way this could possibly go well.

"Lift your chin, tuck your hair behind your ear and smile. You're a Stoss, damn it! Act like one."

The detectives had been seated in the living room under the watchful eye of Estella, as if she didn't trust them not to pocket some of the priceless trinkets that were part of the room's decor.

She gave them a dubious look, and left as Michael and Elaine walked into the room.

Frank stood. Al was still sitting until Frank kicked the toe of his shoe.

Embarrassed, he stood as Michael escorted Elaine into the room, then seated her in one of a pair of eighteenth-century chairs opposite the sofa where the men had been sitting.

Michael patted Elaine's arm and then turned to the cops. "Gentlemen, to what do we owe the pleasure of your company?"

Barber responded immediately. "That would be the attempted murder of Savannah Slade and the murder of her grandmother, Phyllis Palmer."

Michael blanched. Before he could speak, he heard a faint squeaking sound, then a thud. Elaine had just fainted and slid out of the chair onto the floor.

"Well, crap," he muttered.

The detectives were already on their feet. "Al, you get one arm, I'll get the other," Frank said, and they pulled Elaine up off the floor and had her back in the chair before Michael could object at the ungainly retrieval.

She was already giving indications that she was about to regain consciousness, which made Michael panic again. Unfortunately, alcohol had just become a necessity. He needed her to be calm and liquor would do it. He hurried toward the antique armoire and threw open the doors. Its conversion into a bar had happened ages ago, and for that he was grateful. He poured a double shot of bourbon into a glass and rushed back.

Elaine came to almost as quickly as she'd gone out, which led Frank to wonder how much of the faint had been real and how much had been for show. Before he could speak, Michael Stoss had a glass of whiskey in her hand. She downed it like a pro and then blinked, waiting for the alcohol to numb her senses.

Michael had started to refill the glass when Frank pointed. "You. Have a seat. I don't mind if you're here, but you're not the one I want to talk to."

Michael frowned. He would have liked to be more forceful, but it wasn't in him to defy real authority.

"I'm right here, Elaine," he said, patting her arm, and then sat down in the chair beside hers.

Embarrassed that she'd fainted, Elaine began fussing with her hair and her clothes, mumbling that she must look a mess.

Frank sat down. "Mrs. Hamilton, my name is Detective Barber. This is my partner, Detective Soldana. We need to ask you a few questions."

"About what?" Elaine asked.

Michael winced. The tone of her voice was just below scream level. *God, please make her shut her trap.*

"About Savannah Slade," Frank said.

Elaine lifted her chin in a haughty manner as her voice oozed disdain. "I'm sorry? Are you speaking of that woman who's filed a lawsuit against our family?"

"Why, yes, I am," Frank drawled. "The same woman

you met at the InterContinental the day before the attempt on her life."

Elaine's disdain turned into dismay. She looked to Michael, who shrugged and looked away.

Frank leaned forward, resting his elbows on his knees, knowing that the seemingly innocent action had just invaded her space. Exactly what he'd intended.

"I didn't exactly 'meet' her," Elaine said.

"That's not what *she* said," Frank countered.

Elaine panicked. "I don't know what she told you, but I'm at a loss to understand why you would believe an obvious gold digger over one of us."

"By 'us,' do you mean the Stoss family? Do you believe yourselves outside the parameters of the law?"

"Why no, of course not," Elaine muttered.

"I see. So if you believe Savannah Slade is a gold digger, then I'm sure you'll be happy to provide a DNA sample to refute her claim."

Elaine panicked again.

This time, so did Michael.

"Look, you can't make us do—"

"You do know your refusal to cooperate is going to be viewed by the court as fear, and as proof that you already acknowledge the legitimacy of her claim and don't want to confirm it."

Elaine jumped up. "You're confusing me. That's not what I said. I don't understand why you're doing this, and I'm not talking to you anymore. I want my lawyer."

Michael sighed. *Thank you, God.*

Both detectives stood, as well, and Frank spoke again. "Really? You aren't under arrest, so asking for a lawyer seems a bit drastic. You do know that this only adds to the perception of guilt?"

Elaine's face crumpled as she began to wail. "I don't know what to do. I don't understand."

All of a sudden they heard the front door open and then shut with a slam, followed by hurried footsteps.

Michael breathed a quiet sigh of relief. "I do believe Joseph is home."

Frank stifled a grin. Perfect. He was ruffling all kinds of feathers. Exactly what he'd hoped to do.

Moments later Joseph Stoss burst into the living room. His color was high, and the look of indignation on his face was matched by the indignation in his voice.

"Am I to understand that my family is actually being questioned about that unfortunate incident on the causeway?"

Al hated that he felt intimidated, but damn, a billion dollars bought a whole lot of friends in high places. He wished he had Frank's attitude.

Frank knew his partner was nervous, but he had an ace in the hole that Al didn't know about. Because of his own unfortunate phone call, Joseph had been fore-warned about Savannah Slade's presence in Miami, so any claims of innocence Stoss made about not knowing what she'd intended weren't going to fly.

Joseph glared at Frank.

Frank didn't budge, nor did he bother to respond to Joseph's less than subtle disapproval. He decided it was time for a little throw down of his own.

"So, Mr. Stoss, I've spoken to Miss Slade's lawyer. I'm sure you've spoken to yours. It appears Miss Slade's presence here in Miami is on the up-and-up. She brought some pretty convincing evidence to the table, don't you think?"

Joseph was so pissed that he didn't trust himself to speak as the detective continued.

"Since Mrs. Hamilton has just invoked her right to have an attorney present when I talk to her, I expect her to be in my office tomorrow morning at 9:00 a.m. All I had were a few questions. Thanks to this obvious refusal to cooperate, I will have a few more, some of which will be addressed to all of you. Please make it your business to come with her." He looked at Elaine. "In the morning, Mrs. Hamilton, 9:00 a.m. sharp. Failure to show could easily result in an arrest warrant. Do you understand?"

Joseph stepped forward, pointing at Frank in a defiant gesture. "I will have your badge for that remark."

"No, you won't, and we both know why. Don't bother to show us to the door. We'll see ourselves out."

Al frowned as he fell into step beside his partner. Why did he feel like everyone knew a secret but him?

Joseph was so frustrated he was shaking. He turned on his cousins—because he could and because they were there.

"One thing. You only had to worry about one thing, and that was don't fucking talk to anyone. So what do I learn? The police are in our house. What part of 'keep your damned mouth shut' don't you understand?"

Furious, Michael turned on Joseph and slapped him in the face.

"You shut up!" he snapped.

Joseph's cheek was throbbing, and he was so startled by what Michael had done that he couldn't even react. He hadn't known Michael was capable of this kind of rage.

Michael jammed a finger into Joseph's chest, punctuating each word with a jab. "I have something to say, and I'm only going to say this once. You brought this on us. You and you alone. You've been pissed off at the world ever since the day you popped out of your mother's belly two minutes behind Gerald. He did not instigate the stupid clause that designates who inherits. He just got born. What I've never understood is why it mattered. Thanks to our ancestors and their sharp business acumen, we all live like royalty. Why does it matter who holds the purse strings? Why couldn't you just be a part of the family without wanting control? We were all fine. You're the one who didn't like the status quo, so from now on, you figure out how to fix what you've done and just back the fuck off of blaming us."

Then Michael walked out, taking Elaine with him.

Joseph was speechless. The emotions from his past came flooding back and he was, once again, the almost-heir—his father's other son. Neither the designer suit, the Rolex watch nor the ring on his finger bearing the Stoss family crest had really changed the mind-set of the inner man—the man who would forever see himself as second best.

Then he thought of his son, the one accomplishment of his life for which he felt true pride. The shocked revelations and dismay in Tony's voice could not be left to fester. He needed to speak to him, to convince him that he'd simply misunderstood. But when he tried the call, it wouldn't go through. He tried again, then again, before the phone finally began to ring as he waited to hear his son's voice.

But it didn't happen. The call went to voice mail. He left a message, similar to the ones he'd gotten from Tony.

"Call me. We need to talk."

Beyond that, he was helpless to do a thing.

Savannah slept away most of her first day in White-side's home, with Judd maintaining a steady vigil nearby. He'd finally been able to get in touch with Bud and Holly, reassuring them that Savannah was safe and filling them in on what was happening. Then he told them to go online and read the front page story in the *Miami Herald*, because the baby of the Slade family was making news, and cautioned Holly to stay safe.

After that, he'd checked in at his ranch and learned that the film clip of Savannah's wild ride on the causeway, ending with a nosedive into the harbor, had finally made the national news. He'd had to reassure his father that she was safe and healing, with no lingering aftereffects. Savannah was the daughter Judd's dad had always wanted, and his father charged him with telling her to take care, and that when she came back to Montana, they would have the biggest barbecue Missoula had ever seen to welcome her home. Judd was still thinking about their lifestyle on the ranch long after he'd hung up, and wondering how Savannah's newfound fame and fortune were going to translate to what they'd known. He loved ranching. It was his life and who he was. And if everything went according to plan, Savannah was about to step so far outside that life, he wasn't sure she could—or even would—want to come back. He kept trying to figure out ways to make things work, then realized he was jumping the gun. While Savannah was healing, it would be Thomas Jefferson's job to get the court to recognize her claims to the Stoss estate. It was his job—and Whiteside's—just to keep her alive.

Water was flooding through the car window into Savannah's face and up her nose. The flow was fierce, the pressure deadly against her body, as she scrambled to get past the air bag. She could still see daylight when she braced herself to climb out, but then all of a

sudden it was gone. She had time for one last gasp of
air, and then the car was completely submerged. The
window of time she had left to get out was over. It was
now or never. She struggled with every muscle in her
body, pushing past the air bag. The car was beginning
to roll as the upper half of her body emerged. With one
foot on the steering wheel and the other on the driver's
headrest, she pushed—and suddenly she was out. She
began swimming upward toward the light. The need
to breathe was overwhelming, the burn in her lungs a
physical ache, but she knew she could do it. Then all
of a sudden something hit her from behind as the car
rolled. She gasped in shock, the burn of water filling
her eyes, her lungs, her nostrils, and then…nothing.

Savannah sat up with a gasp, breathing in deep
drafts of oxygen, not the water of which she'd been
dreaming.

"Shit."

She hated this feeling of being out of control and
gently eased her fingers through her hair, taking care not
to bump the spot with the stitches. Still struggling with
the remnants of the dream, she threw back the covers
and got out of bed. After a quick trip to the bathroom,
she stepped into a pair of soft pink slippers and eyed
herself in the mirror. She wasn't in the mood to change
clothes, but her tummy was growling. She decided the
pink-and-white pajamas Laura had picked out looked
enough like a T-shirt and sweats to pass, and went to
go look for Judd and their host.

She hadn't gone far when she realized she was
lost. The layout of the house made no sense. It was
like walking in a maze, coming up on walls with no
doors, and doors to rooms that somehow led right back

to where she'd been. Frustrated, she stopped in the middle of a hallway and yelled.

The two men were in the living room, watching the evening news, a good portion of which was dedicated to continuing coverage of the building scandal surrounding the Stosses. One story after another was emerging— people coming forward from Chloe Stewart's past, confirming the fact that Gerald Stoss and Chloe Stewart had once been an item. A brief film clip of Phyllis Palmer's bridge partners saying how elated she'd been to learn of her granddaughter's existence, and the plans she'd been making. Even a man who managed the office at Graceland Memorial North cemetery telling about Savannah Slade's search for her mother's final resting place. Another station was running clips of people who'd come forth claiming they'd witnessed a dark SUV swerving toward Savannah Slade's car time and again, until she was forced onto the causeway. The fact that someone had tried to kill her was evident. Public opinion was definitely on Savannah Slade's side.

"This is good, right?" Judd said as Whiteside flipped to another station.

"As good as a situation like this can get," the ex-agent said as he glanced at the clock. "It's getting close to dinnertime. Do you want to go check on your lady and see if she's awake? Rest is good, but she hasn't eaten since breakfast."

Before Judd could answer, they suddenly heard her voice, echoing somewhere within the house.

"Hey! Hey! Somebody come get me!"

Whiteside grinned. "She sounds mad."

"She's probably lost," Judd said. "I'll be right back to help you fix dinner."

"I'll be in the kitchen," Whiteside said as Judd dashed out of the room.

Savannah didn't have to wait long. She heard running footsteps and turned to see Judd coming through an arched doorway. There were no words to describe what the sight of him did to her heart. And then he smiled, and all her tension and frustration disappeared.

"Here I am, baby," Judd said, and leaned down to kiss her. "Did you get lost?"

Savannah rolled her eyes. "Yes. What's up with this place, anyway? I felt like a rat in a maze, and a dumb one at that. I couldn't find the way to the cheese."

Judd laughed out loud as he scooped her off her feet and into his arms.

Savannah grinned. "You don't have to carry me."

"Maybe I just want an excuse to put my hand on your butt without making a total pass at you."

This time it was Savannah who laughed. "You are such a man."

"Your man, and don't you forget it," he said, then kissed her again—longer, harder, until she moaned.

Judd jerked. "Oh, damn, your poor little mouth. I wasn't thinking, baby. I'm so sorry."

Savannah cupped the side of his face. "You didn't hurt me. You just made me want you."

Judd held her closer. "When you're better, baby... when you're better, okay? For now, Whiteside is making dinner. How about we join him in the kitchen and help out?"

"Yes, please," she said, and wrapped her arms around his neck as he carried her through the maze into the main part of the house.

Once they reached the kitchen, he put her down on her feet.

Whiteside turned as they entered the room, his eyes twinkling with mirth. "Still getting those piggyback rides, I see."

"I hope the layout of your home is not indicative of your sanity," she shot back.

Whiteside laughed out loud.

Neither Judd nor Savannah were aware that Whiteside's laugh was actually a momentous event. After a lifetime with the CIA, he'd lost the ability to find much humor in life. Still, there was something about this woman that spoke to him. Her looks belied her heart. She had a warrior's spirit. He liked that.

"I hope you two like steak," he said.

Judd grinned. "You forget where we're from. We raise what you're about to cook."

"Oh, yeah, that's right." Whiteside looked at Savannah. "So how do you like your steak?"

"On a plate," she fired back.

Whiteside laughed again, and the feeling that came with it was almost euphoric. She already had Judd Holyfield wrapped around her little finger. If he wasn't careful, he would be next.

Judd slipped an arm around Savannah's shoulders and gave her a quick hug.

"We both like our steak medium rare. As for the attitude, she's a little sensitive about people thinking her physical size is indicative of her coping abilities. It's made her touchy."

Judd's apology was a reminder of her missing manners, and Savannah was instantly filled with regret. "Sorry for sounding snippy. That was very rude of me, especially since you've gone out of your way to offer your home and your protection."

Whiteside was still grinning. "You don't need to

be touchy about your size. You're probably the biggest little woman it's ever been my pleasure to meet. I spent my life protecting people who didn't always deserve it. You're an exception to that fact. Happy to help, even if you get lost in my house."

"Why did you build a house so confusing to get around in?" she asked.

The smile died. His eyes narrowed, and his jaw tensed. "I have enemies. Think of the maze as my last defense."

Savannah thought of the joy in the house in which she'd grown up. Knowing a person's life had been so dark that he still felt the need to protect himself even in the design of his home, she reacted before she thought.

"I'm sorry. I'm so sorry. I've been acting horribly, and that's not me," she said, and hugged him.

Whiteside felt her arms slide around his waist. A wisp of her hair brushed against his chin. With that simple act, she scaled defenses that had been in place for years.

A little startled, he looked over her shoulder at Judd, who just shrugged.

"You're gonna have to hug her back if you want her to let go," he said.

This was so far out of Whiteside's comfort zone, he didn't know how he felt, but it was impossible not to react. The hug back was instinctive—a kind of reluctance to let go of something special.

"It's okay, kid," he said softly. "I'd be a little touchy, too, if I'd gone through what's been happening to you."

Savannah patted his arm. "Thank you for being so understanding. Is there anything I can do to help?"

"How about Judd fixes you something to drink, I give

you some cheese and crackers, and you watch a master at work prepare the steaks?"

Savannah beamed. "Perfect. I'd love anything with ice in it."

Judd already knew his way around the kitchen. "I've got that covered. One cold iced tea coming up."

Seventeen

Judd woke up to the sound of footsteps in the hall outside their room and rolled over. The room was in darkness, highlighting the readout on the digital clock: 2:15 a.m. Whiteside must be making a sweep though the house. Damn, didn't that man ever sleep?

He looked over at Savannah. She was still asleep. Careful not to wake her, he got out of bed and stepped into the hall. There was no one there. Satisfied that all was well, he quietly closed the door and then slipped into the bathroom. When he came out, she'd rolled over onto her back. As he crawled back in bed, she began to push and kick at the covers, thrashing her head from side to side.

All of a sudden she sat straight up in bed, gasping for air, her eyes wide with shock. She seemed disoriented, unable to figure out where she was.

Judd slid a hand beneath her hair and pulled her into his arms.

"It was a dream, baby.... You were dreaming. You're okay, you're okay."

Savannah was trembling, her eyes welling with tears. "The water... I couldn't breathe... I couldn't get out.

God, am I going to have this dream every night for the rest of my life?"

"I think it will fade in time," Judd said. "Do you want to get up? Do you want a drink of water?"

"I need to go to the bathroom," she said.

"Need any help?"

"No, I'll be back in a minute."

The carpet was soft against her feet as she walked across the room, but the bathroom tiles were cold. After a quick trip to the toilet, she moved to the sink to wash her hands. She reached for a towel, pausing to look at herself in the mirror. She had to admit, the sight was startling. The bandage on her head had come off earlier in the day, leaving the stitches in plain sight. The bruises on her face were purple. Her puffy lips were almost down to a normal size, but the bruises on her body were faintly visible beneath her pajama top. Out of curiosity, she pulled up her shirt for a better look.

Even though she'd seen them before, the sight was startling—especially the imprint of the steering wheel on her chest. She traced the shape with her hand, unable to remember the exact moment of impact, only that it had happened. Her ribs were sore. She ran her fingers along her side, grateful none were broken. That she was even standing here right now was nothing short of a miracle. Shivering slightly, she dropped her shirt, got a drink of water and went back into the bedroom.

Judd was sitting up in bed waiting for her.

"You are such a good man, Charlie Brown," she said softly as she eased herself in beside him.

Judd smiled as he pulled up the covers, then stretched out beside her so he could see her face. The peace of lying there with her within arms' reach was beyond measure.

"Are you okay? Need any pain meds?" he asked.

She reached for his hand. "I don't need anything but you."

"Thank you, baby," he said softly, then cupped her face and brushed an easy kiss across her lips. But when Savannah wrapped her arms around his neck and pulled him closer, he stopped her.

"Sweetheart, you don't know how much I would love to take this farther, but it's not going to happen. Not until I can look at you without wanting to cry."

"Oh, Judd, it looks worse than it feels. Yes, I'm sore, very sore, but so blessed to still be alive."

He rubbed his thumb along the curve of her chin. He didn't need the light to remember the shape.

"I'm so sorry all this is happening."

"I'm sorry I pushed you away."

"But I'm here now."

Savannah slid her hand down the length of his arm, feeling the strength of the muscles beneath.

"You know what I was thinking when I thought I was going to die?"

He touched his forehead to hers. "I can't begin to imagine."

"I was thinking about you. Remembering the look on your face when you asked me to marry you and I said I wanted to wait. I was wishing I could have lived that moment over, because I would have said yes."

There was a knot in Judd's throat. If he'd had to bury her, it would have killed him.

"You didn't miss out," he said. "I *will* ask you again."

Savannah cupped his cheek. "When?"

"Whenever you're ready to hear it, I guess."

"Ask me now."

Judd's vision blurred as he tried to laugh.

"You would pull this shit with me now. Your ring is back at the ranch in my dresser drawer."

Savannah sat up in bed. "I don't care about that ring. I just want a second chance."

Judd thought for a moment; then a slight smile crossed his face as he got out of bed. He turned on the light and then dug through the dresser drawer, pulled something out of his wallet, returned to the bed and sat down beside her.

"It's not a ring, but in the long run, it's total proof of my intentions." He turned her hand palm up, dropped something in it. "Don't look, yet," he said as he curled her fingers over it.

Savannah's heart skipped a beat. After the way they'd parted when she left for Miami, she'd been afraid he would be so fed up with her that this would never happen again.

Judd ran a finger down the curve of her cheek, gently tucking a lock of hair behind her ear.

"Savannah, you are the love of my life and the reason I draw breath. Will you marry me? Bear my children? Grow old with me?"

She was crying again, but this time for joy. "Yes, oh, yes," she said, and threw her arms around his neck and kissed him senseless.

By the time she'd turned him loose, he was grinning from ear to ear. He pointed to her hand.

"About that thing I gave you, you can look now."

Savannah unfolded her fingers to see what he'd given her. Her eyes widened, and then she started to laugh.

"Are you serious? How long have you had this?"

"About as long as I've had your ring."

"I love it. I *love* it. I can't wait to grow old and tell

our grandchildren that you gave me a credit card before you gave me a ring."

"I thought it was a nice twist, although you'll notice there's still a hitch."

"Like what?"

"The name. Savannah Holyfield. She doesn't yet exist."

Savannah smiled. "We'll activate her after the ceremony."

Judd kissed her lips, then her cheek, then the little indention at the base of her throat. By the time he was finished, she was moaning.

"All you have to do is set a date. I'm there."

"We'll do it when both my sisters come home."

"Perfect." He kissed her once more to seal the deal. "You are now officially my fiancée."

He crawled back onto the bed, slid beneath the covers and pulled her into his arms. For the moment, it was enough.

Joseph couldn't sleep and had come down to the main floor to raid the refrigerator. On the way back to his room, he'd stopped off in the library to get a bottle from Elaine's bourbon stash, then carried everything back up to his room. He ate, but without relish. He drank, but he couldn't dull the growing sense of impending doom.

Nothing seemed to satisfy him tonight. It had been a while since he'd been with a woman. Maybe that was what was wrong. A buildup of testosterone that needed a release. A simple fact of chemistry, not a guilty conscience.

There were plenty of the proverbial skeletons in his closet, but they'd never caused him to lose sleep before.

Things happened. It was something his father had said right up to the day he died.

He walked to the window, looking out into the night with the bourbon in his hand, then took a drink from the bottle, savoring the bite and the heat as the liquor rolled down his throat.

If only there was a way to go backward in time—to have a do-over. If he could, it would begin with the day Gerald had come home full of the news that he had a ready-made family he was about to bring into their midst. He'd been oblivious to what an insult his new plans had been to Joseph, or how he might feel.

All throughout their childhood and then while they were learning to be adults, Joseph had done all the right things. He'd followed Rupert Stoss's every order and edict, while Gerald romped his way through Europe, ignoring the family businesses for the good life. Then Gerald came home to Miami, had an affair with a young woman and walked away, unaware he had left her pregnant to bear his bastard child.

All of a sudden the woman was dying, and she'd reached out to Gerald in desperation and, lo and behold, Gerald had gained a conscience. He'd walked into the house announcing he was finally ready to step into the role to which he'd been born—the role of the eldest son. He even had a ready-made family, complete with a conveniently dying woman and a two-year-old daughter.

For Joseph, it had been too much. He'd snapped, then done what he had for the good of the family, and because he deserved to inherit, not his ne'er-do-well brother.

But instead of completely solving their problem, Joseph's one moment of weakness had been that baby girl. By then he was married himself, and if it hadn't been for his own son, who had just had his first birthday a week before, he wouldn't have given her disposal a second thought. He'd operated under the "got a problem, get rid of it" mantra for years.

But he hadn't followed through.

It was his first mistake, and twenty years later, it was a loose end that had come back to haunt him.

He knew exactly when his moment of regret for his earlier kindness had begun: with the phone call from the detective. The news had been a shock. He'd reacted badly. He should have given Mateo the go-ahead the first night and taken her out in her hotel room. Make it look like a date gone bad, and then it would have been over. But no. He'd overthought it, and that had been his second mistake. His third mistake was sending in a used-up cleanup man like Mateo. At least he'd rectified that one. Problem now was that no one knew where the Slade woman had gone. Not even the cops, as far as he could tell.

Frustrated with the situation in general, he set the bourbon on the dresser and had started to turn out the lights when his cell phone rang. He frowned. Who the hell would be calling at this time of the morning?

He looked at the caller ID, but it was blank. He started to let it go to voice mail, then changed his mind and picked up.

"Hello."

"Hello. Am I speaking to Joseph Stoss?"

The caller had a distinct accent, but Joseph couldn't place it. "Yes. Who are you?"

"I am Pierre DeGaulle, President of the University of Geneva. I am most sorry to have to tell you this, sir, but your son Anthony is dead. It was a suicide."

Joseph's legs went out from under him. One moment he was standing near his bed, and the next thing he knew he was on the floor. There was a roaring in his ears, as if his body was moving through some kind of a tunnel at a rapid rate of speed. This wasn't real. It couldn't be happening.

"Mr. Stoss. Mr. Stoss? Are you there?"

Joseph looked down at the phone he was holding, then put it back to his ear.

"Mr. Stoss. Are you there?"

"I'm sorry. Yes, I'm here." He meant to breathe, but it came out in a sob. "Are you sure there's no mistake? I just spoke with him this morning."

"No, sir, there is no mistake."

Joseph began to shake. The food he'd just eaten was going to come up. He could feel it.

"How? Can you tell me how?"

"He shot himself in the head. I'm so sorry. We had no idea that he was depressed. The authorities have his body, but—"

"I'm coming to get him," Joseph mumbled. "You tell them, his father is coming to get him."

Then he threw down the phone and crawled into the bathroom, vomiting as he went. He threw up the food and the bourbon, and then he kept throwing up until there was nothing left but bile.

When his stomach was as empty as his heart, he rolled over onto the cold tiles of the bathroom floor, closed his eyes and prayed to die.

It was Estella who found him the next morning, when she went in to make his bed. She saw the vomit on the floor and traced it to the bathroom, where she saw Joseph on the floor, his eyes half-open, his body motionless. Certain she'd just found a dead man, she ran from the room, screaming Michael's name.

* * *

Michael was just getting out of the shower when he thought he heard a scream. His first thought was that something was happening with Elaine, and he began to towel off quickly. He was reaching for a pair of sweatpants when the screams became louder. When he heard someone calling his name, he yanked on the sweats and dashed out into the hall, but there was no one there. A door opened behind him. It was Elaine, still in her gown and robe. She ran her perfectly manicured fingers through her hair, not bothering to hide a yawn.

"What's going on?"

At that moment Estella raced around a corner toward them, crying and waving her hands. She was talking so fast in Spanish that Michael couldn't understand a word she was saying.

He ran toward her, grabbing her by the shoulders and shaking her as he spoke.

"In English, *por favor*. In English!"

Estella made the sign of the cross over her heart as she took a deep breath.

"Mr. Joseph! He is on the bathroom floor. I think he is dead!"

"Oh, my God." Michael turned and yelled at Elaine, "Call 9-1-1. Something's happened to Joseph! And if you take a drink in the middle of this crisis, I swear to God I'll put your ass in rehab and leave you there to rot."

Elaine bolted back into her bedroom.

Michael grabbed Estella by the shoulders. "You go downstairs and wait for the ambulance. When they get here, show them up. Understand?"

"Yes, yes, I understand," she said, and made a run for the stairs as Michael headed for his cousin's room.

He'd no sooner entered than he began to gag from the

stench. Then he accidentally stepped into what looked like dried vomit and realized it was the source of the smell.

The bathroom door was wide open. From where he was standing, he could see Joseph lying on the floor, his eyes open, a trail of dried spittle hanging from his mouth.

"Oh, Jesus, Jesus," Michael muttered as he ran into the bathroom and knelt beside the body. Like Estella, he thought Joseph was dead as he felt for a pulse. A strong, steady thump beneath his fingers shocked him as he rocked back on his heels.

At that point, Elaine came flying into the bedroom, her eyes shimmering with tears.

"He's not dead," Michael said. "Hand me a wet washcloth, and hurry. I don't want the EMTs to see him like this."

To Elaine's credit, she never even commented on the trail of vomit. She quickly did as Michael asked, then began cleaning up the site. She put the lid down on the commode and flushed it. Then she grabbed a stack of bath towels and began throwing them over the trail of dried vomit. When the toilet quit running, she poured half a bottle of Joseph's aftershave into the bowl, then flushed it again.

Michael was surprised and grateful for her presence of mind as he slid a folded-up towel beneath Joseph's head, then began cleaning his face.

"Joseph, it's me, Michael. Can you tell me what's wrong? Can you move? Can you talk?"

Joseph blinked, dislodging a tear that pooled, then slid down the side of his nose.

Michael was scared. He'd never seen Joseph in this condition and feared he'd had a stroke or some kind of mental breakdown. He jumped up to rinse out the washcloth, then knelt again, this time washing Joseph's hands. It wasn't until he noticed the dried vomit on the knees of Joseph's pajamas that he realized he must have crawled into the bathroom, which also explained the mess on his hands. But why? Was something wrong with his legs?

"Joseph. Are you hurt? Can you show me where you hurt?"

Joseph inhaled suddenly, as if coming out of some kind of trance, rolled over onto his back and stared blankly at the ceiling.

Startled, Michael grabbed hold of Joseph's shoulders. "Joseph! For God's sake, man, what's happened to you?"

Elaine touched Michael's arm. "I hear the ambulance."

"Thank God," Michael muttered. It couldn't get here soon enough.

Joseph groaned and began to struggle to sit up.

Elaine reached for Joseph's head, smoothing the hair back from his face in soft, repetitive motions. "Lie still. You need to lie still. Help is on the way."

Joseph pushed her hand away. "Too late. It's already too late."

Michael was frantic. "Talk to me, damn it! The ambulance is almost here. I need to know what's happening so I can help you. Talk. Now!"

Joseph blinked as his eyes began to focus, and with that came the memories and the pain.

"Tony's dead."

"Oh, no, no, no," Elaine whispered, and began to weep.

Michael felt his body go numb. This didn't make

sense. "Dear God! What happened? How did you find out?"

"A call from the president of the university." Joseph's face crumpled as a fresh set of tears began to fall.

Michael could hear the footsteps of the EMTs coming up the stairs.

"What did he say? Was it a car accident?"

Joseph shuddered as he struggled to get the words out. "Suicide. Tony shot himself in the head."

Michael felt faint. He kept picturing his young cousin, handsome and smart, living life to the fullest. What in hell had happened to him that he'd taken this turn?

"What would make him do that?" Michael asked bleakly as the sound of running footsteps echoed in the hall.

Joseph shuddered, his voice thick with new tears. "He saw the story in the *Herald*. He was upset. I told him I would fix it. I told him not to worry."

Michael froze. It was the wording that gave Joseph away. "He believed it, didn't he? Did he ask you? Did he ask you if it was true?"

Joseph nodded, then slumped. It was the first time Michael had ever seen Joseph looking his age.

"I have to get to Switzerland. I told them I was coming to take care of my son," Joseph muttered.

Then the EMTs were in the room. Michael could hear Estella's voice, pointing out the way. Suddenly the bathroom was filled with rescue workers and their paraphernalia. He and Elaine were moved back as the crew began to assess Joseph's condition. When one asked Joseph what had happened, he didn't answer.

Michael spoke up. "I don't know if he had a heart attack, or if it's just shock, but he got bad news early this morning that his son had died."

"I need to get packed," Joseph muttered. "Michael, call the pilot. Tell him to get the company jet ready and book a flight plan to Switzerland."

Michael looked at the EMT who was assessing Joseph's vitals. "Not until they say you're okay to travel," Michael said.

"I say I'm okay," Joseph said. The more time that passed, the more he was regaining his sense of self.

Suddenly Elaine gasped, then whispered in Michael's ear, "We were supposed to talk to the police this morning."

Michael wasn't used to making decisions, but this was no time to be hesitant. He glanced at the man who was still working on Joseph, then took Elaine by the arm and pulled her out of the bathroom to the bedroom beyond.

"Go call Paul Stern. Tell him what's happened and to please notify Barber that we can't come in, and that we'll need to reschedule this after we get back."

Elaine's eyes widened. "Are we going with him?"

Michael frowned. "Tony is dead. He committed suicide. We are not letting Joseph face this alone."

Frowning, she pulled away. "He wouldn't do it for one of us," she muttered.

"Just do as I ask—please."

Elaine rolled her eyes, but she left when Michael hurried back into the bathroom.

"Is he okay?" he asked.

The EMT stood. "His blood pressure is a little high, but not unusual, given what you told us. His heart sounds fine. His motor skills are okay. If he can stand on his own without any vertigo, he's probably all right. I would rather he let us take him to the hospital for a more thorough checkup, but he refuses."

Michael shrugged. "I can tell you he won't listen to me, either."

"Then we're done here," the EMT said.

"I'll show you to the door," Michael offered, then walked them back downstairs and saw them out.

As soon as they were gone, he ran back to Joseph's room. There was an open suitcase on the bed. Joseph was moving slowly but already packing. Michael hesitated, then walked over to the dresser where Joseph was standing and put his arm around his cousin's shoulder.

"I'm so, so sorry. I thought the world of Tony. He was an amazing kid."

Joseph turned, his eyes blazing with hate. "It's her fault. None of this would have happened if she hadn't come back."

Michael was stunned. "But you said Tony was upset, that he asked you if it was true. When you told him you would fix it, he had to believe you were behind what was happening."

Joseph moved until there were only inches between them. "Get out!"

"We're going with you," Michael said.

"Then you'd better hurry, because I won't wait. Did you call the pilot?"

"I'm doing it right now," Michael said, and ran down the hall to his room.

Joseph tossed a handful of clean undershorts in the bag. He opened the next drawer to get out some clean shirts just as his cell phone began to ring. He began following the sound until he found it under the edge of his bed. By the time he got to it, the call had gone to voice mail. He saw it was Paul Stern and ignored it. Whatever was going on was less important than the task ahead of him.

Unable to live with his son's death on his conscience, he'd assigned guilt and was out for revenge. He was on a quest to see Savannah Slade on a slab. There was no more caution. No worry about the police pointing the finger of blame at him. He'd been too careful, and this was what had happened. Because of her, she'd put doubt in people's minds—doubt that demeaned the good name of his family. *His* family—not hers.

He sat down on the side of the bed and scrolled through his address book until he found the name he was looking for.

Carl Tyson.

He'd paid him well to remove Mateo from the organization, and a cash retainer to remain at his beck and call. Tyson had happily agreed. Joseph wanted Savannah Slade gone from the face of the earth, and he wanted it to happen before he got back from Switzerland.

He started to make the call, then went and closed the door to his room first. When the call was answered before the second ring, it affirmed Joseph's belief that he'd hired the right man for the job.

"Tyson speaking."

"This is Stoss. I have a job for you."

Tyson laid down the barbell he'd been hoisting and wiped the sweat from his forehead. "Thank you, sir. I appreciate the work."

Barber had a fresh cup of coffee and was headed for his desk when his phone rang. He set the coffee aside and grabbed the phone as he plopped into his chair.

"Homicide, Barber."

"Detective Barber, this is Paul Stern. My firm represents Stoss Industries, as well as the family. As you know, we were due to come in to visit with you this morning."

Barber frowned. He already didn't like this. Stern was speaking in the past tense.

"I'm listening," he said.

"Joseph Stoss has just received word that his only son, Tony, who was in school in Switzerland, has died."

Barber frowned. "Are you serious?"

"Unfortunately, yes," Stern said. "Mr. Stoss and his two cousins are already en route to the airport. They're flying out today to reclaim the body. They will need time to plan the services and see to his burial in Montreal before they can come in as you've requested. I'm sure you understand."

Things were happening too fast. Barber had already lost control of the interview before it even started, and now they were telling him when they would be available? No way.

"I understand this was an unexpected and unfortunate event, and I am sorry for the family's loss. But I am also not comfortable with the fact that they are all leaving the country in the middle of a murder investigation. I'm sure you can understand that."

For a moment Stern didn't answer, and then he cleared his throat. "At this point, the family is free to go anywhere they choose, and you know it. They have not been charged with any crime, and we certainly don't expect it to go that far, if you know what I mean."

Barber flinched. "I'm going to assume that was not in any way an implied threat, because I have a great big mess on my hands, and the Stoss family is right in the middle of it. One woman is dead, another's life has been threatened twice, and she has a very valid claim to a cool billion-plus dollars of their money, which is always a motive for murder."

"But, Detective, surely—"

"You tell your clients that they have five days to get themselves back to Miami and into my office. If they have not returned by that time, I will file warrants for their arrest. Do we understand each other?"

"Perfectly," Stern snapped. "Thank you for your understanding."

The line went dead in Barber's ear. He cursed beneath his breath, and then made a call to Thomas Jefferson's cell. Just when he thought the call was going to go to voice mail, Jefferson answered.

"Good morning, Detective. To what do I owe this unexpected pleasure?"

"Joseph Stoss's son has died. They're flying to Switzerland this morning to claim the body."

"Wow. That's a shock. I wonder what happened?"

"Paul Stern called me. He didn't say."

"Are you sure they'll come back? I mean, once they're out of the country, it could prove difficult to get them back."

"I'm not sure of anything except that, at the moment, they haven't been charged with any crime, and are free to come and go as they please. However, I told Stern they have five days to do whatever it is they need to do, and if they aren't back in Miami in my office by then, I'll have arrest warrants issued for all three."

Thomas sighed. "I don't like it."

"Neither do I, but for now, my hands are tied. I need concrete evidence linking them to the Palmer woman's murder or to the attempted murder of Savannah Slade, and I don't have it. I've got a dirty cop who doesn't know the name of the person who hired him to kill

Miss Slade. We haven't been able to trace the money that was deposited into his account. No one's seen an SUV matching the description of the one that caused Savannah's accident. All I have is a whole lot of circumstantial evidence."

"So we'll get some proof. We have five more days before you confront them. Hopefully we'll get lucky."

"Yeah, well, I'm assuming you'll be giving Miss Slade this news."

"Yes."

"I'm also assuming she's okay?"

"Yes."

Barber hesitated, then felt compelled to add, "Tell her I'm sorry."

Thomas frowned. "Sorry for what?"

Barber shifted uncomfortably. "You know...for what's happened to her here on my turf."

"Oh. Of course."

"Does she plan to have a funeral service for her grandmother? I ask because I'd be happy to see about getting some police protection for her."

"I don't know her plans," Thomas said. "But I'll pass along your message."

"Thanks," Barber said.

"Thanks for keeping me in the loop," Thomas said. "I'll be in touch."

Barber hung up the phone and headed for his lieutenant's office to update him on what was happening. This case was a train wreck, and all he wanted was for it to be over.

Eighteen

Savannah had been given carte blanche to use whatever she wanted inside Whiteside's house. Since her phone had gone down with her car and she was dying to tell Holly that she was officially engaged, she'd made the call from his living room.

Holly squealed when she heard the news, then relayed it to Bud. It was the first Savannah knew that he was there. She sensed something was going on with them and was about to grill her when Judd came into the room. She could tell by the look on his face that something had happened.

"Hey, Holly," she said quickly. "Something just came up. I've got to go, but I'll talk to you later. Take care of yourself."

"I will," Holly said. "You, too."

Savannah hung up and turned to Judd. "What?"

"Your lawyer just called. Joseph Stoss's son, Tony, died yesterday at his school in Switzerland. All three of the Stosses are on their way there to claim the body."

"That's awful," she said. "Did Thomas say what happened?"

"He made a few calls. Said the kid committed suicide."

She gasped. "Oh, my God! Oh, no!"

Judd watched the changing expressions on her face. He knew his woman. She was measuring the impact her arrival might have had on the boy's death. Her next shaky question was proof that he'd been right.

"What if it was because of my lawsuit and the threat I represented?"

"Savannah, stop. We don't know why he did it. For all we know, he could have had emotional issues for years and this is nothing but a coincidence."

"Maybe, maybe not."

"Don't go there, Savannah. We don't know a thing about him or his relationship with his family, remember?"

"You're right. It just took me by surprise." Then the rest of what Judd had just said sank in. "They went to Switzerland? If they're out of the country, what if they never come back?"

"It wouldn't change the validity of your lawsuit. However, Barber has given them five days to get back or he's issuing warrants for their arrests. I can't see people like them living a life on the run."

"Good Lord. Just when I think this couldn't get more complicated… Which reminds me. I need to call Thomas. I don't know what's happening with my grandmother's body. I don't want her to go unattended." Her chin quivered. "That sounds so cold. I still can't get over the fact that she's gone. I just found her, and now she's dead. Murdered. It doesn't seem real."

Judd put his arms around her, pulling her close. "I know, baby. It's a bad deal all around, but you can't blame yourself."

"But I do. If I hadn't come to Miami all ready to assert my right to inherit, none of this would be happening."

"Look, the bottom line is, you've done nothing illegal. You've committed no crime. Stop trying to take on the burden of guilt for someone else's actions. Understand?"

She sighed. "Understood."

Judd tilted her chin, eyeing the stitches, then gave her a quick kiss on the forehead.

"I found a checkerboard and a deck of cards in Whiteside's library. Want to play?"

"I'd rather play doctor with you," Savannah said.

Judd groaned. "Don't tempt me. What'll it be? Cards or checkers? Keep in mind, I won last time."

"That was poker. I don't like poker. I choose checkers."

"Want to make it interesting?"

Savannah poked him on the arm. "I don't have any money, remember?"

"I take IOUs," he said, and tugged on her hand until she complied and went with him.

Tyson was a man who liked to work alone. He was an asexual, thirty-one-year-old killing machine whose only passion beyond the spray of his enemy's blood in his face was his addiction to technology. He had ten years of military experience and a dishonorable discharge for time served. He had issues with authority and a genius ability to hack into people's personal info via the internet. But there was nothing he liked better than the satisfaction of a clean kill. He considered himself most fortunate to be in the employ of Joseph Stoss and was already on the job, running a dump on the names Stoss had given him. According to the boss, one of two men would most likely know where Savannah Slade was in hiding. One was her lawyer, Thomas Jefferson. The other was Frank Barber, a homicide detective. The info he was downloading on the men should give him a good starting point.

Tyson was betting on the lawyer and started with him first, hacking into his personal info and running his credit card numbers to see what recent purchases he'd made. When he saw that the man had purchased several hundred dollars' worth of women's clothing, he grinned. Considering everything Savannah Slade had brought with her to Miami had been in the car when it went into the bay, the logical assumption was that Jefferson had been buying her replacements.

Tyson identified Jefferson's car from DMV, along with a photo for his own satisfaction, and did a double take when he saw the man's statistics on his license. Forty-seven years old. Six feet seven inches. Two hundred and forty pounds. He looked like a professional wrestler but dressed like Stoss. When he saw the man's home address and net worth, he was even more impressed. A very large black man who'd made a legal fortune outside the field of athletics and entertainment. Commendable.

He printed out the info, then began a rundown of the man's phone logs, checking out the personal information of every person he'd called since Savannah Slade became his client. One number in particular popped up several times right before her accident. The interesting part was that it was unlisted. This signaled a point of interest to investigate. He began hacking into bank records, utility company records, anything that might cross-reference with the phone number and give him a name. Once he had a name, he would find an address and then, presumably, Savannah Slade.

He left the search programs running and headed for Thomas Jefferson's office. He didn't think the man would be stupid enough to lead him straight to her, but he wasn't about to ignore the obvious. The key to Tyson's success rate was patience. After ten years in the military, pulling duty in both Iraq and the mountains of Afghanistan, he had all kinds of patience with stakeouts.

It was a few minutes after 8:00 a.m. when he reached the building in which Jefferson had his office, found a good place to wait and settled in. Within ten minutes Jefferson arrived, drove into an alley and didn't come out. As soon as Tyson was convinced the man had gone into the building, he did a little recon, checking out the parking lot in back. One way in and the same way out. Perfect. Only one place to watch.

He jogged back to his car, snagged a banana from the stash of food that he kept on hand and a bottle of water from the cooler in the backseat and waited.

When Jefferson drove out later, Tyson followed him to the courthouse, where he stayed for three hours before driving back to his office. He followed the man home when the workday was over and waited until he saw lights go on in the kitchen, which almost certainly meant Jefferson was staying in for the night. At that point he bugged Jefferson's car so that he could follow it online, then headed back to his own place to see what kind of info had come up on his search. He had five days to prove his worth and didn't intend to fail.

Whiteside had been outside, making his daily sweep of the exterior of his property. He walked into the house from the back, kicked off his muddy shoes and stepped into some slippers just as he heard a small alarm begin to sound. It wasn't one of the perimeter alarms. They had a different ring. Frowning, he headed for the computer room to check his machines.

Savannah was in the shower and didn't hear the alarm, but Judd was in the living room watching TV when he heard it go off. He was up and running toward the sound when Whiteside came out of the kitchen.

"It's not a perimeter alarm. It's something I have on one of my computers."

"Can I see?" Judd asked.

Whiteside hesitated, then nodded. "Follow me."

It only took Whiteside a few moments to see what was happening. "The alarm is part of a firewall I have on anything related to my personal information. If someone starts hacking into my personal business, it lets me know."

"Damn, I didn't know there was such a thing," Judd said.

Whiteside sighed. "Unfortunately, technology has outpaced the law, and I'm still waiting for it to catch up."

"Can you tell who's doing it? Do you think it has something to do with Savannah?"

"I'm running a trace right now," Whiteside said as he activated a search program. "I won't know if it has anything to do with Miss Slade until I find out who's doing it. Like I said before, I have enemies who were my enemies before she was ever born."

Judd glanced at his watch. He didn't intend to leave Savannah stranded again, although she'd pretty much figured out how to navigate within the walls of the house.

Ten minutes later Whiteside leaned back in his chair. "I can't get a lock on the point of origin."

"So what does that mean for us? For Savannah?"

"It means tonight I begin an hourly grounds sweep, which means I need to get in a couple of hours' sleep today."

"I'm no spook, but I can shoot a gun," Judd said.

Whiteside smiled. "No worries. I've got you covered. It's why you're here, remember?"

"I don't know how Thomas Jefferson talked you into this, but we're very grateful that you were willing to do it."

"Thomas is a good man. We go way back," Whiteside said, and then let it drop.

Judd didn't push for more information. All he needed to know was that the man had Savannah's best interests at heart.

"I'm going to check on Savannah," he said.

"And I'm off to bed. I only eat a couple times a day, but there's plenty of food for sandwiches in the refrigerator, if you two get hungry before dinner."

"Don't worry about feeding our bellies. Just keep my girl safe."

"Absolutely," Whiteside said. "She's definitely one of a kind."

Two days later Tyson finally got a hit. Alan Whiteside. Ex-military. Ex-CIA. Retired to Miami in 2007. Owned property due west of Coral Gables, inside the boundary of the Everglades National Park. He frowned. That couldn't be right, but after a quick research check, he discovered that not all the lands in the northeast corner of the Everglades had been acquired by the federal government.

Okay. Interesting. Good place to hide someone. Time to check it out.

* * *

Whiteside stared at the computer screen with a brief moment of disbelief. Someone had acquired the location of his property. A long list of possible scenarios had presented themselves over the past couple of days. Bottom line, he could either move Savannah Slade to a new location or wait and see what happened. The plus side to staying was that the property was only accessible by air. But that left them open to an air attack. One heat-seeker and they would all be toast.

He wanted to call Thomas, but he had no way of knowing if Thomas's phones had been bugged. Without a guarantee of a secure line, it was too dangerous. That left the decision making to the woman herself, and the cowboy who loved her. Neither one was the kind to back down from a threat, but this situation even had him worried. Whoever was behind this was good.

Aware that time was no longer on their side, he went to look for his guests. The moment he stepped out into the hallway, he smelled something baking and followed his nose to the kitchen.

Savannah was taking a sheet of cookies out of the oven and Judd was loading dishes into the dishwasher when Whiteside walked into the room. He paused inside the doorway and took a slow, deep breath.

"Have I died and gone to heaven?"

Savannah smiled. "I didn't think you'd mind."

"And you would be right," he said as he picked up a cookie from an array cooling on the table and took a big bite. "Oatmeal-raisin. My mother used to make these. What a treat."

"I'm not used to doing nothing, and the better I feel, the harder it is to stay hidden like this," Savannah said.

"I can echo that," Judd said as he took the cookie sheet she'd just emptied and stuck it in the sink to cool. "I haven't been this inactive since I fell off a horse and broke my leg."

Whiteside reached for another cookie. "When was that?"

"About twenty years ago," Savannah said, and then laughed. "He hasn't been still since."

Whiteside got a cold can of Coke from the refrigerator, then sat down and finished the second cookie.

Judd could tell by the look on his face something was wrong.

"Are you going to tell us, or do you want to play Twenty Questions?"

The smile slid off Savannah's face. "Tell us what?" she asked.

"You're good, cowboy," Whiteside said.

Savannah sat. Judd walked up behind her chair and put a hand on her shoulder.

"What's happened?" she asked.

"For the past two days, someone has been running a search on my phone number. It's unlisted, but you can get past it if you know what to do. However, they didn't stop there. Long story short, as of three o'clock this afternoon, whoever it is knows this house exists and knows its location. I told you before that I have enemies, but I find it too coincidental that one of them would be looking for me at the same time someone is looking for you. If I were going to lay odds, I'd say you're the target, not me."

The good spirits of only moments ago were gone. Once again she'd been pulled back to reality.

"So what does this mean?" she asked.

"We need to move her, don't we?" Judd asked.

Whiteside nodded. "I think it's best."

"But where to?" Savannah asked. "If they found me all the way out here, they can find me anywhere."

"I have an idea," Whiteside said. "But I need to contact Thomas, and I suspect all our numbers have been compromised."

"Use Judd's phone to call Barber," Savannah said. "Tell him to bring Thomas into the police station. They can call you here on Judd's phone. Those two numbers should be inconsequential enough to get by with one call. Right?"

Whiteside stared at her. "You trust the cops? After a cop tried to kill you in the hospital?"

"I trust Barber," Savannah said.

"Then so be it," Whiteside said. "We need to make this happen quickly. I don't think it's safe to spend another night here."

"Are you saying something might happen to your property because of me?" she asked.

"Four years ago this house didn't exist. If it's gone tomorrow, big deal. I'll either build it back or find a new place to retire."

"I'm so sorry. This is awful," Savannah said.

"No, this is just stuff. The only thing in life that matters are people you care about, kid. You've got your whole life ahead of you. I'd like to think I was a part of helping you live to a ripe old age."

He looked over at Judd. "Make that call for me, will you?" He grabbed another cookie and smiled as he popped it in his mouth. "Might as well enjoy myself while I wait."

Thomas was finishing up a phone call when there was a knock on his door. To his surprise, Laura escorted Detective Barber in.

"He says it's urgent," she said.

"That's fine, Laura. Hold my calls while he's here."

The door closed. Barber moved toward the desk.

"I got a call from a man who called himself Whiteside. He said to come in person and tell you their location has been compromised, and he believes someone's still trying to kill her. If Stoss was crazy mad before on account of his fortune being threatened, I'd guess he lost it completely after the death of his son. At any rate, Whiteside wants to talk to you."

Thomas was horrified. "Damn it! I would have bet my life that no one could compromise that location. So why didn't he just call me?" Thomas asked.

"Because they traced him through your calls, meaning both of your phones have been compromised."

Thomas cursed as he rubbed his hand across the slick surface of his head. "That's my fault. I didn't think. I didn't *think*."

"So you need to come with me. For all intents and purposes, you'll be calling a man named Judd Holyfield on a Miami P.D. phone. You two can figure out the rest."

Thomas grabbed his cell phone and dropped it in his pocket, then stopped.

"Habit," he said. "In case Laura needs to get in touch with me. After you." Thomas stopped by Laura's desk. "I'm going out with Detective Barber, but that's not for public knowledge. I won't be gone long."

Whiteside was waiting. When Judd's phone began to ring, he motioned for the cowboy to answer.

"Hello?"

Thomas recognized the voice. "Judd, it's me."

"Hang on a sec. Whiteside is right here."

Whiteside took the phone. "I need to move her."

Thomas felt sick. "I take full responsibility for this breech. I should never have used my personal phone. I should have used a pay phone or something. I'm not a very good spy."

"What's done is done. The issue now is to keep Savannah safe. Besides, it's pretty hard to find a pay phone these days."

"What do you have in mind?" Thomas asked.

"I'm thinking about the first place we talked about. It wouldn't be for more than a couple of days."

Thomas frowned. "Do you think we can get them there unobserved?"

"What's the name of the cleaning company your building uses?"

"Uh, Russell Industrial Services, I think."

"Okay. That's all I needed to know. I assume you'll be waiting for us?"

"Of course," Thomas said. "When should I expect you?"

"After dark."

Tyson had been in the air since noon. His first flyover had been in a two-seater rental plane, just to make sure of the location. He'd stayed high and on the farthest perimeter of the property, so that if anyone was watching, they would assume it was just a plane on a flight path out of Tamiami Airport.

Once he'd located the property and checked out the surrounding geography, he was impressed. It looked like a damn fortress. However, there was only one way into the property and one way out: by air. But not in a plane like this. He needed something that could go in low, like a chopper, and he was going to need a pilot.

He couldn't fly and shoot at the same time. But it would be just as easy to get rid of the pilot afterward as it was going to be to get rid of Savannah Slade. The military called it collateral damage. Tyson called it leaving no witnesses behind.

Judd didn't ask how Whiteside was able to get a van and uniforms from Russell Industrial cleaning, but when their chopper landed at the airport, their disguises were waiting.

It was sunset. The time when cleaning crews began the task of cleaning big empty office buildings. Judd and Savannah stowed their bags in with the cleaning gear, dressed in the uniforms and got into the back of the van as Whiteside drove them into the city and on toward Thomas's law office.

It was dark in the back of the van. Savannah's heart was pounding, and she kept clutching Judd's hand, imagining that at any moment the van would come to a screeching halt, the doors would fly open and someone would gun them all down where they sat. And all because her mother had fallen in love with the wrong man—with a rich man's son.

"It's going to be all right," Judd said. "Whiteside's on top of this. If he wasn't, we'd still be hiding out in the swamp and unaware that your hideout had been compromised."

"Mentally, I know that, but I'm an emotional wreck. I know I was all full of myself when I left Missoula, swearing that this was something I needed to do on my own. And now look at me. The Miami P.D., my lawyer, you and an ex-CIA spy have me under wraps, and it's still not enough."

"We'll get through this," Judd said. "As long as we're together, we can do whatever needs to be done."

Savannah scooted closer and laid her head on his shoulder, taking comfort in his presence.

Judd kissed the top of her head, then hugged her. He'd been optimistic when he spoke to her, but he was far less so than he'd let on. Until someone was arrested and the court proceedings for her lawsuit were behind them, the future was still up for grabs.

Then they felt the van beginning to slow down. "We're here," Whiteside said. "As soon as I stop, we're going in the back door. Take all your stuff the first trip. Don't worry about the cleaning gear. We're going straight up the freight elevator to Thomas's floor. He'll be waiting."

Lights from the parking lot came through the windshield and lit up the interior of the van well enough for them to gather their belongings. As soon as the doors opened, they stepped out. Judd took both their bags, and they calmly walked into the building.

Whiteside led them through a hallway and then to the freight elevator, which they took up to the ninth floor and Thomas's office. The moment the doors opened, Whiteside stepped out, did a quick scan of the area, then motioned them to follow.

Savannah quickly realized they were at the far end of the hallway, and that they would have to walk all the way down to get to the right door. Every step they took, every tiny sound they heard, was magnified in her mind and turned into a possible threat. If it hadn't been for Judd and Whiteside's presence, she would have run screaming all the way to the door.

Finally they got there, and Whiteside turned the

knob. The door wasn't locked. It swung inward, where they came face-to-face with Thomas.

His face was grim. "You weren't followed?"

"No. I checked all the way from the airport," Whiteside said.

Thomas shifted his focus to the cleaning crew and managed a grin. "I hate to say this, Judd, but those pants are too short."

Judd snorted softly. "I already knew that. I'm the one wearing them."

That lightened the moment enough that Savannah actually relaxed.

"Why are we here?" she asked.

Thomas motioned for them to follow and led the way into his office. Then he walked behind his desk, took a small remote control from the top drawer and aimed it at the wall.

A six-foot section parted without sound, three feet of paneling sliding into the walls on either side, revealing an entire living space behind it.

Savannah remembered that she'd seen it once before.

"This is going to be your home away from home for a while," Thomas said.

"What is this?" Judd asked.

"I put in a lot of all-nighters when a case is in court. I had this built as a convenience for myself. It's small in comparison to my real home, but it's a thousand square feet of comfort, just the same." He led the way in. "The bedroom and bath are over there. The living area is, of course, here. And there's a small but well-stocked kitchen just around that wall. If there's anything you need, all you have to do is ask me. I'll check in on you from time to time, but Laura will not know you're here."

"What if we make too much noise? Will this compromise your meetings with your clients and your attorney/client privilege?" Savannah asked.

"Nope. The place is soundproof. I've tested it before. I left a CD of Guns and Roses playing full blast once, then went into my office and closed the doors. Couldn't hear a thing."

Savannah sank down on the sofa, and then leaned forward and put her face in her hands. Judd dropped their suitcases and sat down beside her.

"Are you crying?" Thomas asked nervously.

She leaned back. "No. I'm just overwhelmed by all you two are doing on my behalf. This is so far beyond what a lawyer should do for a client."

"I was getting bored in my old age," Whiteside said.

"And I owed Coleman Rice a huge favor," Thomas added.

Judd stood. "You're both full of shit, and we thank you—more than you will ever know."

Thomas showed them where the remote was that opened the doors from inside, and where the override switch was in case of a power failure. "If you hear the fire alarms, evacuate the building. Otherwise, keep yourselves inside and out of sight."

"Absolutely," Judd said.

It wasn't until Whiteside started walking out with Thomas that Savannah realized he wasn't staying.

"Wait! Whiteside! What about you? You can't go back to that place on your own. They might kill you."

"Oh, don't worry. I'm not going to do anything stupid. You two just stay put. Talk to you later."

The door shut behind the two men, sealing them out, and Judd and Savannah in.

She frowned as she eyed the one-piece jumpsuit he was wearing.

"If the guys back at the ranch could see you now, you would never live it down."

He grimaced. "It feels even worse than it looks. I'm going to change."

"Me, too," she said, and went into the bedroom, where he'd left their bags.

She was reaching for her zipper when Judd stopped her with a touch.

"Let me, baby," he said softly.

Savannah's heart skipped a beat. Finally! But still...

"What if they come back?"

Judd shut the bedroom door, then turned the lock. "They'll get the message."

Nineteen

As soon as Savannah's clothes came off, Judd paused.

"Lord have mercy, Savannah. I don't know if this is such a good idea, after all."

"Strip, Judd. If we're going to have this conversation, I'm not going to be the only one who's nude."

Judd grinned. She might look like she'd been beaten within an inch of her life, but the fire was still there. This time he didn't hesitate. He stripped out of his clothes, turned back the bedcovers, then turned to face her.

"Is this better?"

Savannah moved closer. "Than that damned jumpsuit? Lord, yes." She put her hands on his chest. "Better than chocolate." Her hands slid downward. "Better than ice cream." Her hands encircled him. She looked up, locking into the heat of his gaze. "But not better than sex."

"Nothing is better than sex with you," Judd said as he scooped her off her feet and laid her on the bed, then crawled in beside her and cupped her face. "Ever since you walked out of my house, I've been afraid this would never happen again."

Savannah's eyes welled. "I'm sorry. I never meant to

hurt you. I never meant to hurt anyone, and yet it seems
that's all I've done since Daddy died."

"It isn't you, Savannah. It's what's happening *to* you.
I love you so much. Honestly, I can't remember when I
didn't."

"I remember when I fell in love with you. You were
riding your black horse in the Fourth of July parade
down Main Street in Missoula. You had on blue jeans,
a white long-sleeved shirt and a gray Stetson. Your left
arm was in a cast, and everyone was calling your name.
You looked straight at me and smiled. That's when I
knew you were the man I was going to marry."

"No way, sugar. That was the summer I graduated
high school. I was eighteen years old, which would have
made you—"

"Nine. I had just finished fourth grade."

She watched Judd's eyes widen with surprise. Suddenly she was in his arms and his mouth was on her lips.
Savannah gave herself up to the passion as Judd moved
up and then over her. She already knew the steps to the
dance, and when Judd started the music, she couldn't
wait to step in.

He had a hand on either side of her head, his arms
braced, his elbows locked to keep his weight off her
body. He eased inside her, watching her face to make
sure there was no pain, and then he began to move.

At the first thrust, Savannah moaned.

Startled, Judd paused. "Did I hurt you, baby?"

"No, God, no. It just felt so good."

"I can do better, way better," he said softly, and began
to prove it.

Savannah grabbed hold of his wrists and closed her
eyes. Just for a second she flashed on that moment when
her car had been airborne above the bay. How blue the

water had been, how the sun had sparkled on the ripples.
How cool the breeze had felt coming in through the open
window just before she hit.

Then Judd whispered her name and the image was
gone. There was nothing in her world to hang on to but
this man and the way they made love.

Thrust after strong, steady thrust, Judd rocked her
world. They lost track of time, locked in the pleasure,
and when she suddenly shifted and her legs locked
around his waist, he knew within a heartbeat when she
started to come. Her muscles tightened around him,
then began to swell. When she got hotter and tighter,
he thought he would die from the pleasure.

Suddenly her body was on fire, and she came in a
burst of heat and joy. It was his signal to let go. Her arms
were around him as Judd spilled himself in her with a
deep, guttural groan.

One second followed another as he waited for his
heart to stop thundering. His arms were trembling, his
body weak from his release, but he remembered enough
not to fall onto her. He pulled out and rolled off, then
collapsed on his back on the bed.

"Don't leave me," Savannah begged, and turned
toward him until she was against his side, her arm flung
across his chest.

Judd was still shaking as he pulled her closer. "Never,"
he said, then took her hand in his and closed his eyes.

Every instinct Whiteside had told him that he was
flying back into a waiting hell. Thomas had tried to get
him to tell the police, but he'd told the lawyer that there
wasn't anything to tell. All he had was a gut instinct, but
if there was a chance to take out this killer, he wasn't

going to let it pass. He came in low and fast as he neared his property, not sure what was waiting to greet him.

At first glance, everything looked the same. Hoping that he'd beaten the killer to the target, he headed for his landing pad. It was three hundred yards—the length of a football field—away from the house. He landed, shut everything down, then jumped out before the rotors stopped spinning and began to run, unlocking the gates with a remote. He ran through the gates in the wall surrounding the house and hit the veranda at a sprint, locking the gates behind him as he went. Within seconds he was inside. There were so many mementos of his past in here, but they were just things. He still had his memories, and if he was lucky, when this was over, he would still have his life, too. He ran into his bedroom, then into the room beyond. He hit the switch, flooding the small, windowless room with lights. He grabbed weapons off the wall, clipping them to his belt, then jamming extra clips of ammo into his pockets before he went for the rocket launcher. He hadn't used it in almost five years, but it was one of those things you never forgot. The duffel bag with the launcher's ammo was in a corner. He threw the strap over his shoulder and ran.

If it had been possible for a man to make a chopper strut, Tyson would have done it. He was so sure of himself, and of making this happen, that he'd been smiling ever since takeoff. The pilot, a man who called himself Chewy, was always ready to make some extra bucks. When Tyson contacted him about a night flight, his response made it clear that he figured it had something to do with a drug pickup and had no problem with that. If he'd known about the rocket launcher Tyson had on the floor beside his seat, he might have changed his mind.

The trip was so reminiscent of a night raid in Afghanistan that Tyson almost forgot where he was. Strapped into the seat, with the sides of the chopper open to the night, the wind whipping through the cabin and making his eyes tear from the sting, with the automatic rifle lying loosely across his lap, he had never felt more alive.

He tapped Chewy on the shoulder, pointing off to their right. The perimeter of the target was lit up like a church.

"Thanks for making this easy," Tyson muttered.

Chewy nodded and circled toward the light. "Where do you want me to put down?"

Tyson shook his head. "I don't," he said. "Just circle."

Chewy frowned. It seemed weird, but whatever.

Tyson traded the rifle in his lap for the rocket launcher and settled it on his shoulder.

Chewy freaked. "Hey! What the hell, man?"

"Shut up and do what I paid you to do," Tyson snapped. "Take it around again, and when I yell, you hover this sucker and hold it still or I'll make you sorry."

It was obviously too late to change his mind about the job. Chewy had no other option but to do as he was told.

He took the chopper in a wide sweeping circle, waiting for the order. When Tyson tapped his shoulder, he pulled up, holding the chopper as steady as he could.

When it suddenly dipped, Tyson fell forward, nearly losing the launcher. If he hadn't been strapped in, he would have fallen out. Chewy quickly pulled it up, but Tyson was already pissed.

"Hold it still, goddamn it!"

"Wind gust!" Chewy yelled.

"Whatever," Tyson muttered, then put the launcher back on his shoulder and took aim.

Whiteside was in a hunting stand built high in a tree nearly a thousand yards from his house. He'd been there for over an hour before he'd heard the distant sound of an approaching aircraft. He pulled on his night-vision goggles and knew within seconds it was a chopper. His muscles tensed. This could be a coincidence. He had to be sure before he decided to shoot something out of the sky.

As he waited, a slight breeze came up, drying the sweat running down his face and neck. It was a welcome relief. The rocket launcher was primed and on the floor beside him. Finally he saw the lights of the chopper. It was on a course straight toward his house. He held firm, waiting. When it got into his airspace and then began to circle, he knew.

He settled the rocket launcher on his shoulder. The chopper came back around, close enough now that Whiteside could see the pilot, and then the man beside him. When he realized he wasn't the only one with the same toy, he tried not to think of what was about to happen.

Suddenly the chopper dipped, and for just a second Whiteside thought the shooter was gone. But he managed to catch himself and the weapon, and pulled himself back just in time.

Whiteside took aim. To make one thing work, it was going to take losing another. He gritted his teeth, trying not to watch as the shooter fired from inside the chopper.

The rocket went straight into the middle of the roof.

The ensuing fireball blew the roof up and off in a thousand burning pieces. The rock wall began to crumble. He saw the pilot's face. He was in shock. Too bad. He was in for another.

Whiteside moved once, shifting his sight until he was staring straight at the smile of the man who'd launched the rocket.

"We'll see who has the last laugh," Whiteside said, and fired.

Then he watched, and he could tell they never saw it coming. One moment they were looking at a fireball, and then they *became* one.

The chopper flew into a thousand pieces, while what was left went end over end into the ground.

"Motherfucker," Whiteside muttered, then climbed down from his tree stand and started jogging toward his own chopper, thankful for his foresight in building the helipad well away from the house.

Within minutes he was airborne.

Thomas had tried to sleep but hadn't been able to get Whiteside out of his head. He knew what the man was facing and wondered if he'd been right—if the killer had really come tonight to take them out.

It was less than an hour before daybreak when he went into the kitchen to make coffee. Just as he slid the carafe into place and hit the on switch, his doorbell rang.

He turned abruptly and sprinted toward the front door. The outside light was on, spreading just enough illumination for Thomas to see a city cab backing out of his drive. Then he glanced through the peephole and saw Whiteside.

"I'll be damned," he muttered, and quickly let the man in. "Whiteside! What a nice surprise," he said.

"Not now, Jefferson. Because of you, I'm homeless."

Thomas gasped. "You were right? They hit your house?"

"With a rocket launcher. I regret to inform you that it appears all the residents perished, most likely from an explosion caused by a gas leak. Unfortunately, a chopper that just happened to be flying past the house became an unwitting victim and crashed due to flying debris."

"For real?"

"No. I had my own damned rocket launcher. But that's the story you and Barber are going to feed to the media. You keep her hidden. You let the world think she's dead. You'll get Stoss and his band of cohorts back in Miami so fast your head will spin. They'll think they have it all under control and will have some kind of story concocted that will give them a plausible alibi for everything that's been happening. Just when they think they've drawn a pass, you pull her out of your hat and watch them fall apart. If you're a betting man, I've got a hundred on the Hamilton woman as the one who gives them up."

Thomas slapped him on the back. "You are the man! You are the big fucking man!" He yanked Whiteside off his feet and into a bear hug that nearly killed him.

Whiteside struggled futilely. "Put me down, damn it! I can't breathe!"

Thomas dropped him on his feet, then shoved him toward the kitchen.

"I'm making breakfast. Name your poison."

Whiteside sighed. The man was crazy, but crazy smart. It was a trait anyone could appreciate.

* * *

Barber had the beginnings of a headache as he pulled into the parking lot at the station. He was in a mood that wasn't going to go away until Joseph Stoss and his two cousins were back in U.S. airspace. Al had taken two personal days and wouldn't be coming in. His wife was having surgery. Part of the time Barber was envious of Al's home life—a wife, two kids, four grandkids and a dog. But most of the time he was glad he didn't have anyone to answer to when he went home, and this was one of those times.

The sun was already working toward hot as he got out of his car. As he started inside, he heard someone calling his name. He turned around just as Jefferson pulled up in his Hummer.

"I need to talk to you!" Jefferson yelled. He pulled into a parking spot, then jumped out and headed toward Barber on the run.

Barber's gut knotted. Something had happened. "What's up?" he asked, trying to sound casual.

Jefferson loomed over him as he grabbed his arm and pulled him away from the stream of people coming and going at the P.D.

"There was another attempt on Savannah's life last night."

Barber felt sick. "Is she all right?"

"Yes. Thanks to Whiteside, she and Judd are in a new location. But a whole lot of shit has gone down. Last night a chopper flew over Whiteside's house. Someone used a rocket launcher and leveled his place, thinking Savannah was in it."

"How do you know this? How could Whiteside know? What if it was actually someone coming for him?"

"He knew, okay? He's known for days that someone

was hacking into all kinds of records, trying to trace the owner of an unlisted number on my calling log. He said they'd hacked utility records, credit cards, land records—everything you can think of where a phone number might have been listed that would lead them to a name. His name. He figured out yesterday afternoon that he'd been made, and that they had his location. We moved Savannah and Judd after dark. He went back and waited, knowing if they came it would be by air."

"How could he know that?" Barber asked.

Thomas smiled. "It was the only way in or out."

"Damn. That's taking solitude a little too far for me."

Thomas sighed. "Yet obviously not far enough. You need to understand that he willingly let them level his home to keep Savannah safe."

Barber's mouth dropped. "He let them do it?"

"Yes. And that's where you come in. We need the media to believe that Savannah Slade is dead, that she was staying with some friends, and their house had a gas leak, exploded and everyone perished. People can think what they want about another attempt on her life, but that needs to be the official statement. As an added bit of info, a passing helicopter was hit by flying shrapnel when the house exploded. It crashed, as well, killing everyone on board."

Barber started shaking his head. "Hell, no, we can't use an accident like that to further another story."

Thomas frowned. "I'm going to have to work on my summation skills a little bit. You aren't following me. It wasn't just any chopper flying by. It was the frigging hit man, get it? Whiteside let them blow up his house, then he took them out."

"What time is it?" Barber muttered.

Thomas frowned. "Why does it matter what time it is?"

"Because I need a drink, and I'm trying to figure out how many more hours I'm going to be on duty before that can happen."

"Oh." Thomas grinned. "So here's the reason you're going to want to get on board with this."

"I can't wait to hear," Barber said.

"If Stoss thinks his nemesis is dead and the threat to the family money is gone, he'll come back so fast it'll make your head spin. He won't care if his hit man went down in flames. There are no shortages of replacements. What he and his cousins will think is that they're home free. They'll have some kind of alibi cooked up that will completely exonerate them from all these other accusations, and I can guarantee you won't be able to break it. But get them into the precinct, then drop your evidence in their laps—along with a living, breathing Savannah Slade—and it's a done deal. For what it's worth, Whiteside has a hundred dollars on Elaine Hamilton being the one who cracks first."

Barber started to smile. "I think he's right. I wouldn't take that bet."

"Think you can get the powers that be to sit on the truth long enough to make this work?"

"Yes. The lieutenant was not happy that Stoss's lawyer got him off the hook, but a dead kid trumped an interview. We don't have enough evidence to arrest him, and we had no choice."

"Then I'll leave the rest of this up to you. If I get anything else that will strengthen your case against them, I'll let you know."

* * *

Judd was in the shower, and Savannah was in the kitchen making brunch. They'd slept late and missed breakfast, but were too hungry to wait for lunch. The television was on in the living room, but she was paying no attention as she began whisking eggs to make an omelet.

All of a sudden she heard the doors open, and Thomas came running into the apartment, yelling. The doors closed behind him as she dropped her whisk and ran out of the kitchen. Judd bolted from the bedroom with his fists doubled up and a towel wrapped around his waist. He was dripping wet but ready to fight.

"You have to hear this," Thomas said as he upped the volume on the TV.

"What the hell's going on?" Savannah asked.

"It's the report of your demise. Very sad, but most opportune for Mr. Stoss. Now that the story's broken, we expect him back in the country any time."

"The report of my *what?*"

Thomas pointed. "Pay attention. If you hadn't still been sleeping when I got to work, you would already know this."

Savannah sat down on the sofa. Judd started to join her, then stopped, since he was still dripping water on the floor.

"...shocking news just in. Savannah Slade, the woman who filed a lawsuit against the Stoss family claiming she was the rightful heir, has perished in a fire while visiting friends outside of the city. Authorities suspect a gas leak, but the fire marshal has yet to file his report. In a tragic aside to the incident, a helicopter with two passengers was flying past the house when it exploded. The helicopter was hit by flying debris and went down near the house. There are no survivors to either incident."

Savannah suddenly pointed toward the screen. "Whiteside's house. It's gone! Oh, my God! Was he inside? Please tell me he wasn't inside! Everything I've touched since this whole mess began has gone wrong. I shouldn't have come here. It was wrong. Wrong."

She began to cry, heartbroken that the man who'd saved her life had just lost his home and maybe his life.

"He's fine. He's at my house as we speak," Thomas said. "As for his house, this isn't something he will tell you, but I will. He let them do it. He was in the woods well beyond the helipad. He waited until they fired on his house, then took them out with a rocket launcher. Feeding the media this line that you've died was his idea. Now Stoss will think you're gone. He'll know it wasn't a random chopper that went down. He'll think his men got caught in the explosion and died accidentally, and he won't give a damn. Just two less people to pay off."

"For some reason, I can't hear this shit and be naked," Judd muttered. "Don't say anything more until I get back."

Thomas sat down beside Savannah. He felt her pain, but this was playing out the way it had to. He put an arm around her shoulders and gave her a quick hug, then handed her his handkerchief.

"Here. No need for crying. Everything is finally going according to plan."

"But his home...that crazy, beautiful home. It's gone."

"Again, his choice. He said it was just stuff."

Savannah began wiping tears as she tried to regain

control of her emotions. All of a sudden she jumped up and screamed.

Judd came flying back out of the bedroom with a pair of jeans half-buttoned and his fists doubled up once again. When he saw she was still standing, he shoved a shaky hand through his hair.

"Damn it, sugar. Either stop screaming or wait for me to get back before you do it again."

"We have to let Holly and Maria know I'm not dead."

Thomas frowned. "Oops. My bad."

"I'll do it," Judd said. "That's something I can handle that no one's going to trace."

"I don't think anyone will contact them, but be sure and tell them if anyone does try to get a statement from them, not to say anything other than that they're in mourning."

"Will do," Judd said, and walked into the kitchen to make the call.

"Sorry," Thomas said. "I thought I had all the corners tucked in. Good catch."

Savannah shuddered, then laid a hand on her heart. "It's still beating, which is no small miracle." Her jaw firmed as a glitter of anger swept over her face. "If I *am* named the Stoss heir, you tell Whiteside he's getting the biggest, fanciest house he could ever want to live in, with a state-of-the-art security system and all the firepower he can dream of."

"Wow. That might actually put a smile on his somber-ass face."

Savannah could hear Judd in the kitchen. It was obvious from his side of the conversation that one of her sisters had already seen the news and had been in the throes of hysterics when they received his call.

"I'd better go smooth this over," she said.

"Again, sorry I didn't think of that," Thomas said. "I'm going back to work. Shouldn't be bothering you anymore today unless something new breaks. In the meantime, check out the cabinet below the TV. There are a couple dozen DVDs if you get bored."

He patted the top of her head, then gave her a thumbs-up as he left.

Savannah hurried into the kitchen and slid beneath Judd's arm. He put the phone up to her ear.

"You talk," he said. "It's Holly, and she needs to hear your voice."

Twenty

It was raining in Montreal when the Stoss jet landed carrying the body of Anthony Stoss. The face Joseph presented to the world was one of stalwart grief. Michael and Elaine were grace personified. Quiet tears. Expressions of shock and disbelief. Their faces appeared in newspapers all over the world. The death of the heir to a multi-billion-dollar fortune was news anywhere. Already the tabloids were speculating on who Joseph Stoss might turn to in hopes of fathering yet another heir. Although he was in his fifties, he was by no means too old. Names of movie stars, daughters of industry moguls—no one was off-limits when it came to the possibility of bearing another heir.

Joseph came off the plane last and walked bareheaded to where his son's casket was being unloaded. He watched in stoic silence as it was transferred to a hearse. Michael and Elaine had already been seated inside a waiting limo. When Joseph finally joined them, his silver-gray hair was beaded with moisture, as was his face. Michael couldn't tell if it was tears or raindrops, then realized the point was moot and looked away.

Elaine was wearing sunglasses even though there

was no sun. It had seemed appropriate to her to hide her grief in some way, since the days of black hats and veils were gone.

By the time they reached the cemetery housing the Stoss mausoleum the rain had become a downpour. The casket was unloaded and wheeled inside. There was a brief ceremony as a waiting clergyman read a chosen passage. The torrent of rain was muted inside the structure but still made a suitable accompaniment to what was happening. Soon it was over. Anthony Joseph Stoss had just joined his ancestors in their final resting place.

Elaine clung to Michael, her head bowed in grief. Tears were shimmering in Michael's eyes. But Joseph was dry-eyed and grim. Only the tic of a muscle at the side of his jaw gave away what he must have been feeling.

On their way out of the cemetery, Joseph gave the driver the order to take them back to the airport.

Michael frowned. They'd been on that plane since leaving Geneva, and he had been hoping to at least spend the night in the family home nearby.

But it was Elaine who saved him the trouble of complaining.

"I was hoping to stay overnight at Pine Hill."

Joseph had been staring out the window, but at her remark he turned his head.

"This is the fourth day. Because you stuck your nose into business that didn't concern you and confronted Gerald's bastard, we have to be at the Miami police station tomorrow or face arrest, remember?"

Elaine paled.

Michael sighed. Joseph was being a bastard, but he didn't have the heart to start a fight.

Within an hour they were back on board. Elaine went straight to her seat and buckled in. Michael took a glass of bourbon and Coke with him to his seat. The irony of his drink and Elaine without was not lost on him.

The pilot handed Joseph a sealed envelope as he came on board.

"A message from your office, sir. It came by fax while you were at the cemetery."

Joseph stuck it in his pocket, then pulled off his jacket and laid it on the back of the seat beside him. He buckled in without looking at either of the others, his thoughts already in cleanup mode. It had taken grief to remind him of something he'd nearly forgotten. Gerald was the one who'd gotten them into this mess. It was going to be Gerald who got them out.

Very few knew it, but when Gerald was nineteen, he had wrecked a car. The girl who'd been with him was killed. He'd walked away with hardly a scratch, and her family had been devastated. Rupert Stoss had paid the family a huge sum of money to soothe their grief. Now Joseph had woven a story to release to the media that once the girl's family, still grieving and resentful, learned Gerald had a daughter they had decided to enact a retribution of their own. It wasn't perfect, and there were only three members of the immediate family still living in the area, but he was sure it would be enough to take the heat off of his own family.

The plane took off. They'd been in the air almost an hour before Joseph remembered the envelope. He got up to get himself a glass of wine and then took out the envelope as he sat back down.

"What's that?" Michael asked.

"Probably another letter of condolence," Joseph said, and ripped it open. Within seconds, his face became animated. "Finally!" he said, and downed the wine in one gulp.

Elaine glared. She'd been barred from any liquor during the entire four days and was suffering from withdrawal as well as from grief. "What could you possibly have to celebrate?"

"She's dead," Joseph said.

Breath caught at the back of Michael's throat.

Elaine gasped. "Who's dead?"

"Gerald's bastard. Here's the story that ran in the *Miami Herald*."

He tossed it to her, then got up to get himself another glass of wine. He'd lost his son. Gerald's daughter was dead. An eye for an eye.

She looked up, her voice shrill with disbelief. "A gas leak?"

Joseph smiled. "Which do you want more? The truth...or this glass of wine?"

Elaine jumped up from her seat, dropping the fax on the floor. "I hate you," she said, and stumbled toward the bathroom.

"You are one cold son of a bitch," Michael said as he retrieved the letter. He scanned it quickly, then shook his head. "All this has done is get us in deeper with the police. You know they're not going to believe this."

"They will when I tell them what I remembered as I was burying my son."

"God almighty, Joseph! You'd use Tony's death as part of your lies?"

A trace of true anger slid across Joseph's face before he got himself in check. "I'll use whatever it takes to get our lives back."

Michael just shook his head, as if he couldn't believe what his cousin had just said. "Do you know how pitiful that sounds? You'll use your son's death to get *your* life back. That's what you mean."

"I didn't kill Tony. He killed himself. He should have been stronger. My heart is broken for what is gone, but I'm still here, and I have a dynasty to preserve."

"There is no dynasty. Not anymore. We just buried the Stoss future back in Montreal."

"I'm not dead yet," Joseph said. "It's my duty to produce an heir, and I will."

Michael sneered. "So that means you're getting married again."

"Why?"

"I just assumed you'd have to. I mean, you wouldn't recognize Gerald's illegitimate child, surely you aren't so two-faced as to think your bastard would be any better."

Rage swept through Joseph so fast he had his fists doubled before he knew it had happened.

Michael saw the response and smiled.

"What? You're going to beat me up for speaking the truth? How original of you, Joseph. You paint yourself as the epitome of virtue when you are one lying son of a bitch. So the girl is dead. God bless her. I hope she haunts your sorry ass every night for the rest of your life."

Ignoring the fact that Joseph was pretty much ready to punch him, Michael reclined his seat and laid the newspaper he'd been reading over his face. It was useless to try to reason with a crazy man.

Joseph was pissed that Michael had called him out, but he didn't care to push the issue. He'd figured out how to accomplish what he'd set out to do. Within twenty-four hours they would be out from under police radar and back in the good graces of polite society.

* * *

At four o'clock the door to Thomas's office opened and Paul Stern stepped in. He walked up to Laura's desk with an apologetic expression.

"My name is Paul Stern, of Stern and Stern. I just received an express letter from Geneva, Switzerland, that was to have been hand delivered to Miss Savannah Slade. However, since her recent demise, I thought the proper thing to do was bring it to her lawyer. May I speak to Mr. Jefferson? I assure you, it won't take long."

"Of course," Laura said. "Just a moment, please." She buzzed Thomas's office. "Mr. Jefferson? Mr. Paul Stern to see you regarding Miss Slade's estate."

"Send him in," Thomas said, and then got up and met the other attorney at the door. "Come in, Paul. Would you care for something to drink?"

"No, thank you. This is an awkward moment, but I have something for Miss Slade from Anthony Stoss. I just received it by special delivery this afternoon. I was to hand deliver it to her myself, but now, with her demise, I thought it best to bring it to you, as her representative."

He handed the FedEx packet to Thomas without hesitation.

Thomas didn't bother to hide his shock. "From Joseph's son?"

Paul shrugged. "I know, it's a bit awkward, but I got a phone call from Tony right after the story about her ran in the paper. He was very upset. He informed me that he was sending something special delivery that I was to put in her hands. I had no idea that I would be the last person on this side of the Atlantic to speak to him alive."

"Does Joseph know about this?"

Paul frowned. "He knows Tony called me, but he has no knowledge of why."

"You're Joseph's lawyer. Miss Slade was suing your client for control of the family fortune, and yet you agreed to bring this?"

Paul didn't falter in his answer. "I admit it gave me pause, but in the long run, I was also Tony's lawyer, and I am a strong proponent of attorney/client privilege."

"Then thank you," Thomas said. "Whatever it is, I'll see that it gets to her family."

Paul nodded. "I'll be going, then. Just so you know, Joseph and the rest of the family will be back in Miami sometime today. They will be speaking to Detective Barber tomorrow in his office. I'm sure we'll have this misunderstanding cleared up soon."

Thomas frowned. "'Misunderstanding' is an odd word to use in regard to murder. However, we're not in court, and I'm not going to debate semantics with you."

Paul smiled as he stood. "I like you, Thomas. You are a wise man and a damned good lawyer."

"Thank you," Thomas said. "I'll walk you out."

It was a blunt indication that their conversation was over, but that was fine with Paul. He'd done what he had to do. His last responsibility to Anthony Stoss had just been dispatched.

As soon as the other man was gone, Thomas closed the door. "Laura, I'm shutting down business for the day. Whatever you're doing can wait until tomorrow. Take an early night. Have dinner. Go to a movie. Do something that makes you thankful you're alive."

Laura's face crumpled. Like the rest of Miami, she believed that Savannah Slade was dead.

"I'm so sorry, Mr. Jefferson. She was a wonderful young woman. It isn't right what happened."

"Maybe we can make it right," he said. "For now, just go home. I'll lock up."

She saved the brief she'd been typing onto her computer, got her purse and quickly left the office. As soon as she was gone, Thomas locked the door and then loped back into his office, grabbed the pack Paul had given him and paid a visit to his guests.

"Hello, hello!" he said as he strode into the apartment.

Savannah was sitting on the living room floor surrounded by an assortment of DVDs. When she heard the doors sliding open, she looked up and smiled.

"Judd! We have company!"

Judd came out of the kitchen carrying a bowl of popcorn.

"What's up?"

Thomas grabbed a handful of the hot fresh popcorn as he sat down on the sofa.

"I'm not sure, but I have a gut feeling it could be good." He handed Savannah the packet.

"What's this?"

"Paul Stern was just here. He said he was supposed to hand deliver this to you, but since you were dead and because I'm your representative, he left it with me. But that's not the surprising part. The surprise is that it's from Anthony Stoss."

Savannah gasped. "You're not serious!"

"Yes, I am. So hurry up and open it, or I'll do it for you."

Savannah fumbled with the packet, trying to open it from one end, then the other.

Judd crouched down beside her.

"Let me help," he said, and used his pocket knife to open one end, then handed it back and stood.

Savannah grabbed his hand, tugging him down onto the floor beside her, then pulled the contents out into her lap.

"It's a letter. Oh, my God, it's a letter to me."

"For Pete's sake, read it out loud before I have a stroke," Thomas said.

Savannah's hands were trembling as she began to read.

"My Dear Cousin,

It is with a saddened heart that I have just learned of your existence, and of what you have been forced to endure at the hands of my family. Honor is without price, therefore it seems we have none. At this moment in my life, I am horrified that I bear the Stoss name, and fervently regret what my father has done to you and those you love. You bear no guilt in any of this. I am the one who bears the shame. I was given no choice as to having been born into the family, but I have a choice to remove myself from it. I do so with the hope that when it is time, we will finally meet in heaven.

Tony."

By the time she got to the end, Savannah was crying. Thomas was in shock. He hadn't opened his mouth once since "my dear cousin." They'd just been handed the last piece in the puzzle that they'd needed for court acceptance and recognition from the heir himself.

Judd took the letter out of her hand and read it again.

"I sure didn't see this coming," he said as he handed it to Thomas.

"No one could have. This is going to tear the lawsuit wide open."

"They'll say we made it up," Judd said.

"All I have to do is subpoena their own lawyer, Paul Stern. He hand delivered the package."

"Did he know what was in it?" Savannah asked.

"Most assuredly not. But it's handwritten, not typed. And there have to be examples all over the place of Tony Stoss's handwriting." He stood. "Needless to say, this is going in the safe."

"It's a good thing you asked for my journal and the pictures, and all the other papers I brought, or they'd be in the harbor."

"I think ahead, although I will admit I never thought any of that would ever happen."

Savannah's shoulders dropped. "Poor Tony."

Judd cupped her face, then made her look at him. "Poor little rich boy. Poor little rich girl. You both learned the hard way that money can't buy happiness."

"I'm still so sad. I think we would have liked each other," she said, and then climbed into his lap and hid her face against his shoulder.

"One more thing," Thomas said. "The Stosses will be back in Miami before the night is over. They're meeting Barber at police headquarters tomorrow. So try to get a good night's rest. As the old saying goes, 'All is about to be revealed.'"

"We'll be ready," Judd said.

"I'll get you some disguises, so I can get you into Homicide unobserved."

"Just make sure it's not another damned high-water jumpsuit," Judd muttered.

That made Savannah laugh, which was what he had intended.

"It's a promise," Thomas said. He gave them a thumbs-up as the doors closed behind him.

Savannah was too still, Judd thought. She hadn't moved and wouldn't look at him. He could tell she was still overwhelmed by what she'd read.

"What are you feeling, honey?"

"I don't know. Sad. Regretful. Determined. And basically pissed off."

"That's my girl." He kissed the top of her head, then pulled the bowl of popcorn toward them. "What did you pick out for us to watch?"

"I was leaning toward a romantic comedy, but after all this, I've changed my mind." She scooted out of his lap, crawled over to the corner of the cabinet and pulled out another DVD. "What do you think about this one?"

"Avatar?"

She nodded. "Still has a love story, but a whole lot of bad guys die and the underdogs win."

Judd grinned. "Works for me," he said, and put it into the Blu-Ray and pressed Play.

Savannah leaned against his shoulder as the movie opened, but was back in his lap before the opening credits were over.

The parking lot and the entire public area outside the Miami P.D. were swarming with news crews, some from as far away as Orlando. Everyone wanted a photo of the bereaved family who were still under investigation. Considering the recent death of the woman who'd challenged their inheritance, it was an O. J. Simpson moment to the power of ten.

Journalists shouted out questions and kept calling Joseph's name. In contrast to his usual habit of courting their favor, he didn't acknowledge their presence. The trio walked in stoic silence into the Miami P.D. accompanied by all six of the lawyers from the firm of Stern and Stern.

Joseph felt like swaggering, but it wouldn't be seemly, considering his recent grief. He had his sad face on, his steps purposefully slower, as if laden with a burden too heavy to bear. They were taken directly to Homicide and from there into an interrogation room. Extra seating had to be brought in for all of the lawyers, and then they settled in to wait for Detective Barber to show up.

Joseph was the first one to look up into the mirror, well aware it was two-way. He almost smiled, as if he knew he was being watched, then casually looked away, too important to be concerned.

Frank Barber was in the darkened room on the other side of the glass, watching the family's arrival, gauging the mood of the group by the expressions on their faces.

Savannah and Judd were on his left. Jefferson stood on his right. Savannah stepped closer to the window, studying the faces of Joseph and his cousins, and more than a little startled to see a bit of herself in each of them.

Suddenly Joseph looked straight at the mirror again, as if sensing he was being watched.

Savannah jumped. Judd caught her hand. It was all she needed to remind her that she was not alone.

"He's not worried," Thomas said.

"He doesn't know he should be," Barber said.

"What do we do?" Savannah whispered.

Barber could hear the tremor in her voice.

"Don't worry, Miss Slade. By the time you make your appearance, they're going to be too shocked to confront you."

"And I'll be right behind you," Judd said. "You're no longer alone in this fucking mess."

Barber tried not to take that personally, but it was yet another reminder of his part in what had happened. Today was his chance for redemption, and he was going to enjoy every second of it. With a nod to the others, he left the room.

Moments later, he and Soldana walked into the interrogation room. All eyes turned to watch them.

Barber made a production of sitting, then laying out a number of file folders. Soldana began setting up a video camera he'd brought, making sure it was aimed so that it would catch the faces of all three Stosses.

Joseph frowned, then leaned over to his lawyer, who promptly addressed the issue with Barber.

"Detective, nothing was mentioned to me about taping this interview," Stern said.

"That's because you're in my house now, and I make the rules," Frank said.

Joseph frowned, but when Paul would have pushed the issue, he stopped him with a single motion.

"He won't be so cocky when Frank gets through with him," Thomas said.

Savannah was standing between two very large men, both of whom were there for her, but there was a part of her that felt the presence of several other people. Her father, Gerald, and her mother, Chloe. Phyllis Palmer, the grandmother she'd never gotten to know. And Tony Stoss, a throwback to the time when his family name meant more than how much money they were worth. She wondered what they would think about the house of Stoss coming to this.

Sensing her emotional state, Judd moved behind her, slid an arm across her breasts so that she was enclosed within his grasp and whispered in her ear, "If you get tired, lean on me."

Quick tears rose, but she held them at bay. A few seconds later, the interview began.

Barber had his opening questions planned a dozen different ways, but when the time came, he cast them aside and jumped in with both feet. He reached for the first folder lying to his right and flipped it open.

Joseph's gaze immediately slid to the contents, but he was too far away to read what they said.

"For the record," Barber said, "I would like each of you to state your name. And by each of you, I mean the three members of the Stoss family. Not your representatives." Then he pointed at Joseph.

The man's color was high, evidence of how incensed he was to be here, but he answered politely enough.

"Joseph Anton Stoss."

"Michael Stoss."

"Elaine Stoss Hamilton."

"Thank you," Frank said, and then pulled the folder closer to him. "I have two cases pending in which your individual names or your family name has come up time and again. It is for those reasons that I've asked you here today. Mr. Joseph Stoss, did you have anything to do with the attacks on Savannah Slade?"

"No, I did not," Joseph said. "Nor have any members of my family."

"I'd rather they answered for themselves," Frank said.

"I have not," Michael said quickly.

"Nor have I," Elaine said.

"This is the report from the crime scene investigators regarding Miss Slade's car, the car that was involved in the accident that nearly took her life on the causeway. The accelerator had been tampered with. There was no way she could have stopped her car. At the time, she claimed that a dark SUV with heavily tinted windows tried to ram her several times, then forced her onto the causeway, knowing there was nowhere for her to go but into the bay. We have several sworn affidavits from eyewitnesses attesting to that same fact. After that attempt on her life, yet another was made at the hospital the same day. One of our own, a policeman named Allan Daly, confessed that he'd been offered a million dollars to make sure she didn't live through the night. He didn't know who was behind the money, but we know who in this room has the money to give."

Joseph reeled as if he'd been slapped, but to his credit, he remained silent.

Savannah kept watching their faces as the detective talked. After Joseph's initial response, they appeared bored, almost insulted by having to be there. But it was early. She hoped the more Barber revealed, the more desperate they would become.

"A couple of days ago, a hunter found a black SUV with dark windows abandoned in the Everglades. Upon its removal from the water, CSI learned the VIN had been removed. But the SUV was equipped with a security feature that allowed the security company to remotely stop the car's engine should it be stolen. After consulting with the company, we learned that the car was part of a fleet belonging to Stoss Industries."

Joseph's eyelid twitched, but it was his only sign of

emotion. Michael looked shocked, and Elaine was in the first stage of panic.

"Detective, is it appropriate for me to rebut this fact now, or would you rather I wait until you've finished?" Stern asked.

Frank eyed the lawyer. "Actually, you don't get to rebut any of my facts. If the district attorney thinks we have enough evidence to charge your clients, you'll get ample time to rebut during trial."

"Trial? You said everything was going to be okay!" Elaine cried, glaring at Joseph.

His nostrils flared. "Shut up. Now."

Elaine hiccupped on a sob and put her fingers over her mouth, as if words might otherwise get out without her permission.

"And we continue," Frank said, and reached for yet another file. He flipped it open. On top were crime scene photographs of Phyllis Palmer's body crumpled pitifully against a wall. He casually pushed them aside, well aware that they were in full view of the trio on the other side of the table, as he reached for the accompanying report.

"That same SUV was also identified as being of the same make and model of a car seen at the residence of Phyllis Palmer, Savannah Slade's maternal grandmother, only minutes before her murder."

Michael grunted. He hadn't meant to, but he felt like he'd just been sucker-punched. He wouldn't look up. He couldn't face the glare he knew would be on Joseph's face, so he dug at a hangnail instead.

Stern spoke up again, this time more forcefully. "Detective! I object to this line of questioning. You are trying to point blame at a family who are in the midst of a most shocking and devastating grief, and you know of what I speak. The suicide of Joseph Stoss's son, Tony."

"I am pointing blame at a family who had everything to lose and nothing to gain by allowing Savannah Slade to live." Barber reached for the third folder. When he opened it, Elaine actually leaned forward, her eyes wide with shock.

On the other side of the mirror, Thomas groaned. "Whiteside is so going to win his money."

"What do you mean?" Judd asked.

"He bet me a hundred dollars that the Hamilton woman was going to be the one to break first."

Savannah barely knew they were speaking. She was as locked into Barber's story as Elaine Hamilton appeared to be.

Judd could feel the tension in her body. He feared for her endurance and wished she could sit down, but knew she wasn't moving for anything but the truth. All he could do was hold her.

Back inside, Frank began pulling out copies of everything Savannah Slade had presented as evidence of her right to inherit.

"Don't try to tell me that you weren't concerned, or that Savannah Slade didn't have a case. You all know exactly what it was, but I will repeat it for the record. She had a birth certificate with your late brother's name on it, naming him as her father. Her DNA test. A test none of you will submit to for purposes of refutation. Photos of her mother, Chloe Stewart, and your brother, Gerald, in an obvious embrace, laughing, kissing, hugging and mugging for the camera, proof of a relationship that was obviously close. A letter from her birth mother in which she tells her daughter why she gave her to a stranger to raise. A letter that states that on the day Gerald Stoss died, she received a phone call from Joseph, a call in which he told her that if she tried to make a claim on the family money on her daughter's behalf, he would kill her daughter just like he killed Gerald."

Michael moaned and laid his head down on the table.

Joseph's face was flushed. His hands were doubled into fists.

"Paul!" he snapped.

"The detective still has the floor," Stern said.

Barber pulled out a thick stack of papers that had been bound together. "This is a copy of a journal left to her by the man she knew as her father. She received it less than a month ago, during the reading of his will. Before that, she knew nothing of her past. And it was because she learned her birth father had been murdered, not because she knew he was rich, that she decided to come forth."

"You say that now!" Joseph said. "But everybody wants what we have."

Stern grabbed Joseph's arm, digging his fingers into the muscle to make his point.

"Joseph! I recommend you let the detective finish and don't argue the point."

Barber reached for the last folder. The moment he opened it, Stern recognized the packet. It was what Tony had sent to Savannah Slade. He didn't know what was coming, but wondered if, in hindsight, he would still have delivered that letter to Jefferson.

Barber pulled a piece of paper from inside the packet. "This letter will be entered into evidence, too."

"We have not been charged with anything!" Joseph yelled.

"I'm not finished," Barber snapped.

Joseph regretted the outburst, but it was too late. He hadn't even had a chance to use his story, and as he sat there, he realized it wouldn't have worked, anyway. Not with all this evidence pointing straight at them and not at an old enemy of Gerald's.

"This letter was sent special delivery from Geneva, Switzerland, to the law firm of Stern and Stern, with a request for it to be personally delivered into Savannah Slade's hands."

In the other room, it was all Thomas could do not to shout, "Oh, man, oh, man, here it comes!"

Savannah clutched Judd's arm as he held her close.

Inside, Joseph had turned on Paul with a look of disbelief. Michael felt sick to his stomach. Elaine was on the verge of hyperventilating and no one seemed to notice.

Barber tilted the letter to the light. "I will read this in its entirety, and there will be no outbursts.

"'My Dear Cousin, It is with a saddened heart that I have just learned of your existence, and of what you have been forced to endure at the hands of my family.'"

Joseph jerked as if he'd been slapped. Paul grabbed him by the arm as Barber continued.

"'Honor is without price, therefore it seems we have none. At this moment in my life, I am horrified that I bear the Stoss name, and fervently regret what my father has done to you and to those you love.'"

"No," Joseph mumbled, and began shaking his head from side to side, refusing to believe this was real.

Barber glared, but kept on reading. "'You bear no guilt in any of this. I am the one who bears the shame. I was given no choice as to having been born into the family, but I have a choice to remove myself from it. I do so with the hope that when it is time, we will finally meet in heaven. Tony.'"

"That's not real!" Joseph shouted. "You made that up to strengthen your case."

Barber laid the letter down in front of them.

Joseph grabbed it, but Barber didn't react, only said, "I believe this is your son's handwriting, which can easily be verified. And it's just a copy, so ripping it up would be futile." Then he turned and nodded toward the window.

"This is our cue," Thomas said. "Stay tough, Savannah. We're right beside you."

Savannah was ready. She needed to confront them on behalf of so many people besides herself. She clung to Judd's hand as they walked out to the hall and into the interrogation room.

Joseph was cursing at his lawyers and both cousins when he saw the door open. Thinking it was the police come to officially arrest him, he was ready to react. Then he looked up and saw Thomas Jefferson.

"You have no business here!" he shouted.

"As a matter of fact, I do," Thomas said, and stepped aside, revealing the woman behind him, still bearing the marks left from the Stosses' attacks—and still bearing the marks of the Stosses themselves: round blue eyes and the telltale white-blond hair.

"No!" Joseph screamed. "They said you were dead! You're supposed to be dead!"

"We lied," Thomas said.

Joseph leaped, screaming, "Bastard!" as he went for Savannah's face.

Savannah heard a roar, and then Judd flew past her, hitting Joseph Stoss with a blow to the chin that sent him careening past his chair and into the wall. Joseph tried to fight back, but Judd hit him again, and then both men went down. At that point several officers raced into the room and began pulling them apart.

Lawyers scrambled to get up and out of the way, unwilling to become more deeply tainted by their clients' problems than they already were.

"Let him go," Barber told the other cops, pointing at Judd. "He was only reacting to a threat to his fiancée."

Elaine suddenly exploded from her chair, screaming and pointing at Joseph before anyone could react.

"It was him! It was all his idea! We didn't know! He doesn't tell us anything."

Joseph turned on her, cursing and shouting. "You stupid bitch! You never know when to keep your mouth shut! And everything you're saying is a lie. You knew. You both knew and said nothing. All you cared about was that the money kept rolling into your pockets, too."

Michael sighed. No need to talk. He would let the lawyers do it for him at trial.

Elaine was all but foaming at the mouth, and Joseph was slowly coming undone. It was Tony's letter that had unhinged him. Seeing it written in his son's own hand, that he was ashamed of the family and of his father, had been too much.

All of a sudden Savannah was pushing herself forward, her shoulders squared, her head thrown back in a gesture of defiance.

"I have something to say." When no one seemed to be listening, she said it louder. "I have something to say!" The furor was still in progress, although Judd had heard her and was already moving toward her when she

suddenly put her fingers between her lips and let out a
whistle so shrill it startled the room into silence.

"Thank you," she snapped. "Now that I have your
attention, I have something to say."

Joseph opened his mouth.

Savannah pointed at him to shut up.

Judd spun, physically putting himself between Savannah and the others. Then he felt her hand on his back.

"I've got this one."

He stepped aside but not away. Not while the devil
was still in the room.

Savannah was shaking, but she was the only one still
living who could speak for the dead.

"You know the sad part about all this crap? You did
all of it for nothing. I was just a baby. You would still
have been in charge. Did no one ever think of that?
Now you're getting exactly what you deserve. Gerald
can finally rest in peace, and my grandmother's murder
has been avenged. You live behind your status and your
money, but at heart, you are curs. I may be illegitimate,
but you are the people without honor. I will inherit the
money, but it will take a lifetime to live down the shame
of what you've made of the family name."

Joseph wanted to retaliate, but the words wouldn't
come. He was looking at her, but he kept seeing Tony's
face. It made no sense, so he looked away as they handcuffed him and removed him from the room.

Elaine began to wail as they led her away in handcuffs.

It was Michael who asked them to wait and turned
toward Savannah. "'Sorry' doesn't cover what has been
done to you, but I *will* say it, just the same. I *am* sorry,
Savannah Slade, on so many levels. I hope you have a
long and happy life."

Barber motioned to the officers. "Get him out of here." Then he turned to the lawyers. "All of you, out. We're done here."

Soldana followed them out, but Barber had something of his own to say to Savannah.

"I owe you an apology. That day you came to me asking for help, I blew you off. It was a far-fetched story, and I told myself you were just someone out to con the family. I'm the one who told Stoss you were here. Like Michael Stoss said, I, too, am sorry on so many levels."

Judd gasped. "Damn it, man! You nearly got her killed!"

Savannah grabbed Judd's arm as he started toward the cop. "No. Don't, Judd! It was a crazy story. Even I struggled with the truth. What's done is done, and he's the one who has to live with it on his conscience."

Barber nodded, she was right, and it wouldn't be easy.

"The important thing is that it's over," Thomas said.

"All except the shouting," Judd added, then took Savannah in his arms. "Ready to go home?"

"Yes. Dear God, yes," she said.

Thomas frowned. "Hey. You have to be back for all the court dates, remember?"

"There are flights between Miami and Montana that go both ways. I'll be back when I have to be back," Savannah said. "In the meantime, I have a wedding to plan."

"And a ring to go with your credit card," Judd said.

Barber frowned. "What's that mean?"

"Don't ask," Savannah said, then laughed, and when she did, it felt like the first laugh in a lifetime of laughter to come.

Epilogue

Four months later

Whiteside was right behind them as Judd and Savannah walked into the mansion on Palm Island. A small Latino woman stood by the staircase with a nervous expression on her face.

Savannah walked up to her, hoping her smile would ease this moment.

"Estella, right?"

"*Sí, señora.* Estella."

"I'm Savannah Stoss-Holyfield. This is my husband, Judd, and this man is Alan Whiteside, the new head of security for Stoss Industries. He is also the new owner of this home."

Estella smiled nervously. "*Bienvenida,* Señor Whiteside."

"Just Whiteside, and in English," he said, then managed a quick smile to ease the bite in his words.

"*Sí,* Whiteside," Estella said.

Savannah laughed, then turned around and dropped the keys to the house in his hand.

"It's not a maze, but it's a replacement," she said.

Whiteside's fingers curled around the keys as he took in the elegance of the foyer, well aware that there was much more to discover.

"It'll do," he said, and gave her a wink.

"Don't forget the board meeting in an hour," she reminded him.

He nodded. "I'll be there."

Judd slipped an arm under Savannah's elbow. "You ready, sugar?"

Savannah nodded.

"Being the new man of the house, I'll see you to the door," Whiteside said, then waved them off as they drove away.

Savannah leaned back and closed her eyes as the limo began to move. They'd been to the cemetery earlier to make sure the tombstone on her grandmother's grave had finally been set. It was heart-wrenching to see mother and daughter together in death when they'd been so estranged in life.

Judd knew she was struggling, and how much this meant to her. He just wished he could make the nausea go away.

"I'm so sorry you're not feeling good."

Savannah laid a hand across the slight swell of her belly. "Morning sickness is supposed to pass. Hopefully before your child is born."

Judd laid his hand on her stomach. It was too soon to feel the baby kick, but it was the closest he could get to it until it was born.

"Are you nervous? About facing the board of directors? Do I need to check and see if they have Skype hooked up yet?"

Forced to return to the present, Savannah agreed. "That would be good. Whether they like it or not, I intend to hold as many as possible at home through Skype."

Judd was still stunned that she'd been determined to relocate her office and personal staff, and run the company from the ranch. She'd made it perfectly clear that after what she'd gone through, she didn't want their children growing up with the dangerous sense of entitlement that came from living in the lap of luxury.

"Whatever you need to do, we can make it happen," he said.

"I know. I really appreciate the wing you added to the house. I can't wait to get everything hooked up and I'm not the only one. My poor secretary is tired of working from the extra bedroom. I've been wading through reports for months, so I'm confident of what to expect. One day soon I'll get a handle on all this and it will become a matter of course."

"Spoken like a true business czar."

She snorted lightly. "Not yet. Not by a long shot."

The limo began slowing down.

She looked out, then frowned as she began to shift mental gears. "I guess we're here. Remember, once I go into the meeting, you make yourself scarce. I can't let them think I'm too scared to face them on my own. And I won't really be alone, anyway. I'm introducing Whiteside as the new head of security, and I'll have legal counsel there, as well."

"I'm not worried. You're one tough lady." Then he tweaked her nose. "However, tough lady, just remember I'll be as close as a phone call if you need me."

Savannah squeezed his hand one last time, then flicked a piece of lint from her dark slacks. The black pantsuit she was wearing was a stark and stunning contrast to her hair and eyes, as was the red knit top she'd added for contrast. Red and black were power colors, and today she needed all the power she could get.

Once inside Stoss Industries, she was met in the lobby by one of the managers, who proudly escorted her to the top floor of the building, where the board of directors met.

"Here we are, Mrs. Holyfield. It was a pleasure to meet you," he added, then left her at the penthouse door.

But she wasn't alone. There was another group in the hallway obviously waiting for her arrival. She eyed them curiously, then smiled as the new head of their legal department turned and saw she'd arrived.

"You made it!"

Savannah was engulfed in a hug. They'd been through too much together to stand on ceremony.

"Thomas. So good to see you again."

Thomas Jefferson beamed. "You, too. You're glowing. I hope you and the baby are well."

"We're fine. I have my moments, but it's nothing that won't pass." She looked past him to the lineup of lawyers waiting to be introduced. "Are these the members of the firm?"

"Yes, ma'am," Thomas said, and quickly introduced her to the five lawyers he'd handpicked to work with him, most of whom specialized in some form of business or international law. Then he checked his watch. "It's time. We don't want to keep the board waiting."

She paused. "Where's Whiteside?"

He stepped out of the doorway behind her. "I'm right here."

He winked as he walked past her, then opened the door. Inside, twenty pairs of eyes turned toward the sound. The board of directors of Stoss Industries awaited her arrival.

Savannah lifted her chin, her eyes gleaming.

* * * * *

  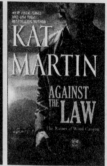

REQUEST YOUR FREE BOOKS!

2 FREE NOVELS
FROM THE SUSPENSE COLLECTION
PLUS 2 FREE GIFTS!

YES! Please send me 2 FREE novels from the Suspense Collection and my 2 FREE gifts (gifts are worth about $10). After receiving them, if I don't wish to receive any more books, I can return the shipping statement marked "cancel." If I don't cancel, I will receive 4 brand-new novels every month and be billed just $5.74 per book in the U.S. or $6.24 per book in Canada. That's a saving of at least 28% off the cover price. It's quite a bargain! Shipping and handling is just 50¢ per book in the U.S. and 75¢ per book in Canada.* I understand that accepting the 2 free books and gifts places me under no obligation to buy anything. I can always return a shipment and cancel at any time. Even if I never buy another book, the two free books and gifts are mine to keep forever.

191/391 MDN FDDH

Name	(PLEASE PRINT)

Address	Apt. #

City	State/Prov.	Zip/Postal Code

Signature (if under 18, a parent or guardian must sign)

Mail to the **Reader Service:**
IN U.S.A.: P.O. Box 1867, Buffalo, NY 14240-1867
IN CANADA: P.O. Box 609, Fort Erie, Ontario L2A 5X3

Not valid for current subscribers to the Suspense Collection
or the Romance/Suspense Collection.

Want to try two free books from another line?
Call 1-800-873-8635 or visit www.ReaderService.com.

* Terms and prices subject to change without notice. Prices do not include applicable taxes. Sales tax applicable in N.Y. Canadian residents will be charged applicable taxes. Offer not valid in Quebec. This offer is limited to one order per household. All orders subject to credit approval. Credit or debit balances in a customer's account(s) may be offset by any other outstanding balance owed by or to the customer. Please allow 4 to 6 weeks for delivery. Offer available while quantities last.

Your Privacy—The Reader Service is committed to protecting your privacy. Our Privacy Policy is available online at www.ReaderService.com or upon request from the Reader Service.

We make a portion of our mailing list available to reputable third parties that offer products we believe may interest you. If you prefer that we not exchange your name with third parties, or if you wish to clarify or modify your communication preferences, please visit us at www.ReaderService.com/consumerchoice or write to us at Reader Service Preference Service, P.O. Box 9062, Buffalo, NY 14269. Include your complete name and address.

MSUS11

SHARON SALA

32941	BLOOD STAINS	___ $7.99 U.S.	___	$9.99 CAN.
32802	SWEPT ASIDE	___ $7.99 U.S.	___	$9.99 CAN.
32792	TORN APART	___ $7.99 U.S.	___	$9.99 CAN.
32785	BLOWN AWAY	___ $7.99 U.S.	___	$9.99 CAN.
32677	THE RETURN	___ $7.99 U.S.	___	$8.99 CAN.
32633	THE WARRIOR	___ $7.99 U.S.	___	$7.99 CAN.
32544	THE HEALER	___ $7.99 U.S.	___	$7.99 CAN.
31264	BLOOD TIES	___ $7.99 U.S.	___	$9.99 CAN.

(limited quantities available)

TOTAL AMOUNT	$ _____
POSTAGE & HANDLING	$ _____
($1.00 for 1 book, 50¢ for each additional)	
APPLICABLE TAXES*	$ _____
TOTAL PAYABLE	$ _____

(check or money order—please do not send cash)

To order, complete this form and send it, along with a check or money order for the total above, payable to MIRA Books, to: **In the U.S.:** 3010 Walden Avenue, P.O. Box 9077, Buffalo, NY 14269-9077; **In Canada:** P.O. Box 636, Fort Erie, Ontario, L2A 5X3.

Name: _____
Address: _____ City: _____
State/Prov.: _____ Zip/Postal Code: _____
Account Number (if applicable): _____

075 CSAS

*New York residents remit applicable sales taxes.
*Canadian residents remit applicable GST and provincial taxes.

MIRA | H HARLEQUIN®
www.Harlequin.com

MSS0611BL